THE ICING MAN

THE ICING MAN

Jonathan D. Lindley

The Book Guild Ltd
Sussex, England

First published in Great Britain in 2001 by
The Book Guild Ltd
25 High Street
Lewes, East Sussex
BN7 2LU

Copyright © Jonathan D. Lindley 2001

The right of Jonathan D. Lindley to be identified as the author of
this work has been asserted by him in accordance with the
Copyright, Designs and Patents Act 1988.

All rights reserved. No part of this publication may be
reproduced, transmitted, or stored in a retrieval system, in
any form or by any means, without permission in writing
from the publisher, nor be otherwise circulated in any form
of binding or cover other than that in which it is published
and without a similar condition being imposed on the
subsequent purchaser.

All characters in this publication are fictitious and any
resemblance to real people, alive or dead, is
purely coincidental.

Typesetting in Baskerville by
SetSystems Ltd, Saffron Walden, Essex

Printed in Great Britain by
Antony Rowe Ltd, Chippenham, Wiltshire

A catalogue record for this book is
available from the British Library.

ISBN 1 85776 517 6

For the Mothers

Who struggle on against the odds,

Lonely but never alone

Always in our thoughts

CONTENTS

1	Pervert	1
2	By the Light of the Silvery Moon	18
3	Twister	36
4	Tainted Ice	55
5	Butterfly	75
6	Black and White	94
7	Plight of the Fairies	112
8	Ariadne's Thread	130
9	Home of the Depraved	149
10	Suffer the Little Children	170
11	36D	188
12	AC/DC	207
13	Come into My Parlour	227
14	Men Don't Mind, Boys Don't Matter	248
15	Northern Lights	267
16	Of Gog and Magog	285
17	Revelations	304

1

Pervert

Here I stand, a man approaching his fifty-second year some twelve months into semi-retirement. An illustrious career spanning two decades to my credit, the last five years of which spent as a respected and stalwart corporate mover/ shaker. By all accounts, although not always liked, I'm acknowledged as a mature, distinguished and honest individual; and it would therefore seem only natural that lack of any moral turpitude could be appended to my list of enviable qualities. Alas not so, for I, Dr Jeremiah Orville Clock, have come to realise an abhorrent truth. My character is not just flawed, but corrupt, perverse and riddled with lasciviousness. Too pompous? – probably. Too strong? – not necessarily. Should I be repentant, contrite? – definitely not. In my defence, I'm justifiably able to cite my current status as a gainfully self-employed servant of society. As a part-time forensic adviser-cum-volunteer magistrate and an active member of the Neighbourhood Watch scheme, my eminent credentials surely outweigh my ignominy, I would note. Admirable maybe, and by most definitions certainly the attributes of a model pillar of society, yet at this precise moment my base character is again on open display for all to observe and ridicule. Ashamed as I am, I just can't help myself. Isn't that great? So, clinging furtively to a half-filled trolley of groceries, I dodge suspiciously between the baked beans and spaghetti shelves of my local supermarket. I can see the roaming pack of store detectives salivating at the prospect of a new victim. Little do they know that the only pickings they'll claw from me this crisp and bright autumn afternoon will be the taste of bitter disappointment. 'And the reason for my unseemly behaviour?' I hear the chorus chanting. Well that, as they say, is a complicated story. To be honest though, my primary motivation is nothing more sinister than a little voyeurism. In common with the majority of my fellow men, the fascination of watching others, from a secluded vantage point, conduct their lives is irresistible. Sexual, domestic; dramatic, monotonous; whatever the activity, it doesn't really matter. The thrill, the undiluted excitement of invading someone's privacy shrouded by a veil of secrecy, is guaranteed to fire up the old adrenal glands every time . . .

For the third time in as many months I find myself transfixed by the antics of my nearest neighbours, Julian Stammers and Kathy Murkett: an odd and ill-matched couple if ever there was one. In general they keep themselves to themselves, which is perhaps just as well since their primary occupation is scouting for young and sometimes innocent girls to appear in so-called soft-porno videos.

Details of this shady although admittedly intriguing profession were revealed to me quite openly by Julian shortly after I first made his acquaintance. It's sometimes hard to believe that that was just less than a year ago, after I'd finally chucked in my sparkling career as Vice President, Scenario Planning and Corporate Communications at Van der Heijden Pharmaceuticals. I'd become well and truly 'ratted off', as Julian would say, with the corporate ant's nest. The life of a high-flyer had cost me dearly: a cold marriage, a messy divorce and the development of numerous character defects I was still trying desperately to shed. And then one miserable fog-laden morning, my Guardian Angel, whom I'd thought long since cast down into the fiery bowels of hell for underachieving, decided to throw me a lifeline. As if a collection of blocks and bypass wires had been flushed out of my commercial brain, the truth was revealed. My life had been in the shithouse where I, as chief shithead, had made life for those unfortunate enough to be around me equally shitty. I was approaching the magical tax-friendly age of fifty and my least favourite aunt had recently passed away, leaving me the proud but astounded owner of a large, albeit run-down, property in a small village just outside Haverhill, Suffolk. What further prompting did I need? To the horror/delight of my colleagues, off I went to start my new life as rural landowner, DIY devotee and master decorator of cakes. Yes, I can still see the condescending faces at my retirement wake when I revealed my secret passion.

'Oh my God, Tick-tock's into icing cakes. Silly old bugger. D'you think he's always been that way inclined, if you know what I mean? – Sweetie.'

I couldn't be bothered to set the sarcastic bastards straight, but for my long-suffering secretary who'd overheard the comment and had seemed overly concerned by it, I had. Yes, I'd long held an interest in the fine art of cake decoration; but no, I was still old-fashioned and preferred female sexual partners. My clarification had seemed to please her. I preferred not to speculate as to the reason why.

Unshackled and freed from my self-constructed straitjacket, I'd set about working on the fixer-upper with gusto. I think it was on the second day, as I was hurling a tirade of abuse at some tool or other, that Julian came sauntering along the narrow private road towards me. Being an old village, most houses had, over the centuries, grown up Heath-Robinson fashion on either side of the main thoroughfare connecting Cambridge with Colchester. My residence was, however, an exception, having been constructed a hundred yards or so back from the road. Nobody seemed to know why this anomaly had occurred, but I for one was glad of it. No traffic noise, no prying eyes and, more often than not, no visitors, as the place was impossible to spot from the carriageway.

'Howdy partner, I'm Julian,' my new neighbour had greeted me. 'Julian Stammers,' he'd drawled. 'Me and the brains of the outfit live at the end of yer track. Thought I'd mosey along and make yer acquaintance.' One hour after this somewhat confused 'Count of Monte Cristo meets John

Wayne' encounter, Julian had declared that I was 'all right for a city dude' and now ranked as one of his best buddies. It transpired that the man actually hailed from Sheffield, but there was no doubt that the good Lord had made the tiniest of screw-ups. Mr J. Stammers was definitely created for the American prairie-lands, but somewhere along the way a heavenly admin wallah had mistaken Yorkshire for Montana. The error, once discovered, apparently couldn't be rectified, but despite the incorrect location Julian had still developed as his maker originally intended.

Despite his affectation with all things Western, I'd taken to my new neighbour straight away. Always a friendly, amiable character, Julian was a touch over thirty years old, five feet eight inches tall, well built, with jet-black hair greased back to emulate his singular hero, Elvis Presley. One couldn't help but be absorbed by his striking facial appearance: large, smiling blue eyes – the right one affected by a slight glide – and complementary pair of equally smiling Mick Jagger lookalike lips. I don't think I've ever seen him dress in anything but a combination of blue jeans, white T-shirt and leather jacket, yet this choice of attire suits him remarkably well. His clean-shaven features create an impression of smartness; and his relaxed, methodical, almost robotic way of moving betrays years of studying US and Italian cowboy movies.

A week or so after our first encounter, Julian had returned one evening to ask if I needed any help with my endeavours. At that time I was pretty tired so I'd declined his offer and instead invited him in for a drink. One or four whiskies later, Julian was well into the story of his life. Much of what he described was vague and difficult to follow, but three points were clear enough. Number one – he'd had a hard time as a child due to his surname and the fact that, when agitated, he did actually have a slight stammer. Number two – since leaving school at sixteen he'd held various jobs as car/motorbike mechanic, and number three – the brains of the outfit, aka his partner Kathy Murkett, was the love of his life. Interestingly enough, Julian had gone on to tell me that it was Kathy, when they'd met some five years earlier, who'd introduced him to his current part-time career as a video talent scout. At first I found it odd how easily he'd accepted the role and been absorbed into a business which didn't at all seem to fit his character. By the end of our male-bonding session, however, I was left in no doubt that Ms Murkett's influence over him was absolute. If she even hinted it would please her if he stood in front of a bus, he wouldn't hesitate.

From time to time – never allowing too long an interval to pass – Julian wanders round to see me. We drink, talk a lot of nonsense and slowly but surely get to know each other. So far I've never been invited to their house and, strangest of all, my companion has shown no inclination to formally introduce me to the enigmatic and largely invisible Kathy. It's true she sometimes passes the bottom of my road when I'm working on the hedgerows. If our eyes meet, she nods and I wave, but that's as far as we've got. One night I thought of going round uninvited – take a bottle, 'break the ice' sort of thing – but, as if my intentions had been telepathically intercepted, Julian miraculously turned up on one of his impromptu visits. Definitely weird! But then, who am I to label anyone as weird given my present performance alongside the endless shelves of tins, bottles and jars . . .

I think the root of my enchantment is the way in which Julian and his mate operate in perfect accord, almost as if they're acting out a well-rehearsed play or ballet. Kathy, without question, does indeed come across as the 'brains of the outfit'. Like a graceful bird of prey she hovers from aisle to aisle, surreptitiously regarding potential targets. Once a candidate's been located, Julian skilfully makes an approach. The pattern is always the same – a casual remark about some product or other, a brief introduction, then somehow the switch to the business at hand. This part of the operation still remains a mystery to me. There always seems to be a critical moment when the unsuspecting victim may take offence, lash out and storm off, but I've yet to witness such an event. Invariably, the negotiation is successful or at least in part. Failure, when it does occur, is perhaps the most remarkable and entertaining part of the whole process. Julian, smiling throughout, deftly manages to quell any alarm or anger and within seconds departs from the mark as one might expect an old friend to . . .

It's now less than five minutes since the last campaign and already I sense that Ms Murkett has identified the next contestant. Correct, Julian's on the move! Basket in hand, he sidles up to what appears to be a young mother no more than nineteen years old. The girl has two children in tow – one toddling beside her; the other a baby propped up in a trolley. She's a pretty girl – tall, dyed-blonde unkempt shoulder-length hair and trim figure teetering on the voluptuous side in certain areas. Her make-up is decidedly overdone and less than skilfully applied. Julian seems to be passing her by then suddenly bends down to retrieve something the toddler's dropped. The harassed girl is grateful. Julian smiles, picks up the child and points to an item on a nearby shelf. The vivid image of a 1960s encyclopaedia salesman with his foot well and truly in the door flashes across my mind. This is indeed an unsung art form. But wait! All is not well. The girl's becoming agitated. She's hastily retrieving the toddler from Julian's arms. A crisis is developing. . . but my friend shows no sign of concern. His smile broadens; he picks a jar or bottle from the shelf and shows it to the flustered woman. Words tumble from his mouth and in a moment the girl's face relaxes. She blushes. A further brief exchange and the woman accepts Julian's card. They smile; nod to each other and, following a US-style military salute, the master takes his leave. Another triumph. Truly amazing. At this juncture if I were watching with a female partner, I'd be tempted to say something clichéd like, 'Was that good for you too?' As things stand, however, several fellow shoppers are eyeing me with a mixture of concern and suspicion. Definitely time to move on to the cereals and crisps section . . .

Almost two-thirty. Time to end the excitement for today, collect the shopping I came for and head back home.

Idling the time away while queuing at the checkout, reading about this week's special offers, a characteristic voice gave me an unwelcome start.

'Hi, Doc. How's it goin'? Looks like you're stockin' up for a bit of a siege there to me. Guests comin'?'

I turned to discover that Julian had joined the back of my queue. The three ladies separating us looked at me expectantly, their interest in my as yet undelivered response clearly spellbinding.

'Hello Julian,' I replied a little sheepishly. 'Yes, a trifle more than usual. I'm expecting someone from the Work Experience programme tomorrow.'

'Oh right,' he beamed with enthusiasm. 'Great! Teach the kids a trade. Wish I'd had the chance. By the way, did ya catch today's show? Not bad, eh?'

I knew full well what was being referred to, but the thought that Julian was aware of my role as voyeur both robbed me of speech and delivered an acute injection of embarrassment. At this point the trio of shoppers, if seated, would certainly have been perched on the edge of same, hardly able to contain themselves; desperate to discover the topic under discussion. Unfortunately, the prolonged silence prompted my friend to answer for me.

'Of course ya did – daft question. A fair selection for a Tuesday, if I do say so myself,' he continued. 'And what about the girl with the legs up to the Mississippi and 747 upper deck? Definitely a star in the makin'. What d'ya think, Doc?'

If it had been anyone other than Julian you'd be forgiven for concluding that he was either playing to the gallery or deliberately trying to embarrass me. This, however, was Julian; and I'd come to appreciate that malevolence wasn't in his nature. Also, the assumption that I would without doubt have witnessed his efforts was interesting. Probably it stemmed from a misunderstanding of my role as part-time, or more correctly these days, very occasional, forensic consultant to the police. For most people, the mention of forensics instantly conjures up images of Sherlock Holmes and more modern TV investigative marvels. In fact my area of expertise was restricted to esoteric poisons and, although I'm by nature an observant individual, I lack the star qualities of Mr Holmes or his contemporaries.

In response I smiled and nodded my agreement. The ladies frowned and shook their heads in disgust, still none the wiser regarding the topic. As for Mr Stammers, he just carried on beaming, oblivious that anything was amiss. Thankfully it was at last my turn for the ubiquitous barcode scanning ritual, and ten minutes later I was more than relieved to signal a fond farewell to my neighbour.

As I drew out of the car park in my newly restored pride and joy – a red 1970 Triumph TR6 – I caught a glimpse of Kathy re-arranging the contents of the Stammers/Murkett VW bus. In time-honoured fashion when our eyes met nods were exchanged, but my supplementary gesture – in this case a smile – was left unacknowledged.

If Julian was to be labelled a trifle eccentric, then Kathy definitely had to be pigeonholed in the 'really strange' category. Her general appearance, like that of her partner, never seemed to alter significantly. A throwback from the hippie days, Kathy fitted the old-fashioned description of a 'drink of water' perfectly. Basically, there was nothing to her at all. It was almost as if she'd been squeezed out of a tube and was constantly on the verge of succumbing to gravity by reverting to a blob on the floor. About five and a half feet tall, she had long, straggly, light-brown hair parted in the centre, and her face, somewhat gaunt, almost corpse-like, was dominated by frameless hexagonal glasses. These, in turn, covered perhaps her most attractive feature – a pair of doleful grey eyes, which seemed to contain hidden depths of wisdom. This observation interested me greatly, since on superficial inspection Kathy's practice of rarely speaking or smiling afforded her a somewhat gormless appearance. Nothing, I'd come to appreciate, was further from the truth, however. Older than Julian by a decade, she nonetheless looked much younger than her age; an impression aided in part by the flowing, early-Seventies-style frocks she favoured and the tiny flowers she used to decorate her hair. Never having spoken to the woman, I knew nothing of her background or whether she held down any other jobs apart from her involvement in the pornography trade. This aspect of my neighbour's life still didn't sit at all well with my vision of the order of things. If you ignored their seedy cottage industry, Kathy and Julian would just be your average odd but cute village couple. But then you couldn't ignore what they did or the completely open and unself-conscious way in which they did it.

As I joined the main road heading for Haverhill, I couldn't help but recall one of my more entertaining drinking sessions with Julian. I remembered that during the course of the evening I inwardly vowed to find out more about Kathy and the whys and wherefores of her involvement with the cheesecake video game. My plan had initially seemed to fail miserably. I discovered nothing of interest about Ms Murkett but instead wound up reeling off a fairly detailed account of the life and times of Doctor J.O. Clock to my ever-receptive guest. To my surprise, Julian regarded a lengthy scientific and corporate career as ideal training for setting up a one-man cake-decorating business. His interest had seemed, as always, genuine so I'd kept on going. Of the list of hobbies I went on to describe, three, i.e. collecting antique tarot cards, herbal medicines and car/motorbike restoration, attracted the best response. It seemed that when it came to motorbikes our relationship took an unexpected leap from 'buddy' status to 'kindred spirit'. The only 'fly in the ointment', so to speak, was that while I favoured old British bikes – Francis Barnett, Norton, Royal Enfield and the like – Julian was, surprise, surprise, a staunch Harley man. Then came my only breakthrough to date. Joy of joys, Mr Stammers revealed that Kathy was a devout herbalist – food, cosmetics, medicines, the lot.

Before parting that evening I gave Julian a sample of my patent cold/flu snake oil as a gift for his good lady. The next day a small floral card fluttered from the letterbox. A thank-you note from Ms Murkett – game on, at last.

The light was slowly fading as I turned into my narrow lane/surrogate driveway. By the time I'd unloaded my purchases, the eyelids of day were flickering closed, their toil and labour of the past ten hours finally complete. Before unlocking the front door I took a few moments to stand back and survey the state of the Clock residence.

'Still a long way to go,' I groaned. A year of backbreaking effort, injury and expense, not to mention several volumes of abuse, expletives and cursing already sunk into the place had barely scratched the surface of the restoration work needed.

The main problem was that over nearly four centuries two separate cottages and a barn had been systematically cobbled together. By all accounts the last major cobbling exercise had been completed in 1895, just after my aunt's parents took possession of the holding. Grandfather Clock, a name the old boy understandably hated, was a reasonably successful solicitor on my mother's side. Not unlike myself, he had become disenchanted with his chosen career and decided that life as a farmer would best suit him in his retirement. Fate, however, had disagreed. No sooner had he completed annexing the barn to the already coupled pair of cottages to generate a relatively pleasing T-shaped plan than a dose of typhoid carried him away. Luckily, sufficient funds were available for the family to live reasonably well. Proposals for the creation of a working farm were scrapped, along with the construction of a new barn. Instead, widow Clock invested in making the place comfortable. She installed electricity, did away with the thatched roof in favour of tiles and three splendid chimneys, and landscaped part of the garden. This period had unquestionably been the property's heyday. In subsequent years little was spent on maintenance, and by the time my aunt took over sole possession during the Second World War, the place was already in need of much love and attention.

'Well,' I sighed to myself. 'Don't worry, old girl. Somehow or other I'll raise you back to your former glory. For now though, I'm just about drained and tomorrow's a big day. We're expecting a young visitor.'

After putting the car to bed for the night I stumbled into the hallway, trailing my cache of shopping behind me. Yes, tomorrow was likely to be a big day and in more ways than one. To my amazement, the Doctor Clock one-man cake-decorating business had proved remarkably successful. Orders, sporadic at first, had swelled to a trickle, progressed rapidly to a stream and had recently merited flood status. Prompted by my newly acquired community conscience, I'd decided to create a Work Experience position rather than cut back on the business. Initially the local Job Centre had seemed to regard cake decoration as a less than attractive idea. Nevertheless my years as a senior exec had stood me in good stead when it came to not accepting 'no' for an answer. Once in the system, it had taken less time than anyone expected for a candidate to be found, and so tomorrow I'd be taking on yet another new challenge – that of trainer.

I'd almost completed stowing my supermarket supplies when an acute sense of anxiety poked its head above the parapet. For several moments I stood motionless, listening for what I'd no idea, but I was sure something was amiss. The problem with old houses, particularly those in a state of ill repair, is that they possess a constant chorus of their own. If it's not the creaks and groans of the long-suffering structure then it's the scratches and scuffles of the little furry squatters roaming around in the roof or in between the floor joists. On this occasion, however, it was beginning to sound as if at least one of the visitors wore size nine boots. Before moving in I'd been told burglary was rare in this part of the country. Later, when the house contents insurance turned out to be an order of magnitude less than I'd expected, I accepted the claim unequivocally. That aside, unnatural noises were definitely emanating from the bedroom above me. It looked like I was experiencing the exception that proves the rule.

Meat cleaver in hand, I gingerly moved towards the stairs. A cursory scan of the area around the front door and adjoining rooms gave no indication of breaking and entering. This observation was, however, of little value, as in reality any of the fifteen or so windows would present little challenge for even the most unaccomplished thief. On the bottom step of the staircase, two points of logic rudely questioned my current course of action. One – whoever it was must have heard me arrive and therefore know full well that I was now inside, and two – whatever kung fu abilities I could call upon would hardly prevent at least half a dozen stairs from whining and moaning the minute I stepped on them. There was nothing for it. An SAS rush and surprise attack was called for if Jerry Clock was to win the day. Two deep breaths and I scrambled up the stairs. The initial ascent went well but then I missed my footing, lurched backwards, slipped and crumpled to the bottom step. Undeterred, I mounted a repeat performance; this time accompanied by a roaring battle cry. The assault was a success. I reached the top of the stairs; heart pounding, eyes flashing in all directions. Then I realised – no meat cleaver. As I stood frozen, torn between pushing on unarmed or affecting a tactical retreat to recover my weapon, a loud crashing sound came from the target bedroom. Without thinking I raced along the landing and ploughed into the room. At that instant a figure leapt from the window. I vaulted over the intervening bed, sure of catching a glimpse of the intruder, but luck was still playing hide and seek. Dusk was fast approaching, and with so many ledges and outhouses within easy reach, whomever it was just evaporated like a phantom. I made to scuttle back downstairs and out into the yard, but that would have been no more than a futile gesture. By the time doors were unlocked, a torch dug out from somewhere and a search plan formulated, even a burglar on crutches would have been halfway to Colchester.

A little shaken, out of breath, but most of all frustrated, I flopped onto the bed. For several minutes I sat in the gloaming, trying to decide the next and best course of action. Logically this was a police matter and, given my connection with the forensic boys at Scotland Yard, also my role as a volunteer magistrate, I'd have expected my hand already to be clutching the phone. For some inexplicable reason though, I felt a strong reluctance to involve outsiders. Possibly in my semi-retired state I'd gradually become a hermit without realising it. On the other hand, perhaps it was just another case of fearing embarrassment. Without doubt once a particular group of police colleagues found out about the break-in, there'd be more than a few jokes devised at my expense. Two years ago such a prospect would have had zero effect on me, but today? Could be I was actually turning into a sensitive and complex human being after all.

By degrees I calmed down and began to receive the messages of pain being transmitted by my knees and right shin. Not surprisingly, my tumble on the stairs had probably been harder than I'd realised. Okay, I decided, first order of business, a double brandy followed by an inspection of the premises to determine the extent of any damage and see if anything's missing. With less drama than I'd ascended the stairs, I headed for the main downstairs living room. On the way I collected the meat cleaver from the bottom step, which reminded me that my few knocks and bumps could have been much worse. The brandy, although not as effective as adrenalin at masking pain, provided the boost I needed to embark on my tour of inspection. As I systematically meandered from room to room, I began to feel quite relieved. So far nothing appeared to be damaged or missing. I checked upstairs, and apart from an old wristwatch that hadn't kept good time for years and, of all things, my newly purchased electric razor, I seemed to have got off lightly. As far as I could tell, the invader had gained entry through the window by which they'd departed. To my annoyance, I found several other open windows, all of which I'd intended to close before my shopping expedition. So now the list was growing – decrepit, over-sensitive, misanthropic and senile. Great! Looking on the bright side though, at least I wasn't faced with a hefty bill to replace broken glass or, worse still, a smashed window frame. All in all, I was pleased that my uncharacteristic aversion to involve the police had surfaced. The only remaining puzzle was why the burglar had settled for such a limited haul. I felt sure he must have been in the house for some time. Although I still hadn't retrieved many of my valuable possessions from storage, I'd at least have expected the video, CD player and such like to take a walk. From whichever angle I approached the problem it seemed inconceivable that the person was searching for something specific. It had to be an opportunistic venture, surely.

Well it was now quite late and I still hadn't eaten or prepared for my Work Experience visitor. Given the hour, I decided to settle for a microwaved marvel, leftover apple pie and another couple of drinks. By the time I'd consumed my bachelor's feast the temperature of the room had become distinctly chilly. Fortunately the fire was laid from the previous evening so it took only a small aliquot of my fading energy to crank it up. As the logs finally caught light, I sat staring into the flames. A series of whisky-promoted images pirouetted through my mind and, cloaked in a haze of crackling heat, I drifted . . .

No! A particularly unpleasant spectre unceremoniously rose up, kicking away my malaise and dragging me back to a state of full alert. 'Bugger!' I exclaimed. 'That's all I need, nightmares.' Just gone eleven, I discovered, and I still hadn't made the necessary preparations for the next day.

Reluctantly I sloped off to my icing room like an old hedgehog heading for its hibernation bed. I flicked on the light switch, yawned, then nearly screamed. 'Oh no, Jesus Christ, not the cakes. Shit and to hell.' Greeting my eyes was a scene of pure carnage. My delicate and painstaking masterpieces were battered, flattened, squashed – utterly destroyed. Pieces of cake and icing were strewn everywhere. The walls had been daubed with colouring agents then pelted with bags of icing sugar. Individual mouldings carved from royal icing, having been drenched with water, were reduced to a sticky mass. Nothing seemed to have been left intact. So now I knew the reason behind the visit. But in God's name why? Who on earth could be motivated to unleash such a monstrous degree of fury on a handful of cakes? Was it an attack on me: some kind of threat or a warning? Surely not. As I struggled to take in the full extent of this mindless act of destruction, the most horrific of consequences hit me like a hammer. Fortunately, the majority of work was for events some time in the future. With a determined effort I probably had enough time to order new cakes and repeat the work. One project, however – a particularly spectacular three-tier wedding cake – had a deadline of less than two weeks. The bride and groom held a fascination for all matters related to the royal armoury. Needless to say, the order was for a cake adorned with a selection of some of the more elaborate coats of arms belonging to local militia units and aristocracy. Even if I could work thirty hours a day, it would be impossible to recreate the same level of detail in less than three weeks. I held my head in my hands and cried out. But at that moment I had a premonition – somewhere I was about to discover one final insult to add to the injury already sustained. I wasn't to be disappointed. On the back of the door my raging nemesis had painted the word 'WaNKER' using cochineal. In comparison to the rest of the handiwork, not particularly exceptional – that is until I followed the trail of red leading from the letter R. The line crossed to the adjacent wall then descended to the floor, where it ran along until it reached the table on which most of the ruined cakes rested. At this point the red streak ascended one of the table legs, traversed the surface of the table and ended in a large circle drawn on the base layer of the mutilated wedding cake. In the centre of the circle, I'd been left a little gift – a small amount of opaque viscous liquid of human origin, I suspected, spread out on a piece of cling film.

'Very nice,' I exhaled. 'Very nice indeed.' The only question remaining was whether the term 'wanker' referred to my visitor or to me. Now I had no choice. The police would have to be brought in. In terms of cost, the damage wasn't that great, but the nature of the attack posed a number of serious questions about the perpetrator's state of mind. I could easily have been a random target and, if so, others may be at risk. Unlike my previous episode of hesitancy, I made straight for the phone.

I'd barely begun dialling when an almighty thumping sound echoed from the front door.

'This can't be happening,' I seethed. 'Who the bloody hell can that be at this time of night?' I replaced the receiver and approached the door. Once again my tardiness in the DIY stakes returned to haunt me. For months I'd been meaning to install a security inspection glass but had always managed to justify a postponement. Mark up another screw-up notch for Clock the Flop. The pounding, which by now I'd decided was probably someone kicking the door, continued with ever-increasing urgency. Charged with curiosity, too tired to care and totally brassed off, I threw caution to the wind and flung open the door. I was fully prepared for an abuse hurling session if it turned out to be kids messing about – a real possibility with Guy Fawkes Night just around the corner. But it wasn't kids or anything remotely related to 'messing about'. Teetering on the porch, trembling, his face covered in blood, stood Julian, his partner Kathy cradled in his arms. His eyes were glazed and wild, an effect markedly accentuating his glide. I opened my mouth to speak, but Julian beat me to the mark.

'D-Doc. Thank God!' he stuttered, completely devoid of his affected Western accent. 'You've got to help my Kathy.

16

The bastards've killed her. Please, please bring her back. You can do something, I know.'

Any verbal response I might have made would clearly have been redundant. My distraught neighbour needed help not words, so I simply jammed open the door and ushered him into the living room. At first he resisted my encouragement to lay Kathy on the four-seater couch near the window. It was clear that if his lady had passed away, irrespective of whether she was destined for heaven or hell, Julian was determined to go with her. Finally he gave in to my entreatments and allowed me to examine the stricken woman.

Superficially, the signs weren't good. Kathy appeared totally lifeless, exhibiting no evidence of a heartbeat or breathing. Her head, ghostly pale face and upper torso were soaked in blood, but the source wasn't obvious. Although not medically qualified, my various careers had afforded me an extensive knowledge of medicine. As a result, rightly or wrongly, I was usually able to make a comment about most conditions, but trauma on this scale was way out of my league. Nevertheless, I set about ministering to the poor creature as best I could, although already convinced she was beyond help. Julian stood motionless at her side like an ancient guardian of a regal tomb. His conviction that Kathy must be revived was so strong that if the angel of death had yet to come for her, he'd be prepared to fight him off for eternity if necessary.

As I conducted a second, more detailed inspection of my patient I discovered several remarkable if not incredible findings that at first had escaped my notice. The nature of these observations was such that I felt it unfair to delay sharing my conclusions.

'Well, Julian,' I said finally, patting him on the back, 'good news. Not only is this young lady not dead but, unless I'm seriously mistaken, she's not your Kathy either.'

2

By the Light of the Silvery Moon

Julian blinked several times, glanced momentarily in my direction then resumed his previous posture. It was like watching a TV set suffering a temporary power interruption. A brief picture distortion, perhaps the odd flicker, then back to the original programme without leaving the slightest trace that anything had happened. Without doubt the man was in an advanced stage of shock and, on reflection, I should have considered this fact more carefully before blurting out my revelation. Well, it was too late. Julian's brain was whizzing round like the tumblers of a slot machine after someone yanked its handle. My job now was to ensure that each of the three rotating drums stopped in the right order and displayed the jackpot three-bell combo. Contrary to medical opinion, I find a stiff whisky has an immediate and beneficial effect on most conditions. In my neighbour's case, a double dose turned out to be necessary before I was finally able to effect my one-armed bandit manoeuvre.

'So she's not dead?' he repeated after I'd explained my findings for the third time. 'And it isn't Kathy? Same looks, same frock, but not Kathy?' Since Julian had refused to relinquish his sentinel's post, he'd accepted his treatment while standing at the injured woman's side. This was far from ideal as, despite my faith in the therapeutic value of alcohol, when applied to cases of shock it's advisable for the patient to be seated. Nevertheless, Julian seemed to be holding up well so, not being one to look a gift horse in the mouth, I decided to continue my exposé and capitalise on the merits extolled by the adage, 'actions speak louder than words'. To begin with I thought it best to demonstrate that life still pervaded our victim's body. The old 'breath on a cold mirror' did the trick and, although Julian wasn't totally convinced at first, he noticeably began to relax. To prove my doppelganger theory, I first pointed out several scar remnants around the neck and face, which I explained were probably the result of plastic surgery. Next I gently opened the woman's mouth and, with the aid of a small penlight, described how she'd recently undergone extensive reconstructive dental work. Finally, the *pièce de résistance* lay in the windows to the soul – the eyes. On several occasions Julian had commented on his partner's spellbinding grey orbs. When in full health, the lady in question may also have possessed the same attribute, except that her eyes were dark brown.

'B-bloody hell!' Julian said almost in a whisper. 'What in tarnation's goin' on?'

Myself, I'd have probably opted for 'What the fuck?', even though I usually reserve that particular expletive for DIY mishaps. Under the present circumstances, however, my neighbour's choice of words and Western-style delivery were perfect. He was definitely well on the way to recovery.

My performance successfully complete, I had little trouble in guiding Mr Stammers to a seat. I fixed him one of my herbal wonders and, while he slurped it down, returned my attention to the woman. Given her dilated pupils, dramatically suppressed breathing and pulse rate, I was reasonably sure she'd been deliberately shot full of one or more drugs. The question was whether the intention was merely to effect a state mimicking death or to achieve it in actuality. As far as I could tell, her condition was stable and, to my relief, I could detect no evidence of wounding. There was no doubt that the blood still clinging to her body was genuine, but it was equally certain that it had been indiscriminately applied by a third party. These observations triggered my own personal recovery programme. The initial crisis was passed. No one was dead; no one was bleeding to death. I was calm; Julian was calm. So now what? Once again the logical course was to call in the authorities; and boy, would that be a red-letter day for the uniformed brigade. Breaking and entering, GBH, unlawful use of drugs; not to mention some bastard beating himself off on my cakes. But this just wasn't the night for dialling 999. No sooner had I settled on my course of action than Julian was off on his amateur telepath routine.

'Say, Doc,' he began pensively. 'You're not thinkin' of callin' the cops, are ya?'

'Well,' I replied. 'Don't you think we should? At the very least the woman needs proper hospital treatment. God knows what's been pumped into her.'

For once Julian's face adopted a serious expression. He nodded. 'Sure, Doc, I know it's the right thing to do, and the last thing I want's for the little lady to suffer but . . .' He paused long enough to shoot me an ace of a hangdog look.

I half-smiled. 'But you'd rather we didn't involve the police.'

'That's about the size of it, sir,' he confirmed. 'You know the business Kathy and I are mixed up in. I ain't sayin' it's good, but it ain't that bad neither. We don't do nasty stuff, and all our gals are treated with respect and get paid fair.'

I didn't feel qualified to agree or disagree with the young man's claim. In our drinking sessions the porno topic rarely arose, and out of courtesy I invariably gave it a wide berth. Interestingly, Julian never tried to justify the business – I'd assumed because he didn't think it necessary. He had on one occasion referred to the girls they used as 'unfortunates', and in a way I think he honestly believed he was helping them. As he put it, 'A hundred quid for ten minutes touchy-feely in your birthday suit wasn't bad,' and I suppose if you viewed it in that way it probably wasn't.

'Anyways, Doc,' he continued. 'I don't have many real friends. Hell, apart from you, I don't have any. But I appreciate our chats. You've shown me respect, and even if inside you think I'm just trash caught up in an American fantasy, you don't show it.'

For Julian this was quite a speech and, although I felt

uneasy at stemming his flow, my concern for the unattended woman was growing. 'Okay,' I interjected as he made to resume. 'What d'you propose?'

He slapped his knees with both hands and stood up to face me. 'As I see it, some creep's got my Kathy. Why, I dunno. Most of my associates are slime. They'd kill your grandmother for a nickel and still offer ya change. So I need time to see some people; find out what's happenin'.'

'Don't tell me,' I protested. 'In the meantime I play Doctor Kildare and look after the patient.'

'Thanks, Doc,' came the grateful reply. 'I knew you'd understand. You're the chief cowpoke.' Before I could react, Julian mumbled something about cleaning up and shuffled off to the bathroom.

Not the outcome I'd expected, that was for sure, I moaned to myself.

Without realising it, I began to consider the consequences of my neighbour's proposal while giving my newly assigned patient a further examination. Admittedly, her condition did seem to be improving and, as far as I could tell, she was physically sound. What her mental state would be when the drugs wore off was anybody's guess but, as things stood, hospitalisation, although desirable, perhaps wasn't essential. I brought a bowl of hot water, soap and towels then set about mopping up the blood and wiping her face and arms. As I rubbed the hot towel over her dress, I began to detect the strengthening odour of paraffin. Instantly my mind slotted all the jigsaw pieces I'd been toying with into place. The resulting picture was not good; not good at all. I abandoned my clean-up operation and, with a pair of scissors, carefully cut away the ruined frock. After effecting a makeshift bed-bath, I dried her limbs as best I could and wrapped her in a mountain of blankets. Luckily Julian hadn't emerged from the bathroom so, frock in hand, I made for the kitchen. Time for several impromptu experiments . . .

As expected, a thin film of paraffin rapidly formed on the surface when I placed pieces of the garment in a little hot water. Furthermore, significant traces of a white powder remained after a portion of the aqueous residue was evaporated. Finally, when ignited with a match, the cloth exploded with the force of a Roman candle. There could be no doubt – someone wanted the world to believe that Kathy Murkett was dead. But why such an elaborate charade? Clearly considerable time and expense had gone into creating a superficial lookalike, even though the body was destined for incineration. That would leave only dental records, spectacles and perhaps – if things were arranged very carefully – conveniently undamaged locks of Kathy's hair for my forensic chums to drool over. If I was right, the victim's clothes had been impregnated with some form of fine paraffin wax mixed with sodium chlorate weedkiller. In combination, the heat generated on ignition would pretty much char the corpse thereby hampering detailed analysis. All very fine, yet my hypothesis still failed to explain the rationale behind the use of plastic surgery, blood splattering and the detailed attention to clothing. At that moment I heard footsteps entering the living room.

'How d'you feel now, Julian?' I enquired, exiting the kitchen as nonchalantly as possible.

The young man smiled. 'If Kathy were lying there recoverin' I'd be fine and dandy; but as things stand I feel pretty beat up.' I gestured him to a chair but, as he responded, I caught a glimpse of blood trickling down the side of his neck. My reaction didn't go unnoticed. 'Sorry to trouble you, Doc, but perhaps you could take a quick look at my head. There's some kinda gash. Can't seem to stop it oozin', and it hurts like the devil.'

The wound turned out to be superficial, but I couldn't pinpoint the cause. It was as if something blunt like a length of steel rope had been yanked across the scalp. In the few minutes or so it took me to attend to the laceration I was overcome by a remarkable sense of clarity. Given my conclusions about the intended fate of Kathy's double, it seemed certain that for some reason the plan had gone awry. Maybe the assailants had been interrupted or their window of opportunity had expired – who could say? Nevertheless, with the level of investment involved, it was more than reasonable to assume that they'd be anxious to finish the job. All my senses told me that Kathy herself was, for whatever purpose, wanted alive. The understudy, however, had to be disposed of, and checking her into hospital – even with the police involved – would be a sure-fire way of facilitating this objective. With luck no one except Julian and I knew the woman was here. Better to let Mr Stammers have a few hours to contact his underworld cronies and see if anything turned up. In the meantime there'd be more vital information to be gained from the patient when she came round. After all that, the next step could be decided.

My snap decision-making aberration complete, a hefty chunk of self-preservation rolled up for duty. What the hell was I doing? When did my admission to the Joe 90 Club take place? And the answer to these weighty conundrums? Well, quite frankly, I didn't care. Sure it was madness to get involved in criminal goings-on, but Julian and Kathy needed help. There was real danger; risk; dire consequences, etc. etc. and that was fine too. If I was brutally honest, I was scared out of my wits, but I was also having the time of my life. The bottom line – whatever happened couldn't be worse than the annual pre-budget meeting at Van der Heijden, and I always survived that. Time for old Tick-tock to rock and roll . . .

As I put the finishing touches to patching up Julian's injury, he grasped my arm. 'So you'll leave the cops out of this, then?' he questioned.

I deliberately delayed my response. Instead I carefully collected my medical paraphernalia, placed it to one side then took the seat opposite him. 'For the moment, yes,' I confirmed. 'But on three conditions.' Julian made no objection so I continued. 'Number one – you give a full account of what happened after I left you at the supermarket. Number two – we decide a plan of action and follow it through together. And number three – if at any time I think the police should be notified then no argument. What d'you say?'

Julian shrugged. 'I guess I say what you want me to . . . Okay. But if you don't mind me sayin', for an educated guy you're one hell of a crazy SOB – and I luv ya for it.'

Quite frankly, his response left me momentarily speechless. After a few seconds, however, the idea of being a crazy SOB began to develop a strange appeal. As to the expression of affection, I just hoped it was a cowboy guy thing and nothing more.

'Done!' I finally announced. 'Let's get to it, starting with number one.'

Over the next few minutes Julian gave a remarkably graphic account of events leading to his arrival at my door. After loading up the VW bus, the pair had stopped off to collect their video equipment before driving on to the Gogmagog and Wandlebury hills. It seemed that a number of Julian's associates favoured this location for shooting their erotic video backdrops. On this occasion, however, they'd visited the location themselves to film a selection of dusk scenes at the behest of one of their clients. As I understood it, an overseas distributor had become interested in this particular filmmaker's work and he needed help to meet a ridiculously tight deadline.

'So you and Kathy aren't involved in actually making the videos?' I enquired.

'Not usually,' Julian confirmed. 'One of us always hangs by the set when any of our gals are performin'. Like I said; we try to look after 'em. These days ya've gotta be real careful. There's some seriously sunken cakeheads around in our line of work.' My curiosity satisfied, I encouraged the young man to resume his account, but apparently he'd yet to complete his reply. 'Since you've asked though,' he persisted. 'My Kathy's written and directed a couple of clips for compilation videos. The one I like best starts with a schoolgirl catching this guy givin' it to a couple of nympho nuns. Then . . .'

'Yes, fine,' I interrupted. 'I get the general idea.' Although I respected Julian's pride in his partner's achievements and his reminiscences no doubt afforded his troubled mind a brief respite, we had to move on. Maybe when all this was sorted out, I'd ask about the conclusion to the nympho nun story.

The remaining account was brief. One minute the two of them were surveying the lay of the land; the next Julian was knocked unconscious. When he came to, he found Kathy lying in some bushes about twenty feet away. He'd tried to revive her, failed, dragged her to the van then flaked out.

'And you can't remember anything else?' I prompted.

'Nope, that's about it. Must've been out quite a spell. The rest y'know, Doc,' he replied.

It wasn't much to go on. I had hoped for at least one decent clue to feed my amateur detective cravings, but nothing. As I'd witnessed my CID colleagues do a thousand times, I asked for the story to be repeated. Somewhat reluctantly, Julian obliged, but second time around he mentioned that Kathy was holding the video camera.

'Was she filming when you were attacked?' I almost shouted.

The young man closed his eyes and visibly attempted to suck the memory from whichever recess in his mind it was lodged. 'Come to think of it, Doc,' he announced finally, 'Kathy'd just replaced the battery and was about to record a few test shots. So yep, it could've been runnin'.'

'And you didn't see the camera when you regained consciousness?'

Julian shook his head.

I glanced at the old grandfather clock labouring away by the door – four a.m. Gee, doesn't time fly when you're having – well, whatever. I regarded my injured and still-bewildered neighbour carefully in order to assess the accuracy of his answer to my next question. 'Do you feel fit enough to take me to where you were attacked?'

'Now?' he exclaimed.

'Yes now; immediately; this very instant,' I stressed dramatically. 'If the video was running at the time, it might have picked something up. It'll soon be light, and if the person behind this hasn't already got the tape, we'd better get a move on. An expensive video camera just lying about won't stay there long with all the people that wander around that area.'

Since I judged Julian's somewhat belated affirmative response to be more than fifty per cent true, I decided to proceed. I hastily threw a few essentials like a flashlight, rubber gloves and a crowbar for protection into a tattered sports bag. Ready for action, I grabbed my coat but then froze. In my enthusiasm I'd forgotten the woman. She couldn't be left alone – it was too risky.

'Damn!' I cursed, rapidly trying to conjure up as many options as I could muster. I was about to enter a free-fall into despondency when the powers that be decided to give me a break. Our patient stirred, groaned a little then opened her eyes. I asked the usual dumb questions like, 'How d'you feel?', but she was clearly still in too much of a daze to comprehend. Julian handed me a glass of water and, after a slight tussle, she took a few sips. Gradually her eyelids began a graded descent and, within a few moments, she fell into a normal state of sleep. With luck, she'd be fine now for several hours, so rightly or wrongly I resolved to continue as planned . . .

We took my car for the obvious reasons that Julian was unfit to drive and I didn't fancy cruising around in his clapped-out VW while it sported a bloodstained interior. As we whisked along the largely deserted road towards Wandlebury, Julian sat motionless, deep in silent thought. So far I hadn't told him about my worrying discovery regarding the pyrotechnic properties of our Kathy lookalike's frock. I wasn't sure how he'd react, and for the next hour or so at least I needed him to be focused. Later, I decided, much later.

It took only twenty-five minutes to reach our destination. The darkness of night was just beginning to fade as fine sprays of morning light set to work bleaching their way through the heavens. I drew the car to a halt in the visitors' parking area and from there we proceeded on foot.

If not mistaken, it must have been nearly twenty years since I was last in this particular neck of the woods. Generally, Cambridge and the surrounding countryside are as flat as a fluke. The Gogmagog Hills, just less than three miles south-east of the city centre, are therefore something of a geological anomaly. That is, of course, unless you believe the legend of Gogmagog, a huge giant who fell in love with the nymph, Granta. Unfortunately the lady rejected his advances and, as a result, the spurned fellow later metamorphosed into the hills that now bear his name. If not, then the area is just a ridge: home to an ancient Iron Age fortress, now the Wandlebury estate. Stories of witches and occult practices have made the site popular with tourists in recent times. At the very least there are picturesque walks and splendid views over the university town, marred only these days by the grotesque twin chimneystacks towering above the nearby Addenbrooke's Hospital.

Today, however, my companion and I had no time for sightseeing. After a few moments' uncertainty, Julian finally led me to a small clearing surrounded on three sides by tall lime and silver birch trees.

'This's the place, Doc,' he said in a low voice as if afraid of prematurely waking the local flora and fauna.

Aided by the flashlight and the rapidly brightening skies, we began a systematic search of the undergrowth. Almost immediately I spotted the camera tangled up in brambles, pointing in towards the clearing; and upon initial inspection it seemed to be undamaged.

In contrast, Julian screwed up his face. 'Darn it! The tape-loading mechanism's jammed and the aperture's locked shut,' he recited.

'Sounds bad,' I observed, not really sure of the implications of this type of damage.

'Maybe not,' he concluded after completing a round of switch-flicking, button-pressing and catch-releasing.

'So can you fix it?' I enquired hopefully.

'Not me, Doc,' Julian scoffed. 'If Kathy caught me tinkerin' with this baby – man . . .' He stopped short, his face suddenly woeful. No doubt images of his partner's plight had unceremoniously started gnawing away at him with renewed vengeance.

'How about any of your colleagues?' I responded quickly, endeavouring to divert his train of thought. 'There must be at least one DIY camera repairman in their ranks.'

'Sure is,' he replied. 'Old Bob Saunders down near Abington. He's usually got the magic touch where these things are concerned.'

'Good, well that's about all we can do here for now,' I announced. 'Better head back to my place and check on the woman.'

We'd travelled perhaps thirty yards back along the track when Julian slowed, hesitated then came to a complete stop.

'What's the matter?' I asked, concerned that the blow to his head was beginning to act up.

Julian put his hand out towards me, I assumed to indicate that I should 'wrap up' and wait.

Several seconds passed and I was finding it difficult to obey my instructions. 'Come on, Julian. What's happening?' I insisted. 'This isn't helping my blood pressure.'

'Sorry, Doc,' he said finally. 'I just had the strangest feeling. It was as if I'd forgotten somethin' or maybe passed somethin' I should've paid more attention to. Either way, we've gotta go back.'

My first instinct was to put up an argument and repeat my concern about leaving our patient alone any longer. Nevertheless, whatever had caused a blip in Julian's CPU was having a profound effect on his psyche. Better, on second thoughts, to play along – for a short time anyway. We trailed back along the path, Julian taking the lead. A short distance from where I'd discovered the camera, a clump of long-dead tree stumps was huddled together in front of a tangle of brambles. There, Julian drew to a halt, carefully inspected the surroundings then seated himself on the highest of the stumps. Still puzzled, I opted to remain silent and sat down alongside him.

'What now?' I queried when it seemed he was on the verge of drifting off into a trance.

'Oh, Doc. Yeah, right, er,' he babbled. 'Well, don't honestly know what to say, but d'ya mind just squattin' here a spell. Not long, mind.'

'O-kay,' I agreed slowly. 'Any chance of an explanation while we wait; or do we need silence?'

Julian smiled briefly. 'Now, Doc, don't think I can't tell when ya're takin' the Michael.'

'My apologies,' I croaked. 'I didn't mean to be sarcastic or anything. Too many years listening to brain-dead department heads where I used to work.'

'No need to be sorry, Doc,' came the friendly reply. 'I like it when ya use that city style – what d'ya call it?'

'Banter?' I suggested.

'Yep, that's it – banter.'

With this word hanging in the early morning air, we fell silent. Gradually the sun lit up a clear blue sky and we seemed set for a fine day. Over the past week the weather had been very changeable with much rain. Temperatures for the time of year were somewhat above average, and so far there'd been no frost. Nevertheless, that night had been relatively clear and I remembered noting that a passable number of stars had taken the trouble to come out on parade. The combination of saturated earth and fluctuation in temperature had caused a relatively thick mist to form among the trees and some of the denser clumps of bushes. The effect was quite eerie and, sitting there in the midst of this Macbethian spectacle, watching the wisps of vapour eddy and flow through branches of withered leaves, I was becoming decidedly unsettled. Conversation seemed the most expedient remedy, at least until the ghostly fog evaporated.

'If you don't mind my asking, Julian,' I began quietly, 'how did you and Kathy get together? I know it's none of my business, but I wouldn't have guessed she was your type.'

'You certainly got that right, Doc,' he agreed with a smile broad enough to guarantee him a role in any US daytime soap opera. 'The funny thing is that she sort of chose me, and for the life of me I don't know why.' This recollection had patently hit the right spot when it came to unearthing fond memories. Without further prompting, Julian launched into the story of his first encounter with the one and only Kathy Murkett. He began by admitting that for a time in the early nineties he'd been less than a model citizen. More often than not bored by his numerous jobs as a junior car mechanic, he'd just lived for the weekends. Together with a bunch of reprobates from around the area, he'd liked to frequent clubs, bars and discos – get drunk, start fights, then throw up on the pavement after being roughed up by the establishment bouncers. This life suited him fine since most of his favourite cowboy movie stars seemed to share the same enthusiasm for this slapstick-style existence. Late one summer about five years before, however, he and his chums had travelled down to London for a Harley-Davidson motorcycle owners' rally. In reality only Julian had a bike, but that had been in a million pieces on his mother's living-room floor. True to form, he and two of his buddies were drinking in a 1950s revival pub when they'd spied 'three good-lookin' gals'. In time-honoured fashion the men had flipped a coin to decide how they'd pair off. Needless to say, Julian wound up with Kathy who, to his dismay, seemed to represent the short straw of the trio. The girl failed to respond to his premier chat lines, didn't want to dance and said almost nothing. It wasn't long before the two other couples had sloped off. Julian, faced with defeat, had finally decided to call it a draw and got up to leave. As he did so Kathy had taken his hand, led him over to the jukebox, fed in a few coins, and the rest, as it's often said, 'is history'. When it came to parting, it was discovered that not only was Kathy also on a day trip but she too lived near Cambridge and had recently moved into the house they presently occupied.

'Truly a match made in heaven,' I commented at the end of the narration. 'But you've got to tell me; what was the record Kathy first played?'

'You'd never guess it in a million years,' Julian beamed. 'At the time I'd never heard of it. Turned out to be some song from a 1950s movie with Doris Day. Movie had the same title – *By the Light of the Silvery Moon*.'

My friend was right. I'd never have guessed it in ten million, never mind one million, years.

I glanced around to find that most of the mist had dissipated. My ploy had worked. The sun was now shining brightly through the trees, banishing the imaginary band of amorphous spooks and ghouls back to their subterranean dwelling places. Although Julian's story had taken little time to relate, we couldn't tarry any longer.

'I'm sorry, Julian, but unless you can tell me clearly what's happening, I'll have to go, with or without you,' I explained forcibly. Throughout his account I'd sensed that he hadn't been entirely successful in evading the trance that threatened him earlier. Now, as I regarded him closely, I couldn't help but feel that he was a man possessed by another, more powerful spirit. As a rule, I'm not the supernatural type, but these days the unwritten laws, which for thirty years had dominated my existence, were systematically being overturned one by one. I was becoming very concerned – no, more than that, I was frightened. Had the blow to his head caused a haemorrhage? Was he suffering from concussion? Or was he actually caught in the grip of an astral anomaly? Whatever it was, I had to shake him free of it. 'Julian,' I shouted. 'For God's sake, snap out of it. Look, it's me, Jerry Clock. You know, all fancy words and cakes.' As I made my appeal, I stood to face him and grasped both of his arms. At first nothing happened. His eyes had lost all trace of their smiling, congenial quality and were staring sightlessly right through me. I made to shake him again but, without warning, he stood bolt upright, flinched, then with an almighty shudder seemed to break free of whatever sought to shackle his essence.

'Over there,' he gestured, then louder, 'look over there.'

For what seemed an eternity I scanned the location indicated by Julian's raised arm. Nothing. I looked again, but it was only when he pushed past me that I caught sight of something on the ground glinting in the sunlight. Together we hastened towards the reflecting light source about ten yards from the tree stumps.

'Let me,' I entreated, kneeling to inspect the site. A brief forage and there it was, peeking out from beneath a few fallen leaves – a small metallic effigy. I was on the point of retrieving it when I noticed what appeared to be a syringe needle clinging to its rear surface. My forensic experience still intact, I donned the rubber gloves I'd brought along and carefully removed the needle, wrapping it in my handkerchief for investigation later. At least now I had my first piece of data – the effigy was magnetic therefore probably made of iron. It was a curious object completely unfamiliar to me. If I'd been forced to guess, I'd have said it was extremely old, but I couldn't begin to assign a date or period. In terms of size, it was small: only about half an inch long, fashioned in the form of a figure which didn't seem human – perhaps a demon or gargoyle. Its surface was smooth and highly polished, so it seemed reasonable to assume that if it were an ancient relic then it had been carefully restored and only recently mislaid. I passed the object to Julian, who thankfully appeared to have fully recovered from his transcendental interlude.

'Any idea what this is?' I asked in the vain hope that his desire to remain until the artefact came to light, so to speak, might in some miraculous way be connected.

He scrutinised the effigy for a good half-minute before revealing his conclusion. 'Nope. Can't say I've ever seen anythin' like it. Mind you, could've been a pendent if that ring thing in the head comes out.'

'Very impressive,' I congratulated him after a further inspection. 'I'd missed that. Thought it was probably just a circular etching, but you're right. I'm sure if we had a set of watchmaker's tools, we could probably prise it up. Anyway I'm cold, tired and hungry, not to mention worried sick about our injured guest. So if it's okay with you, can we go now?'

'Sure, Doc,' Julian agreed. 'I was only hangin' around cos I thought ya wanted to.'

For the second time we retraced our steps to the car. Julian seemed partially preoccupied, but showed no sign of a repeat mystical performance. At one point I felt compelled to look back over my shoulder, half-expecting to find a couple of hit men running after us. I felt distinctly uneasy and was, to say the least, relieved to see the car parked where I'd left it. With all this weird stuff going on, a vanishing car trick would have been all the encouragement needed to send me rushing off to the nearest Catholic church, seeking sanctuary.

Seat belts engaged, I couldn't resist another look at the relic Julian had, albeit subconsciously, unearthed. I collected together a few metal objects I could easily call to hand – a pen, metal-framed sunglasses and paperclip. To my companion's puzzlement, I then set about trying to assess the magnetic strength of the find. As I suspected, it was quite significant, but even so the syringe needle could only have been attracted if positioned in close proximity. Whoever used the syringe probably owned the artefact, I concluded. If so, and the article was of any value, that was another good reason, besides the woman and the camera, for the owner to return to the scene of the crime. The more I thought about it, the more I knew it was time to get the hell out of there and quick.

We drove back as the morning rush hour was gaining a stranglehold on the roads. All the pre-programmed commuter types, mobile phone in hand, suit jacket hanging from the rear side window, scuttling off to London. It was like spawning salmon fighting their way up-river – two to three hours to get there then, eight hours later, the same haul back. As my American colleagues would say, 'Enjoy!'

Just as we approached Horseheath I thought it wise to interrogate Julian about his recollection of events from the time he'd faltered during our initial attempt to leave Wandlebury up to the discovery of the icon. Not unexpectedly, the poor man had no idea what I was talking about. As far as he was concerned, I was the one who'd wanted to go back to dig around for more clues. Interestingly, he did recall reeling off the Stammers/Murkett 'love at first sight' saga, but not the circumstances. At the end of my impromptu debriefing session I asked him if he remembered ever having any episodes of heightened sensitivity, premonitions or sixth-sense phenomena before.

His reply was both fitting and comical. 'To be frank, Doc,' he said, 'I don't quite know what ya mean, but if it helps, when Kathy's annoyed with me she says I'm about as sensitive as tortoiseshell and as perceptive as a cow.'

As Mr Eric Morecambe of the famous comedy duo Morecambe and Wise often declared, 'There's no answer to that.' Best let the topic drop, I decided.

We were only a short distance from home when the significance of the syringe needle poked its way into my mind again. The relationship between it and the effigy was a mystery. If I stretched my imagination a little, however, the needle could have been the one used to deliver drugs to Kathy's substitute. If so, then that would support my hypothesis that the perpetrators were interrupted before the dastardly deed was complete. Being forced to break off the administration halfway through could have resulted not only in the needle parting company with the syringe, but also in saving the substitute's life. With luck, chemical analysis of its contents should confirm things one way or the other.

'Better come in for a moment, Julian,' I recommended.

34

'I'd like to take another look at your head before you go chasing up your colleagues.'

'Fine with me,' he nodded. 'I could do with another one of your brews and half a bottle of aspirin, if that's okay.'

On the way in we passed the infamous VW bus parked in the drive. Unfortunately, its original plastic seat upholstery had been replaced with fabric. As a result, the bloodstains were going to be a bitch to remove. If Julian was planning to drive around town to seek out his friends, we'd have to find something to cover up the mess or there'd be a queue of people phoning the police everywhere he stopped.

Tired and worn out, we reached my front door. Once inside, Julian indicated his need to make urgent use of the facilities, leaving me to make a beeline for my neglected patient. Unfortunately, I found that my neglect had had a far more profound effect than I could ever have foreseen – the woman had gone.

3

Twister

A cursory search of the house proved fruitless. My first and probably last patient had either been kidnapped or done a bunk.

'Truly excellent!' I exclaimed as Julian, having vacated the bathroom, watched me career down the stairs, his expression questioning. From my perspective, it was the end of the line. No survivor meant no vital information and no explanations. The small metallic effigy wasn't about to 'spill the beans', 'download the goods' or whatever else the modern parlance was. We'd been dropped off in Brick Wall City and I was seriously pissed off. But as Julian so succinctly remarked, 'It wasn't worth blowing a gasket over.' The substitute had vanished and we couldn't do anything about it.

Once I'd calmed down and reluctantly accepted the situation, I whipped up a makeshift breakfast. Julian only picked at my offering, but did put away three mugs of the herbal tea he'd requested earlier. As he drained the remnants of his last refill, he stood up and announced that it was time for him to go. I offered to assist him clean up and camouflage the bloodstained seats in his VW, but he wouldn't hear of it.

'No problem, Doc,' he assured me. 'I'll drive the old girl into my garage and fix 'er up there. Won't take a minute. Ya get some rest.'

Rest – yes, that was a good one, I thought to myself. The image of my ransacked icing room tapped politely on my weary memory, entered then exploded in a sea of sparks. I showed Julian the damage then, despite his protestations, ushered him to the door, mumbling something profound like, 'Don't worry, everything'll be okay.' Half-heartedly I set about tidying up the living room-cum-makeshift clinic, but the result didn't even qualify as a cat-lick. My wise neighbour was right – I needed rest. Not as young as I used to be and all that malarkey. Seated in the most comfortable of my fancy armchairs, I had no energy to prevent my eyelids from drooping. The events of the past twelve hours or so meandered through my mind like a group of drunks on an ice rink. A couple of collisions and a major pile-up later, I sank into a restless doze.

Somewhere in the distance I could hear an irritating knock. Probably a workman hammering, I decided, shifting my posture for the umpteenth time into another muscle-cramping position. The noise persisted, as did my resolve to ignore it. Finally, a welcome silence heralded peace, but only for seconds. Once again someone bloody knocking: this time closer, louder and – oh shit! – on my window. I jerked forward with a start. A glimpse of a figure moving away from the window in the direction of the front door confirmed I had a visitor, and a persistent one at that. Bringing myself round as best I could, I hobbled into the hallway at the maximum pace my collection of stiff joints, aches and pains would permit. All I could imagine was that it was Julian. Probably forgotten something, I surmised. I opened the door but, instead of Julian, a young girl – or an effeminate boy – was standing on the threshold, face expressionless.

'Yes?' I exhaled less than cordially.

'Bates,' the youth announced. 'Norma Bates. Work Experience. You Mr Clock?'

'Oh, for God's sake,' I groaned inwardly, 'surely it can't be that time already?' I squinted at my watch. Bugger, eleven a.m. 'Sorry,' I rasped, my brain still stuck in second gear. 'It's not convenient now. Come back tomorrow. Better still, next week.' Without waiting for a response, I started to close the door. At the halfway point, however, I made the mistake of making eye contact with my rejected caller. The sight caused me to check the door mid-swing. I don't think I've ever seen a face so disappointed, so crestfallen; not even my own when Trisha, my ex, blurted out she was leaving me. As if my arm was a coiled spring, I swung the door open. Third gear grated into position and my level of awareness began to tick over more smoothly. 'Sorry,' I apologised. 'I've had some trouble, and no sleep hasn't helped. Look, forget what I said. Please, come in.'

After a slight hesitation, the girl I now knew her to be accepted my invitation and stepped into the hall. I directed her into the living room and encouraged her to sit. Instead, Miss Bates remained standing and looked around as if contemplating buying the place.

'Interesting,' she remarked. 'But really, if it's not convenient I can come back.' Although she only uttered a few words, her manner of speech caught me by surprise. The tone was reasonably educated, the accent neutral. I did, however, get the impression that she was putting on a performance to some degree. Whether it was to conceal a local dialect or merely affected to impress me, it was a good effort.

'No, it's okay,' I reassured her, finally persuading her to sit. 'Again, please excuse my rude greeting back there but, as I said, I've had a bit of a harrowing night. We should start again. I'm Doctor Jeremiah Clock, pleased to meet you.' I rose and shook her hand.

'Norma Bates,' the girl repeated. 'They didn't tell me you're a doctor.'

I smiled. 'Well, I'm not a medical doctor, which is all most people recognise. I'm a doctor of philosophy, a PhD. It means . . .'

'That's okay,' Norma interrupted politely. 'I know about degrees. What's yours in?' she continued.

'Chemistry,' I explained. 'But I haven't been involved in science for years.'

Miss Bates nodded and resumed her survey of the room.

I couldn't help but berate myself for falling for the oldest mistake in the human relations book. I'd assumed that because she was under twenty, she'd be pushy and over-confident, typical of the teenager that dominates the TV these days, but it was looking very much like I was mistaken.

Norma Bates was probably about five feet six, seventeen to eighteen years old and very slim. If she did have breasts, they were well hidden, but even so her figure was attractive. My male chauvinist observations apart, she was genuinely a very pretty girl despite the large amount of bold makeup she obviously favoured. Her hair was short, a natural lustrous black, and in places it contained a few dark-green highlights, which I had to admit didn't look too bad. She had large hazel eyes, pencil-thin eyebrows and a gold nose stud but no earrings. Dress-wise, I suppose her overall appearance wasn't dissimilar to Errol Flynn, Douglas Fairbanks Jr or any other swashbuckling hero you could think of. Black suede fashion boots, black tights and an over-sized white cotton shirt, tied in at the waist with a sort of green/purple chiffon scarf to complete the ensemble. When I first saw her standing at the door, I must confess I wasn't smitten, but in less than ten minutes my opinion was changing for the good.

'Guess we've got to have an interview now,' Norma said suddenly, fixing me with a stare. 'I expect you've read my notes from the Job Centre. That's what people usually start with.'

It didn't take a 'one hundred and fifty pounds an hour' psychologist to see that the girl didn't relish the prospect of being asked a lot of standard interview questions. If my assessment was correct, she probably had trouble with that sort of thing and had notched up quite a few bad experiences. For good or ill, I couldn't say, but since I had my own style of interview technique deliberately designed to irritate and dumbfound Human Resources drones, I suspected we were in for an interesting time.

'Sorry to disappoint you,' I replied. 'But that's not my way. Reading about people tells me what others think and want me to think. That doesn't interest me. While we have a cup of coffee, I'd prefer you to tell me what you think I should know. From time to time, I'll have questions, but mainly in response to your comments. Does that sound okay, or are you ready to make a dash for the door?'

Norma smiled nervously. 'Sounds okay,' she agreed.

Deal made, I prepared the coffee and laid on a few of my special cakes and biscuits. As I watched patiently, the girl demolished half the confectionery and eagerly accepted the offer of a second coffee.

'Cakes are really good, Mr – sorry, Dr Clock. Did you make them?' she inquired, apparently uncertain as to whether it would be appropriate to go for yet another.

I nodded and gestured for her to help herself.

After a moment's contemplation she slowly sat back in her seat. 'I think I should tell you something first, then maybe later . . .' she elected. 'Okay, let's see. I'm eighteen, an orphan from the age of five. Parents divorced, disappeared and dumped me.'

'Not such a good start,' I said softly.

'Doesn't matter,' Norma shrugged. 'I've been okay. Knocked around a few foster homes, but I've been with my current family, the Knotts, since I was thirteen. They're good people. Do the best they can.' Miss Bates paused.

Probably deciding how deep to go, I surmised. 'Don't feel obliged to tell me anything you're not comfortable with,' I threw in. 'I'm just someone you're thinking of working with. Not a social worker, psychologist, or anybody else with an office.'

'It's cool, I'm fine,' she acknowledged. 'Let's just say then that the Knotts foster quite a few kids and I've been there the longest. I left school at sixteen. Generally did well, but I've a problem with exams. You know the sort of kid? Passes the mocks, screws up the real thing. Over the past year I've not been able to get a steady job, so wound up on this Work Experience programme.'

'And how've you found that?' I enquired.

The girl grimaced. 'Not great. I suppose you might as

well know since I guess most of the paperwork talks about it. I suffer from some sort of behavioural dysfunction. At least that's what all the head doctors call it.'

'Megalomania, schizophrenia?' I suggested jokingly.

'You'd think so sometimes the way people go on,' Norma observed. 'Actually nothing so spectacular. Just, if I get annoyed, occasionally things go a little crazy. Nothing really serious, but it frightens Mr and Mrs Normal so they prefer to pass me over for a tamer model.'

So far I felt the girl was doing a good job. She'd bitten the bullet, revealed her dark secret, but perhaps more significantly she'd allowed her speech to become relaxed and seemed less concerned about putting a foot wrong.

'How about interests, hobbies?' I asked, deliberately not picking up the thread of her quirky behaviour.

Norma seemed surprised at my glossing over what for her must have been a stumbling block rarely, if ever, overcome. 'Okay,' she remarked. 'I like to paint. Mostly watercolours, but usually I can't afford the materials. Music – rock, techno – and, although the Knotts think I'm weird, I really like church music. You know, choirs, chants, requiems and stuff.'

I involuntarily raised an eyebrow. 'A fair list – anything else?'

'I'd like to be involved in fashion,' she replied after a thoughtful pause. 'And Mrs Knott's taught me to read palms.'

As my interviewee completed her account, I noticed a copy of what I thought to be *Vogue* magazine peeping out from the top of her tote bag. More intriguing, however, was a copy of the *Oxford Book of Verse* half-buried beneath a knitted scarf or shawl. Unfortunately my wandering gaze was detected and its focus traced.

'I see you've spotted my secret passion,' she smiled, somewhat embarrassed.

'Who d'you like?' I enquired.

'Not fussed really,' came the dismissive reply. 'But if pushed, I like Ogden Nash. Robert Burns is good, but I don't always understand the meaning of the words. And last but not least, there's Hilaire Belloc – gobbledegook, but I get a kick out of it. . . So, Dr Clock, how'm I doing?' Norma suddenly blurted out, a little surprised herself at the openness of the question. She immediately tried to make a retraction but I assured her it wasn't necessary.

'You're doing just fine. Better than I would if our roles were reversed. A performance definitely worthy of another cake if you're interested.' She was, so I let her eat it in peace while I made another pot of coffee. When she'd finished I thought I'd risk a couple of questions since she now seemed reasonably relaxed.

'D'you mind telling me why you decided to come and see me about my humble position?'

'The truth?' Norma asked.

'The truth'll do nicely to start with. You can tell me the lies later.'

Confused by my response, the young girl nevertheless went on to explain her story. As I'd half-guessed, she'd applied for or been sent to other jobs, but for a variety of reasons things hadn't worked out. Either the interview had gone south, or after she'd started work a problem had arisen and her behavioural dysfunction had reared its ugly head – so back to square one. Basically, she wanted to do something involving art – fashion, design, window-dressing – it didn't matter what, but she couldn't get a foothold. With most avenues tried, failed or blocked, the only option left from both the authorities and her point of view was my opening. I had the feeling that Norma knew she could do much more than those around her believed. Alas, the vicious circle created by her 'problem' seemed indestructible, so slowly but surely the small amount of confidence she possessed was being progressively drained away.

'Well, that's about all I need,' I announced semi-formally for effect. 'Your turn – any questions?'

Norma looked puzzled, as if I'd asked her to solve a complex mathematical equation.

Another first, I suspected. 'Never mind,' I ventured after

a few moments. 'You can ask me any questions as we go along.'

The girl's eyes widened. 'And "as we go along" means . . . ?'

'It means, madam, that I explain my work, your role, and then if you feel like giving it a go, you've got the job.'

'You're joking?' she exclaimed. 'What about my history? And, and you haven't looked at my papers or given me a test.'

'Okay,' I conceded in a manner I hoped would be interpreted as light-hearted. 'I'll give you a test, then we'll see. . . What I do requires attention to detail. So you've been in my house for about an hour now? Close your eyes then describe my appearance and the layout of the room in as much detail as possible. Fair enough?'

Miss Bates frowned. 'You're definitely not like the others. If you're serious though, I'll give it a try.' I was, so she did. 'Right then,' she began, her eyes tightly shut. 'You're Dr Clock. Clever, well-spoken and polite. Probably about six feet tall, medium build, not a bad physique so maybe you work out now and then. You've got short grey hair, blue eyes and are clean-shaven. Looks? Good. Reminds me of a cross between Harrison Ford and that guy out of *Cadfael*. What's his name?'

'Sir Derek Jacobi,' I obliged.

'Yeah, that's him. Oh, and I guess you're about sixty.'

'Not bad at all,' I complimented her, thankful that she hadn't settled for a much less flattering description I'd once heard – a daft old fart with a posh accent. 'But don't expect a Christmas card. I'm only fifty-one. Thanks for the Ford/Jacobi comparison though. Anyway, don't stop. Carry on with the room.'

'Well,' she began slowly. 'We're sitting in two of three armchairs facing an old brick chimneybreast and fireplace. There are wooden beams on the ceiling and on all the walls, I think, except where the bookcase is. The floor's polished wood, covered mostly by a big Persian carpet, and there's a long couch piled up with blankets by the window.'

'Okay, that's very impressive,' I interrupted, reminded of the missing woman by mention of the blankets and couch. 'You've passed the test with flying colours, so open your eyes and I'll show you where I work.'

It wasn't until we reached the door of the icing room that I remembered the break-in. As a result of my impromptu doze I'd forgotten all about it.

'God above,' I blasphemed under my breath. I hadn't called the police; made arrangements for new cakes to be made, or even tidied up. I hastily apologised to Norma and trotted off a potted version of what had happened. 'Better we do this when things are straightened up,' I recommended. 'It's a complete mess in there. Hardly an encouraging sight for your first day.'

But Miss Bates turned out to be especially persistent. She seemed unusually anxious to be allowed inside the room – so much so, I began to wonder about her motives. In the end – probably because my resistance was at an all-time low due to lack of sleep – I agreed to a quick glance. As I opened the door, the girl's face turned a stony grey. She entered the room and looked around with such a profound expression of shock and dismay you'd have thought it was her own workplace that had been violated. Before I could prevent it, she looked behind the door and in a flash traced the path of red stain from graffiti to cake.

'Oh shit!' she exclaimed angrily, her change in tone catching me off-guard. 'The stupid fucking idiot.' Her eyes flashed with rage, her teeth clenched. 'Bloody moron. I knew he'd tried to fuck things up for me. What a bastard, rotten fucking bastard. I'll fucking kill him.'

Obviously I was being treated to a full-blown demonstration of Norma's behavioural dysfunction. The question was, how to react and, more importantly, how to calm her down? There was no way to know what would prove effective: taking hold of her, uttering soothing words, perhaps even shouting. But this was not the time for prolonged consideration. She was becoming more distressed and was exhibiting signs of physical agitation. My gut feeling was to grasp her firmly by the hands and try to talk her down. It didn't work. At the first touch, she wrenched her hands away and began flailing her arms about. Still convinced that a physical component was essential, I clumsily encircled her with my arms then drew her to me in a kind of bear hug. I held on for dear life as I felt her tormented frame rail against my restraining hold. Telling her that everything was going to be all right seemed more than a tad feeble, so I opted for the 'nothing's happened, let's get on with it' approach.

'Norma, we've got to tidy this place up quickly. We need new cakes and a plan of campaign. I can't do it all on my own. I need your help. Will you help me, please?' Until I used the word 'help', my strategy seemed to be failing. However, the 'H' word possessed the magic shutdown code, and within a couple of breaths I felt the tension drain from her body. A moment later she was calm.

'Oh God, I'm so sorry, Dr Clock,' she coughed, almost in tears, 'really sorry. Things were going so well, then the sight of all those cakes smashed to bits just set me off.' I guided her back to the living room and insisted she sip some water. Before I could ask my first question, she answered it for me. 'It's not a fit or anything like that. I know what's happening. I'm just, just . . .'

'Extremely annoyed?' I offered.

She nodded then visibly summoned up an extra slug of courage. 'My language's pretty gross at times like that. I know I've upset you and you're probably freaked out. Most people are. I don't know why you bothered to help me, but thanks anyway. Normally I'd have been slung out by now. Lots of hot air, finger waving, sometimes even the police. All that just makes me worse. It's often an hour or more before I can get my head together. By then it's too late. Nobody wants to know. Nobody wants to listen.'

'Well, it isn't like that today,' I assured her. 'You're a bright young lady. I think we can work well together. As far as I'm concerned, you were angry at what you saw. Now you're not. So you're one up on me.'

'I don't get it,' Norma said puzzled.

'No big deal. I was furious when I found the mess and I'm still furious now.'

'You're crazy,' the young girl smiled. 'I know you're trying to be nice, understanding and all that. Apart from you, only one other guy claimed to have an interest in me, but all he wanted to do was get his hand down my knickers.'

'Is that what you think I'm trying to do?' I interjected.

'Well, to be honest,' she admitted, 'we've only just met, and I've learnt the hard way not to trust anyone right off, if ever. But you seem okay so far.'

'Thanks for the vote of confidence,' I replied.

'You're welcome,' she nodded. 'But I think it's time to cut the – well, you know what. I might be weird but I'm not stupid. You heard what I said back there and guessed I knew something before we even went in the room. You've just been feeding me slack, waiting to see if I'll come clean. Right?'

'Partly,' I agreed. 'But I haven't been feeding you slack. It wasn't necessary. You brought up trust. Well, I trusted that when you were ready you'd tell me whatever it is you're about to say.'

'I see,' Norma said warily. 'All right then, here goes. It's odds on that my dickhead ex-boyfriend, Twister, is the one who wrecked your kitchen. He's an ace, top-of-the-class no-hoper. Every time I talked about getting a job he just rubbished the idea. For him, being signed-on meant he was up for a lifetime achievement award. Since they brought in the New Deal scheme though, things got more difficult, so good old Twister thought a life of crime was the way to go. That's when I chucked him.'

I stood up and walked to the fireplace. 'What makes you think this Twister character's involved?'

'Easy,' Norma responded. 'First, I saw him again recently and we had a row about me coming here. Second, the letter "a" in "wanker" painted on your door is small; the rest's capitals. The pillock liked to think that was his trademark.

Last, when he used to come, he never produced much stuff. Just about what he left you.'

'Pretty conclusive then,' I remarked, deciding it best not to question the evidence further. 'But why Twister?'

Norma scoffed. 'We met at my last school about three years ago. Everybody had nicknames. He was always trying to cheat at exams. Never got away with it though. Anyway, that was his handle.' I suddenly became aware that the girl was staring at me, this time with an air of expectancy. 'Well, go on then, ask me what my nickname is.'

For effect I shuffled a few ornaments around on the mantelpiece then sat down again. 'Not necessary,' I finally remarked. 'I already know.'

'No way,' the girl retorted excitedly.

'Okay, I'll make you a bet,' I offered. 'Basically, I'm as nosy as the next person. So if I guess your nickname, you tell me more about life with Twister.'

'And if you're wrong?' Norma demanded.

'You can ask me a personal question,' I conceded.

'Okay,' my opponent agreed. 'What's the name then?'

To be honest, I hadn't a clue. My strategy was simple. Continue to make the girl feel at ease and hopefully further cement our newfound acquaintanceship. I didn't know why, but Miss Bates intrigued me. Not having experienced bringing up a young family, I was out of touch with the current batch of teenagers. Due to the nature of my work I rarely came across this particular group, so my experience was limited to contact with the offspring of colleagues, distant relatives and my ex-wife's friends. Sure, I was a cynical stuffed shirt but, even allowing for that, I didn't really understand what it was like to be a youth of the new millennium. Norma, as the Americans would say, was special. She wanted to get on in life despite the tough breaks she'd been handed so far. Maybe I was deluding myself, but I thought I could be of some help. A smile spread across the girl's face like the sun hitting the horizon.

'Something amusing?' I enquired

She nodded. 'You and me. I know you're a smart guy. I

heard you used to be a big wheel in one of those blood-sucking multinationals. Even though we've only just met, I like you. I still can't believe I'm talking to you, a complete stranger, like you're my best friend. Anyway, you've worked hard at being cool, even though I can tell you don't know much about people like me. I understand what you're trying to do, but you don't need to treat me like a glass ornament. If you drop me, I may bounce but I won't break.'

This was a turn of events I hadn't expected. Norma seemed to have quickly learnt how to see right through me and my various ploys. Nothing left to do but come clean.

'As they say, or probably used to say, it's a fair cop,' I admitted. 'If you're willing to forgive me, no more psychological games – promise. Nothing, however, has changed. I might be old as far as you're concerned and have limited experience with, shall we say, young adults. Nevertheless, I do need help with my business and I honestly think you'd do just fine. As to your temperament, we'll see how things go. If you want it, the position of deputy cake decorator for Clock Icing Limited is still open. Oh, and one more thing. You win the bet. I've no idea what your aka is.'

'Thanks a lot for the job, but you'll probably want it back when you know my nickname,' she warned. 'I'll give you a clue. My name's Norma Bates and I act crazy.'

'God above,' I sighed. 'Of course, Psycho.'

'Bull's-eye for Dr Clock,' Norma exclaimed. 'Since you got it in one, maybe later I'll tell you more about Twister, the biggest mistake of my life to date.' Then, just as everything seemed to be going swimmingly, Norma's expression darkened.

'What's the matter?' I asked with concern.

It took some time for the girl to articulate the problem. 'Well, Dr Clock, you've been great about everything. Trouble is, Twister broke into your house and messed up all your hard work. When you tell the police and they pick him up, he'll start shouting that I drove him to it and all kinds of stuff like that. By the time he's finished, someone's bound to think I was involved and they'll stop me working with you.'

Very interesting, I mused. Yet another time when contacting the authorities wasn't as straightforward as it should be. Oh well, it was too late now anyway, and not far short of impossible to explain why I hadn't called them last night. What's more, I'd promised Julian no police, at least for the time being.

'Don't worry,' I insisted. 'Now I know what's happened, I don't think we need the police. Instead, I'll make you a deal. You help me clear up and repeat the orders, then next time you come across your mate you have my permission to exact your own retribution. Sound fair?'

Norma agreed, and with that we were off and running . . .

Two bone-shaking explosions set Miss Bates on the edge of her seat. I hastily explained that it was one of two possibilities – a farmer discharging a double-barrelled shotgun or my neighbour's VW coughing its lungs up. A quick recce through the window confirmed the latter. Julian, videotape in hand, was out of the van in a flash and making for the door at uncharacteristically high speed. Time to head him off at the pass, I decided, given the presence of my young guest. Having made some excuse to Norma, I opened the front door just as Julian was about to knock.

'Hi, Doc,' he gasped, breathless with excitement. 'The camera's electrics are a goner, but Bob says the tape's okay. And look, there's a heap of recordin' on it.' The cassette was thrust under my nose to confirm the finding. I tried to squeeze a word in but Julian was at full tilt. 'While Bob was working on the camera, I visited a couple of guys who usually have their ear to the ground. One of them . . .'

'Sorry, Julian,' I finally butted in. 'But my Work Experience person's here. Wise to keep stumm for the moment. Come in for a second until I can work something out.' I was planning to say, 'better leave it till later' or the like, but the level of urgency in my friend's eyes told me he couldn't have handled that. As he entered, I asked to look at the tape again. 'Shit!' I whispered under my breath. 'Just as I feared – VHS format.'

Julian looked puzzled.

'My machine only takes Betamax,' I explained. 'Trish got the VHS.' We were too close to the living room for further exchanges even at a whisper, so in a normal voice I went into thespian mode. 'Thanks for coming over to tell me. Sorry, I can't look at it now but I've got a visitor.'

Norma was already standing as we entered the living room, but I didn't think she'd overheard any of my clandestine comments. I introduced the pair while still struggling to think of a way forward. As I listened to Julian launch into his Svengali routine, automatically triggered, I'd come to appreciate, by the proximity of any woman under the age of ninety, a ray of light sparked into life at the end of the proverbial tunnel. The young girl didn't like to feel responsible for apparently interfering with a pre-arranged plan and wanted to be helpful. Julian spotted the opportunity, and that was it – plan agreed.

'So you're sure it's okay for you to stay here and start cleaning up the workroom while I go over to Julian's house for half an hour?' I asked Norma, taking the cue created for me.

Before I knew where I was, my neighbour was dragging me out of the door in response to Miss Bates shooing us away. Life's full of surprises, I thought, not the least of which on this occasion was the fact that I was about to enter the Stammers/Murkett abode for the first time – and by forced invitation.

'The Ranch' as Julian preferred to call it was, in fact, a semi-detached cottage. Like many in the village, it had begun life a few centuries before as a single dwelling place. With the influx of people not overly flush with cash, two homes had been created and extensions added by subsequent generations. The property in question now comprised four eras of construction, all rendered together as one. So for a cool 200K you essentially got three one-up-one-down units and a single floor block tacked on the end. All in all, a DIY merchant's dream come true and an owner's worst nightmare.

Without ceremony Julian unlocked the front door and led me into the 1960s-style lounge. I was positioned in front of an enormous widescreen TV while my companion switched everything on and loaded the tape.

'What d'ya think we'll g-get, Doc?' he asked, his obvious anxiety having reactivated his stutter.

'Don't get your hopes up,' I warned. 'It's only a long shot.' My comment, however, fell on deaf ears. Wrong response, I judged.

Space-age remote control at the ready, Julian changed his mind in mid-action and dropped the device in my lap. 'Go on, Doc,' he encouraged. 'You start 'er rollin'. Lady luck's never been too sweet on me.'

I did as instructed. For about thirty seconds we watched static then another minute or so of woodland scenery at dusk. The picture then flickered violently, distorted, but re-focused to depict a prolonged close-up view of some trees. Suddenly there was a flash, a blur and the screen went back to static.

As I expected, Julian was disappointed. 'Hell, that was close,' he remarked. 'I thought we were goin' to see somethin' there at the end.'

From my perspective, I wasn't sure we hadn't. Obviously the distortion had occurred when Kathy dropped the video at the time of the attack. If I was right, the subsequent footage was recorded while the substitution was in progress. Then came the interruption I'd suspected all along. The question now was the cause. At my behest, Julian set up the tape to replay the interruption sequence frame by frame. Luckily the mistress of good fortune smiled in our direction. The blur was unquestionably the running figure of a man. There were a few frames where his profile was almost discernible, but neither Julian nor I could identify any recognisable features.

'So what d'you reckon the flash was?' my neighbour asked

51

inquisitively, his previous depression stalled by the winds of optimism.

'I'm almost certain it's the flash from a camera,' I replied, quite excited myself by the implications of the discovery. 'We still don't have much to go on,' I added hastily, 'but if I can confirm that the needle contains certain drugs I suspect, then at least a picture's beginning to form.'

My friend's expression lit up as I spoke, as if he were about to brim over if he didn't blurt out something that had occurred to him.

'Come on then,' I offered. 'Let's have it before you blow one of your gaskets.'

'This's great, Doc,' he began unintelligibly. 'It's what I was tryin' to tell ya before. One of the guys I spoke to said there'd been trouble recently with someone hangin' around the hill. Probably a peeper got wind of the type of filmin' we do there. Trying to get a few photos for some serious knee-tremblin' sessions.'

'Could well be the best lead so far,' I agreed, 'especially if he got a shot of Kathy's double being laid out and doped.' Under different circumstances I may have been even more jubilant, but the mention of peepers and knee-tremblers brought back memories too close to home.

After a few moments' cogitation, I asked Julian if he'd had time to look around the house for any clues – recent letters written to Kathy, which she might have tried to conceal; missing items; new, unexplained or strange purchases. He confirmed he hadn't, but seemed to think it unlikely he'd come across anything odd.

'Kathy's real tidy,' he stressed. 'Come on, I'll show you the room she uses for writin' and stuff. She won't mind.'

I had to admit that the prospect of being allowed to view Kathy Murkett's inner sanctum was quite exhilarating. A feeling of guilt that my curiosity was about to be satisfied only because of the present circumstances put in a brief appearance, but was shamefully batted away. Without further ado, I was taken to the upstairs room of extension unit one – probably of late-Victorian construction, I suspected.

Julian's comment about his partner's penchant for neatness was not exaggerated. The small room, decorated with discreet floral patterned wallpaper, was immaculately kept. It was like a room in an elaborate doll's house with ornate lace curtains and rich Edwardian-style soft furnishings. A chest of drawers, bookshelves and a tiny desk were packed with a variety of miscellaneous items, all precisely arranged. Half the bookshelf, which extended from floor to ceiling, was filled with CDs, most of which seemed to be of Hollywood musicals and show tunes. Well at least that explained Julian's *By the Light of the Silvery Moon* story, I concluded. Perhaps most extraordinary was a collection of dolls displayed in individual cases, all arranged on a bank of shelves adjacent to the window. The basic figures closely resembled Barbie dolls, but each was decked out in a different set of exotic lingerie. Stockings, suspenders, panties and bras were expertly tailored in what appeared to be genuine materials such as leather and silks, with a few in rubber. The designs were varied, ranging from items you could purchase generally to others that I assumed could only be ordered through certain men's magazines.

'One of Kathy's hobbies,' Julian announced proudly, noticing my keen interest. 'Pretty darn good, eh? All real stuff: designed and made by her. Anyway, Doc. Ya can see she's a real tidy gal. All the drawers and cupboards are the same.' Julian took a quick peek in each of these locations as he spoke. 'Nope. Don't see anythin' strange. Our bedroom's next door, but most of our work-related tackle's in there. Kathy wouldn't be right pleased if I took ya in. Sorry Doc, but I promise I'll check it out later.'

I indicated that I understood perfectly and that his proposal was fine. Nevertheless, I'd have given a hefty sum to stick my head round the door for a quick look. There was never much doubt that Ms Murkett ranked high among the unique souls of the world but, having seen her home, her workplace, and of course the Barbie dolls, it was now a certainty . . .

Before going downstairs, Julian felt I should see his 'den'

for comparison. Not unexpectedly, the place was a tip. All manner of tools and books merged seamlessly with a myriad motorbike parts strewn haphazardly over half the floor space. There was a bench on which several British Second World War fighter-plane kits were being assembled and, on the walls, countless movie posters. Three in particular dominated the rest – Arnold Schwarzenegger in *The Terminator*, Raquel Welch in *One Million Years BC* and Clint Eastwood in one of the *Dollar* films.

My neighbour smiled broadly. 'I know. Looks like a kid's room. Guess that probably says it all. . . Come on, Doc. I'll fix ya a drink.'

Given my chronic lack of sleep, I declined the offer of liquor and settled for tea. I couldn't resist asking for the videotape to be played again, but could glean nothing more.

'Who the hell can it be?' I said rhetorically.

'Your friend and mine,' a girl's voice rang out behind us.

Julian and I swivelled around in unison to find Norma standing in the doorway.

'Who else but my darling Twister,' she rasped.

4

Tainted Ice

Julian and I looked at each other then back at Norma.

'How'd you know?' I asked softly, acutely aware that the girl was rapidly approaching another flash point. She shook her head, and for one dangerous moment I thought I'd lost her. But to my abject relief she took a deep breath and the crisis passed.

'Something really weird's going on here,' she accused. 'I only came over to ask what to do with the damaged cakes, and I find the two of you watching Twister on video. Somebody better explain or I'm off.'

'You'd best sit down,' I suggested. 'It's okay, there's nothing to be alarmed about.' Not smart, I immediately recognised, as the girl tensed and retreated a step in response to my appeal.

'Two of you an item? Mixed up in dealing with that crackhead?' She jabbed a finger at the screen. 'You talked about trust, Dr Clock. You also said I was bright. So don't treat me like a dumb kid.'

I could sense she was trying to keep it together but there was no way of knowing how long she'd succeed. My next remark could easily seal it one way or the other. The last thing I wanted was to drag the poor girl into this, but then I urgently needed to know more about Twister, if that really was him on the TV screen. What a bloody mess, I wailed to myself. Like they say, once you get mixed up in crime it's like quicksand – it just sucks you deeper and deeper till you disappear without trace. I glanced at Julian. He was shaking his head very slightly, a gesture I took to mean, 'Don't say anything.' But it was too late. It was my call, and all or nothing was the only option. At that moment my mind decided to give me a nudge. An image of a shadowy figure lighting a match then letting it drop burst into life in glorious Technicolor. The lighted match drifted downwards, the smallest detail of its flame captured in slow motion. Finally it landed on the prostrate body of a woman. Her clothes exploded in a ball of flame, her shrieks of agony ripped through me. Terrible, unspeakably terrible. I had no choice. 'All' was the only option.

'Look, Norma,' I began. 'What I've told you is true. Mr Stammers and I are just neighbours. From time to time we have a drink and chat. I know we might not seem likely drinking partners, but for some reason we just get along. That's all there is to it.'

'Okay,' Norma said, still suspicious. 'But what's with the tape?'

I nodded, and in that split-second I knew that nothing less than the stark truth could win the day. 'You remember when I almost didn't let you in? I told you I'd had some trouble. Well, Mr Stammers' partner, Kathy, has gone missing. They were up near Wandlebury yesterday when they were attacked. Julian – Mr Stammers – was knocked out. When he recovered, Kathy was gone. At the time they had the video camera running, and that's what we're looking at now.'

Norma retook the step she'd retreated, apparently appeased to some extent by my explanation so far. 'What are the police doing about it?' she asked.

For the first time Julian spoke in his uniquely calming and reassuring way. 'I asked the Doc not to call the cops,' he admitted. 'My line of work isn't too kosher, so could be some of my associates are involved. Don't worry none though. Doc's keepin' an eye on things. Soon as he thinks they're needed, he'll bring in the law.'

Norma remained silent for a while then finally entered the room and closed the door. 'Sounds like a pile of BS to me, but since it's Dr Clock shovelling, I guess I'll buy it.'

Catastrophe averted, Norma agreed to join us and, huddled round the TV like a bunch of conspirators, Julian and I explained matters in a bit more detail. By unspoken agreement, we made no mention of the doppelganger, and I, of course, kept quiet about my experiments on the bloodstained frock. In return, Norma pointed out the marking that was just visible on the running man's anorak. A red cross – the symbol of St George – turned out to be another of Twister's trademarks. This observation, coupled with the video footage of a boy's shaven-head profile, was all the proof she needed to make a positive ID.

For me the most astounding aspect of our debate was Julian's explanation to the inevitable question about his 'line of work'. In essence he told the truth, the whole truth and nothing but the truth, but in a way that would have been acceptable to a nun. Well, maybe a nun wasn't a good choice in light of the film Julian had told me about. Anyway, Norma didn't seem fazed by it – in fact she even laughed. My young friend had definitely missed his way. As a psychologist he'd be up there with the greats.

Since it was already well past lunchtime, Julian offered to knock up a few sandwiches. Norma lent a hand, leaving me alone again to contemplate perhaps not the universe but at least the world surrounding our mini-drama. I tried to undertake a full review of events to ensure that nothing had been overlooked, but my lost night's sleep was beginning seriously to tell on me. As I reluctantly abandoned my mental manipulations, it occurred to me that it was still less than twenty-four hours ago that the saga had begun. At that moment it felt like I'd been involved in nothing else for at least a week.

When the repast arrived, I noticed that Norma seemed to have not only regained an even keel but was, if anything, buoyant. Amazing what ten minutes alone with Julian could do, I observed. While chomping our way through our host's doorstep-like creations, the topic of how to locate Twister came up. Norma confirmed that the lad had rapidly progressed from shoplifting to petty theft to stealing cars within a few months of his decision to become a professional criminal. The previous week, when their paths had crossed and sparks flown, Norma had tried once again for old time's sake to bounce him off his chosen course. Things hadn't gone well though. His reaction to her demand that he quit and join her on the Work Experience programme had been blitzed by a tirade of scorn and ridicule. A description of my position and her upcoming visit drew only further mockery. Finally, any remaining vestige of civilised debate had foundered when Twister started to brag about his new association with drug dealers.

'Any idea where he's peddlin' dope?' Julian asked, less than inspired by what he'd heard.

Norma started to shake her bowed head, but then something must have hit a chord. She looked up. 'He didn't say in so many words,' she recalled. 'But he went on about how great everything was. Sleeping all day and then spending most nights buzzing the rave circuit.'

I frowned. 'Well, at least I think I know what a rave is, but aren't they supposed to be spontaneous? Those in the know only find out the location at the last minute?'

'Close enough, Dr Clock,' the girl confirmed, 'Not exactly a doddle when you want to track someone. Trouble is, I've only been to one or two around here, and that was a while back. There are a few people I can think of who may still be part of the rave scene, but I'm not real friendly with them. Don't think they'd tell me – not straight off anyway.'

Julian's lips were already mobilised and well on the way to one of his mega smiles even before Norma had finished her explanation. 'Local raves, you say? In that case, no problem. It's not somethin' we're into cos there's some bad stuff goin' down. These raves are attractin' some heavy-duty hombres. Young kids, booze and drugs, a couple of fast-talkin' dudes with cameras and a caravan, and bingo – instant cheapo porn.'

Another five-minute powwow and it seemed as if we were in business. Julian confirmed that some of his contacts would be able to fill him in on details of possible rave venues in the area. Since the phoning around would take time, it was agreed that Norma and I would return to my house and finish off restoring the icing room while we waited. By the time we left it was nearly three-thirty. Norma assured me that her foster parents wouldn't be worried by the length of time she'd been gone for the interview. Nevertheless, I insisted she give them a call: explain she was safe and that I'd bring her home in the car later. I could tell my new assistant was uneasy about accepting a lift, given the long distance. She had to admit, however, that it had taken her the best part of three hours to reach me. Infrequent buses – late, if actually arriving at all – with a couple of tidy hikes thrown in for good measure: bad enough in daylight but after dark, I wouldn't hear of it.

I was halfway through agreeing plans for completing the mopping-up operation when my mind and body suffered a brownout. I felt terrible. My legs turned to jelly, my limbs ached and what was left of my cognitive powers was definitely on the wane. I had to concede that a fifty per cent resemblance to Harrison Ford wasn't enough to keep an old relic like me going without sleep. Norma was touchingly concerned by the onset of my feeble condition. She insisted that I consume one of her patent but, as it turned out, disgustingly sweet carbohydrate-rich snacks then lie down until Julian made contact. Protests proved futile, so eventually I succumbed. I collapsed onto the bed like a deflating balloon and in the blink of an eye plummeted into a deep, deep sleep.

I awoke in hell. Roasting hot, unable to move: I could see only the silhouettes of countless prancing flames. In the darkness, two shadowy figures bent over me, one of them prodding and goading. I flinched, cried out, then struggled to sit up when suddenly the lights flashed on.

'Jesus!' I exclaimed, my eyes momentarily dazzled by the brilliance.

'You okay, Doc?' one of the figures asked.

'Julian?' I muttered.

'That's me,' came the confident reply.

Finally my mind emerged from the treacle enveloping it and the dazzling effect of the lights faded. 'God above,' I whined. 'That was a shock I could've done without.' I looked about. Norma and Julian were standing on either side of the bed. The fire had been lit and was roaring away with a vengeance. Someone had evidently gone to the trouble of manoeuvring me fully clothed from on top of the bed to beneath the covers, then of tucking me in tighter than a baby in a papoose. 'What's happening?' I spluttered. 'What's the time?'

'It's nearly eleven-thirty,' Norma responded. 'Julian called about fifteen minutes ago to say he'd got a tip-off that there's a major rave going down tonight near Halstead. I was supposed to wake you, but you wouldn't budge. In the end I decided to wait for him. Luckily he had the knack.'

'That's nice,' I said under my breath.

Julian seemed strangely pleased by my sarcastic remark and smiled hugely. 'Well, it's up to you, Doc,' he proclaimed. 'Are we up for a little boogie-woogie tonight? Track down this Twister fella and get my Kathy back. Charlie Boy, he's my contact, says it'll likely be another week or so before there's another one of these shindigs in this neck of the woods.'

'Well, if that's the case,' I said stoically, 'there's nothing to decide. I'll probably pass on the boogie part but otherwise, yes, let's give it a try.' Then it hit me just exactly what I was agreeing to. 'Whoa. Just a minute,' I ordered. 'Who's this "we"? Norma should've been home hours ago. Her parents'll be climbing the walls.'

'It's okay, Dr Clock,' the girl hastily explained. 'I called them again. Hope you don't mind. Told them I'd stay with some friends in Haverhill. It's no problem, really.'

I felt a double dose of innate parental outrage and pomposity rise in my throat. I opened my mouth to sally forth, but caught sight of Julian giving me one of his looks. This particular one couldn't have been clearer. 'She was a grown woman; I wasn't her father; so basically, sit on it.'

'On two conditions,' I insisted as forcefully as my position – sitting up in bed like a half-dazed porcupine – could command. 'You stay close to Mr Stammers or me at all times, and at the first sign of trouble, you're out of there. Is that clear, young lady?'

'Yes, sir!' Norma replied in a way that gave me little confidence that my role as surrogate father figure had been in any way successful.

I opted for nothing more than a quick swill to wake myself up, then threw on a set of old clothes considered by Julian to be the only things I had suitable for the occasion. A mug of life-saving coffee later, courtesy of Nurse Nightingale, and we were ready for the off. All we had to decide was whether to travel in the VW or the TR6. Fate, however, apparently didn't fancy either choice. My companions convinced me that a classic car wasn't the best conveyance to be seen in, even if parked some distance from the site. That left the VW, but the junk heap wouldn't start. Out of time and out of options, I reluctantly unveiled the beat-up Norton Commander motorcycle and open sidecar I'd been tinkering with for the last five years. Despite the seriousness of our quest, my companions seemed to regard a late-night bike ride along dark deserted roads with cold damp air blasting in their faces as a treat. Myself, I didn't catch the appeal. In fact, I couldn't decide which was the more worrying – my passengers' warped idea of pleasure or the thought of the three of us heading off to crash a rave. John Wayne, Ms Errol Flynn, and myself in old gardening trousers and shabby overcoat presumably as Lt Columbo, didn't instil too much confidence.

By twelve-thirty we were in the vicinity Julian had described and, after a few backtracking episodes, we finally discovered the turning we'd been looking for. A few miles of narrow lanes, tracks, and an off-road experience later, and a huge barn loomed before us with flashing lights and booming sound billowing from its groaning structure. This was definitely the place and the rave was in full swing.

We hid the bike, riding gear and helmets at the back of a small, dilapidated shed a few hundred yards from the target. As I completed my security routine, I noticed Julian and Norma surreptitiously exchanging whispers obviously, they believed, out of my earshot.

'I might be older than the pair of you put together, but I'm not deaf,' I called out. 'I know I don't exactly look your typical rave devotee, but I'm not letting you two waltz in there without me.'

'Don't worry, Doc,' Julian reassured me, 'just chewin' over a few options. I think the little lady's got the best plan, though.'

'Which is?' I enquired, already certain I wouldn't like it.

'To start with,' Norma began. 'Julian's going to check out the entrance and hopefully spot someone he knows who can get us in.'

'That's the easy part,' my neighbour boasted.

'If all's well,' she continued, 'Julian will signal us, and after you've been introduced, we'll be home free.'

I looked at my companions. 'Okay,' I said slowly. 'And just how am I to be explained away?'

'Well, it's got to be believable,' Norma took pains to stress. 'The organisers of this kind of gig are really suspicious. If they think you're an undercover cop or anything, they'll just shut everything down, then we'll never find Twister.'

'Let's have it,' I prompted. 'We haven't got all night.'

Norma coughed nervously. 'Basically, you're one of Julian's clients: an old guy with money who sometimes produces girlie movies for his own interest. I'm going to be the star of the next production, and we're looking for some new talent to play supporting roles.'

I was right. I didn't like it, especially the part about me being an old guy. Nevertheless, I wasn't exactly on home turf so better to leave it to the professionals.

'Couldn't be better,' I declared sarcastically. 'Just what

I've always imagined myself as. Come on then; let's get on with it. At least the plan ensures you, madam, stick to me like superglue at all times. And besides, any story that'll get me out of this cold damp air can't be all bad.'

The plan went extremely well. One might even have been tempted to say it went like clockwork. My role as rich dirty old man not only impressed Julian's contact, but also resulted in our party being afforded the equivalent of VIP treatment. We were escorted to one of only a handful of knockdown tables that had been set up toward the rear of the barn, and three bottles of beer and two cracked plastic cups plonked on the table by a pair of hands apparently not connected to anyone in particular completed the welcome pack. Given the bone-rattling thump of the music, the totally deafening noise and the crush of gyrating youths, alcohol was the last thing I needed. Over the din Julian shouted that he was off to scout around to see who else he knew. Norma seemed quite at home grooving – or whatever it's called these days – to the music and almost enjoying her beer until I took it from her.

As we sat waiting for Julian to return, I tried to fathom the attraction of this kind of event. The majority of revellers were cavorting around what little floor space there was almost in a stupor. Some appeared to favour slamming into one another while others seemed hell-bent on shaking their heads and limbs free of their respective joints. The atmosphere was a fog of smoke, incense and other burnt chemicals. It was hard to imagine that there'd be sufficient oxygen left to keep people alive, never mind flailing about like demented apes. Blinding high-powered spotlights bathed the scene in vivid colours, their motion in some way linked to the relentless pace of the drone – for drone was the only description I could think of that fitted the bill. Take a single phrase, feed it into a synthesiser, add a pounding beat and repeat two million times. Result? – Well, I suppose the result was a good time for all, judging by the response, I scoffed quietly to myself.

My age, prejudices, pomposity and outdated values had all been summarily dredged up to the surface by the spectacle before me. Perhaps I was better off retreating into my sheltered world of icing cakes after all. I still felt the excitement I'd experienced when all the trouble started, but was this really what I should be doing? I was about to conclude with three of my least favourite words, 'at my age', when I noticed Norma jump up from her seat. She grabbed my arm and suddenly I found myself propelled into the body of the reeling mass. It was like finding yourself hurled from the deck of a ship into a raging sea. Unable to make my protestations heard over the clamour, I could do little more than strive to keep her in view. Deeper and deeper we plunged into the spinning vortex, completely at the mercy of synthesisers and electric guitars, which like electronic sirens were driving the multitude to ever-greater heights of abandon. A boy leapt from a nearby platform onto a carpet of waving arms, like wheat swaying in a summer breeze, then another and another. Supported by the countless tendrils, the divers seemed to float across the solid pack.

Rotated helplessly this way and that, I momentarily lost my footing, stumbled, but then miraculously recovered. I strove to regain my visual lock on Norma, but to my dismay she'd vanished. Panic instantly grasped what little composure I had left and started to throttle the life out of it. I cried out, but I knew it was a complete waste of breath. Suddenly a rift appeared in the crowd to my right. Irrationally I lurched towards it, entering the mid-section just as it began to reseal. In the split-second of freedom granted me, I managed to edge myself a good ten yards back towards the perimeter of the crush. The gap zipped together as I moved, eventually closing shut around me and jerking me to a standstill.

'Great isn't it, Dr Clock? All this raw energy.'

'Norma?' I yelled, fighting to swivel around and confirm

my suspicion. 'Thank God I've found you,' I shouted at the top of my lungs. 'This is worse than bedlam. We must get back to the table. Julian could be looking for us.'

Reluctantly Norma allowed me to extricate her from the throng and escort her under close guard back to our table. Predictably our oasis had been taken over by another group of VIPs, and it didn't take a soothsayer to predict that the chance of finding alternative seating was subzero. My hand tightly grasping Norma's arm, I mounted a determined search of the barn as far as the jostling crowd would permit. Julian was nowhere to be seen, and after a good ten minutes I was forced to conclude that he must be somewhere outside.

We entered the still night air through a damaged section of the barn wall at its rear. For some reason the organisers had decided that this was not a likely breach point, so fortunately no heavies were in evidence to bar our escape. Free at last from the seething cauldron of sweating bodies and igniting hormones, I felt immensely relieved. Norma, still captivated by the infectious primeval atmosphere, was breathless with excitement. As I looked at her, memories of my own somewhat staid youth slotted into view, and for one brief moment – just one – I understood what all this was about.

'Sorry to give you a fright, Dr Clock,' Norma panted. 'Everything was cool though. I'd never have left you. Just for a while there I guess I got carried away.'

'Carried away being the operative phrase,' I said sternly, my tone hitting the mark with greater force than I'd intended.

The light in Norma's eyes visibly dimmed and an expression of remorse instantly unravelled across her face.

Time to initiate damage control, I realised. 'No need to look like a squashed lemon,' I smiled. 'You know us old fogies – worry, worry, worry. It goes with the territory. What can I say? Come on, buck up. Let's find out where Mr Stammers has got to.'

My efforts met with success, and with the young girl's

optical illumination bumped up a few dozen watts we reconvened the search. A circuit of the barn and a couple of nearby wooden huts revealed nothing. To my amazement, people were still arriving and what I took to be several head-smashers hired by the organisers were unsuccessfully trying to turn them away. I was on the point of contemplating the horror of a second sortie inside the building when I noticed lights flickering in the distance. With less than sound reasoning, I decided it was probably worth a quick look, then if we had no joy, back to the human sardine can. As we approached, it was just possible to pick out a line of four Portakabins in the weak moonlight. Each was mounted on a trailer, which in turn was hooked up to a fair-sized truck. Before we could gain a clear view, though, engines burst into life, sending the fear of God rocketing through me. Seconds later a small group of people exited one of the cabins before it trundled away across fields in the direction of the main road. The procedure was repeated with a second rig, but the third and fourth stayed put.

'What d'you reckon's going on, Dr Clock?' Norma whispered.

'Difficult to say,' I admitted. 'I imagine the organisers need trucks to haul around the equipment, but not Portakabins. I suppose they could be the porno caravans Julian mentioned.'

Under cover of an intervening hedgerow and sections of damaged fencing, we crept along to within twenty yards of the target. Never having been one for games like hide and seek, I didn't find myself warming to the experience now. Crouching near the ground, ears pricked, eyes flashing hither and thither, might be okay for children or rabbits but not for JOC. Curiosity, however, is a difficult mistress to deny at the best of times, and since we'd come this far . . .

From our new position I could detect no sign of life in the second cabin, but in the first flickering light was definitely visible in one of the windows. After a few minutes, which seemed more like half an hour, still nothing had stirred. The only sounds I could detect were those of my creaking knee joints and a rather large hedgehog shuffling through the undergrowth. Time to risk a foray, I decided. As in all the best movies, I instructed my partner to wait while I tiptoed over to the illuminated window. Norma was less than ecstatic about the idea, but dutifully agreed to assume the role of lookout. The mission went well. I reached the side of the cabin, managed to get a foothold on the trailer and hauled myself up to one side of the window. My precarious position allowed me only a restricted view, but it was enough. About half the interior was aglow with dozens of burning candles. All shapes, sizes and colours; they were positioned mostly on makeshift shelves around the walls, but a few taller ones were packed together on the floor. In the midst of this eerie spectacle were two young girls, their arms tied behind their backs and their expressions fearful. A rope had been attached from their bound hands to the ceiling, forcing them to bend over. Both girls wore remnants of what appeared to be US-style policewomen's uniforms, but the garments had been torn away or carefully arranged to expose their naked breasts and buttocks. The only items still intact were their hats, abnormally high stiletto heels and suspendered stockings. As I watched, a much older, pot-bellied Hell's Angel reject swaggered into view. For a few moments he taunted the girls, slapped them on their behinds then whipped out his huge willie and started playing with it. Up to that point I couldn't be absolutely sure either way whether this was a horrendous crime in progress or an example of the darker side of Julian's world. But then the two captives suddenly grinned, looked at each other and began to squabble over who should have the dubious pleasure of sucking the mammoth appendage first. Two other men – one wielding a video camera, the other sound equipment – emerged from the shadows and, with exaggerated stealth circled the players, obviously intent on capturing all the action in graphic close-up.

Relieved that at least it hadn't turned out to be the first

of my conjectures, I couldn't help but feel deeply saddened. What was so-called civilised society coming to when young people barely in their teens allowed themselves to be subjected to such degradation? The purity of youth, at one time held in high regard, had become polluted. No doubt though, in a few years time, the spin doctors would simply capitalise on the change and begin extolling the virtues of a new 'tainted ice' youth culture.

Ah well, that was probably enough hypocritical soapbox preaching for one session. In fact I should be the last one to criticise, my voyeuristic tendencies just having been unexpectedly topped up for the present.

Still no closer to locating Mr Stammers or the inimitable Twister, I climbed down and retreated to base camp but, to my horror, Norma had evaporated.

'Shit!' I exclaimed.

'Looking for yer little girlie?' a gruff voice called out mockingly from somewhere in the darkness. I spun around, most of my internal organs jostling for position in my throat. 'Over here, squire,' the voice continued. 'That's right. By the truck.'

No sooner had I focused on a spot close to the trailer coupling of the first vehicle than someone grabbed me around the neck. Before I could react, my arm was wrenched almost out of its socket, twisted then jammed up behind my back.

'Welcome to Hotel Shithole,' the crude voice of my attacker rattled in my ear. 'Shall we join yer baby-face cute piece of ass?' Having dispensed with the niceties, my less than congenial host hurled me headlong through the hedge. Gasping, I was dragged to my feet and frog-marched over to meet his colleague. As we approached I could see Norma, her eyes wild, her mouth covered with tape, struggling against the gorilla clutching her hair.

'Ya wanna teach yer fucking tart some manners,' the gorilla snarled as I was jerked to a halt. 'Fucking cunt's got a real mouth on 'er, and she tried to boot me in the balls –

didn't ya, bitch? Now round 'ere we takes that as not right friendly, don't we, Bulldog?'

'Not friendly at all, Mr Z,' came the dutiful response.

Perfect, I thought. Bulldog and Mr Z. If I hadn't been half-frightened out of my wits and the situation not so dire, I'd have laughed out loud.

'Have a nice time beakin' through the window, then?' Mr Z rasped. 'Cream yer pants, did ya? Well sunshine, d'ya wanna know what pisses me off? Perverts. But what really gets on my tits is perverts like you who don't wanna pay for it.'

A quarter-century of education, over twenty years in industry, and I couldn't think of a thing to say. Norma was becoming highly agitated, obviously having entered one of her 'states'. I shuddered to think how this might escalate when faced with the present terrifying situation.

'Don't say much do 'ee, Mr Z?' observed Bulldog.

Mr Z grinned. 'Oh, don't ya go worryin' yer head about that, me old mate. Loverboy 'ere's goin' to tell us 'oo 'ee is and all about what 'ee's been up to before I beat the shit out of 'im, ain't ya, son?'

Up to that point I'd been unable to get a clear view of Mr Z since he held Norma directly between us and his face was partially obscured by shadow. In preparation for my interrogation, however, he signalled Bulldog to exchange places, allowing me a brief glimpse of his features. Not as tall as I'd imagined, Mr Z was, to my surprise, about my age but much fatter. He sported a long wispy grey beard, tinted glasses and a peak cap covering an apparently completely bald head. His clothes were fairly nondescript – jeans, some kind of logo T-shirt and a heavy leather jacket. As he took over from Bulldog, he brought his face close to mine. He grinned, exposing a partial set of tobacco-stained teeth and, as he exhaled, the stench of his breath almost made me retch. I couldn't tell much about his partner as he was dressed all in black except for a daft multicoloured ski mask.

The transfer of responsibility clearly made Bulldog's day.

He immediately started to paw Norma and caress her face with his gloved hand. It was then that I noticed her ankles had been bound together with the same tape used to seal her mouth. In struggling to escape her new keeper's unwanted attentions, she jerked sideways, overbalanced and crumpled to the ground. Bulldog giggled like a demented hyena. He knelt over her then allowed a huge gob of saliva to splash onto her face. Tongue flapping lizard-like, he started to lick her, spreading his spit over her cheeks and forehead. That was it. I couldn't stand it any longer. I struggled violently, kicked out, but Mr Z hadn't the slightest trouble in quelling my rebellion.

'Naughty, naughty,' he goaded. 'Ya ain't seen nothin' yet. You wait till Bulldog starts lickin' her little . . .'

'You boys havin' fun?' The question cut Mr Z off in mid-sentence. Bulldog immediately abandoned his meal and sprang to his feet. I was swivelled around.

'Julian!' I hissed. 'Thank God.'

'Who the fuck're you supposed to be?' Mr Z smirked – I thought most discourteously. 'Tex Tucker?'

From somewhere my neighbour had acquired a distinctly beat-up cowboy hat, and I was immediately reminded of one of the posters in his room. The stance, the look, even the four words he'd uttered – there could be no mistake: Clint Eastwood. True, he didn't have a poncho or a couple of six-shooters, but who cared?

Without waiting for a reply, Bulldog rushed at the intruder. He swung wildly with his fist, but Clint just casually stepped out of its path. In reply, Clint stuck his attacker with a perfect blow to the solar plexus. The man doubled up, the wind knocked clean out of him. For a moment he looked up, surprised by his quick defeat, but Mr Eastwood's other fist smashed him to the ground.

A suggestion of a smile briefly touched my friend's lips. '"Man's got to know his limitations",' he quoted from one of his idol's later police films.

'Fuck you!' growled Mr Z, apparently having left his dictionary of swear words at home. 'I'm goin' to tear yer fuckin' head off and shove it up yer arse.' My captor unceremoniously knocked me to the ground, whipped a large flick-knife from his back pocket and advanced towards his prey. 'Fucking this' and 'fucking that' tumbling from his lips in a constant stream, Mr Z lunged and parried. On this occasion Clint held his ground, biding his time, I assumed, waiting for the right moment. It came sooner than I expected. A lightning kick with his foot and the young man sent his assailant's knife flying into the air. Disarmed and dismayed, Mr Z hesitated then made the same mistake as Bulldog – he charged. Three 'ers' – slower, fatter, and older than his colleague – the one-man swearing machine suffered the same fate. A second blow failed to finish the job, but a third sent him staggering towards me. I scrambled to my feet to avoid a collision, but then realised that Mr Z had spotted his knife and was heading straight for it. At that moment my pent-up fear, rage and anger hit supercritical. Basically, I just snapped. I launched after the man at full tilt, slammed into him with a not half-bad rugby tackle and punched him squarely on the nose. My opponent yelped, covered his face and lay still. The conflict was over.

I couldn't believe I'd just thumped someone. It had to be forty years since I was last in a fight and, if my memory was correct, the duration had been about a minute and I'd lost. My hand stung like hell, my emotions were in turmoil but, as I began to regain control, one thing couldn't have been clearer – I was bloody well pleased I'd walloped the fat bastard.

'Fuck me, man,' Mr Z whined. 'You've broke my fuckin' nose. The fuckin' old pervert's broke my nose.'

By now Julian was standing over us. 'Not bad, Doc,' he remarked, smiling. 'That's the trouble with these tough guys – all mouth and glass jaws.'

As we released Norma, Bulldog, having partially recovered, led his boss across the field towards the barn. The girl was shaken but seemed to have passed the crisis point of her condition and was relatively calm.

'Thanks Julian,' I said, looking around to see if the coast

was clear. 'But what happened to you? We looked everywhere.'

'Sorry,' he apologised. 'I managed to get a lead, but it meant meetin' a guy back near where we parked the bike. Anyways, we should be gettin' out of here. Those two old boys'll be fixin' to raise the cavalry then they'll be back, and it won't be for polite conversation.'

'But what about the lead?' Norma breathed, her teeth chattering slightly. 'Did you find out where Twister is?'

'Sorry, mam,' Julian apologised. 'The guy I spoke to knew the boy but said he hadn't seen him. Funny thing was though, seemed I was way back in a long line of folks mighty eager to find the young fella.'

Not too encouraging, I thought, and by the look in Norma's eyes she harboured the same concern. 'Anything else?' I asked out of habit.

'Nope,' Julian replied. 'Nothin'. When I returned to the barn I got the tip-off that an old-timer and young gal were wanderin' loose outside. When I couldn't find y'all, I thought I'd mosey on down here. I'd been told Marcus Hamilton had three of his mobiles on point tonight. Figured ya might've been attracted by the lights.'

'Good thing you did,' I said rhetorically. 'But wait a minute, you're certain it was three rigs, not four?'

'Why sure,' he confirmed. 'Marcus only uses three.'

Norma and I exchanged glances, but before I could pursue the matter the door of the cabin behind us flew open and the flabby Hell's Angel cast-off waddled down the steps.

'Oh, Jules my love, are you all right, dear heart?' the man crooned. 'Those Marcus boys are so rough, but you certainly sorted them out. You're so macho these days. The hat's a mistake though.'

'Who the hell's that?' I whispered, stunned that even with all the commotion I could have forgotten about *LAPD Girls Go Undercover with Free Willie 2.*

My neighbour stood up to greet his admirer, apparently not having picked up my question. The two embraced.

'Toby Farthing!' Julian exclaimed. 'Haven't seen you in a good while. How's the bondage flick business these days?'

Unfortunately Toby wasn't in the mood for social chit-chat. All of a fluster, he hastily explained that Mr Hamilton wasn't known for his peaceful temperament. Retribution for the attack on his boys was a given, and Toby didn't fancy his crew being the only ones left at the scene when the seriously pissed-off Mr H arrived. Without further ado he bade Julian farewell, nodded to Norma, blew a kiss to me then joggled back to the cabin. A moment later the film crew transferred to the truck and started the engine. As the rig rocked away Toby stuck his head out of the window.

'Sorry we didn't help out with the fight, Jules, but you know how it is? An actor's face and all that. Bye, Sweetie. Take care.'

'And then there was one,' I chanted to myself, still trying to come to terms with the concept of a gay porno actor disguised as a Hell's Angel. I couldn't speak for the others, but I for one was picking up some very peculiar vibes about the last remaining unit. Julian had confirmed that Marcus Hamilton generally only used three rigs. Two of same had already left, and Toby clearly believed he was the last. Despite the imminent arrival of the forces of vengeance, my companions agreed that the presence of the fourth truck/trailer was odd. No persuasion was necessary to gain a consensus that since we'd come this far a quick reconnaissance of the cabin was worth the risk. I could tell from their eyes that Julian and Norma would have agreed to almost anything if offered even the slightest chance of finding Twister: Julian, because the lad was possibly his only real lead to Kathy, and Norma because, in some strange way, I believed she was beginning to fear for his safety.

The cabin was in total darkness, its doors and windows tightly secured. Julian volunteered to work the lock so, while Norma and I accepted lookout duty, he got to work with a small penknife. No more than thirty seconds later the muffled sound of breaking glass set the hairs on the back of my neck jumping to attention.

'Sorry, people,' Julian whispered as we ran towards him. 'I'm a touch rusty at the old lock-pickin' game, but this baby did the trick just fine.' The baby – a half brick wrapped in the young man's hat – was something of a misnomer, but it had achieved the objective.

Since there'd been no response to the noise, it was safe to assume that no one was home, so we entered. Instinctively I started to fumble along the wall in search of a light switch. Thankfully there was one – the only question was whether it was connected to the truck battery. Again we were in luck. A couple of ceiling lights struggled into service – distinctly miserable, but at least we could now make out the cabin's interior. Apart from a table, a handful of chairs and some general bric-a-brac, the place didn't appear to have been recently occupied. It seemed we'd wasted precious 'fleeing' time, and I was about to recommend a tactical retreat when Norma cried out.

'Oh Jesus! Dr Clock, hurry, in here.' The young girl was standing about two-thirds the way down the cabin, peering through a dividing curtain she'd drawn. I reached her side in a second, Julian only a pace behind. There, lying on an old-fashioned surgical table and connected to a bewildering array of tubes, wires and monitors lay a young boy.

'My God,' I breathed. 'Twister?'

5

Butterfly

In all of my years associated with the medical fraternity I'd never seen anything like it. The complexity of the monitoring system was fiendishly convoluted, the IV line array outlandish. A preliminary examination of the boy revealed little except that he was in a deep coma. If my reading of his life signs displayed on the monitors was correct, however, several of his vital organs were on the point of collapse. There was precious little time remaining – but what to do for the best? My instinct was to shut everything down and yank away the lines, but without knowing the purpose of the set-up this could simply result in Twister's instant death. My companions were hovering at my side with bated breath.

Norma, silent since her shocked discovery, suddenly regained the power of speech. 'Come on, Doctor Clock. Please help him, please,' she pleaded. I glanced at Julian, who took the hint and guided her gently but firmly back into the main body of the cabin.

Without the pressure of anxious eyes boring into me, I could think more clearly. The key lay in the computers. If I could glean some information about the program, I'd at least stand a chance of determining whether the system was designed for good or ill. Quite sure the answer would be the latter, I worked the keyboard as fast as my fingers could move. Strangely, there seemed to be no password protection and, after racing down a couple of dead ends, I hit the jackpot. A menu of detailed schematics popped up on-screen offering a range of options including a 'properties field'. Once selected, I was presented with a long list of titles and instructions on how to access the 'primary settings' dialogue window. From there I was able to view the set-up, section by section, and effect changes to the associated parameters. It took only a minute or two to view the entire file and only another ten seconds before the penny finally dropped.

'Jesus,' I hissed, unable to suppress my astonishment.

Attracted by my outcry, Julian stuck his head round the curtains. 'Everythin' okay, Doc?' he enquired in a low voice. 'Anythin' I can do?'

I turned to face his hopeful expression. 'I'm sorry to say there's nothing anyone can do.' An overwhelming feeling of helplessness rapidly flooded both body and soul. Julian held the curtain back for me as I rose and made to re-enter the main cabin. Norma was standing by one of the windows, staring sightlessly towards the barn. 'Any sign of movement?' I asked weakly.

The young girl spun round as if mounted on wheels. 'How's he doing?' she demanded, ignoring my question. 'Is he out of that thing? Will he be okay?'

I pulled up one of the seats and sat down with the backrest facing me. For a moment I hesitated, caught in the familiar dilemma of 'tell it as it is' or 'tell it how others would wish it to be'. But this was Norma, and I'd already learnt the answer to that one. 'I'm sorry, love,' I began. 'There's nothing to be done. He's too far gone.'

Norma's eyes glazed, her body tensed, then she detonated. Like an Olympic runner released from the starting blocks, she jetted away, clattering past any and all objects that barred her direct line to the curtain. Two steps away from the target, Julian caught hold of her. She struggled violently, determined to reach her goal, but his grip was too powerful.

'Come on, little lady, ya can't help yer friend none in this state,' he advised sympathetically. 'Best take a couple of deep breaths and listen to what the Doc has to say before . . .'

'It's okay, Julian,' I interrupted. 'You can let her go. Just stay with her.'

I waited a short while before following. Somehow I knew that in those few fleeting moments a presence would come and, where I had failed, swiftly release Twister from his bed of thorns. When I arrived, a single glance at the monitors confirmed my expectation. It was all over. Norma was sitting by the young lad's side, his lifeless hand gently cradled in hers. Julian, his arm wrapped around the girl's shoulder to comfort her, stood as he had earlier when guarding our Kathy lookalike. Like droplets forming in a springtime thaw, tears splashed onto Norma's cheeks and traced a meandering path to the crease of her lips.

'He's gone?' she murmured, half-question, half-statement of fact.

'I'm afraid so,' I confirmed. 'There was nothing anyone could've done. I'm really sorry.'

'Someone did this to him,' she continued as if the idea were incredulous. 'But why kill him? Why all this?'

Neither Julian nor I could manage a reply.

Suddenly Norma shot up from her seat. 'No, wait a minute,' she exclaimed, seemingly mesmerised by the mass of wires and tubes. 'This wasn't just rigged to kill, was it? This fucking mess is some kind of torture chamber.' The young girl's voice, although harsh, was steady and controlled.

Julian, who as yet knew nothing of Norma's behavioural quirk, looked anxiously in my direction, uncertain of how to react. I raised my hand to indicate that we should remain on standby. If I wasn't too far from the mark, the girl was merely expressing normal frustration and grief. Over-reacting every time she displayed strong emotions seemed a sure-fire way to make matters worse. Sure, it might not always be possible to read the signs correctly, but if there were mistakes, so what – all part of the learning curve, as they say. On this, my first test, it looked as if I'd got it right. Norma's anger quickly subsided and she resumed her post at Twister's side.

'Some kind of fancy drug-overdose kit then,' she said without diverting her eyes.

'Yes,' I agreed. 'A very elaborate one.'

'What's with all these bloody TVs then?' she continued. 'Why not just beat him up, shoot him up and have done with it?'

I drew up a seat at her side and pointed to the main computer monitor. 'It's certain that whoever did this is very clever and very sick. All the screens and wires were used to monitor Twister's vital signs – heart rate, pulse, body temperature and the like. Somehow – and to be honest it's beyond me – all this information was fed into the computer and used to regulate the IV drip.'

Norma fixed me with a piercing glare. 'So you mean the amount of shit being pumped into him was regulated by his physical condition?'

'Exactly,' I confirmed. 'The horribly sadistic part is that an increase in any of these parameters caused an increase in the speed of the IV drip.'

'Nasty,' Julian grimaced. 'Real nasty. I ain't no scientist, but what that means to me is if the young fella tried to escape or even thought about it, he'd be speeding up his own end.'

The comment met with silence, as we each contemplated the fear and dread Twister must have endured until the level of drugs in his body robbed him of his senses.

Barely had the vigil begun when an almost supernatural event broke the respectful peace. The bank of monitors flickered then simultaneously displayed the photograph of a wooden cross supporting the dying figure of Christ. A moment later the scene was replaced by text from the Scriptures and a rich, deep voice reading the lines:

'And they brought unto him also infants, that he would touch them: but when his disciples saw it, they rebuked them. But Jesus called them unto him, and said, Suffer little children to come unto me, and forbid them not: for of such is the kingdom of God. Verily I say unto you, whosoever shall not receive the kingdom of God as a little child shall in no wise enter therein.

Luke, Chapter 18 v.15–17.'

One by one the screens then faded to darkness. I started to make a comment – something about the context being skewed but the sentiment quite appropriate – when Julian waved me into silence. As we listened, a faint wailing sound could be heard in the distance, becoming louder as the seconds ticked by.

'The cops,' Julian pronounced. 'I should've known somethin' mighty fishy was goin' on when the lynch mob didn't turn up. A dime to a dollar we're sittin' pretty in the middle of a set-up.' He received no questions, no debate. I somehow knew he'd hit the proverbial nail, and Norma was in no doubt either.

As we made to leave, Norma hesitated at the curtain and turned towards the fallen soul. I could tell she knew there was nothing we could do and it was better to let the authorities take care of him, but something had to be said.

'Bye then, Twister boy,' she said softly. 'Remember now, don't be such a silly bugger this time when you get to wherever you're going.' She blew him a kiss then joined the exodus.

With Julian in the lead, we jumped down from the cabin and scurried across an open field parallel to the barn. The faint wail was now clearly the sound of police sirens and, as we drew level with the monolithic structure, flashing lights pierced the darkness. Exhausted, panting for breath – or more succinctly, just plain knackered – we reached the bike undetected. An anxious few minutes clambering into the motorbike gear and frantically trying to kick-start the bike didn't do my heart any good, but then we were on our way. I was thankful that in the end the motorbike had, to some extent, chosen itself to be our mode of transport. It was small hence had been easy to conceal, and it was great for beetling down narrow equestrian tracks and footpaths, thereby proving too elusive to follow or even notice.

It was just shy of four-thirty a.m. when I turned into my drive. Julian again conveyed his sympathies to Norma then took his leave, promising to contact me later in the day if he discovered more information. Despite a fair degree of resistance, Norma agreed to let me drive her home in the TR6. The pact, however, wasn't sealed until I agreed that she could return once she'd had a rest and some time to recover from the ordeals of the ill-fated night.

As I drove towards Cambridge, re-acquainted with the wee small hours for the second time in as many days, I began to wonder what extraordinary events lay ahead. I had the disturbing feeling that my experiences to date might prove to be little more than the tip of a rather hefty iceberg. Certainly, Julian's conjecture back at the Portakabin that we'd in some way been set up hadn't helped one iota.

For the first half of the journey Norma sat quietly at my side, absorbed in her thoughts. As I regarded her profile, an acute pang of guilt thrust a six–inch steel blade into my heart then slowly twisted the handle for good measure. Since I'd rather rudely entered the poor girl's life, she'd experienced stress, anger, remorse and grief. Add to that an impromptu journey into the sleazy world of pornography, a terrifying encounter with Bulldog *et al*, and you could be forgiven for thinking that a nervous breakdown would be a welcome relief. Yet there she was – most certainly down but definitely not out.

As we approached Babraham, Norma emerged from her contemplative state and turned toward me. 'Dr Clock,' she began thoughtfully, 'do you think Twister was in pain?'

It was a difficult question, and I took a good few seconds before replying. 'Very hard to say for sure,' I said honestly. 'My guess is that the drug used was some form of heroin, perhaps China White.'

'That's the really pure stuff, isn't it?' she questioned.

I nodded. 'If that were the case then he'd have felt nothing. In fact, he'd probably have experienced a period of euphoria then simply gone to sleep. Over quite quickly, I suspect.'

Norma smiled. 'You know, this is about the most horrible thing that's happened to me, but there's a funny side. Poor old Twister. All he wanted was to be famous. You know, be the main man. And now I guess he's made it. Killed by some Frankenstein freaks with a religious bent. Shit, it's bound to make the big newspapers, TV, maybe even *News at Ten*. I really hope so. He'll be over the moon, as he used to say to annoy me.' My expression must have betrayed a degree of puzzlement, as an explanation was immediately forthcoming. 'I hate football,' she said simply. With that we retreated once more into our own sanctuaries of thought.

Since Norma lived on one of the newer estates in Bar Hill to the north of Cambridge, I elected to take the fastest if not the most direct route and picked up the M11 at Duxford. Having bypassed the city, I joined the A14 at the end of the motorway. When Bar Hill was in striking distance I thought it best to have a few more words with my passenger. Primarily, to check she'd be okay returning home unexpectedly when she was supposed to be staying with friends in Haverhill. I no sooner began to speak, however, than Norma abruptly broke off the conversation.

'Look,' she remarked, pointing to the dashboard clock. 'It's five o'clock. Can we hear if there's anything on the news yet?'

I agreed, but unfortunately there was no mention of the murder – only that police had been called to a drugs-related disturbance at a rave near Halstead. Norma looked disappointed.

Six o'clock had just finished chiming on my grandfather clock as I unlocked the front door and literally staggered into the hallway. I crawled upstairs, discarding clothes as I went, and by the last step I was completely naked. Although the fire in my bedroom had burnt itself to cinders, the room was still warm. I dived under the covers and, as I switched off the light, went out with it.

I awoke with a start. One of those awful dreams where something grotesque suddenly jumps out at you unexpectedly. Horrible! Still tired, I glanced first at the clock –

eleven thirty-six, then through the window – miserable and damp. For a few moments I couldn't decide which depressed me more: the late hour or the lousy weather. Then I remembered all the trials and tribulations of the past couple of days and promptly dismissed the contest as ludicrous.

I was in the process of washing up the dishes from my dietician's mindbender of a brunch when someone knocked at the door.

'Norma!' I exclaimed, somewhat taken aback by her earlier than expected return.

'You're not going to try and send me away again, are you, Dr Clock?' she chided me in response to my dumbfounded expression.

'My humble apologies,' I grovelled. 'I'm ashamed to say I've only just risen and finished feeding my cravings for fat and grease. You can't have had much sleep. Three or four hours at most.'

Norma shrugged. 'Well, to be honest, I couldn't rest. All I could think about was poor, sad Twister. Odd, since we were never that close but, like they say, your first is always special.'

Unintentionally, I showed surprise at this private if not in fact intimate revelation.

'Sorry, Dr Clock,' Norma said, a trifle embarrassed. 'I didn't mean to gross you out or anything.'

'You haven't,' I replied smiling. 'I'm honoured you felt comfortable enough to talk about your personal life, that's all.'

'So, what's the plan now?' she deftly changed the subject.

It was an excellent question. Our primary lead had passed beyond the veil, so we were back to one missing lookalike, one needle possibly containing a lethal cocktail, and a magnetic effigy.

'Well,' I sighed. 'I must admit there isn't much of a one at the moment. All we can hope is that Mr Stammers picks up a few more clues from his associates.'

'And if not?' Norma ventured.

'If not then, like it or not, I'll have to insist Julian goes to the police. Mind you, I haven't the slightest notion of how to handle that particular oversized can of worms. I must have been mad to agree to delay in the first place, but in the light of Twister's fate God knows how the situation can be explained away.' Suddenly feeling distinctly trapped and the onset of a maiden panic attack looming in the background, I decided it was time for another switch of topic. 'Cakes,' I announced. 'New cakes. High time we started your training, young lady.'

In the midst of my bullish display, the implications for Norma of working in the icing room to replace the damage caused by Twister clipped me on the back of the head. I quickly caught hold of myself but, as always seemed to be the case, her observant eye had already seen, processed and deciphered my actions.

She threw me a reassuring smile. 'No need to worry, Dr Clock. I can handle the ghosts and I want to learn. A team,' she concluded, holding an upturned palm towards me.

'Low five?' I sought confirmation.

She nodded, we slapped hands and the pact was sealed.

Norma then proudly showed me the job she'd made of cleaning up the workroom while I'd been asleep the previous evening. It was an impressive effort. Most things were back to normal, and even the graffiti had been almost completely erased from the door.

'Time to maintain my reputation,' I declared. 'Step one, replacement cakes.' This was a daunting task, but if anyone could do it then my unofficial partner, Sondra Warwick, was the one person who could.

Sondra and I went back quite a way. I first met this bright Philadelphian lady as I commenced my second postgraduate year at Cambridge. After working as a graduate in chemistry for a few years, I'd realised that without the magical letters 'PhD' dangling off the end of my name, progression opportunities would be slim. It was 1978; I was thirty, unmarried and ambitious. So I blew off my job and became a full-time mature student. My first year was uninspiring. Cambridge was fine, but at my age the wonder of student life had lost a fair proportion of its lustre. Then, at the beginning of my second year, I'd been cycling down Lensfield Road towards the University's chemical laboratories when I'd witnessed some fool in a BMW nudge a girl off her bike. Since it was late evening, few people were about and, in the event, I proved to be the only soul willing to play Sir Galahad. And thus our friendship had begun. Back then Sondra was nineteen going on thirty-five. She was five feet seven inches tall, had short, dark-brown hair with a fringe, and innocent green eyes – if such a description has any meaning. Most unusually for an undergraduate, she'd been wearing a suit – a dark-navy pin-striped effort – which gave her the daunting appearance of a senior civil servant. After I'd helped her up and confirmed that no medical treatment was required, I'd done what any self-respecting knight in shining armour would have – recommended coffee. The damsel, no longer in distress, had to my delight accepted.

I'd applied to Churchill College once the offer of a PhD came along. It was one of the newer colleges, and therefore didn't have the same mystique as King's or St John's, but it suited me just fine. Located on Storey's Way, the building was well away from the tourist-infested city centre, had modern facilities and boasted an excellent reputation in science. I'd rented rooms in Morbalisk Lodge, a large house owned by the College located at the edge of the campus in a sleepy cul-de-sac surrounded by trees. It was to this humble abode that I invited my new American friend, and later, as our relationship blossomed, where we'd spent many glorious afternoons making love.

Sondra, I learned during our first encounter, had won a scholarship to study English history at the former all-female college, Girton. It was her first term and, as it turned out, I was her first lover. For my two remaining years we'd been inseparable. We'd studied together, read together, listened to music, talked a great deal of nonsense, but most of all we'd loved. Of course we'd debated marriage, but that was as far as it ever got. With my impending return to industry looming large before us, I'd begun to press for a commitment, but fate cruelly turned its head away. One day my beautiful American lady was spirited from my grasp, summoned home by her family to help tend her father who'd suffered a massive stroke. We'd written constantly, but days turned into weeks and weeks inexorably spawned months. Sondra had not returned. Heartbroken, I resumed my career, immersed myself in the corporate delusion and piece by piece allowed the love of my life to be dismantled, stored and indexed.

It was only after Trisha and I had divorced a couple of years ago that Sondra's name came to my attention quite by accident. From time to time I still receive a copy of the *Churchill College Review*, a magazine designed to bind past and present members to the ever-magnanimous host. Not being one who clings to the past, I usually remove the publication from its envelope, flick through the pages without intending to read a word, then deposit it together with any reunion notices and the like into the nearest bin. On the occasion in question, however, I was in mid-disposal routine when the booklet slipped from my hand. Cursing, I retrieved the wayward item only to find myself staring at a familiar face – Sondra's. The piece accompanying the photograph described her two years at Girton, her abrupt return to the States and subsequent academic achievements. Many years later and a messy divorce behind her, she'd decided to take a sabbatical in the UK. By then a celebrated US authority on the British involvement in the two World Wars, Professor Warwick, as she'd become, joined the faculty of Churchill to study in the famous Winston Churchill Archives. We began to correspond; met up occasionally to reminisce about old times then, when I retired, Sondra unbelievably volunteered to be my part-time cake supplier. The offer not only proved to be genuine but also was quite practical. To her colleagues' dismay Professor Warwick suddenly announced that, following her sabbatical year, life as an academic superstar had lost its appeal. Drawn by the tranquillity of the Cambridgeshire fens, she resolved to set up residence in the UK, finally settling in the picturesque cathedral city of Ely.

I don't think anyone had the slightest inkling what triggered this change of heart. I for one certainly didn't. Sondra still seemed the same cheery soul, but there had to be something she wasn't letting on about. Try as I might though, any attempt to discover the truth was always softly but firmly deflected. So that was it – end of story. These days, when not rustling up my cake orders, she seems content to be an active and no doubt formidable part of local community life. She still turns out an impressive quantity of weighty historical tomes, carries out her research and presents the odd lecture. All in all, a remarkable turn of events. I can't help feeling though from time to time how strangely contrived life is. Who'd have guessed that nearly twenty years after Sondra vanished from my life, our paths would cross again in such extraordinary circumstances? Even more bizarre was the idea that our mutually compatible hobbies discovered at university would one day form the basis of a new thread capable of binding us together again . . .

I was in luck. Sondra was at home when I called. She willingly accepted my simple explanation that some freak but unexplained accident had devastated my creations. My lady professor knew me well enough to realise there was serious trouble afoot and that the phone wasn't an appropriate medium for lengthy explanations. Since I'd announced some time ago my intention to apply for a Work Experience candidate, Sondra was fascinated to hear about Norma. She insisted we come over to see her immediately, offering tea and a free assessment of my new employee as inducements.

A touch of discord between the hired help and myself about the merits/demerits of another motorcycle ride quickly put to bed, we set off for Ely in the Triumph. The murky morning weather had quite effectively fended off all attempts to significantly weaken its grip and now, as the afternoon was drawing on, we seemed set for an early dusk. Norma was noticeably intrigued by my association with Sondra, and spent the entire journey prodding and poking around for more information. Still with most of my corporate brainwashing intact, however, I had no trouble in demonstrating my prowess for being irritatingly evasive. In essence I told the poor girl nothing but the barest outline of our past relationship.

'You're no fun,' she complained petulantly. 'There must be more to it than that.'

I gave an exaggerated smile. 'Well, of course there is,' I teased. 'But you should know – a gentleman never tells.' Fortunately I was able to avoid a debate about my claim to being a gentleman as the awe-inspiring outline of Ely Cathedral, sombrely majestic in the gradually fading light, distracted my interrogator's attention.

'Jeez, that's one amazing building,' Norma observed. 'Stuck out in the middle of nowhere like that. I can never decide whether ancient travellers passing this way for the first time would be comforted or frightened when they came across it.'

It was an interesting comment and one worthy of deeper exploration, but we were already within striking distance of our destination.

'That's the house straight ahead,' I pointed out as we turned down a narrow street just beyond the shadow of the great house of worship.

'God, it's huge,' Norma exclaimed.

'That's for sure,' I agreed. 'The mausoleum I call it.'

Sondra's house was indeed an oddity. A detached Edwardian three-storey mansion set in about one-third of an acre of land, it had so many rooms I arrived at a different answer every time I counted them. For one person to be rattling around in – it was nearly as bad as my situation. Nevertheless, Sandy, as I always called her, apparently saw the place, loved it and had to have it. All I can say is that these US academics get paid far too much . . .

As we drew up in front of the imposing oak-panelled door, Professor Warwick was already on the porch steps to greet us. We exchanged platonic kisses and I introduced Norma.

'So you're Ms Bates?' Sondra repeated, carrying out a detailed inspection of her new guest. 'Well, I'm very pleased to meet you. Clock's such a miserable old bugger usually; he doesn't like anyone. You must be someone really special. I'll have to study you. Anyway, come on in. I'm glad you made it before dark.'

We entered, and were shown into the dining room. The table was laid with a veritable feast of sandwiches, pies, salads and cake. Sandy insisted that we eat first and talk later, which seemed eminently agreeable to my young friend. Halfway through the repast a couple of pizzas and an American cinnamon apple pie materialised. I was well and truly defeated by these late additions, but Norma didn't let the side down. She managed to demolish about a third of each and still find room for a second wedge of toffee cake.

'That was really great, Professor Warwick,' Norma gushed. 'You're a fantastic cook.'

Sondra scoffed. 'Thank you kindly, but Clock here can knock spots off me if he sets his cap to it. Mind you, he usually doesn't, or more likely won't. Anyway, first things first. Call me Sondra or, if you like, Sandy. The Professor Warwick thing makes me sound more of an old maid than I am.'

For a moment my young assistant weighed the choices then announced her decision. 'I like Sondra best if that's okay.'

Decision made, I could see Sandy eyeing me mischievously, and I just knew she was going to put me on the spot. I wasn't to be disappointed.

'Tell me, Norma,' my American troublemaker pretended

to speak as if I couldn't hear, 'what do you call Clock? Bet you tenpence you're still on Dr Clock.'

'Sandy!' I protested. 'You're not only embarrassing the girl, but encouraging her to gamble. What next?'

The two women broke into laughter, a sight that pleased me greatly. The girl from Philly always was much more full of life than I. She had the God-given knack of putting people at their ease, and in times of crisis or great sorrow you couldn't ask for anyone better to ease the pain of those affected.

To my secret annoyance, a debate ensued to determine how Norma should address me in future. Dr Clock was rubbished, Jeremiah or Jerry rejected, and at one point I thought we were down to 'hey you'. Fortunately, the final recommendation, which I had to admit gave me a modicum of pleasure, was Dr J.

With the initial pleasantries set aside, Sandy addressed the issue of replacing the cakes. A schedule was set and a phased plan of action agreed. Since the main business of the day had gone much better than expected, I mentioned my young friend's interest in art and fashion. No sooner had I delivered the remark than I realised my grave error. I'd almost forgotten that Sandy's one other great interest was theatre costumes and make-up. When at Cambridge she'd often been involved in college or local productions and acquired quite a reputation. There was now no stopping them. Norma wanted to see Sandy's photo albums and costume designs, and Sandy was interested in the girl's ideas. Even though I don't usually frequent the local hostelries, I was strongly tempted to announce that I was 'off down the pub'. In the end, the dreaded topic of makeovers raised its ugly head and, before I knew what was happening, I was dismissed to the lounge and instructed to quietly watch TV.

For over an hour I paced up and down in my designated prison, switched the box on and off about three times, then finally sat in darkness, watching the amber street light at the edge of the drive struggling to stay alight. Again my thoughts turned to Sondra. In twenty years she really hadn't changed much at all: same hairstyle, pretty much the same slender figure, even the same dress sense. The only notice-able difference was in her eyes. Sadly, the indefinable innocence, which so perfectly complemented her free spirit, had faded. Thankfully not entirely, but I could tell that the grinding wheel of life had taken its toll. Since our reunion there'd been a sort of unspoken agreement that detailed discussion of the past was best avoided, at least for the time being. Every time I saw her face though, the years fell away, the memories returned and I'd find myself wishing that that day would see our stupid taboo finally shattered.

At last I heard voices nearby. I switched on the light and, as the room illuminated, I couldn't help but ask myself the same question I'd asked a hundred times before. What was Sondra doing in this old dungeon, hidden away in the back of beyond? She could be the toast of the academic com-munity anywhere, but instead she'd opted for a semi-hermit-like existence, baking cakes for a worn-out antique like me. The question, however, was as always destined to remain unanswered for the lady's had returned.

'Well then, what d'you think, Dr J?' Norma beamed, giving me a twirl.

'My goodness, you look – well – fantastic's the only fitting description,' I uttered, totally flabbergasted.

The young girl's new appearance was indeed spectacular. Her make-up had been completely reworked – lighter and far more subtle. Nothing remained of the green highlights in her hair. Instead a small area of dark blue had been introduced on one side and the old style re-jigged to create a very sophisticated effect. Even her clothing had been changed. Today's ensemble of blue jeans and a woollen sweater had been replaced by black leather fashion pants and black chain-mail-like short-sleeved top, presumably culled from Ms Warwick's special collection.

'Well, all I can say's I hope they haven't printed this

month's cover of *Vogue* yet. And if I was thirty years younger . . .'

Sandy frowned. 'If you were thirty years younger, I'd be nine and you'd be stuck for someone to make your cakes. Anyway, we haven't finished with you yet. We girls have had a fair old chat, and Norma's told me about her somewhat less than flattering nickname.'

'So we'd like you to choose a new one,' the young girl interrupted excitedly.

'A great honour,' I conceded. 'But are you sure it's wise to ask *me*? Remember, when I was sixteen the Beatles, Gerry and the Pacemakers and the Hollies were all the rage. Now, don't even think about saying "who?" Okay then, you asked for it . . .'

I studied Norma carefully. She was by any standard quite striking; so much so that my mind spontaneously conjured up the image of a butterfly recently freed from its cocoon. For a brief while I toyed with the idea of 'Butterfly' as a nickname, but somehow it just wasn't right. Then, like a lighthouse beacon splitting the darkness, it dawned on me: the perfect name. Norma's streak of blue hair, her manner and the initial of her middle name, J.

'Blue Jay.' When I announced my proposal both women appeared stunned, and for several pounding heartbeats I thought they both hated the suggestion. Finally, the verdict was delivered almost in stereo.

'Great!' They both declared. Ms Bates beamed; Ms Warwick winked. Good old Tick-tock had managed to come through again – praised be the Lord!

Now that everyone had been reassigned suitable monikers, Sondra suggested that a small commemorative drink was in order. While our hostess disappeared in search of white wine, Norma sheepishly admitted that during their tête-à-tête she'd revealed some details about my neighbour's disappearance and Twister's involvement in destroying the cakes. Although I'd planned to be the sole conveyer of our macabre story, I wasn't put out by her confession. Quite the reverse in fact. It was good that the two ladies in my life were getting on so well and had already begun to exchange confidences. Equally pleasing was that Norma was willing to include me in the loop, so to speak.

Soon after our toast Blue Jay sprang up and announced that she was off to wash the dishes. It was the worst example of staged contrivance I'd witnessed in a long time, but I pretended not to twig. As was her way, Sandy sat in silence while I reeled off a full account of the scarcely credible occurrences of the recent past. By the conclusion, her face had adopted an expression of deep concern. She asked several questions and sought clarification on a point or two then resumed her silence. Finally, having processed all the data, she was ready to deliver her conclusions.

'Well, Jerry,' she sighed, 'you've certainly fallen in it, right up to your neck with this one. Excluding the police will definitely be back to kick you where it hurts most. As things stand now, I think you're out of options. The logical – no – the rational, sane thing to do is call them in right now.' Gradually her features softened and she managed a faint smile. 'But that's not the Clock way, is it? Okay, I'm your partner-in-cakes, so I may as well live dangerously and be your partner-in-crime too.'

I jerked foreword in my seat to protest. This wasn't what I'd anticipated at all. I saw Sondra as my confidante: someone to mull things over with and toss in a good dose of common sense when required. The last thing I wanted was to suck her in too. But the obstinate Professor would hear no protestations of any kind. Instead she began to lay down the law in the form of a four-point action list. Firstly, Norma was to be told the rest of the story. This was based on the premise that the young girl was going to find out sooner or later, and if I wanted to retain her trust sooner was the better option. Secondly, she would arrange for the contents of the needle that I'd found to be analysed. A contact of hers at Cambridge could apparently be relied upon to perform the tests on the quiet as a favour, thereby avoiding at least one further link to me. Next, I should arrange for her to meet Julian, and finally, she wished to examine the mysterious icon.

I seriously considered restating my objections, but I knew I'd lose the ensuing battle. Reluctantly I agreed. 'Okay then, you win,' I conceded. 'I'll speak to Norma on the way home and send you the needle tomorrow. If I introduce you to Julian though, don't blame me if you end up starring in one of his videos. I've told you what he's like. As to demand number four, I think I still have it with me. Yes, here! Make of it what you will.'

Sondra regarded the object intently, her expression betraying instant recognition.

'You know something about it?' I asked with anticipation.

'I believe I do,' came her confident reply. 'Could be wrong of course, but I'd say it's a representation of the mythical giant Gogmagog, ancient champion of the Britons.'

'I'm impressed,' I marvelled. 'You history buffs certainly know your stuff.'

Sondra winked. 'I'd like to leave you labouring under that impression but I'm too soft. No, the only reason I recognise this little fella is because of some pornography scandal in Philly a few years back. I'll have to check on the details, but I'm sure it involved a video shop. Gogmagog Video, I think it was called. Anyway, no prizes for guessing what the company logo was.'

6

Black and White

Another late night. Restless, unsettled and taunted by dark terrifying dreams. To be frank, I was relieved to be awake and beginning to dread the prospect of sleep ever again. I think if it weren't for the endless cups of Maragogype coffee I was swilling back, I'd have sunk into a depression so deep it would have taken no less than a late Jacques Cousteau protégé to haul me out. It was decidedly worrying to acknowledge that it was already past one a.m. when I finally returned home after dutifully chauffeuring Norma back to Bar Hill. Of greater concern now was the fact that the old clock had only struck six times. However much my body and soul cried out for hours, days or even weeks of deep peaceful uninterrupted slumber, my overactive mind refused to co-operate. Perhaps on reflection though, I shouldn't complain too much. The trip to Ely had actually worked out exceptionally well. Sondra had been her usual practical and helpful self, Norma had been transformed into Blue Jay, and replacement cakes were on the way. True, I wasn't exactly thrilled by Ms Warwick's four-item shopping list but, although I'd never admit it to anyone, I felt a greater sense of stability and confidence now she was involved. By the time we'd finally departed, Norma had been in fairly high spirits. After much persuasion she'd accepted Sondra's assurances that she could keep the clothes and the selection of make-up used to effect the metamorphosis. The young girl had later wept quietly to herself when the story of her ex-boyfriend's demise wasn't announced on *News at Ten*. Nevertheless, the reminder had prompted her to tell a few tales of their time together before things had gone sour.

Laden down with an enormous doggy bag each, filled with the extensive leftovers from our feast, we'd headed back to Cambridge. As promised I used the opportunity of the quiet drive to reveal the missing pieces of Kathy Murkett's disappearance except that related to the chemically-treated frock. Norma's reaction was far more receptive than I'd anticipated. She listened carefully, showed no sign of annoyance at not being trusted with the whole story originally, and at the conclusion simply said, 'Thank you.' Surprised by her calm response, I couldn't help but initiate an interrogation aimed at trying to understand her feelings. I wasn't entirely successful, but in essence I suspected she already knew that there was more to the situation than I'd explained to her. Nevertheless she exhibited great maturity in accepting that there was actually no real reason why she should have been told anything. After all, she was just 'a kid with a behavioural problem', as she put it.

Weighty issues put behind us, I'd once again been bombarded with a barrage of questions regarding my past relationship with the good professor. I endured salvo after salvo – everything from how we met to why we hadn't married. In general I maintained a resolute silence. The only occasion when I decided to make an exception was in response to the question of why Sondra's accent was more English than American. I explained that at some college party or other I'd bet Sondra five pounds she couldn't pass herself off as the daughter of an English aristocrat. I'd lost, but thereafter my spirited soulmate for some reason never quite regained her native mode of speech. Ironically, Norma didn't believe me.

Once back home I'd found a message from Julian waiting for me on the answerphone. Nothing of any consequence, only that he'd mostly drawn a blank but was awaiting a call from someone in Colchester who might have some valuable information.

So here I was: stoked up on caffeine with a full day stretching out before me and, if I so chose, nothing in particular to do. Norma had other commitments, and it would be at least the next day before Sondra would have the first batch of new cakes ready for collection. If I didn't have the worry of Ms Murkett's disappearance and Twister's sadistic demise to harry my brain, I could have been quite content... Rubbish! I chastised myself. The truth was I'd have been bored.

After a review of my potential options, I decided that the first order of business should be to parcel up the syringe needle and arrange for it to be couriered over to Sondra. Having prepared the package, I was on the point of contacting the agents to arrange collection when I caught the sound of someone running towards the house.

'Julian!' I exclaimed, opening the door as he leapt onto the porch. 'Come on in. Any news?'

'Morning D-Doc,' he panted, clearly about to burst if he didn't blurt out whatever it was he had to say. 'Yep, maybe got a little somethin' to chew on at last.' To avoid the explosion and a possible total speech lock, I quickly sat him down and insisted he take a few deep breaths. He took one then launched into his spiel. 'G-Got the call I'd been waitin' for a couple of minutes ago,' he stuttered. 'One of the guys I deal with in Cambridge told me yesterday that a mate of his had heard somethin'. This guy mostly hangs out in Colchester. Real mean hombre by all accounts. Anyways, I called in one or two favours, doled out a few bucks, and bingo. Gaz, I think he calls himself, phones me up to arrange a meet. So I'm eastward bound. Just figured I'd let ya know.' Julian was already halfway out of his seat before I could respond to his hastily delivered monologue.

'Just a second,' I cautioned. 'I know you're anxious to get on your way, but are you sure you'll be okay? If you like, I'd be happy to come along and ride shotgun.'

The young man grinned. 'Thanks, Doc, but I'll be fine. No offence, but guys like Gaz hail from my side of town. He sees you in tow and he'll smell cops then be off like a jackrabbit. You just sit tight and I'll be back real soon. Never know, may even have the little lady with me.' I could see that further debate would prove fruitless, so I let him go. As he rushed off down the drive he suddenly paused and turned. 'Hey Doc, you wanna be careful,' he called. 'Could be you're spendin' too much time in my company. Beginnin' to sound like me.' He waved and with an, '*Adios, amigo,*' dashed on.

I closed the door and sloped into the living room. Gradually I became aware that the air seemed tinged with a delicate, musk-like fragrance. Odd, I thought. I had no flowers and Julian was a dedicated Fabergé Brut man. Initially, I dismissed it as just the remnants of a discharge from one of the factories situated on the Haverhill industrial estate. The strength of the aroma continued to increase, however, and I was on the point of considering lodging a complaint with the authorities when I heard a scuffle coming from the adjacent lounge. I went to investigate.

'Dr Clock, good morning. My, we are looking handsome today.'

Frozen to the spot, I thought for a second I was hallucinating. But no, the fragrance was real, the voice real and the stunning woman standing by the mantelpiece was definitely real. My faculties flooded back, but too late to avoid being pre-empted by my heavenly visitor.

'Let me guess,' she purred. 'You're a "Who the hell are you? What are you doing in my house?" kind of guy. Not a more demanding, "What do you want?" person at all. Are you, lover?'

'Fair assessment,' I croaked, unable to find my normal voice. 'So now we've agreed on the questions, any prospect of a reply?'

'Oh, clever boy,' she gushed, 'slick response. You know, men with big intellects really make me... Well, more of that later. For now, since you haven't ordered me out, how about being a gentleman and offering a girl a seat?'

Still operating partially on autopilot, I gestured towards

the two-seater couch next to the fireplace. I felt as if I'd been transported to a Hollywood movie studio, where my visitor and I were rehearsing a scene for an erotic thriller. There was no argument that the vision before me could be the front-runner for sultry screen goddess of the year, or more likely the decade. She was not far short of my height, perhaps in her mid-thirties, with a figure equal to any Vargas creation. Her gently waving strawberry blonde mane, which extended almost to her waist, was quite breathtaking and complemented her enormous, deep-blue eyes perfectly. Structurally her face was that of a classic beauty – strong lines, full lips and a small but well-proportioned nose that gave her the air of a Viking warrior princess. Although clothes seemed an unnecessary evil, her completely white outfit was an inspired choice. Basically a suit, both jacket and tantalisingly short skirt appeared to have been sprayed on. Even her impractically high stiletto heels might well have been moulded into position, leaving no discernible means of removal except to be cut away.

'Dr Clock,' she said thoughtfully, somehow managing to cross her legs. 'Interesting name for quite an interesting man. Scientist; corporate renegade; confectioner; and now amateur detective. Let me see, we've had Ironside, Shaft, Morse and Kojak. I suppose there's no reason not to add Clock to the austere list of celebrated sleuths. What d'you think, lover?'

I tried to harden my expression and, as Norma would say, look cool. 'I'm not much of a TV fan, as you must know since you've obviously researched my background,' I countered in the strongest voice I could summon. 'However, in my capacity as amateur detective, am I correct in assuming you're behind Kathy Murkett's disappearance and the death of that young lad?'

'Cheeky boy!' she said coyly. 'Now I'm disappointed. You didn't ask my name first. No matter, I'm not *too* offended. It's White – just plain White.'

'How appropriate,' I mused.

'And I think I'm going to call you Jeremiah, but only if I'm feeling strict, mind. It suits you.'

'Good,' I pronounced. 'Now that we've been properly introduced, I think I'm entitled to a reply to my earlier request. You know, the purpose of your visit: that sort of thing.'

'I'm not sure "entitled" is quite suitable,' she criticised. 'But since it's you, lover boy . . .'

I had hoped her remarks were a prelude to an explanation but I was wrong. Ms White seemed content to allow her last words to hang in the air while carrying out a leisurely inspection of the room. The whole situation was bizarre to say the least. Was I being interrogated, threatened or just entertained for a while pending some more sinister event? This latter conjecture seemed on the surface to be the most feasible, since I had the distinct feeling my guest was using her penchant for suggestive banter merely to mark time. Well, if that were the case, I just hoped I wouldn't have to wait much longer. Despite my laid-back performance, I was becoming more anxious and apprehensive by the second. Another few minutes of this verbal swordplay and I'd be forced to open the door to fear and panic as well.

'Quite comfortable,' the young woman concluded at last. 'You know, lover boy, it's a shame you've allowed yourself to become embroiled in this business. Not really your cup of tea, is it?' I started to speak, but my guest's expression suddenly became questioning. She leant forward as if to impart a secret then asked, 'Do you like the word "embroiled"? I do. It's got a sort of rolling energy. What's your opinion?'

After a moment's consideration, I agreed, thinking it wise to humour her just in case insanity was yet another of her peculiar characteristics.

'Well, I've enjoyed our informal chat,' she abruptly modified her tone. 'Unfortunately, time marches on and we've yet to address the business of the day.'

I glanced over my shoulder to see if anyone else had

arrived, prompting the blip in Ms White's behaviour, but could see no one.

'In a few moments my colleague will be joining us,' she continued, now sitting straight-backed. 'You'll find him rather quiet, but please don't let that mislead you. He's a man for whom actions speak louder than words. But more of that later. For the moment, all you need to know is that his primary role is as adjudicator.'

Reference to an adjudicator was all the stimulation fear and panic needed to begin hammering on the door. It was beginning to look like the entertainment phase of my three speculative options was over. Time to grit my teeth and prepare for interrogation and threats, I decided.

'So Ms White, if you don't mind my interrupting,' I ventured. 'The *modus operandi* I can expect is that you pose a series of questions and your colleague decides if my answers are acceptable or not? In the absence of a response, I presume he also reserves the right to apply certain inducements.'

'If you like, Jeremiah,' the young woman agreed, apparently amused by my speculations. 'Given your expectations then, it may be better if I provide you with a hint or two about the questions before he arrives. That way you'll have time to ensure your answers meet with his approval.' At this point Ms White rose, adjusted her skirt and glided to the window. I had a strong feeling that she was, to a degree, apprehensive of her mysterious colleague, if not actually fearful. Could her performance be taken as genuine, or was I being treated to an elaborate version of the good cop/ bad cop interrogation routine? Well, I guessed, I'd soon find out.

Without removing her gaze from the window, the lady in white invited me to join her. We both stared silently out onto the grey shingle covering the driveway and the equally dull autumn morning. Then, in what could easily have been a sequence from any good romance novel, the young women turned towards me and ran her delicate hand slowly down my cheek. Her expression once again flicked from authoritarian back to seductress in the blink of an eye.

'You want to be nice to me, don't you, lover boy?' she pouted. Her close proximity, the hypnotic effect of her perfume and the steaming intensity of her fathomless eyes – yes, every part of me wanted to be nice to her. 'Look,' she commanded, dangling a heavy, silver charm bracelet encircling her wrist in front of my face. 'This was a present from my colleague. Sometimes he's very generous.'

'Very attractive,' I mumbled.

She smiled. 'Yes it is. And you know what? Every time we complete a difficult assignment . . .'

'Mr Generous buys you another charm,' I predicted cynically.

Her eyes flashed in confirmation.

In a slow, deliberate manoeuvre Ms White headed back towards her seat, ensuring that her body just brushed against mine as she went. She fell silent and I knew, as clearly as if handed carved tablets of stone, the one or two hints had been delivered. As far as black comedy sketches were concerned, I felt confident the present effort was off to a rousing start. Most of the essential components were in place, ready and waiting for the arrival of the all-important catalyst to set the whole thing ablaze. Yet the plot was still hidden from me. Yes, the relationship between the charm bracelet and the effigy was clear enough, but who the hell were Ms White and her invisible colleague? If by some extraordinary means they did know I'd found the mislaid charm, why not just beat me up and take the damn thing?

It would have been an absorbing diversion to continue trying to solve these fascinating puzzles, but the sound of heavy footsteps approaching from the kitchen all but erased my logical thought patterns. I subconsciously held my breath; then he was upon us. . . Filling the doorway of the lounge like a huge gorilla stood the young woman's colleague. Flip flop – Ms White adopted her formal persona and set about introducing the hulk.

'Allow me to present the most Reverend Joseph P. Black,'

she proclaimed. 'Native of Lafayette in the great State of Louisiana.'

A Reverend, eh, I thought. Certainly could account for the biblical episode at Twister's execution, if nothing else.

The Reverend bowed but didn't move or speak.

A very odd dilemma, it occurred to me. Leave the man standing there until he decided to pull my arms off, or invite him in for tea and have my arms pulled off later. Oh well, may as well have tea first, I concluded, images of condemned prisoners and last meals rolling around in my head.

'Please come in Mr – sorry, Reverend – Black. Ms White tells me you're somewhat of an adjudicator,' I said, instantly feeling like a complete berk.

Stupid comment or not, at least the desired result was achieved. The colossus edged through the door and, with surprising control, lowered himself down slowly by his partner.

Joseph P. Black, I said to myself. In a way, who else could possibly complement Ms White better? To ensure a clear-cut claim to surrealism, the Reverend was not only black by name but black by nature. His skin was actually charcoal-black, as were his three-piece suit, shirt, tie and shoes. As a result, the whites of his eyes and a huge set of chompers stood out like cats-eyes caught in a stream of headlamps. At least six feet two inches tall, the Reverend was built like a tank. That at one time he'd been a boxer or wrestler seemed more than a reasonable possibility. Now supposedly a man of God, it was hard to imagine the devil being able to drum up any willing volunteers to face him. In contrast to his imposing bulk, his face was remarkably gentle. He was completely bald – probably by choice rather than any influence of nature – clean-shaven, with round friendly eyes and a finely chiselled mouth.

As I sat looking at Black and White before me, hope briefly surfaced. This couldn't be happening. It had to be a dream. With all the stress, late nights and irregular meals, what could I expect? But alas, the two larger-than-life characters were real enough and the nightmare, I suspected, had yet to begin.

'The Reverend considers it might be a good idea if we all have a cup of coffee,' Ms White announced without any visible communication with the man. 'He'd like you to help him later with a little task he has to take care of, so refreshments now would be most welcome.'

To a large extent I suppose I'd given up. I didn't know what was happening or what was going to happen. Two points were reasonably clear, however. Firstly, this couple of seriously disturbed fashion freaks who'd doubtless instigated Kathy Murkett's kidnapping and Twister's murder seemed to have a worrying priority problem. And secondly, life back at Van der Heijden had suddenly taken on a new appeal. As for the Reverend Black's little task, I shuddered to even speculate on what that might turn out to be.

Feeling I had little choice but to continue playing out the drama/black comedy, I prepared drinks under the watchful eye of Ms White. Nothing more was said until we'd finished our refreshments, when to my further surprise the young woman explained that the Reverend needed to purify the room.

'In preparation for our discussions later, you understand,' she added by way of clarification. 'My associate is well-known in certain quarters for his novel ideas concerning lies and the forces of evil. Simply stated, it is his contention that people deny the truth due to the temporary presence of demons. These malevolent creatures inhabit inanimate objects such as ornaments and furniture. As and when it pleases them, they transfer to humans, practise their satanic art then retreat.'

'Fascinating,' I remarked, now quite convinced that each was as mad as the other. 'And no doubt the Reverend possesses a patent method to deal with this plague of demons.'

In response to a nod from Ms White, Black opened his jacket and withdrew what could only be described as a tightly coiled whip. The weapon appeared to be made of hundreds of strands of plaited stainless-steel wires affording an astonishingly flexible cord. Barely had I time to regard the object when the Reverend let fly. Two ear-piercing cracks, and a pair of porcelain paperweights on either side of my chair were reduced to fragments. I swallowed hard.

'And the good gentleman is also blessed with the gift of detecting which objects are infested,' I ventured warily.

'Quite so,' Ms White concurred. 'The device, which has been blessed and is rinsed daily in holy water, has proved remarkably successful.'

Yes, I thought to myself. One could see how it would. Interestingly, by producing the whip, I'd been provided with another piece for my jigsaw. At least now I knew the origin of Julian's head-wound and associated concussion. Just as well this character was a crack shot though. The slightest error and you'd be minus an eye.

'I take it that now the local demon population has been evicted from this area we can move on,' I enquired sarcastically.

Thankfully it appeared that we could. While the Reverend washed and dried the dishes I was instructed to change into old working clothes. Again, with Miss World as my chaperone I completed the task then followed the dynamic duo into the back garden, straight into the arms of another shock.

'Oh Christ!' I blasphemed, much to Joseph P's displeasure. Parked next to one of the outhouses was a hearse. A brand-new model, the vehicle was brilliantly polished, trimmed with black ribbons and fully laden. I glared at the young woman, aghast and totally bewildered.

Her stern expression momentarily softened as she spoke. 'No need for alarm, Jeremiah. The coffin's already occupied. Only since we were visiting you, the Reverend suggested we might kill two birds with one stone, if you'll pardon the unintentional pun.'

'And just what's that supposed to mean?' I snapped, beginning to lose my grip.

'Oh come now, Jeremiah,' came the disappointed reply.

'You've done so well up to now. We don't usually meet people of your calibre. You can work it out, I'm sure. Let me give you a clue. What's missing from the following sequence? Dead body, coffin, hearse?'

'Burial,' I hissed.

'Excellent!' she replied. 'I said you'd prove to be one of our more interesting assignments.'

Well this assignment had just about had it. 'What the fuck are you people about?' I screamed. 'What's the point of these stupid psychotic games? You've kidnapped one poor sod, murdered another. Wasn't that enough fun? Looking for new kicks?' Seized by anger and frustration, I took a step towards Ms White. In the same instant a massive hand clamped around my neck, choked off my air supply and dragged me backwards. My eyes bulged, lost focus and, as the blurred image of the lady in white wavered before me, I saw death. Abruptly the clamp released and, in a panting fit, I collapsed to the ground.

'Almost out of character, Jeremiah,' the woman said, her voice chastising. 'Perhaps not entirely unexpected though. After all you did throw a tantrum the other night when one of those animals you tangled with started molesting your little girl. You know, before we sent the police to coax you away?'

I couldn't reply for coughing, and this latest revelation did nothing to aid my recovery. More incredible by the minute! How could they have witnessed the conflict without being seen? Unless – yes – they must have been in with Toby Farthing. No wonder the old queen couldn't get away fast enough. And the police – a neat way of abruptly terminating our unwanted attentions.

Again my personal cogitations were short-lived. The Reverend hauled me to my feet and dusted me off like an old hat.

'Hopefully you're now quite recovered?' Ms White enquired.

'Perfectly, thank you,' I spluttered. 'Sorry to have to drop in your estimation and all that, but is there the slightest chance of being told who the deceased is and why in God's name – sorry Rev – you want him buried in my back garden?'

For what seemed an eternity Ms White and her colleague looked at each other as if communicating telepathically. At length the woman muttered something inaudible to herself then spoke up.

'Yes, Jeremiah. There is a slight chance. Depends on how much of a good boy you are. Impress us and we'll see. For now, be good enough to do as we ask.'

'And if I refuse?' I demanded.

'Then you'll upset the Reverend,' she replied solemnly. 'Not recommended, I assure you. Oh, but don't misunderstand. He won't hurt you. No, *you're* quite safe. I can guarantee that.'

Although I was sick and tired of the veiled threats and irritating word games, I couldn't ignore this particular one. The emphasis on the word 'you're' was all the warning I needed. Unless I danced to their tune, it would be those around me at risk. I confirmed my understanding, and as a reward the Reverend Black thrust a shovel into my hand.

Not only had I never dug a grave before, I'd never had occasion to even contemplate the task. In the event, it was the hardest work I've ever done. I've no idea how many hours we toiled. The Reverend orchestrated the project and, in fact, did seventy per cent of the work. Sweating like a bull, he hardly took a break. He just kept heaving huge spadefuls of earth from the ground like a machine. Every now and again he'd pause, confirm that the excavation dimensions were to his satisfaction, then resume digging. All the while Ms White seemed content to lean against the hearse and watch. It was almost as if she were gaining a kind of erotic pleasure from watching the two of us pit our spirits against the back-breaking endeavour. Once or twice when she thought I wasn't looking, she retrieved an oddly shaped palmtop computer from the hearse. I'd never seen the like yet, judging by the dexterity with which she manipulated the device, she was obviously no slouch when it came to computers. Another piece of the puzzle? The memory of Twister caught like a tiny fly in the middle of a complex web of medical malevolence sprang to mind. Perhaps behind the camouflage of her multiple personalities and sexy exterior, a brilliant mind was at work. A clichéd male fantasy, quite possibly, but the more I analysed her behaviour, the more I became convinced that Ms White was the evil genius behind both the Kathy Murkett and Twister incidents. Clever as she may be, one thing was also certain – she was only a technician, an operative. Somewhere above her, conceivably far above, was the top man or woman. Question was, who?

It was late afternoon when the Reverend Black indicated that the job was done. Still dumbfounded by the purpose of this morbid exercise, I complied with my instructions and helped deposit the coffin into the gaping hole. Before covering it, the Reverend took up a priestly stance at the head of the grave and I felt sure for the first time I'd hear him speak. He bowed his head and his lips moved, but no sound was audible. Finally, and without question most perplexingly, Ms White handed him a device similar to the computer she'd been working on earlier. The Reverend climbed into the hole and, deliberately out of my sight, positioned the contraption somewhere on or within the coffin's structure.

Black himself took charge of replacing the earth. Evidently a man who took pride in his work, he completed the job by carefully replacing the turf we'd originally cut away. While the finishing touches were being made, I was obliged to transfer the excess soil into heavy-duty plastic bags and load them into the hearse. Task complete, we returned to the house, where I was permitted a short break before reporting for duty in the lounge.

'A fine piece of work, Jeremiah,' Ms White complimented

me. 'The Reverend is pleased with your efforts. How might we say? Ah yes – a little money in the bank.'

I shook my head in dismay. 'Look,' I stated emphatically, 'I can see you take your work seriously. Yes, I acknowledge your mastery of intrigue, confusion, deception and the rest. Yes, I've got the message: I can ask any questions I like as long as I don't mind incomprehensible riddles for answers. But tell me honestly – if there's any such word in your dictionary of job ethics – if I answer these questions you're supposed to be asking, will I find out anything?'

Ms White expressed the hint of a smile. 'As I've already explained, there's always a chance. Like they say, while there's life there's hope.'

'So it's tough titties for the poor bastard in the casket then?' I scoffed. 'Oh sorry, I've made another unfounded deduction. For all I know the box is empty, or worse still I've just helped bury someone alive.'

'You learn quickly, Jeremiah. Well done,' came the usual evasive reply.

By now Reverend Black, tea tray in hand, had rejoined the party, and once again taken a seat at his partner's side.

'Guess it's time for *Jeopardy*,' I speculated, sensing a marked change in the atmospheric tension.

'By all means, regard the situation in whatever light pleases you,' Ms White offered.

Still thirsty from my exertions, I eagerly drank the tea. Black and White poured cups for each other but showed no inclination to drink. My suspicions aroused, I forwent a refill and sat back half-convinced that in the next few moments I'd be writhing on the floor in agony. Nothing happened.

'So the tea wasn't doctored then?' I observed to break the silence, which had become increasingly oppressive.

'Not doctored,' Ms White confirmed. 'Although you'll be pleased to learn its effects are most beneficial . . . Well, Jeremiah, time we were on our way. It's been a pleasure.'

'What?' I cried. 'You must be joking. Oh, I get it. This is just another of your mind games.'

108

The young woman ignored me. Instead, she gestured to the Reverend who bowed, rose then shambled towards the door. I leapt to my feet, looking incredulously first at Ms White then at the hulking figure of the Reverend exiting the room.

'Now, now, lover boy, no need to get all excited,' the voice of the re-installed sex kitten entreated me. 'Come and sit next to Nurse White. She'll make everything better.'

Not knowing what to do for the best, I finally decided that the offer to make everything better seemed the most attractive course.

'What about all the answers I'm supposed to be reeling off under threat of retribution from the Rev?' I complained.

Ms White smiled coyly, and I realised what I'd just said. I was actually moaning about not being interrogated. Things were definitely out of hand.

'Calm yourself,' my attentive visitor whispered. 'The ordeal's almost over. You've answered all our questions perfectly. The Reverend's very pleased.'

'Oh, you're completely off your rocker,' I protested angrily. 'I haven't told you a bloody thing and you know it. I'm not stupid. No doubt he'll be in here any minute with a rubber truncheon and start pounding the crap out of me whether I co-operate or not.'

Ms White draped herself over my shoulder and continued her whispering routine. 'Silly boy, what a vivid imagination. It's the new millennium, not the Sixties. We don't use physical violence anymore. Chemicals are the future – nice, easy to use, impossible to trace chemicals.'

'But you haven't given me any drugs,' I questioned, rapidly losing confidence.

'Haven't we?' she teased, gently caressing the side of my head. Her touch was like gossamer, but it alerted me to a stinging sensation I'd felt before but ignored. I untangled myself from her arms and hastened to the mirror above the mantelpiece. Sure enough, on the side of my head just above the ear was a small gash surrounded by traces of congealed blood. As my reflection stared back at me the penny dropped. The demonstration with the whip. No doubt one of the lashes was aimed not only at an ornament but also at me. It seemed almost beyond belief – something out of a Cold War spy thriller. Nevertheless, if the tip had been coated, then maybe . . .

I turned to face my adversary, a mixture of panic and anger brewing in my chest.

'What've you done to me?' I demanded. 'I don't remember talking: just digging that God-forsaken grave.' I was suddenly struck by the idea that the whole episode had been a hallucination, but my aching back and blistered hands said otherwise. My frustration frothed over, but then a wave of dizziness knocked me off balance. I blinked and found myself back beside my surrogate nurse.

'I'm sorry, lover boy,' she purred, apparently with genuine feeling. 'Unfortunately the substance we used, although marvellously effective, generates a class of metabolite toxic to one or two vital organs. The good news, though, is that the tea you drank contained what you might call an antidote. It'll react with those naughty metabolites and flush them right out.'

'And the bad news?' I managed to slur, beginning to lose focus.

Ms White tutted. 'So suspicious,' she chided. 'No need to worry. You'll feel a bit woozy for an hour or so, but that's a good sign. It means the antidote's taking effect.'

With each passing moment I was falling deeper and deeper into what felt like a state of dead drunkenness. I could hardly move. I was aware only of the blood surging through my veins and the thud, thudding of my heartbeat in my ears. Before I completely lost control of my mouth muscles, I succeeded in articulating one last question.

'Why not just kill me now if you've got . . .' I couldn't finish, but Ms White was paying attention.

'More out-of-date thinking,' she smiled. 'We only resort to such measures if unreasonably provoked, like for example. . . Well, never mind. Besides, what can you or your friends do? You don't know who we are or what's happening. I understand you'd probably feel much better if we threatened you and ordered you not to interfere. Trouble is, that sort of thing only happens in movies. This is real life, honeybun. Anyway, must be going now. Mustn't keep the Reverend waiting. Thanks again and oh, by the way, look after our little secret in the back garden. Don't play with it, mind, or you'll be sorry. There, how's that?'

Her closing speech complete, Ms White left my side, carefully ensuring that I was propped up in a comfortable position. She quickly scanned the room, kissed my forehead and left. I heard the front door open and one last remark before it clicked shut. 'Apologise to Julian. Sorry we sent him off on a wild goose chase. All in a good cause though. All in a good cause.'

I was utterly confused, bewildered and distraught, to mention but three of the several dozen adverse emotions I was experiencing. Unconsciousness felt like it was creeping up on me from the feet up. As it reached my knees, I fumbled in my pocket for the effigy – gone. As it flooded my chest, I looked over to where I'd left the packaged needle ready to send to Sondra – gone.

'Oh my living Christ,' I shrieked in silence. 'I've given them everything.'

7

Plight of the Fairies

I was still hopelessly groggy when Julian found me later that day. He'd suspected all was not as it should be soon after arriving in Colchester. Gaz, the mean hombre contact, turned out to be more elusive than the fabled city of Shangri-La, and by lunchtime it was evident that the man probably didn't exist at all. Julian had already resolved to return home when, purely by chance, he'd come across one of his old cronies who'd heard that some very serious and very weird shit was going down thereabouts. In Julian's business this kind of occurrence was commonplace and normally would have raised little interest. That situation had changed dramatically, however, with the mention of stories of people disappearing and being replaced. Details were sparse and highly embellished, but my tenacious neighbour decided to follow up on the lead. A few carefully placed enquires in some of the more notorious illegal drinking and gambling dens in the area revealed odd but generally corroborative snippets of information. Finally, the trail had led back to Cambridge, or to be more precise, the Cherry Hinton area. There, one or two of the locals were prepared, for the price of a pint, to recount tales akin to *The Invaders* TV series. Alas, the trail had essentially gone cold. It had been clear that people in the know were afraid to talk – a finding that pointed to premier-league crime or perhaps even the Mafia.

Although I didn't remember much of what transpired after I was first discovered, I have the impression it took Julian nearly two hours to return me at least in part to the land of the living. I vaguely recall being plied with what seemed to be gallons of a hot, black treacle-like liquid laughingly referred to as Turkish coffee. Also prominent despite my malaise was a sense of being dragged about like a rag doll, all the while being told to 'hang in there'. Now, as I sat facing my saviour across the kitchen table, still marvelling at how difficult it was to stir the witch's brew before me, everything seemed to be in a total shambles. Julian had just concluded his story and was regarding me with concerned eyes.

'Feelin' any better, Doc?' he asked for the nth time. 'Can't risk pourin' more coffee down ya. 'Fraid you'll blaze like a 120-volt bulb in a 240-volt supply, and pop.'

I wasn't sure about the electrification analogy, but one thing was certain – I felt like liquidised cow dung. My head was reverberating with the sound of some sadistic bastard clouting a J. Arthur Rank-sized gong every two seconds, what was left of my stomach would have been abhorrent to Macbeth's three witches, and my mouth – well, best not say. I sighed deeply and fixed the young man with a forlorn stare.

'No, but thanks for asking,' I groaned.

Julian grimaced. 'Gotta try harder, Doc. I have ta know what happened, and time's a wastin'.'

Time – now there was an interesting topic. I asked.

'Goin' on ten,' my neighbour confirmed.

Shock, surprise, surprise, shock – that's all I seemed to live on these days. Ten o'clock was bad enough, but I daren't ask the date!

Despite my sorry condition, I was reasonably satisfied that I'd overcome the worst. Gradually I began to come round. A fistful of aspirins and half a bottle of Milk of Magnesia later, and I just about qualified for re-entry into the human race.

No sooner did I show signs of intelligent life than Julian was anxiously pressing me for an account of my experience. I found it extraordinarily difficult to put into words my encounter with the vivacious Ms White and her gargantuan sidekick. Several attempts adopting a variety of approaches were needed before I felt confident that he fully understood what I was trying to convey. Up to this point I'd omitted the saga of the coffin. It was only when the analgesics and the antacids had finally ceased battling each other that I felt strong enough to broach the subject. As I proceeded, it was obvious that Julian put two and two together and made four. The problem came when he added another two and pulled a seven out of the hat. I don't think I've ever seen anyone so beset by angst and fear, yet for the sake of appearances struggle to remain calm.

'You think it's my Kathy in that there box, don't ya, Doc?' he droned through gritted teeth.

'No, Julian,' I repeated emphatically. 'I honestly don't believe it's her. Look at the facts. Whoever's behind this must need Kathy alive. There's no way they'd have gone to all that trouble with the lookalike. Then there's my visit from Snow White and King Kong. Come on, man; think it through. There's absolutely no sense to it, is there?' Judging by the marginal reduction in the level of tension in Julian's clenched fists, I appeared to be making some progress.

'Okay then,' he sighed, 'if it's not Kathy, then who is it?' This was the question I'd been waiting for. Time to clinch the argument by airing my own hypotheses. At least if they didn't make matters better, with luck they shouldn't make things any worse either.

'As I see it, there are three possibilities,' I began authoritatively. 'One: the box contains something other than a body such as gold, guns or maybe just bricks. Two: it could be the poor girl you rescued; and three: it's Twister.'

Julian shrugged, apparently unimpressed. 'Well, Doc, if pushed I can see your one and two have some substance. But three seems way off. The young fella bought it then the cops came.'

'Precisely,' I proclaimed. 'The cops came. Yet there's been nothing reported. The macabre murder of a young boy in the midst of a porno filming fest – and at a rave to boot. Should have been a tabloid bonanza, but no. TV, radio, newspapers – not one single reference.'

'So ya reckon those visitors of yours got him out of there the second we skedaddled?' Julian conjectured.

I nodded, but refrained from further comment, allowing time for all the evidence against Kathy's demise to work its magic. Eventually Julian conceded the point and began to loosen up.

'Smart figurin', Doc,' he remarked. 'For the time being I'll buy it, but unless Kathy's home real soon, booby-trapped or no, that box is comin' up mighty quick.'

Fair enough, I thought. Now all I had to do was work out a way of explaining all or part of this unholy mess to Blue Jay. To be honest, I was still struggling myself to decide which of the three options was the most likely. In all cases the same stumbling block fell across my path – why bury the coffin and its contents in my back garden? Was it just a form of intimidation, a prelude to blackmail, or something far more sinister?

This last bout of mental muscle flexing generated a sufficient jolt to break the last remaining chains tethering my free will. The mind-dulling effects of the drug cocktail were over. Ironically, the recovery of my cognitive faculties proved more of a curse than a blessing. With the force of two giant juggernauts colliding head-on, I remembered Sondra and what I'd done. It was now painfully obvious that the time lapse between the whip demo and commencement of the grave-digging episode was far longer than I recalled. Who knew for how long the venom from the whip's fang had robbed me of my memory? More than that, the drugs had opened and displayed every thought I possessed for Ms White to pick through as she pleased. There was no point to err on the side of optimism: no hope that by some miracle I'd been able to resist the rape. I had to accept that they'd extracted the lot. Of all the information taken though, only that associated with the three innocent female bystanders – the unknown girl, Norma and Sondra – worried me. I couldn't help the first on my list, but there was a chance to protect the other two. Julian took my concerns to heart and, although after all this time he must have been frantic worrying about his partner, he was more than willing to rally to the cause. The first priority was to contact Sondra. While I used the phone, my neighbour, despite the darkness, volunteered to scout around outside for any clues that might have been inadvertently left behind. An incredible long shot, but I was loath to temper his enthusiasm.

As expected, Sondra took the news calmly and, in between wisecracks, was evidently more concerned for me than for herself. The old chestnut of police involvement raised its head yet again, but for this reason and that suffered the usual fate of dismissal. Of course, stubborn and independent as ever, Sondra politely declined my offer for her to stay with me until the danger passed, so a number of other hair-brained stratagems were discussed. In the end, however, logic won the day. Essentially there was nothing to be done and no point in hiding. Finally Sandy insisted I hang up and get some rest. She promised to remain vigilant and keep in regular contact – nothing really, but at least the sound of her voice from time to time would afford me some degree of comfort.

I found Julian still prowling around outside, a flashlight in each hand. For about ten minutes I followed him here and there while he scanned the ground in the vicinity of the gravesite and where the hearse had been parked. Eventually he agreed to call off the search, but only after I'd given him permission to resume the next day. We wandered back inside, mulling over options for contacting Norma. Julian sauntered off to wash his hands, but within seconds came striding back, clasping a small envelope.

'Look, Doc,' he exclaimed. 'I found this stuffed through yer letterbox. See how it's addressed. "To the kind man who helped me".' We glanced at each other, both acutely aware that the note must be from Kathy's lookalike. 'Go on, Doc, open it,' Julian encouraged. 'I don't reckon the gal saw me. It's intended for you.'

The note was intelligible but relatively confused.

Dear Sir,

Thank you for helping me. I don't suppose I'll have long before they catch me again. Maybe it's too late for me but there could be a chance for the lady I look like. If you can meet me near the mathematical bridge at eleven a.m., hire a punt, I'll come every day until. . . Be careful – hidden danger everywhere.

Yours respectfully, N

I handed the letter to Julian and sat down.

A smile crept across his face then suddenly retreated. 'You think this could just be another one of your friends' tricks?' he asked disappointedly.

To be honest, after my encounter with Black and White anything was possible. On balance though, I believed the note to be genuine and said so. What I didn't impart and what worried me most about the note was the sense of hopelessness reflected in its text. However, now wasn't the time for reading between the lines or conjuring up demons that weren't there – certainly not without the Reverend and his trusted whip at the ready.

My neighbour's optimism had grown about two hundred per cent since I'd pronounced the letter kosher. Like me, I could see he had his doubts, but taken at face value it was the first concrete indication we'd had that Kathy might still be alive. Midnight came and went as we discussed how best to handle the meeting, but an entirely satisfactory conclusion proved difficult to reach. The reason was hardly surprising. As he incontrovertibly pointed out, it was his partner's well-being at stake. If I went alone and things went awry, he'd never forgive himself or me. Fair enough, I could hardly argue with that. On the other hand, it was reasonably clear that the terrified woman only recognised me. If anyone else appeared at the rendezvous or I showed up with a friend, the girl might simply vanish forever.

As the clock struck one a.m., Julian finally capitulated. 'Okay Doc, you win. It's your show. All I can say's I hope the gods are with ya.'

The final hurdle cleared, we agreed that Julian would contact Norma first thing. His task was to provide an outline of my interrogation, an account of his sojourn to Colchester and a summary of my planned meeting.

My neighbour frowned. 'Okay, let's get this straight – outline, account, summary,' he recounted. 'And as far as the outline's concerned, no mention of the box – right?'

'You've got it, partner,' I confirmed.

'Time for bed, Doc,' he concluded. 'You're startin' to imitate me again.'

Unable to leave well alone, I spent a fair collection of tortured moments trying to explain that in some circles imitation was considered the sincerest form of flattery. However, as soon as I got the impression that Julian thought I was going sweet on him, I packed it in!

Next morning it needed a photo finish to decide who was awake first: me or the fabled lark. The weather turned out to be perfect – torrential rain. For hours I rattled about the house like the Ghost of Christmas Past. On numerous occasions I resolved to give Sandy a ring and apprise her of the new development. When it came to the crunch though, I chickened out. I told myself that the news would simply upset her more and unnecessarily. In truth, I was petrified she'd talk me into letting her come along. To my relief, nine fifty-nine reluctantly gave way to ten o'clock after a good half-hour's conflict.

The rain showed no sign of letting up and, if anything, had stepped up a notch. At least one consolation of the atrocious conditions was that the roads were much less crowded than usual and Cambridge itself wasn't quite the assault course it generally is. I parked in the Lion Yard car park then jogged back along Pembroke Street, crossed into Mill Lane and on to Scudamore's boatyard by the River Cam. The punting season was long past, but it was still possible to cruise the College Backs. Elsewhere on the globe it's reputed that only mad dogs and Englishmen are prepared to brave the midday sun. In Cambridge, punting along the Backs in mid-October tended to be the prerogative of the Japanese – dogs wouldn't touch it.

Not at all surprisingly, the river was devoid of even the craziest of tourists on this most miserable of days. The staff at Scudamore's quite rightly thought I was insane and waved me off in my punt like I was on the Titanic. It was some twenty odd years since I'd manoeuvred one of these unwieldy river craft, yet I was pleased to discover I hadn't lost the knack. Feeling reasonably in control, I propelled myself beneath Silver Street Bridge and into the precincts of Queens' College. Directly ahead I had a clear view of the so-called Mathematical Bridge. A wondrous creation built entirely of wood, the original structure was held together by neither nut nor screw. Alas, learned men, unable to leave well alone, had reputedly dismantled the bridge but found it impossible to reconstruct without the aid of extensive metalwork – a good story, but in fact no more than a myth perpetuated to enthral the tourists.

I looked at my watch – five past eleven.

'Am I too late?' I groaned, cursing my reprehensible planning. Certainly no living creature was in evidence on either bridge or bank. It occurred to me that dressed in an oversized anorak, orange waterproof trousers and an old Australian bush hat I favoured on such waterlogged occasions, I might not be recognisable. Since I'd come this far, I decided it was at least worth a few more minutes challenging the elements before conceding defeat. I drew the punt alongside the left bank opposite the Fellow's Garden, removed my hat and waited. With water cascading down the inside of my anorak, it didn't take long for me to resolve to quit and try again another day but, as if in response to my decision to surrender, the rain abruptly scaled back to drizzle. So dramatic was the change that I had the vivid impression of a large heavenly garden spray, its nozzle originally set on maximum douse, accidentally being flipped to a fine mist setting. All I could hope was that the celestial gardener didn't notice the error until I was safely back in the car. I grasped the long punt pole and prepared to shove off but then hesitated, my eye attracted by a sudden change in scene. Looking up, I noticed that where a moment ago the bank had been deserted it was now occupied by at least two dozen people milling about. Had my brief period of distracted thought allowed a parallel universe to slip through the void? Or was this merely the emergence of folk forced to shelter from the rain? In light of my marked increase in fanciful thought, I began to question the wisdom of having exposed my head to the downpour . . .

'Time for the off,' I said to myself out loud.

'No, please wait,' came an alarmed call.

Caught completely off-guard, my balance momentarily deserted me and the image of myself toppling headfirst into the murky waters flashed before my eyes. Fortunately, my expensive hiking boots proved their worth by refusing to slip on the punt's soaking wet deck. Straining muscles in all directions, I managed to simultaneously steady both craft and its commander with the pole.

'Shit!' I exclaimed, more out of relief at not falling than annoyance.

'Are you all right?' the same woman's voice questioned.

I looked up to find a figure, unrecognisable in a long black hooded coat, perched on the edge of the bank. Without invitation the individual clambered into the belly of the punt and huddled up like a forest creature contemplating hibernation.

'Please go on down the river,' she implored in a shouted whisper.

I did as I was told without question – something I was becoming quite good at these days after years of being the one always issuing the orders.

Once underway, the woman drew back her hood. Since she was essentially lying face up, sprawled at my feet, I could see her clearly. The sight made my heart sink. It wasn't the woman I was expecting. This young lady had long black curly hair, round glasses and wore heavy eye make-up –

nothing like Kathy at all. Aware of being inspected, the woman turned her head to one side so I could see her neck. With her fingers she teased out some strands of light-coloured hair from behind her ear. Scars and a wig, I murmured. So it was her after all.

My optimism restored, I navigated the vessel to the centre of the river and on towards King's Bridge. Although the rain had now all but ceased, the punt was totally water-logged. The poor woman was literally lying in a pool of water but, despite my entreatments, she wouldn't budge. Oddly, she said nothing, and eventually, when my curiosity could be contained no longer and I started to speak, I was waved into silence. Beyond King's Bridge the imposing vista of King's College and its famous chapel came into view. Even on such a dull and depressing day, the grandeur of this most British of scenes was nonetheless inspiring. Sadly though, the majesty of Cambridge University and its nine-hundred-year history could do nothing to help the plight of the frightened young woman cowering at my feet.

It seemed that we were fated never to speak, but as we reached Clare Bridge my passenger raised herself into a partially sitting position.

'Sorry,' she said at last in a normal voice. 'They're everywhere. I thought they might try to stop us as we passed King's, but it may be okay now. At least for a while.'

'Who are you?' I asked – the first on my list of a thousand questions.

The woman gave a faint smile. 'Well, I used to be Natalie McCarthy, but now I'm anyone they want me to be.'

'And who are they?' I followed on eagerly.

'Dunno,' she shrugged. 'They're just *them*. The ones with power, money. People that steal human lives, change them, use them, then discard what's left.'

It was all too confusing. 'I'm sorry,' I apologised. 'I don't really understand what . . .'

'No, I'm sorry,' Natalie interrupted. 'I'm talking in riddles. You have to forgive me. Since waking up on your couch, I've just been running, hiding. Half the time, I don't even know what from.'

'But are you all right?' I said unable to express the question more specifically. 'Last time I saw you, you'd been treated with some powerful drugs.'

'It's okay,' the woman assured me. 'There are no sensitive areas you need to tiptoe around. I'm convinced I was supposed to die that night and would have if fate hadn't interfered – assuming you believe in that sort of thing of course.'

My concentration was diverted while I negotiated safe passage beneath the Garret Hostel Bridge, leaving Trinity Hall behind us. Trinity College was next up for review and, as we drew level with New Court, Ms McCarthy advanced another step away from her fears.

'This will probably sound like a line from a bad novel,' she resumed, 'but I feel there's little hope for me. I haven't seen much and I know even less, but they don't agree. Doesn't matter where I go or who I tell, sooner or later I'll find myself starring in another of their special "one night only" dramas.'

'What about the police?' I suggested – as if the idea hadn't ever crossed her mind.

Not surprisingly, I received only a knowing glance. 'Well, that's enough of an intro,' Natalie sighed. 'Sooner or later you'll be asking why I took the risk of contacting you. Well, let me save you the trouble . . .' And so began the remarkable story she decided to impart. I must confess to feeling quite unsettled by the fact she showed no interest in who I was or my role in the scheme of things. It was as if all the usual packaging that makes up polite conversation and logical thought were no longer relevant to her. Not surprising really, I concluded, given what she must have been through. In fact she was far more lucid and articulate than could reasonably be expected. She started by admitting she had no knowledge of Kathy and only knew about Julian from investigations she'd carried out after fleeing my home. All that was actually known to her was a snippet of infor-

122

mation she'd overheard the night of the planned exchange. Two women had been discussing how the mark was to be transported to an airport and something about immigration procedures – and that, unfortunately, was it. I pressed for more details but had little doubt that the young woman had divulged all she knew.

We were now in sight of St John's, last bastion of the all-male colleges. Besieged by the pressures of the late twenti-eth century, the faculty had finally yielded and allowed females to wash away five and a half centuries of bachelor history. What a pity, I thought, that this revered institution couldn't simply spirit my young friend away and conceal her deep within its ancient cloisters. Romantic nonsense maybe, but was it really so much to ask to preserve a life, to give a modicum of peace to this tortured and harried soul? I wished hard but my pleas merely bounced unheard off the deaf and seemingly aloof walls of earthen brick.

Apologising for the meagre facts she possessed, Natalie went on to describe her accidental fall into the shadowy world of illusion and drugs that had blighted her life. Three years before, she and her partner, Elena Pascal, had moved back to Cambridge. They'd met while at university there, brought together by their mutual fascination with the tales and legends of fairies. Friendship had blossomed into love and, after graduating, the pair had opened a bookshop near Huntingdon specialising in all things magical. The venture, successful at first, had gradually foundered, so with what little money they'd been able to salvage it was decided to see if their old *alma mater* would treat them with greater kindness. Natalie managed to secure some work through one of the colleges while her partner took a job helping out in a video store. Everything seemed to be going well until one day Elena didn't come home. Not only that, but as the days passed it became clear that she'd disappeared completely. There was no sign, no trace – she'd somehow simply vanished. The police drew blank after blank, and after several months Elena became just another unsolved missing person statistic. Two years drifted by without a word then, out of the blue, a letter arrived from America. The note, apparently written by Elena, was unintelligible. All Natalie had to go on was an address printed on the envelope – 'The Gellar Psychiatric Institute', situated on the outskirts of Philadelphia. She'd written, attempted to phone, and in the absence of any meaningful progress had finally flown to the US. Upon reaching the Institute, she'd been shown into a waiting room, been furnished with coffee and told to await the arrival of one of the duty officers. No one appeared, and drinking the coffee was the last thing Natalie remembered clearly.

'But that was a year ago,' I exclaimed incredulously. 'What happened to you?'

'Probably best I never know exactly,' the young woman remarked cynically. 'It's only in the last two days, since I've been free of all the drugs and mind control, that what I'm hoping is my true identity and past have trickled back.'

Barely had she completed the explanation when her attention was distracted by something behind me. I turned to see some young people regarding us from the Bridge of Sighs, which spans the river connecting St John's Third and New Courts.

'Only students,' I reassured her.

Not totally convinced, Natalie became agitated as if the sand in some invisible hourglass were running out. 'Like I said,' she continued. 'It's been hard enough convincing myself of my identity, but the last twelve months seems like a bad acid trip. I have impressions of being in a kind of hospital for long periods. Nurses – Americans, I think – telling me I'd been in a bad accident and then suffered a nervous breakdown. Last night I dreamt I was shown my face in a mirror. It was horribly scarred and disfigured. The next instant I had a new face – not my own – not like this.' She touched her lips and cheeks, partly to emphasise her point, but mainly, I suspected, to wipe away her tears surreptitiously. 'Anyway,' she pressed on, 'I also have memories of being taken to strange places, of meeting unusual people. Each time I felt it was the same me inside, but I never appeared to be the same person outside.'

'So it's your belief that you were held a drugged prisoner, then from time to time given a different face and reeled out to perform at the behest of some criminal organisation or the like?' I suggested.

'Far-fetched, I know,' she acknowledged. 'But it's my best guess. This last episode though, it's the real clincher. I think this set-up had to be arranged in a hurry. There were mistakes and times when I think the drugs wore off. A trip on a plane, dental treatment, make up, and two strange characters – one black, one white – are blurred memories but not as obscure as the rest.'

The mention of Black and White sent a shiver spiralling down my spine. As luck would have it, however, this unpleasant jolt was well-timed. I'd been listening so intently to Natalie's explanation, I realised I was no longer piloting the punt with due care and attention. We were about to collide with the bank, and in another few seconds the low bridge supporting Magdalene Street would have taken my head off.

As we headed towards Jesus Green and the lock that marked the turning point of the trip, the heavens opened.

'And you never saw your partner, Elena, again?' I asked, hoping to tie up a few loose ends.

Natalie shook her head. 'Don't expect I ever will now,' she said sorrowfully. 'Probably she suffered the same fate I did, but how and why it all started – well, I guess I'll never know. Here!' she said abruptly, holding out a piece of paper. 'This is as much as I can recall of the psychiatric clinic's address. Sorry, but I don't know what happened to the original letter and envelope. They probably took them along with the rest of my life. I wish I could be of more help in trying to find your friend's wife.'

'They're not married,' I remarked inanely.

Natalie, however, wasn't really listening. Again, her attention was distracted by other craft on the river and cars whizzing past along Chesterton Lane.

'No,' I called through the pelting rain. 'I'm really very grateful. You've been extremely helpful. This must have been very difficult for you as well as a great risk. Is there anything I can do to help?'

'Thanks, but no. Don't worry about me. Maybe my predictions of doom and gloom are just paranoid delusion.'

I didn't agree. 'But what about money. How've you been living?' I persisted.

'Glad you mentioned that,' came the acutely embarrassed reply. 'Stole some of your things actually. Pawnshop was reasonably generous. If I make it, one day I'll send you a cheque.' Natalie gave me a repentant smile then turned to face the heavens. Water bleached against her face, and if I had to guess I think she was hoping it might wash away all the false skin and restore Natalie McCarthy to her original self. 'Well,' she breathed, 'I suppose our clandestine meeting's at an end. If you don't mind, I'd like to go back now. Ask me anything you like. Maybe you're only . . .' The young woman froze, unable to finish her offer. Her eyes glared wildly past me and her lips began to tremble. 'Jesus Christ! They've found me,' she said almost in a whisper.

I turned around and followed her gaze back along the river. There were a couple of rowing boats and another team of punters battling the atrocious weather, but precious little else. Then I saw it – a small motor launch, apparently having just left the bank, was arcing around on an intercept course straight for us. The stinging deluge made it almost impossible to see clearly yet, despite this difficulty, I could just make out two figures on board – one black, one white. Our luck had just run out. Still larger than life and twice as sinister, two of the four horsemen of the Apocalypse in the guise of Ms White and the Reverend Joseph P. Black were abroad, hunting souls – our souls. I had no idea whether they were after Natalie, after me, or after both of us. As to their real intent – again not a clue. Rational thought disengaged, instinct took over. Ramming the punt pole into the riverbed, I strained to bring the vessel about to face our pursuers. Natalie had collapsed in a catatonic state on the bottom of the punt, apparently resigned to whatever fate was destined to befall her. But I wasn't. The punt came around just as they approached. Like a knight of old, I hauled the pole out of the water and, jousting-fashion, prepared to repel boarders. Anticipating my intent, the Reverend Black, acting as helmsman, made a last-minute course correction and effectively wrong-sided me. I tried to swing my jousting pole to match the manoeuvre, but it was too heavy and I was too slow. Before I could gain a sound footing, the motor launch glanced against our bow, sending me sprawling on top of Natalie. Momentarily stunned I might have been, but I wasn't about to yield. I scrambled over my startled passenger, grasped an oar in place of the lost pole and advanced towards the bow. Another two seconds and I could have put up a valiant fight, but it was not to be. The punt suddenly lurched forward, hurling me back into the arms of Ms McCarthy. As I looked up I saw that the launch, having pulled back, had effected a crude docking manoeuvre. A metal bracket of some kind fitted to its hull locked in position, pushing us, to my dismay, towards the weir side of the lock. Frantic, I clawed at the mechanism. It wouldn't budge. I looked toward our attackers, cursing and swearing like a trooper. Black, his expression hard as stone, continued his deadly course. Ms White, enrobed in a heavy white coat and holding a large matching umbrella, sat motionless, staring at the bank as if oblivious of events surrounding her. My mind was spinning, trying to fathom a way out. The weir, not at all deep but nevertheless potentially lethal, was in clear view. Suddenly with the partially submerged marker-buoy line that spanned the weir in clear view, the motor launch slammed into reverse. Veering hard to starboard, it headed for the bank, leaving us to be carried by the mounting momentum of the current towards the drop. It occurred to me that if we abandoned the craft it might still be possible to swim for it, but one look at Natalie and I could see the idea was hopeless. We had only seconds. In a last-ditch effort I fought to slow our progress with the paddle stick – futile, completely futile. Convinced that the only remaining course was to protect my charge as best I could, I crawled alongside her and held on for dear life.

Hardly a dozen heartbeats passed when the chugging of another motor, followed by a stomach-wrenching crash towards the stern, almost flipped the vessel over. It wasn't the form of collision I'd expected, but then neither was the fact that we were gradually changing direction amid the howl of a straining engine at full throttle. Although I daren't hope, I raised my head above the side of the boat... Incredible! – it was the only fitting description. Clint Eastwood, otherwise known as Julian, was frantically winching the punt to the side of what looked like a dwarf tugboat. At the helm, his partner-in-crime for this scene at least – Raquel Welch, aka Norma – was dragging us back from the brink of disaster and on towards the bank.

To the applause of the few rain-soaked passers-by that witnessed the dramatic rescue, we moored both craft and helped Natalie ashore. As we did so, I looked along the river in search of our would-be assassins but, as expected, they'd completely disappeared. Unable to spot the film crew they thought were shooting an action-packed movie scene, the onlookers soon lost interest and scuttled off in search of shelter.

'Thanks, people,' I said to our rescuers, still shaking. 'But how the . . .'

Julian silenced me with a pat on the shoulder. 'Don't fret yerself none, Doc,' he drawled. 'Tell ya all about it later. First order of business is to get you and the young missy here out of the rain.'

After considerable encouragement, Natalie allowed herself to be guided to the front passenger seat of Julian's VW. We all piled in, and at my insistence took off for my place.

While caught at the first set of traffic lights, Norma began asking Natalie how she was feeling. Without warning the young woman yanked away her seat belt, flung open the door and bolted. In the couple of seconds it took anyone to react she rushed across the road, miraculously escaped being hit by two passing cars and leapt onto a moving bus. No one was more flabbergasted than I. I knew she wanted to go it alone, but after all that had happened I felt sure she would accept some assistance, at least for a short while anyway. Just goes to show how wrong you can be, I thought to myself. Under the circumstances it was agreed that there was no point in trying to tail her. If in future she needed help, she knew where to find it.

More upset by Natalie's disappearance than I cared to admit, I fell into a morose silence. Halfway home I absent-mindedly withdrew the paper I'd been given. Julian, eagle-eyed as ever, must have noticed me looking at it through his rear view mirror.

'Anything of interest, Doc?' he inquired in his usual friendly and inoffensive manner.

I was about to explain when I realised that in addition to the details concerning the Philadelphia Psychiatric Institute, two other addresses had been scribbled on the sheet. My jaw dropped open almost cartoon-fashion. One in Philadelphia, one in Cambridge: both for Gogmagog Video. Without realising it, the words tumbled from my lips.

'What's that ya say?' Julian exclaimed, jamming the brakes on.

Startled, I complied with his anxious request to view the note. 'You know something about these places?' I questioned in amazement.

My friend's eyes widened as he read. 'Sure do, Doc,' he said, finally looking up. 'The Cambridge shop – why, Kathy's been manageress there since it opened.'

8

Ariadne's Thread

Ironically, a touch of mid-afternoon sun slowly muscled its way through the dark rain clouds as we approached home. A change of clothes, a phone call to Scudamore's and a forfeited deposit later, and it was time for a trilateral exchange of information. Julian began by explaining how he'd followed my instructions and spoken to Norma. Unfortunately accounts, outlines and summaries had, as I'd half-feared, become a trifle confused. To resolve the matter, he'd collected the girl and brought her back to assist in a search of my garden. Needless to say, it hadn't taken Ms Bates long to wheedle out the whole truth, including the sensitive matter of the buried coffin and its possible contents. Interestingly, she wasn't too upset. She regretted that Twister had been denied his posthumous claim to fame, but concluded that he'd probably reached his final resting place with far greater respect and dignity than if he'd been subjected to a police post mortem or the like. By my reckoning I must have just missed them when I left for Cambridge. Their unrewarding search complete, the two had convinced each other I couldn't be trusted out alone and set off in hot pursuit. One of Julian's mates was an easy touch for a boat, which was moored downriver. They'd planned to wait for me in the Jesus Green area, believing I'd be safe enough drifting along the Backs. As luck would have it, however, they'd been in the process of traversing the lock when the trouble began. The rest had been down to the generous hand of fate and Julian's quick response once he'd realised what was happening.

Blue Jay's story – or BJ as Julian was already calling her – was much shorter but equally unsweet. In return for Julian's candid explanations, she'd described our visit to Sondra with special embellishments surrounding my relationship with the professor. As far as I could tell, the keeping of secrets where my new friends were concerned was clearly a waste of time. This being the case, I held nothing back about my encounter with Natalie McCarthy. Then, rightly or wrongly, I finally decided to reveal the results of my tests on the young woman's frock.

Cards on the table all round; the question of what to do next was addressed. Julian, fascinated by the Gogmagog Video shop lead, was in no doubt that the Cambridge branch had to be checked out for clues as soon as possible. During the second half of the car journey home from the river, he'd recounted his partner's involvement with the store. It transpired that Kathy had been working in the shop when they first met. She'd told him that the owners were long-time friends of hers and when the franchise opened they'd asked her to manage it. Julian knew little else except that for the past three to four years the job had become part-time, with Kathy sometimes visiting the shop only once or twice a week. A heated debate soon developed regarding who should undertake the 'checking out'. In the end it was conceded that Julian possessed indisputable advantages that guaranteed his election. Number one, Ms Murkett was his responsibility, and number two, he had the gift of the gab. Votes cast and decisions made, it was well past feeding time for the troops. Norma gave me a hand to prepare a modest repast and during the process relieved me for a few minutes so I could call Sondra to check and chat. To my joy, all was well. No visit from or sighting of the notorious Ms White and the Reverend Black. The cakes were ready for collection and, in addition, she had also taken the liberty of contacting one of my larger competitors about the special three-tier wedding cake. Pending the approval of my client, the firm believed they could deliver on time if I prepared the armoury designs while they took charge of the basic icing. So it was agreed. In the morning I was to telephone the bride's father who'd placed the original order and, if all was well, visit Sondra to give the go-ahead and pick up the other cakes.

Over a less than healthy meal of quiche, chips, sausage and beans, the three of us chatted, each trying to conceal their own personal fears and trepidation about the bizarre situation binding us together. We talked of music – Julian and his Country and Western, Norma about Techno and boring old Clock about Classical. Cinema, my time at Van der Heijden, fashion, motorbikes – whatever topic came up got an airing. Finally, Julian announced his desire to return home and collect any messages. He confirmed that he'd visit Gogmagog Video as soon as it opened in the morning then await my return from Sandy's to make a report. Before I could enquire about arrangements for BJ, however, he suspiciously sloped off and I could see that I'd been left literally holding the baby.

I gave a truncated laugh. 'Now I only think it's fair to warn you that intrigue, deception and all manner of dastardly deeds used to be my stock-in-trade. Not weekly, mind, or even daily, but by the minute. So whatever it is you've cooked up with my smooth-talking neighbour, better spit it out before the icing hits the fan.'

Taking my remarks in the light-hearted manner I'd intended, Norma shook her head and grinned hugely. 'I told Tex you'd catch on as soon as he left,' she grumbled.

'Tex?' I repeated aghast. 'Whatever happened to Mr Stammers?'

BJ's smile was becoming infectious and I could tell I'd already lost, whatever the plot. 'Sorry, Dr Clock – oh no – Dr J, I mean. Guess I'd better come clean then.'

'Recommendable,' I agreed.

'First off, when you get used to him, Julian's a real Cadbury's. You know – fruit and nut, as in nutcase.'

'Yes,' I smirked. 'I've seen the advert and get the drift.'

Norma was evidently having trouble keeping a straight

face, but managed to forge on. 'Where was I? Oh yes. On the trip from home, I told him about our meeting with Sondra and my new nickname. Well, the silly bast – er, bugger – started laughing, so . . .'

'So to get even, you decided Tex was a suitable revenge?' I interrupted. 'Courtesy of Mr Z, if memory serves.'

Norma nodded.

'Good,' I exclaimed. 'I'm glad we've got that sorted. Now all I need to hear about is the conspiracy.'

I received one of the young lady's sheepish looks then she took a deep breath and launched into the pitch. 'It's not a conspiracy really, more of a practical arrangement,' she advocated. 'You said yourself it's a long way to come from my home to here. All that wasted travel time, not to mention the lifts I've been lucky enough to get. Anyway, since you need loads of assistance with the cakes and we have to keep helping Julian, I thought . . .'

'You thought it might be a good idea to stay with me,' I added, finding it impossible not to interrupt for a second time.

'It's okay with the Knotts,' she emphasised. 'They said you could phone them to confirm. Well, not really,' came the immediate retraction. 'But they trust me. They wouldn't mind – honestly.'

Inwardly I smiled. So far it was a reasonable effort. Trouble was I suspected the sting in the tail had yet to be delivered – I was right.

'But if it's not convenient, Julian said I could stay with him until we find Kathy.'

Game, set and match, I mused. The girl could have a future on the board of Van der Heijden. Time to play it cool, I decided. 'I can't deny your proposal has merit,' I remarked in my best corporate tone. 'Needless to say, even though this is the new millennium, you must appreciate the potential dangers for both of us if I let you stay.'

'I told Julian you'd never agree,' the disappointed girl let fly with a full battery of despondency.

'Just a moment,' I cautioned. 'I haven't finished yet. You

can stay for a short time under the following conditions. Firstly, you persuade Sondra to stay here with us. Secondly, I speak to the Knotts and if they agree, you call daily to let them know you're okay. Thirdly, under no circumstances do you stay with or accept an offer of employment from Mr Tex Stammers. And finally, you earn your keep.' I couldn't exactly believe what I'd just said, but before I had time to reconsider, Norma leapt up and gave me a huge hug. It was all over. I'd been well and truly suckered. But then suckered perhaps wasn't quite the right word. Without question I'd be a hundred per cent happier having Sondra where I could keep an eye on her during this crisis. Fiercely independent, she'd already refused, but now... At last the perfect set-up – it had to be heaven-sent. Chivalrous intentions apart, there was one other reason in favour of the idea – basically, I was lonely. Sure, Julian's occasional visits provided a welcome relief, but two spirited females turning my life upside down twenty-four hours a day? Delight or disaster, pleasure or pain, I couldn't say – hell, I didn't care. Crazy, crazy, crazy.

Once Norma had settled down I broached the 'knotty' subject of that night's arrangements. In reality it turned out to be an uncontested bout. I was exhausted after my punting adventure, it was late and, surprise, surprise, she just happened to have brought a holdall along containing at least two kitchen sinks. With the tail end of my energy, I spoke to the very amiable and somewhat over-trusting Mr Knott, who agreed the plan.

At last in the comfort of my own bed my fears for Kathy Murkett, Natalie McCarthy and Sondra intermingled with sadness for the poor unfortunate Twister. The ever-present threat posed by the delectable Ms White and formidable Reverend Black, the coffin buried in my garden and the as yet unsolved conspiracy were up there jiving for position. Then of course there was Blue Jay: complex, strong, vulnerable, craving to be needed. I closed my eyes and drifted towards sleep. In my final moments of consciousness I thought of Julian plotting with Norma how best to handle old Tick-tock. Certainly when this was all over, I'd have to have a word with that young chap . . .

The next morning got off to a whirlwind start. Norma had the same effect as a detonating smart bomb, the whole house being rattled and shaken to its foundations by her effervescent presence. Sondra was given prior warning of our intended invasion and, after checking in with Julian, the agreed plan of action was launched.

As expected, Sandy's commitment to self-sufficiency was formidable. I was left in no doubt that she wouldn't have budged an inch if the proposal for a temporary stay at the Clock residence had been made solely on the 'protection' ticket. The prospect of undertaking the role of chaperone to protect BJ from my evil designs, however, worked like a charm. Genius, sheer unadulterated genius!

Due to a lecturing commitment that evening in Oxford, it was agreed that Sondra would come over directly afterwards, even though the hour was likely to be late. Primary mission accomplished, I telephoned the bride's father who'd ordered the armoury-decorated wedding cake, explained the crisis and fortunately gained agreement to proceed with Sandy's plan. We were definitely on a roll. Less than two hours later we'd dropped off the trio of cakes at my competitor's shop and transported the rest home.

After lunch I gave my young assistant her first lesson in cake icing and managed to make good progress with the first few coats-of-arms. By now time was getting on and I was beginning to feel twangs of concern about Julian's well-being. He too had indicated that, despite his anxiety, there were matters begging his attention.

'Kathy won't be right pleased when she gets home if I've let the business turn to mush,' he'd announced, apparently genuinely concerned by the possible consequences. Fortunately, Gogmagog Video didn't open till eleven a.m. owing to its late closing time, affording Julian the time he'd craved. Nevertheless, I'd assumed that he'd be back by one or two at the latest. In the event, it was just gone four o'clock when Norma called out that the VW was trundling up the drive.

'Where the hell have you been?' I almost shouted as BJ escorted him into the living room.

Julian, somewhat startled by the ferocity of my greeting, flopped into one of the armchairs and exhaled deeply. 'Sorry Doc,' he apologised. 'Things never work out the way ya think. Damn shop didn't open up till nigh on noon. Then the gal in charge turned out to be new and didn't know nothin'.'

'What happened to her predecessor?' I asked, already half-certain of the answer.

'Well, accordin' to the little missy – quite attractive gal as it happens . . .'

'Julian!' I scowled.

The young man opened his arms in a gesture of innocence. 'Don't worry, Doc. I didn't fix 'er up or nothin'. Just settin' the scene for yers. Anyhow, Belinda – that's her name – told me that the fella who usually runs the show when Kathy's not there suddenly upped and left on some hikin' holiday in the Far East somewheres.'

'Sounds mighty fishy to me,' I remarked unintentionally in Julianese, much to Norma's amusement. 'What I mean is,' I tried to recover, 'the whole thing reeks of a conspiracy, or at the very least contrivance.'

Julian shrugged. 'Like ya said in the first place, Doc – mighty fishy.'

This latest piece of information did indeed cloud the picture even more. Slowly but surely Kathy Murkett's life was being erased and the few people that knew her spirited away.

'Were you able to look around the back of the shop?' I asked hopefully.

'That was the interestin' thing,' Julian replied. 'Of course I asked, but Belinda said she'd been given strict instructions

136

not to let anyone go pokin' around. Accordin' to her, shop's about to fold. She was just taken on temporary like to help with the shutdown.'

'The plot thickens,' I murmured.

'But who told her all this?' Norma piped up, apparently not wishing to be left out of the interrogation team.

'Said this fella did a few days ago when she was taken on,' Julian confirmed. 'Told her about his last-minute holiday arrangements right enough, but left her with the idea he'd return soon, and at any rate before the shop closed. In the meantime she could ask Kathy anythin' she needed to know.'

It came as no surprise to learn that Julian knew nothing about the video store's imminent closure. Whoever had stage-managed this melodrama was no amateur. Doors were being sealed at every turn, and I had a sinking feeling in my stomach that unless we could piece the story together in the very near future Kathy would be lost forever. In a way it reminded me of the mythological story of Ariadne using a thread to ensure her lover's escape from the Minotaur's labyrinth. If only Kathy had been able to lay down her own thread for us to follow, we may have stood a better chance of finding her, hopefully before malevolent forces as yet unknown severed the cord . . .

Apart from the revelation concerning the store's future nothing more of interest emerged from the debriefing session. Julian acknowledged that he hadn't pressed the issue of a general search. He believed that Belinda was harried enough by being left in charge of the business. Too much pressure and she might have broken down, perhaps even called the police. For me the way forward was now crystal-clear. Someone had to break into Gogmagog Video, and pretty damn sharpish. The slightest delay and it was a racing certainty that any evidence lying around would be removed, altered or destroyed.

My companions were slow to appreciate the merits of my proposal. I think the main problem was that the recommendation for criminal action had come from me – respected citizen and honourable magistrate. In a strange and touching way, I suspected that Mr Stammers and Ms Bates didn't want to see me drag myself down to a base level. Faced with such deep-seated concern, it wasn't easy to persuade them to go along, but eventually the ex-corporate wizard won through.

The plan was simple enough. Wait until the shop closed then, using Kathy's keys, Julian was to sneak in the back way and disarm the alarm system. Not actually breaking and entering at all really, except that it wasn't our property and we didn't have permission to enter. Of the many bones of contention surrounding the operation, the most resilient was who searches and who stands lookout. Eventually the matter resolved itself in a rather curious way. After much debate it suddenly dawned on me that we were arguing a no-brainer – with due apologies to all present for the corporate-speak. Norma was the only one with a good knowledge of hacking into computer systems, courtesy of her computer studies class. Julian was singularly suited to the role of lookout due to his 'street' appearance and unflappable temperament. And myself? Well, supposedly as the brains of the gang, I was considered to be the most likely to recognise whatever it was we were looking for.

It was five past ten precisely when a distinctly haggard-looking Belinda shut up shop for the night. Gogmagog Video, situated on Hobson Street, was a small enterprise and quite easy to miss unless you were paying attention. Fortunately, the recent bout of inclement weather had continued: it had been raining on and off all day and the temperature had dropped, making it noticeably chilly. The result – deserted streets. Another advantage proved to be the location. There were few shops along the row adjacent to the back of Marks and Spencer, and all had been closed since much earlier in the evening. The opposite side of the road was totally occupied by the grounds of Christ's College and, since Michaelmas term was in full swing, few students were abroad.

While Norma and I hovered surreptitiously around the corner in Sussex Street, Julian insisted on first 'casing the joint'. This process hardly seemed to have begun when he returned bearing news of our first major setback. Try as he might, he couldn't gain access to the back entrance. The gate to the alleyway was locked.

'Sorry folks,' he whispered. 'To be truthful, I hardly ever visited Kathy here. This part of town isn't really my patch.'

'That's great,' I breathed, rolling my eyes. 'Now what?'

'No need to fret none, Doc,' he assured me. 'Have front door keys, will travel . . .'

And so it was. The entrance locks corresponded without too much searching with two of the keys in Julian's set, and deactivating the alarm proved no obstacle. We confirmed that communication would be via mobile phone ring code or verbally, and with that the operation began.

Despite a thorough inspection, the store's ground-floor level revealed nothing of interest. At this stage we employed flashlights, which although far from ideal proved satisfactory for the job of scanning the racks of videos. Next, we ventured into the back room. Here, there were no windows and, since the door was only semi-glazed with a heavy cotton blind, I agreed we could risk using the lights. Essentially a stock room, the area was remarkably neat and tidy. Consequently it took only a few minutes to rummage through the desk, cabinet and boxes of new or duplicate cassettes that made up its content.

So far so good. No hidden alarms, booby traps or infrared security-video cameras, I joked to myself, hoping to bolster my fragile confidence. Apart from a microscopic toilet and almost invisible tea-making area, there was nothing else to see.

'On to the first floor,' I whispered.

The stairs were rickety and creaked horribly on every step, so by the time we reached the summit any creature alive or dead inhabiting the building would have been alerted to our presence. In contrast to the downstairs, the upper level was a complete tip. As far as I could see the entire area was essentially a single room, with a second created in the back corner by means of two steel partition walls. The floor was covered in a variety of partially opened boxes containing videos and mystical trinkets. Two desks and chairs were set side by side adjacent to the front window, and a bank of filing cabinets occupied the opposite wall. Of immediate interest was a rather old and grubby-looking PC on one of the desks and a small steel safe hidden away under its neighbour. By unspoken agreement BJ assigned herself to the computer while I investigated the safe. Since the only window overlooked the street, I decided that even with the Venetian blinds drawn use of the room light was too risky.

To my disappointment, the strong box presented no challenge at all. It was locked but, as I set the combination tumblers to zero in preparation for a spot of amateur safecracking, the mechanism gave a loud click. Filled with disbelief, I nonetheless gave the handle a turn and, voilà, the door opened. Inside I found two small boxes, each stuffed full of bills – one set paid, the other set unpaid, or to be more charitable, awaiting payment. A random review of the contents convinced me that I was wasting my time. Disappointed, I closed the safe door and joined Norma at the computer terminal.

'Any luck?' I asked as she clicked away merrily, causing window after window to appear and disappear from the screen.

'Pretty old-fashioned,' she whispered. 'They're still only using Windows 3.1.'

I tutted to try to ease the tension.

Norma half-smiled. 'Anyway, I'm doing reasonably well. There's some security but not much, and it could easily be bypassed by a twelve-year-old. At the moment I've access to their ordering and invoicing system. Again nothing especially complicated.'

For a few minutes I watched mesmerised as my young accomplice gained access to, then manipulated, a wide range of files and databases. It was all fascinating stuff, but regrettably not of the slightest value to our quest. I was beginning to despair when Norma let out a muffled cry of triumph.

'Yes!' she exclaimed. 'This is something they've gone to a fair deal of trouble to hide.'

'What is it?' I asked limply.

At that moment the mobile phone emitted its irritating jingle.

'Oh shit!' I cursed, grabbing the abomination. 'Perfect,' I muttered, shutting the contraption off after listening to the message. 'Julian says there's a couple of coppers coming this way. Best to lie low until we get the all-clear.'

Unable to resist the temptation, we crept to the edge of the window and peeked through the blinds. Sure enough, two officers of the law were proceeding along Hobson Street heading towards M&S. Drawn like iron filings to a magnet, the pair, seemingly uninterested in all other establishments, made a beeline for the video shop. I swallowed hard and began to imagine all manner of give-away clues we must have left dotted about. Drawn curtains, lights, flashlamps, perhaps even a twenty-foot fluorescent sign saying 'Burglars here'.

A few yards from the entrance, Julian suddenly emerged from the shadows. Judging by his unsteady gait, it looked like he was pretending to be just a tiny bit tipsy. Then I caught a glimpse of the officers' faces. I smiled and breathed a huge sigh of relief.

'What?' Norma demanded, perplexed.

'It's okay,' I whispered. 'It's two young women.'

'So?' came the uncertain reply.

'This is Julian we're talking about,' I explained. 'Another ten minutes and he'll have them doing a striptease outside the Master's Lodge.'

Sure enough, Julian was proving to be more than equal to his reputation. From somewhere in his jacket the old beaten-up cowboy hat had been resurrected and, imaginary guitar in hand, he launched into a not half bad rendition of 'Love Me Tender'. . . and the ladies were loving it.

'Where the hell does that hat keep coming from?' I remarked, not really expecting a reply.

'One of Tex's trademarks,' Norma informed me authoritatively. 'Seems that wherever he goes there's always someone he knows willing to part with their hat. People just love the guy and everyone gets a kick out of his impromptu performances. According to Julian, same thing used to happen to his old dad. Apparently he looked like Winston Churchill. Each time he went down the local, some mate or other would always stand him a big cigar in return for a quick impersonation. You know, "We'll fight them on the beaches": that type of stuff.'

Although under less fraught circumstances I'd have been quite happy to continue listening to my accomplice's account of the life and times of Julian Stammers, Esquire, we still had work to do. Satisfied that our lookout was more than able to keep the local constabulary occupied, I gestured that we should resume the computer search. Within seconds Norma retrieved the screen that had attracted her attention. Basically, the file was a list of names in the form of two columns side by side. Opposite each entry was a sum of money – usually a five-figure amount – and, in parenthesis, the name of an HM Prison.

'What the Dickens is this all about?' I murmured.

'Shall I print it out?' Norma asked, clearly anxious to move on.

I nodded and, while the laser printer spewed out the list, sifted through the rest of the room's chaotic content. I'd more or less completed my assignment when the mobile bleated again. Julian confirmed that the coast was clear but recommended that we soon consider calling it a draw. I tried the door of the partition room but it was locked. Since I could see BJ was finishing up, I decided it was probably wise to make our getaway. We scooped up our gear, made sure the copy of the list was extracted from the printer and headed towards the stairs. Then, as I turned to conduct a final sweep of the room, I heard a faint groaning sound coming from the partitioned room. Norma heard it too, so we held our position and listened. The groaning continued. I raced back to the door and tried the handle again. Definitely locked. Without a word, we headed for the desks in search of any likely keys. Since there was nothing doing, I started on the filing cabinets and, in the second drawer chosen at random, I hit gold – a whole bunch of keys.

In time-honoured fashion, it was the last one I tried that fitted. Once unlocked, the door turned out to be of much sturdier construction than I'd expected. It didn't move at all easily, and I suspected that it had been fitted with heavy-duty springs. As I forced my way in, Norma's flashlight picked up more than furniture and boxes.

'Oh no, not again!' I exclaimed.

Slumped in the corner, arms handcuffed to pipes on either side of him, lay Toby Farthing. He was in a pitiful state. Blood trickling from beneath his hairline, a blackened eye and tape over his mouth – he'd obviously taken a fair beating. As the light illuminated his startled and terrified face, he began to shake his head. Norma and I both instinctively advanced towards him. I knelt at his side and with a swift stroke peeled off the gag.

'The . . .'

Clunk . . .

'Door,' he coughed as it swung to. 'Ah, sweet knights, what folly marks thine entrance?' he crooned.

Spinning around like a top, Norma clawed at the door. 'Shit!' she cried out in frustration. 'There's no handle. We're locked in.'

Despite his appalling injuries, Toby managed a smile. 'Clever bitch you've got there, dear heart. Dangerous combination that: a woman and brains. You'll have to watch out.'

'Who the hell did this?' I rasped, preferring to assess his condition rather than heed his advice.

'Who else?' came his petulant reply. 'That beast of a Reverend and his Jezebel bastard. Just because they didn't like my performance with the lovely Jules... Ooh, that hurts.'

Well at least I was right about the presence of White and Black at the Rave, I told myself, endeavouring to quell my patient's complaints. As I made to resume my examination, the lights flicked on. Norma, having located the switch, was standing beside a small computer desk, which supported a fairly sophisticated laptop. Interestingly, the rest of the room was exceptionally tidy, with row upon row of videocassettes lining all four walls. My companion, her face as white as a sheet, was evidently trying to beckon me with her eyes. I took the hint, made some excuse to Toby and joined her. Without speaking, she pointed behind the desk to something she'd discovered. It was not a find I appreciated one bit – a mass of wires encircling a complex electronic device attached directly to a large pack of incendiary explosives.

'Bugger!' I cursed. Although I knew as sure as night follows day that the system would be linked up to the laptop, I checked anyway. Ten out of ten.

'What're you two scamps up to over there, fussing and squeaking like a couple of squirrels in heat?' Toby's picturesque query gave me a start. 'Something nasty, isn't it?' he accused, becoming visibly alarmed. 'Come now, don't hide it from old Toby. He might be a raving fairy, but he's no dullard.'

I signalled Norma to examine the computer and returned to the frightened man. 'Look,' I said firmly. 'I don't know what it is. Seems to be something related to the computer. Anyway, it doesn't matter. You'll be out of here in a few minutes.'

Toby coughed up a gob of blood, spluttered then choked violently before finally catching his breath. 'Darling boy,' he grimaced. 'So considerate. But no silly games, please. It's a bomb and in case you've forgotten, you're locked in too.'

He had a point, but then we had Julian. 'Norma,' I called in a low voice, 'call Julian. Tell him to get up here PDQ.'

As the Q left my lips, I saw the young girl's still white complexion lose its colour altogether. 'All of the gear plus phone – outside?' I ventured. 'Shit!'

An acute shock of pain suddenly racked Toby's body, causing him to yell out then lapse into semi-consciousness. For the moment there was little I could do, so I rejoined Norma at the computer. The screen was blank except for a selection of icons in the left-hand top corner.

'Main menu, you reckon?' I enquired.

She nodded. 'I daren't touch it though. Chances are, we press any key and . . .'

We stared at the screen mesmerised like a couple of cats caught in a headlamp beam. Then, as if irritated by our attention, the hard disk started to growl and a second later the display flickered back to life. BJ took an involuntary step backwards. I nearly bit my tongue off.

'Jesus, what's happening?' I snapped.

'Screensaver,' she deduced. 'I think it's gone into a screensaver mode – look!' She was right. A series of Bibles followed by a cross circled around the LCD. Eventually the cross came to a standstill in the middle of the display, pulsed for a moment then gave way to a scrolling text and commentary:

'Know ye not that the unrighteous shall not inherit the Kingdom of God? Be not deceived: neither fornicators, nor idolaters, nor adulterers, nor effeminate, nor abusers of themselves with mankind, nor thieves, nor covetous, nor drunkards, nor revilers, nor extortioners, shall inherit the Kingdom of God.

Corinthians, Chapter 6 v.9–10.'

'Your friend and mine again,' Norma remarked.

I didn't reply, my mind fully occupied by a simple and straightforward conclusion. We were well and truly screwed. Reactivation of the computer could mean only one thing –

prelude to disaster. If we didn't act quickly, it would be triple barbecue time. To my companion's horror, I hit the space bar and waited for the explosion. Silence. I exhaled deeply as the screensaver yielded to a schematic representation of the device. The diagram was completely incomprehensible, but towards the centre was the image of an alarm clock. Yes, it was ticking and yes, it was in countdown mode.

'What's the time?' I asked, even though I had a perfectly good watch of my own.

'Ten forty-five,' Norma confirmed.

'Excellent!' I groaned inwardly. 'A whole fifteen minutes.' Okay, Clock – Jeremiah, Orville – time to get it together and get everyone the hell out. Seven years pissing around in Scenario Planning – so what's the exit scenario from a sealed room containing a computer-controlled incendiary device and no phone? I dredged up all my former tricks and techniques one by one, pitting them against the problem. Then I saw it, crystal clear and staring me straight in the face: computer + modem = phone + code. One glance at the laptop and I could feel a 'double six' throw in my bones.

'Norma!' I almost yelled. 'You're a Windows wizard. Can you minimise this screen and see if there's a phone dialler loaded on this thing?'

The girl's ghostly complexion suddenly blossomed as she caught my drift and spied a telephone line going into the LT's modem card.

'Dialler!' she exclaimed excitedly as the phone pad image blazed before us.

Julian responded to the SOS call at lightning speed. He flung open the door and dragged us both out before he caught sight of Toby, now just beginning to stir.

'Eight minutes to get him out,' I bored the message home. Until now I'd paid little attention to the set of handcuffs used to tether Toby's wrists. In a strange way the poor man looked like a prisoner of old left to rot for a generation or more in some rat-infested dungeon. As to the cuffs, they were made of a curious high-density plastic. Rock-hard, they barely closed around the wide metal piping which, extending from floor to ceiling, probably formed part of an antiquated heating system. It took only seconds to conclude that, given the tools at hand, neither pipes nor restraints could be sawn, smashed or snapped in the few minutes remaining.

Toby was now fully alert and had more or less guessed the magnitude of his predicament. 'Jules, dear heart,' he cried. 'Listen to me, listen. Be a good boy and whisk these good people away. No one's going to worry about another dead queen, least of all me. Let's face it, Westminster Abbey's overflowing with them anyway. Tacky, very tacky.'

As he spoke I suddenly detected the same odour I'd experienced when trying to clean Natalie's frock.

'Same MO,' I mumbled. Much to Toby's dismay, I unceremoniously ripped away his T-shirt, tore it into strips and tightly bound each cuff to its respective pipe. 'Matches!' I yelled. 'Please God, let someone be a smoker.'

BJ shrugged. Julian shook his head.

'I've a rather nice lighter my friend Benjamin bought me for Christmas,' Toby volunteered, totally bewildered by what was going on.

I grabbed the lighter, signalled Julian to pull our prisoner's hands away from the pipes as far as the links would allow, then ignited each wrapping. As I'd hoped, the cloth burned brightly and fiercely for a few seconds before completely carbonising. The hard plastic only melted and warped slightly, but most importantly the point of attachment between cuff and link became brittle as it cooled. Julian's penknife did the rest. Toby was screaming, his hands singed in places, but he was free . . .

'Two minutes!' Norma shrieked. We were going to make it.

Then I saw a wire – extending from the explosive's mechanism to beneath a piece of hardboard Toby was sitting on – a fucking wire.

I just wanted to scream my lungs out, curse God in his heaven and every saint in Christendom. It could only be a pressure plate. However quickly we moved, with Toby's weight and injuries we'd never make it to the door. Bedlam descended on the scene. Toby, recognising some last-minute hitch, was pleading with us to leave him. Norma was shouting out the seconds while Julian kept repeating the same question over and over: 'What now, Doc? What now?'

I could think of only one possibility. Everything depended on the computer table and the castors a forgiving God had given it. I started barking orders.

'Norma, take the computer off the table and keep yelling out the time. Julian, drag the thing over here and help me get Toby onto it.'

Thankfully my team responded instantly and as instructed. I planted myself firmly behind Mr Farthing's bulky frame and Julian helped me haul the man face-first onto the table like a side of beef. At my signal Julian dragged the table off the platform and out of the door. All was in place for the final manoeuvre. Unhappy from the outset that I'd insisted on manning the plate, Julian pleaded with me to exchange places. The timekeeper, however, was down to fifteen seconds.

'No time!' I yelled. 'Norma, wheel the table to the stairs and then get outside. Julian, when I'm through the door, heave it to and run.'

There was no time for confirmation. Catapulting myself away from the wall, I took two giant steps then dived. The explosive device clicked demonically as I flew by. I rolled, the door locked. Boom!

9

Home of the Depraved

I can't decide what upset Sondra the most – the fact that I wasn't at home when she arrived back from Oxford or my condition when I finally did turn up. On balance the sight of my charred clothing, blackened face and split lip probably afforded the latter choice a slight edge. Add to that, however, the spectacle of Julian and Norma in a similar state of dishevelment struggling to assist Toby, half-naked and beaten-up, from the VW, and I guess there was no longer any contest.

'Bloody hell, Clock!' she snapped. 'What on God's earth have you been up to? Look at the state of Norma, for Christ's sake. The girl's eighteen. You're supposed to be looking after her, not taking her to street fights with a couple of wasted tramps.'

Despite the hostile greeting, Sandy as always jumped in at the deep end. Summarily dismissing BJ from her supporting role, she grabbed hold of Toby and, with Julian's help, hauled him inside. While Julian and Norma took it in turns to clean up, the professor gave me a hand tending to Toby. We laid him out on the couch and did our best to determine the extent of his injuries. After a double examination, the prognosis wasn't so bad. As far as we could tell, the old boy certainly had a couple of cracked ribs, probably a fractured right leg and a mild concussion. The good news was that the blood he'd been coughing up was only due to the fact that two of his teeth had been knocked out and he'd a nasty bite on his tongue.

'Toby's going to live then?' he enquired at one point, still half in a stupor.

I assured him he was, plied him with a cup of my best wonder-brew and insisted he rest. Sondra, who was busying herself binding up his chest and tending to his other external injuries, was less than sympathetic. When Toby made the mistake of complaining about the pain, she assured him that it was only to promote his speedy recovery so he'd appreciate it more when she finally murdered him. After that, he just gritted his teeth and bore whatever pain he experienced in silence.

Eventually the battle-worn troops were as smartened up as they were likely to be that night and cowered in whatever chair they'd collapsed into, awaiting the wrath of Ms Warwick. Not surprisingly, all eyes turned to me.

'Okay Clock, spit it out,' she instructed. 'The unexpurgated version please. None of your old Van der Heijden "smoke and mirrors" garbage.'

Given little option, I told it as it was. I started by introducing Julian, who had the good sense to temporarily shelve his Svengali routine. In turn he introduced the silent Toby, and then it was back to me. Sondra's face was a picture throughout – in fact a picture of varying degrees of disbelief, horror and just plain despair.

'Interesting,' she mused as I concluded. 'So you were right about the bomb being an incendiary device. But what troubles me is the story after the explosion. Somehow you all managed to get out of the shop and scurry back to Mr Stammer's car unseen before the emergency services arrived. Sounds a bit glossed-over to me.'

'Well,' I commented uncertainly, 'I'm not sure we were unseen, and scurrying's a bit strong. But I think it's fair to say we were hobbling pretty quickly, and I doubt anyone could've recognised us.'

'Good,' came the stern response. 'I just hope you'll take it so lightly if you're wrong and half a dozen squad cars come screaming up the drive.' Sondra surveyed each of us in turn, then gradually her outraged schoolmarm expression softened. 'Bloody idiots the lot of you,' she exclaimed with just a hint of a smile. 'But I suppose I have to be grateful you're all safe. Certainly it's thanks to you that Mr Farthing here will see another sunrise.'

Lecture over, I made everyone a laced chocolate drink, and after a slightly frosty start conversation began to run freely. It didn't take long for the topic to drift back to the problem at hand. As it did, Norma began feverishly searching her pockets.

'The list!' she exclaimed, waving it in front of us.

Like a game of 'pass the parcel', the crumpled piece of paper was circulated around the group. A couple of reviewers believed they recognised the names of criminals whose cases had been followed by local or national media. Toby, who was rapidly returning to form – aided and abetted by a mixture of alcohol and herbal/conventional medicines – proved to be the most authoritative. Two of the people listed were known to him personally and, as a result, he was able to confirm that the individuals were currently serving time at Her Majesty's Pleasure in the institutes associated with their names. Unfortunately the forty-two entries printed in the adjacent column were a mystery to all. It was Sondra who, after the group fell into a period of prolonged introspection, broke the mood by abandoning her seat in favour of floor pacing.

'That reminds me,' she said finally after settling by the mantelpiece. 'The effigy. When Clock told me about the existence of the Gogmagog Video shop in Cambridge, I thought it suspicious but eventually decided it was probably just a coincidence. I assume he's told you about the similarity between the icon and the US Gogmagog Video company logo.'

Embarrassingly, it was the one part of the story I'd forgotten to impart. A few sighs and much groaning later, everyone was put in the picture and the floor returned to the professor.

'Until my trip to Oxford,' she resumed, 'I hadn't been able to locate any information about the story. It's a few years back, and unfortunately I had a clear-out of all my old Americana this summer. As luck would have it though, I ran into an old classmate of mine from Philly at the Oxford conference tonight. He quite clearly remembered the incident, probably because the press had a field day printing all manner of erotic pictures. Completely irrelevant to the case, but it certainly boosted circulation. Anyway, according to him, GM Video was a front for a top-of-the-line pornography outfit. Seems they had two particular areas of specialisation. The first involved male rape by gangs of under-age girls, often Asians . . .'

'Sounds dreamy,' Toby piped up, only to find himself instantly withered by one of Sondra's killer lecture-room stares.

'More interesting,' she pressed on, 'was a series of movies they made in which the female star played the role of a well-known person – actress, politician, model, etc. Now don't get me wrong, these girls weren't just made up to look like the originals. They'd been carefully selected then subjected to extensive plastic surgery so they became exact doubles.'

Julian nodded, his memory obviously stimulated by Sondra's account. 'Just for the record,' he volunteered, 'the general idea's not anywhere near new. Pretty much after all this plastic surgery stuff got started in the States, the prostitution racketeers cashed-in in much the same way. As you can imagine, guys with a stack of cash were willin' to pay big bucks to party with a lookalike film star.'

Sandy raised her eyebrows. 'Well, Clock, I'll give you one thing. You've certainly amassed the ideal group of experts for this case.'

'So what happened?' I asked, neatly side-stepping the uncharitable compliment.

'What usually happens, I guess,' she shrugged. 'People became greedy, started double-crossing each other and, before you could say censorship, dead bodies were cropping up all over the place. A real bloodbath by all accounts. Eventually, the police unravelled the whole sordid story, but – and it's the "but" that'll be of most interest to you – the grey matter – the money behind the operation – was never identified.'

As Sondra reseated herself Julian was quick to pick up the speaking baton. 'It's one helluva story,' he observed. 'Sure, there's some relation to that girl Natalie's situation, but there's no way Kathy and the video shop here could've been operatin' the same kinda business. Jeez, folks, this is my line of work. I'd know.'

'There's no doubt of that, Julian,' I interjected, seeing his distress. 'No one said anything about it being the same set-up. But the facts do suggest some high-level criminal involvement. Kathy's disappearance, Natalie, Twister, and the list, not to mention Ms White and the Reverend – at the very least we're in the middle of a complex and dangerous situation. And to be honest, whether the two Gogmagog Video shops have anything in common or not, they're only small pieces in a very large puzzle.'

'Well, my dears,' Toby spluttered, trying to prop himself up, 'if one of you nice girls will oblige, this seems as good a time as any for Toby Farthing to put his ten-pence-worth in the pot.' Better acquainted with Mr Farthing's terminology than the rest of us, Julian politely waved away Sondra's offer of help and did the necessary himself. 'Gentle folk,' he addressed the room with a pained sweep of his arm, 'first let me thank you most sincerely for delivering this unworthy soul from the gaping jaws of death. There are many, in fact many indeed, who would have simply walked by on the opposite side of the road without a qualm. Thank you, thank you.'

Since the highly theatrical performance evidently begged a response, I decided to do the honours. 'You're very welcome, Toby,' I said with gusto. 'Others might doubt it, but you're a brave man. I'm not sure I'd have been able to behave as selflessly as you did under the same circumstances. Your antics as a patient, however, sadly leave much to be desired.'

Everyone laughed. Duty had been served.

'A kind word, a cruel comment – such is my lot,' Toby sighed. 'But no matter. As I'm sure you know, I have little with which to repay your gallant deeds. Only my ten-pence-worth of information may serve as a partial repayment of my debt.' In his inimitably flamboyant and roundabout way, Toby slowly focused in on the secrets he wished to divulge. To be fair, it was evident to all assembled that the Footlights Show was merely a smokescreen to hide his pain. The shock of being beaten and his narrowest of escapes from a gruesome death had shaken the poor man to the core. It was, in fact, not far short of a miracle that he was capable of putting on any kind of performance at all.

He began by admitting that even before Norma had outlined the present crisis to him in the van, he'd heard one or two whispers on the grapevine. The girl's outline, originally designed to take the victim's mind off his injuries, had become progressively expanded and had included a description of the Gogmagog effigy. This had awakened several forgotten memories.

'The first point is,' he recounted in a low voice, 'about three years ago one of the few ladies in my life – quite a young thing – fell on hard times. However, when I saw her less than a month later she was on top of the world. Said she'd been offered a new lease of life. Told me not to worry if she suddenly disappeared, then wished me a happy future. Silly cow, I thought. Then, quiff my umbrella, if she didn't just vanish. Haven't seen hide nor hair since.'

'Interesting,' Sondra commented. 'Would you say there was anything special or unusual about her?'

'Not really, my dear,' Toby remarked thoughtfully. 'Like many I've met – a lost soul, alone, no roots to speak of. But you must forgive me. All this talking's wearing what little bit's left of me to a shadow. Just one more piece of tittle-tattle. The night of the Halstead rave. I haven't told you yet how we fell in with the Black and White Minstrels. Well,

154

that bastard Marcus Hamilton introduced them to me when we first arrived. Gave me some cock-and-bull story about them being bigwig producers or some such tommyrot. Needless to say, as soon as we set up, the bitch in white started issuing orders, threats – most unpleasant. Anyway, they were in and out a few times till your party turned up. Didn't say much. In fact the oversized golliwog never opened his trap. But I did overhear one thing. Miss Tight-arse whispered something about an American operation then Gog and Magog finally being released.'

This last speech had definitely pushed Toby over the edge. It was, as always seemed to be the case these days, well past the witching hour and time for everyone to turn in. A brief powwow involving Julian, Sondra and myself resulted in the decision that Toby should be offered room and board for the night at the Stammers' residence. In the morning Julian would take him to the casualty department at Addenbrooke's Hospital and have the injured soldier properly tended to. My neighbour felt confident that few questions would be asked, since attacks on the gay community in and around Cambridge by skinheads were sadly commonplace.

So it came to pass and, as the clock struck three a.m., Norma finally sidled off to bed, leaving Sondra and I alone staring into the glowing embers of an almost extinct fire.

'Jerry, my boy,' Sondra sang out softly, 'I've said it before and I'll say it again, you're in one helluva pickle. Now you've got me bobbing up and down in the vinegar with you. Bloody hell, I'm supposed to be a respected history professor – learned, reliable – even though I do come across as a dotty semi-recluse these days.'

'But you're loving it all really, aren't you?' I smiled, fingers and toes tightly crossed.

Sandy fixed me with one of her 'this is what we're going to do' stares. 'Time to face facts,' she announced after a prolonged pause. 'The trail on this side of the pond's cooling down so fast it's making my nose bleed. Natalie McCarthy's partner, the Gogmagog Video saga and Ms

White's comments about a US operation – like everything else on this God-forsaken planet, if it's big, bad and bawdy, it'll thrive best in the good old US of A.'

'So you think that's where Kathy is?' I ventured, less surprised by the idea than I would have imagined.

'Damn right she is,' Sandy insisted. 'Dead or alive, I can't say. Nor do I have a clear idea what's going on as yet. The one thing I'm certain of, though, is that Ms Kathy Murkett's something special in this, you mark my words.'

'Any thoughts on the Gogmagog link that keeps cropping up?' I asked.

Sandy shook her head. 'As far as I know, there are three main legends involving the name. You've got the local version – giant Gogmagog gets jilted by frivolous nymph, Granta, so turns himself into a hill. Then there are endless stories about a couple of giants, Gog and Magog, usually related in some way to the conflict between the ancient Britons and Trojans. Finally, there's the Bible – Old and New Testament versions. You know, the usual "forces of evil" routine.'

I wasn't feeling too clever when Ms Warwick launched into her potted history recital, but being reminded of Toby's remarks, the Bible and its association with the Reverend Joseph made me sick to my stomach.

Sondra could see I'd had enough. 'Come on, Clock, you've done your good deed for the day. Even though I think you're irresponsible, irrational and just plain pig-headed, I'm proud of you. You're a decent man, and I . . . Sleep. That's what we need. Come the morrow I'll get us a couple of tickets to go visit Uncle Sam.'

It was late afternoon when Julian came over to issue his daily bulletin. Thankfully, Toby's injuries were no worse than we'd suspected. Given his excess weight and apparently high blood pressure, however, he'd been admitted to the hospital and was likely to remain there for three or four days. This was good news. I still didn't understand why Ms

White and Co. had attempted to remove the old boy. He was small fry at best and no threat to anyone except the acting profession. It just didn't make sense, especially since the lady had gone to such pains to assure me that killing was by far and away her least-favoured option. Nevertheless, Toby was in hospital and with luck out of harm's way.

True to her promise, Sondra booked seats on the next day's lunchtime flight from Heathrow to Philadelphia. What I hadn't realised was that she'd already made plans to return home for a visit in about a week's time. Hence, this was another case of two birds and a stone – the 'k' word being deliberately omitted due to current circumstances. As expected, Julian and Norma were less than happy to be left behind while we carried the standard to foreign shores. After much heartrending debate, however, they accepted that their role was best played out on home turf. Sondra was a native, and I'd spent nearly half my working life on the East Coast. Rightly or otherwise, our backgrounds made it much easier for us to pass unhindered through the US establishment. Access to government agencies, documentation and the unofficial side of officialdom was our forte. Without question it wasn't fair, but our two companions wouldn't stand a chance in that particular part of the forest. Of course they knew it all too well – it was just difficult under the circumstances to be reconciled to it. In contrast, when it came to walking on the wilder side of Philadelphian society, the shoe was on the other foot and our position undeniably weaker. Here again, though, on balance Sondra's local knowledge and contacts carried the day.

With the matter reluctantly settled, Julian agreed to try to unlock the secret of the list of names while Norma promised to scour the darker side of the Internet in search of more information concerning past, present or potential future entries related to Gogmagog Video. The greatest difficulty came, however, when I had to decide whether or not to let the young girl remain alone in my house. I was against it for a dozen reasons – some rational, some irrational – and I just couldn't be convinced. In the end I agreed to the one option I thought I never would – she should stay with Julian. There was no getting away from the fact that her involvement in this cesspit we'd slid into placed her at risk. Better for her to have Mr Stammers as a guardian angel than no one at all. At least that way she could assist Julian with his efforts, share the load of visiting Toby and keep a watch on my home plus morbid content of the back garden. Last but not least, there was the matter of Natalie McCarthy. Although I doubted she'd make contact again, the thought of her hammering on my door begging for help, only to receive no reply, was too disturbing an image. I gave Julian a spare set of keys and silently prayed to the gods.

Before we left, BJ delivered a creditable performance helping me to push ahead with the task of preparing several more intricate decorations for the wedding cake. At a conservative estimate the project could still be completed on schedule if I returned within five days then worked without sleep for the remaining time. Finally everything was in readiness for our departure. I insisted on one last lecture session with Julian on looking after his charge, and bullied Sondra into doing the same. Daily phone calls to exchange findings and check on everyone's well-being were set down in stone and emergency procedures double-checked. By the time we all turned in that night I had the feeling my shell-shocked neighbour would be glad to see the back of us. As we parted though, he gripped both my hand and arm with the force of a vice.

'Doc, what you're doin' for me – well, I'll never be able to repay ya,' he impressed upon me. 'God speed.'

I was wrong.

Next morning the weather was remarkably fine – crisp, but unequivocally fine. The drive down to Heathrow went without a hitch, and British Airways did us proud by taking off and landing on schedule. We arrived at Philadelphia airport mid-afternoon on the same day. Sondra waited while I cleared Immigration and, with our bags already revolving around the conveyor belt as we entered the baggage reclaim hall, everything seemed to be going well. Perhaps too well, I began to worry.

'With luck, the driver of the car I've arranged should be waiting for us by the time we're through with Customs,' Sondra assured me.

In line with my recollection of this particular flight, which I must have taken hundreds of times in the past, the area beyond Customs was a zoo. Scores of people, most of them waving name placards, were in evidence to greet the tired and bedraggled travellers. As we emerged into the throng, I listlessly glanced from face to face, from card to card, in the vain hope of catching sight of a sign reading 'Professor Warwick'. My eyes soon began to ache, then, for an instant, I thought I saw the word 'Clock'. My attention snared, and I stared through the sea of raised arms until I focused on the huge figure of a black man in a black suit, grinning at me. My heart stopped.

'Over here, Jerry,' Sondra's voice brought me to heel with a start. Her arm suddenly jerked me away from the object of my terror. I railed against the pull, almost knocking my guide off-balance. Feverishly I scanned the area – no sign, no man.

'Jerry, what's the matter?' Sondra repeated. 'Are you ill?'

I quickly drew my wits about me, apologised for the stall and allowed myself to be escorted to a diminutive Asian-looking gentleman carrying the expected placard. Jet lag, daydream or reality? The first two seemed the most likely, but I couldn't help but wonder . . .

Alvin, our friendly chauffeur, chattered away merrily to Sondra as we wended our way out of the airport complex. Our destination was West Conshohocken, a small town outside Philadelphia not too far from historic Valley Forge. We were booked in at the Marriott West, a relatively new hotel built to serve the growth of businesses in the area. I'd stayed at this particular establishment many times and quite liked it. Apart from being away from the city centre, hence not outlandishly expensive, it was comfortable and only a stone's throw from the expressway. The location was also convenient, since it was close to the gargantuan King of Prussia Mall, former home of Gogmagog Video and our first port of call the next morning.

Due to the on-schedule arrival of the flight, Sondra talked me into inviting her to dinner. As a gastronomic point of interest, Philadelphia and its environs boasts some of the highest rated restaurants in the United States. I had hoped to get away with a snack, but in the space of sixty seconds the stakes rocketed through takeaway to room service to local bar to family restaurant and finally ended up at Le Bec-Fin, one of the best. Unfortunately, this hallowed eatery was located back in the centre of Philadelphia, on Walnut Street. My companion, however, in common with many of her countryfolk, paid little heed to distance. 'What was twenty miles or so when the food was orgasmic,' I was berated when foolishly expressing mild resistance.

It was nigh on one a.m. as we exited the city. The meal had been excellent, but due to jet lag and the fact I drank too much, somewhere along the line I missed out on the orgasmic part. Despite my semi-stuporous state I was pleased to see the famous row of boathouses that lines the Schuylkill River still brightly illuminated – strangely, one of the few local landmarks I'd always found a comforting sight – like coming home. As I drifted in and out of my alcohol-induced trance, I couldn't help but feel I'd been hustled. I knew well enough from past experience that trying to reserve a table at the restaurant in question usually required weeks or even months of advance notice, especially for the later of the two nightly sittings. Yet we had landed mid-afternoon, travelled to our hotel and then, following an 'on the spur of the moment' decision, managed to secure a table for the nine p.m. session – no problem? Hmm . . .

Half-baked conspiracy theories continuing to form in my beleaguered brain, I toppled into bed. Lying there in total darkness, it struck me as odd if not downright funny that Sondra and I were in separate rooms. Not that I'd expected anything else really, but given the nature of our assignment

– delving into the murky world of pornography and eroticism – our puritanical arrangements did carry a touch of irony. Directing my thoughts towards Ms Warwick was a big mistake. Always a martyr to jet lag, I invariably suffered the full range of distressing symptoms: sensation of fever, headache, malaise and, of course, sleep disturbance. The minutes laboured by like hours, allowing all my cherished memories of Sandy to unfold before me. Occasionally the images began to transform into dreams, but a periodic 'whoosh' from the heating system kicking in or the distant hooting of freight trains dragged back my consciousness. The sound of the trains and the intensity of my recollections somehow began to link. As the rolling stock drew relentlessly closer, my memories of those lazy afternoons in Cambridge, making love till exhausted we collapsed in each other's arms, intensified. Finally, the engine passed by the hotel bringing in its wake scores of laden wagons – b'dum, b'dum, b'dum, b'dum. The slow, monotonous beat thudded in my chest. I was a man possessed. I had to go to her . . .

Rolling out of bed now fully alert, I quickly dressed and cautiously ventured into the corridor. Sondra's room was on the opposite side of the same floor hence not too daunting a task for a less-than-accomplished late-night prowler such as myself. I reached her door, the sound of my own heartbeat having replaced the rhythm of the passing train pounding in my ears. My hand curled into a fist; I raised my arm, prepared to knock.

Shit! I didn't have the balls.

Ashamed and irritated by this initial failure, I regrouped, ordered my courage back into play and launched a second assault.

'Can I help you, sir?' a suspicious voice rang out from behind.

Startled, I turned to find a young lady, perhaps from room service, glaring at me, apparently disturbed from her task of gathering the breakfast order menus that dangled from the odd door handle. I panicked, mumbled something unintelligible about being lost then, waving my plastic key under her nose in denial of all intention of wrongdoing, shuffled back to my solitary room. Failure.

Five minutes after I finally got off to sleep, the alarm burst into life, shocking me back to reality. I felt bloody awful. My brains had been wrapped in a damp woollen blanket and my stomach filled with slow-drying cement. Sondra, on the other hand, looked the picture of health and, seeing my vulnerable condition, showed no mercy, taking unnatural delight in taunting me. 'Goddamn women – can't live with 'em, can't live without 'em.'

With her usual efficiency, Sondra had arranged for a hire car to be at our disposal and seemed to have received a thousand faxes from a variety of local and UK sources in response to queries she'd made before our flight. Tanked up on coffee, I gratefully accepted the offer of riding in the passenger seat and let my companion brave the roads. It was about ten a.m. when we joined the Schuylkill Expressway, bound for the King of Prussia Mall. In no time at all we reached the complex, which appeared much as I remembered it. There were now new Neiman Marcus and Nordstrom stores and what looked like another annexe, but at least the place still existed. Given what I'd experienced recently, I wouldn't have been surprised if the site had been levelled and turned into a Marine World or baseball ground. From one of her faxes, the boss confirmed that Gogmagog Video used to be located on the first level, not too far from JC Penney's. Sure enough, we found the spot without difficulty, but our hopes of finding anything out were immediately dashed – the whole area was being refitted.

'Bloody hell!' Sandy cursed, glaring at one of her faxes. 'This says work on a new block of stores isn't due to start till next month.'

'How unexpected,' I grumbled sarcastically. 'Another loose end tied up?'

Determined not to leave empty-handed, Sondra shot off

into the construction area and accosted the first workman she came across. The poor man didn't stand a chance. Having failed to eject her on safety grounds, he called for the assistance of a couple of colleagues. They, needless to say, fared no better – but it also seemed that Sandy wasn't making the progress she desired either. Eventually the group dispersed and my tenacious partner made to retreat. She'd just about reached the demolished entrance when a stocky Latin-looking gentleman beckoned to her. After a brief discussion and the occasional furtive look at the other workmen, Sondra exchanged a few notes for what appeared to be a card. Transaction complete, the two parted company, and I quickly closed in to find out what had happened. The upshot – for forty dollars we'd bought ourselves the name of a guy who used to work at the video shop. This gent, now employed at a scented candle and bric-a-brac shop on the ground floor, was purported to be the man to see for those interested in specialist GM adult videos.

Given the subject matter, it was decided that for this second engagement I was far more suited to the task. Once again fate seemed hell-bent on portraying me as the archetypal dirty old man. Kitted out with a pair of snazzy shades and a pocketful of twenties – evidently an essential requirement to aid the transfer of information – I gave it my best shot. Fortunately, it must have been my lucky day. My contact – a wiry young man in his mid-twenties with a ponytail and oversized suit – liked the British and, in particular, the Queen Mother. We got on famously, even though he seemed a little put out that I didn't actually know his idol personally. Nevertheless, 'one thing led to another', and finally I felt comfortable enough to broach the topic of exotic entertainment. London in the Sixties and Seventies was of particular interest to my newfound friend. Christine Keeler, Soho, the Paul Raymond Revue – he was in his element. As the conversation progressed, I learnt he knew nothing of the behind-the-scenes activities of Gogmagog Video, but he did admit to selling XXX material under the counter – a private scam and nothing to do with the shop owners. To push for any more details would definitely be akin to walking into a minefield, I decided. Time to ease off a shade.

When I'd first entered the shop it was empty, but a couple of girls and a family, having hovered around the door for a while, were now on their way in. In order to retain my informant's company, I selected a Jerusalem candle at random. While it was being wrapped, he scribbled something on a piece of paper and dropped it into the carrier bag.

'If ya'd like to pick up some high-quality GM souvenirs while ya're here, check out this address,' he said in a low voice, glancing at the bag. 'Most of the stuff's available in PAL as well as NTSC. Just tell the guy at the door Art sent ya. Oh, and ya might wanna lose the "Burbs" look before ya go.'

Sondra was furious. I'd got the information for the price of a friendly chat and a candle, which it turned out she was in the market for anyway.

'Bloody nerve,' she complained. 'He should have stiffed you for at least a hundred bucks. I would've. And I'd have stuck another fifty on top because you're a Brit.'

Art's piece of paper contained the phone number and address of a private house in Manayunk, an old township on the outskirts of Philadelphia. In recent times this area had seen somewhat of a revival with the opening of several good restaurants, bars and trinket shops. The only problem was that the note concluded with the phrase, 'after ten p.m.' To be honest, I didn't relish the prospect of cruising around the back streets of Manayunk or anywhere else in Philadelphia after dark. This was, however, the only link to Gogmagog Video we had left and, on past performance, if we didn't act immediately it would evaporate just like the rest. At least there were some advantages to our late appointment – time to buy more suitable clothes, time to eat, and with luck, time to catch up on some shut-eye while Sondra fitted in some of her personal business.

164

We left the car in one of the main street car parks not far from the centre of Manayunk. From there, we walked down a handful of decidedly intimidating back streets before reaching our destination a few minutes after ten-thirty. The building – at the centre of a block of five – was quite old and entirely constructed of brick. It was in a chronically ill state of repair, with paint peeling, cracked windows and much of the woodwork rotted away. None of the rooms on the three floor levels were lit, but the front door was open and a ginger cat curled up on the threshold did at least seem pleased to see us.

I regarded Sondra closely. Although I wasn't at all sure what manner of dress would blend in at this particular venue, my partner certainly looked streetwise. In tight maroon jeans, a shabby leather jacket, wearing heavy red make-up and sunglasses, she could have been the sort of gal one might expect to encounter in your average back-street porno shop, I tried to convince myself. I, on the other hand, felt like a complete pillock. As if blue jeans and Country-style boots weren't bad enough, Sondra had insisted on decking me out with a denim shirt, black bolero and cotton head bandana: favourite of the over-forties Harley rider. Well, it was too late to turn back now, so in we went.

At the end of the entrance hall sat a highly unattractive example of a human male. About seventeen stone, scruffy with a matted beard, he was dressed – well, I suppose he was dressed like me. Sandy did the talking and after a few lewd remarks, which I didn't really understand, and the mention of Art's name, we were shown into the 'shop', probably originally a dining room. There, a handful of men were browsing through an extensive collection of videotapes laid out on tables. Each table seemed to represent a particular category or theme – bondage, S and M, lesbian, orgies, etc. The owner or manager – a fat old lady with bleached hair, wearing baggy velvet shorts and a T-shirt advising the reader to 'Just fuck it. I did.' – was sitting in a rocking chair to one side of a makeshift counter. A pair of kittens –

presumably belonging to the ginger at the door – were playing chicken by perilously dodging beneath the base of the chair as it rocked gently back and forth.

My better half indicated we should begin examining the merchandise and try to look inconspicuous.

That'll be interesting, I thought, feeling like a clown at a funeral.

Despite all attempts to blend in as run-of-the-mill customers, our fellow clients kept glaring at us as if we were wearing placards declaring, 'Hey people, look! Martians disguised as Americans.' I was just about to suggest a phased withdrawal when Sandy suddenly draped herself over me, started nibbling my ear and fondling my behind. This was good, I thought, surprised but quite at ease with the situation. And good it was. The incriminating placard evaporated, and the group of potential vigilantes returned their attention to seeking out the best buys and hidden bargains. For about ten minutes we kept up the performance, but in that time discovered nothing of interest. Once again, withdrawal was looking like the most expedient option when the powers that be, apparently sufficiently amused by our antics so far, decided to prolong the proceedings. A neatly dressed man emerged from a darkened room behind the counter clutching two videocassettes. He handed the manager what seemed to be a tidy sum of money then hastily departed. There was no question – we had to gain access to whatever lay beyond the fat lady's rocking chair.

Before leaving the hotel we'd had a heated debate about whether or not I should speak at any time during our mission. To resolve the matter, it was agreed that I should try out my first-rate Sylvester Stallone 'down and dirty' Philadelphian accent on the concierge. By a unanimous vote it was decided I should remain mum. . . This being the case, Sondra signalled that she would speak to the old girl and see how the land lay.

The response to Sondra's enquiry didn't look promising. I could see the manager was making a poor job of playing dumb but clearly wasn't having any. Sandy hesitated for a moment then waved at me to join her. I obeyed, then listened spellbound while she launched into a completely garbled plea employing what I took to be a rarely used local dialect culled from the Neolithic age. At its conclusion she jammed her hand down the front of my jeans and squeezed me where it hurts. I could do no more than gasp with surprise. The old lady burst into laughter and nearly flattened one of the kittens as the speed of her rocking chair abruptly shifted from first to third gear.

'What the hell did you tell the old crone?' I hissed as we entered the forbidden chamber. 'You nearly knocked my eyes out with that little stunt.'

Sondra grinned. 'I told her you were over the hill and having trouble getting it up. Said we tried all the usual porno stuff, but the only time I got any action was after you'd seen some really heavy-duty hardcore.'

I frowned. 'Thanks a lot, I'll not forget that.'

As far as I could tell in the poor light, the new room was divided into two sections. One, in common with its neighbour, contained several tables on which videos were displayed. In the second toward the rear, a series of four booths had been crudely fashioned out of plywood, each fitted with a curtain drawn across the entrance. These cubicles apparently offered clients the opportunity to preview their selections before making a final choice. Judging by the look of the two zombies administering the facility, however, I had the clear impression that once viewed it was a sale or else.

'Jerry,' Sondra whispered, digging me in the side. 'All these videos: they're marked GM, and see the logo? It's the same as the effigy.'

'At last,' I exclaimed inwardly. 'Indisputable evidence linking Kathy Murkett's disappearance with Ms White, the Reverend Joseph P and all things of Gog and Magog.

We set about carefully examining each of the videos. The cases were of remarkable quality, as was the printing on the covers. Then again, at two hundred dollars each you'd at least expect half-decent packaging, I decided. Much of the merchandise was borderline nauseating – bestiality, gang rape, enema shots, S and M – but occasionally the front cover showed a girl with a remarkable resemblance to a well-known actress or supermodel. I'd just about seen enough when one of the covers caught my eye. I inspected it closely, then almost choked. The main character was a young woman identical to Natalie. She was heavily made-up, but there was no question. I hadn't until now considered whether Natalie, or Kathy for that matter, resembled anyone famous. Certainly it wasn't anyone in the movies or related to TV that I could think of. As I racked my brains trying to recall all the well-publicised faces I'd seen recently, I suddenly realised that Sondra had never actually seen either of the two ladies in question. I showed her the cover.

'Would you say this girl looks like anyone well-known you've come across?' I asked softly.

Sandy's reply was instantaneous. 'I certainly would. She's the spitting image of one of the new generation of outspoken Congress ladies. Why? Oh shit, not your lookalike?'

Without another word we approached one of the zombies, listened to the extensive list of rules and regulations and, after parting with a hundred big ones, supposedly as a deposit, received the go-ahead to preview our selection. Amid the gasping and groaning that emanated from adjacent booths, we started the video. The plot centred on the US Capitol building in Washington DC, supporting Sandy's Congresswoman theory. Ensuring good value for money, the director wasted no time in getting to the action. In the first scene a prim and proper politician was caught with a male and two female colleagues in an elevator during a power cut . . .

As things were just getting interesting my spoilsport companion 'paused' the tape then drew closer to the screen. 'Jesus Christ!' she breathed. 'See that guy? A million dollars says it's Wayne Millard. He was a big porno star until about five years ago, when he got life for triple rape and murder. The creep's been in San Quentin ever since.'

'Possible,' I remarked, not really convinced, 'but this video could've easily been made before he was arrested.'

Sondra shook her head violently. 'No,' she rasped, evidently stunned by the appalling implications of her discovery. 'I checked the tape. The movie was produced last year. And besides, you said yourself, Natalie McCarthy only disappeared a year ago.'

10

Suffer the Little Children

Dawn had just cast the first hint of a smile across the Schuylkill River when Sondra was up and raring to go. Even though it was hours before the hotel's business centre was due to open, she harangued and eventually browbeat a hapless night manager into lending her a VCR. Once hooked up, we spent a couple of tortuous hours scrutinising selected sections of our premier two-hundred-dollar video. The more we watched, the more we both became convinced that the leading roles were being played by a drugged Natalie and Sondra's triple rapist. By the time room service delivered a couple of bumper breakfasts the faxes were flooding in thick and fast. The majority contained only general information, but one launched my blood pressure into orbit.

'Oh, for Christ's sake,' I cursed.

'What is it?' Sondra cried, half-expecting me to have been struck down by a seizure.

'It's the Gellar Institute,' I replied. 'You're not going to believe this, but the chap you contacted has just confirmed it changed hands last month.'

To be honest, I don't think Sondra had any trouble believing the news. It was accepting it that caused a minor explosion. 'Shit and bloody shit,' she ranted. 'We just can't run fast enough to keep up with these clowns, can we? At this rate, your buddy Art and the video emporium we buzzed last night'll be dust by lunchtime.' We exchanged glances, knowing that Sondra's cynical comments might not be too far from the truth.

An impromptu strategy meeting concluded that loss of

the video shop might be no bad thing, but Art, who definitely knew more than he'd let on, was quite another matter. A return visit to express my appreciation for his kind introduction and confirmation of a purchase might be enough to take our relationship to the next rung on the ladder of trust. At that moment another fax was slipped under the door. This one, from the same source as the sheet I'd just been reading, confirmed that if we were still interested, an appointment to see the new director of the Gellar Institute had been slated for three p.m. that afternoon. The plan for the day was therefore decided. Initially a quick return trip to the King of Prussia Mall for another session with Art. If I was lucky, back to West Conshohocken for lunch at Billy C's, my favourite Philadelphia cheesesteak sandwich bar, then off to the Institute.

Luckily, there was still a short time before the Mall opened so we took the opportunity to check in with Julian and Norma. To my relief, all seemed to be going swimmingly. Julian had been able to confirm that about half the names on the list were convicted criminals currently serving time and yes, in the prisons parenthetically marked. Perhaps more intriguing though, was that of the few other names he'd been able to check so far, all had recently served time. Meanwhile BJ had been able to find a selection of newsgroup websites with hyperlinks to Gogmagog-related entries. In most cases the trail led to porno video companies peddling GM products, but some were offering special opportunities for adventurous women to make large sums of money – no special skills required. As with Julian's experience, there was more. When Norma tried to revisit some of the sites, she found the pages closed. Sometimes the same details could be found elsewhere; but in general the world of Gogmagog was rapidly shrinking. Apart from their research activities, the pair had taken it in turns to visit Toby. I was pleased to hear that the old boy was on the mend and driving the nurses mad with his outrageous impressions of Alec Guinness and Laurence Olivier. Also good news was that although his blood pressure had been brought under control, the doctors had decided he should remain with them until it became more stable, and that meant at least another few days.

The call ended in good time for us to make it to the shopping plaza a few minutes after it opened. I didn't know what was happening, but the mall was amazingly crowded. Usually an early-morning arrival guarantees a journey of solitude and one of the few times when an 'in and out' shopping expedition is a real possibility. But not today – cars all over the place: people milling about like the end of the world was at eleven thirty-three. The cause of this unprecedented stampede still an unsolved mystery, we wandered along to the candle shop. As we approached I became aware that the population of security guards was increasing. Walkie-talkies in hand, quite a collection seemed to be heading in the same general direction as us.

Bang! A horrendously loud crack seemed to shake the very fabric of the mall's structure. As in a game of musical chairs when the music stops and there's a moment's hesitation before everyone darts for a seat, the scene around us froze – people startled for a split second by the explosion were now scurrying around like ants. Some security staff crouched down by the side of pillars and ornamental plant arrangements. Others tried to assist the fleeing crowd. Then the music stopped again.

'The next son-of-a-bitch to move gets a one-way ticket to sit at God's right hand,' a booming voice echoed through the air.

Instinctively I dragged Sondra behind one of the wooden benches dotted up and down the pedestrian walkways. Peering through spaces in its latticework construction, we encountered a scene that was little short of incredible. Emerging from the doorway of the candle shop was the bulky figure of a man. He must have been about six feet three, no less than twenty stone, with a face of pure evil. His eyes, like his balding head, were rolling as if improperly connected. Massive arms bulged out of a faded short-sleeved

T-shirt, its end roughly jammed into a pair of tight-fitting, paint-stained jeans.

The madman surveyed his startled audience then stretched his arm back into the shop to retrieve a hostage. It was a man: a wiry man with a ponytail. It was Art.

'Oh Jesus!' I whined. 'This can't be happening.'

But it was. One of the passers-by – obviously not one to be ordered about – started to move away. Not the best of decisions. Enraged by this act of wanton disobedience, the swaying menace pulled a huge gun from his belt and blew the offender's chest out. Pandemonium ensued. While some folk just fell to the ground where they stood, others, panic-stricken, ran in all directions. The gunman bellowed, screaming at them to stop, then the shooting began again. Three maybe four people were hit as the whole area became a war zone. By now the police force and SWAT unit had arrived. Wailing sirens drowned out the sound of human cries. Another shot, this time accompanied by the ear-piercing crack of smashing glass. As if a switch had been flipped, silence sucked the clamour out of the air in less time than it takes to blink. His audience of bystanders and police finally paying him the attention he craved, the hulking figure advanced another step. Sweat was teeming from his face and arms, soaking his terrified captive. Art's feet were barely touching the floor, and his face was rapidly turning blue as the python-like arm encircling his neck crushed his windpipe. I glared at Sondra, still struggling to decide what to do for the best. We were so close, perhaps only twenty feet away. Any movement at all and we'd be a sitting target.

As the atmosphere cracked with tension, the man finally spoke. 'Heed the voice of salvation,' he growled. 'The Divine One has chosen me to deliver his word and his vengeance on you, his unworthy servants. Creatures of excess, tainted souls; remember the teachings of Matthew. *"And Jesus went into the temple of God, and cast out all of them that sold and bought in the temple, and overthrew the tables of the moneychangers, and the seats of them that sold doves, And said unto them, It is written, My house shall be called the house of prayer; but ye have made it a den of thieves.*"

'What the buggery's all that about?' I whispered.

Sondra thought for a moment then slowly nodded her head. 'The only thing I can think of relates to this area. Some people believe there used to be an old church here long before the mall was even thought of. Chances are that's what he's on about.'

I frowned. 'Chances are he's been spending too much time listening to the Reverend Black.'

To my horror, the prophet of doom again surveyed his flock then directed his demonic gaze towards us. 'You!' he cried. 'Protectors of demons, Satan's spawn. The Almighty sees you for your true selves – a blight upon the world that must be destroyed. But God is merciful. Sacrifice and ye shall be saved. Be not afraid. Let my example lead you to everlasting peace.' With his words ricocheting from the walls and ceiling, he twisted Art like a lifeless doll, snapping his neck. His duty fulfilled, he dropped the body to the ground and stretched both arms out wide. 'Lord, receive thy loyal servant into the Kingdom of . . .'

His final word fell unheard beneath a barrage of gunshots. I had no idea how many projectiles riddled his body, but when the last bullet was fired he was no longer recognisable as a human being. Despite his terrible injuries, he somehow managed to sink to his knees as if in complete control of his muscles. There he remained like a martyr – hands clasped, his mouth spewing out a mixture of blood and words. Finally he toppled forwards and it was over. He lay face-down on the ground, his arms outstretched, blood oozing from every part of him. It was appalling. I didn't want to look but felt compelled to do so. With one eye open I scanned the pulverised corpse. My gaze traced a line from the crown of his head down the side of his face to the neck and shoulders. And there it was. No larger than a compact disc, but it was still clear enough for me to see. Tattooed on his upper forearm – the image of Gogmagog.

Sondra gripped my arm, her face completely drained of blood. 'Come on, Jerry, this is no place for us.'

I nodded and, as the frightened crowd transformed into ghoulish onlookers moving in for a closer look, we headed for the exit.

For a good ten minutes we sat in the car, paralysed by vivid images of the executions we'd just witnessed. With a fleet of police cars and other emergency vehicles arriving in a continuous stream, somehow Sondra found the strength to start the engine and slowly begin to put some welcome distance between ourselves and the mall.

I'm certain that without the mind's ability to function on autopilot in times of stress we'd never have made it back to the hotel. Not surprisingly, the prospect of Billy C's had lost its appeal, and instead we sat in the Marriott restaurant, each staring at a cup of cold coffee.

'Jesus, Jerry,' Sondra choked, 'you of all people know I'm not a quitter, but this thing's just way out of control.'

I would've agreed, but at that moment a member of staff came bounding up and handed my partner another fax. As a result of years of preconditioning, she automatically opened the envelope, withdrew the sheet and, after a brief glance at the content, offered it to me.

She scoffed. 'Well, according to this, Mr Millard's still breaking rocks in San Quentin.'

'And if so,' I carried on, 'how's he managed to get time off to star in the odd skin flick?'

For a short while we entertained the idea of cashing in our chips. Sondra reckoned that she'd be able to complete her list of domestic and professional chores in less than two days. If so, and we could secure airline seats, we'd be home in time for me to finish the artwork for the wedding cake, then we could resume our boring old normal lives . . .

But it was just all so much crap and we knew it. Too many people whose lives had touched mine were involved. Walking away would solve nothing. Nor would it provide a release from the responsibilities, moral or otherwise, that fate had seen fit to plant squarely on my shoulders. At the very least, I would never be able to live out the rest of my days without knowing I'd done everything within my power to reunite Julian and his lady. Not my problem? Wrong. It became my problem the second Julian came to me for help.

During my brief period of introspection I hadn't noticed Sandy looking at me. When our eyes finally met, she smiled. 'Sorry,' she said, 'I just had a bit of a shaky moment there. Doesn't take much effort to read your mind though, so you know damn well I'd never let you go it alone. How could I? You don't speak the language and, unless you're going to a backstabbing party with a bunch of suits, you'd have trouble blending in at a football match.'

I hit her with my best cynical expression then squeezed her hand. 'No worries on that score, milady,' I joked. 'You don't get away from me until I've paid you back for doing your best to seriously dent my hunting equipment last night!'

Our resolve back on track, a look at my watch confirmed it was time to get ready for the second assignment of the day – a visit to the Gellar Psychiatric Institute.

Feeling decidedly more comfortable in my Armani three-piece, Salvatore tie and matching accessories, I took the wheel of the rental and set out once again along the Schuylkill I-76 heading north-east. Sondra had opted for one of her intimidating pinstripe trouser-suit numbers; not dissimilar from the one she'd been wearing twenty years ago when we first met. The only noticeable differences now from my perspective were that the gear probably cost more than ten times that of the original and she looked even more beautiful.

The sky was a mass of broken cloud, threatening rain. As it turned out a threat was all it was. By the time we joined the local Route 363 heading towards Trooper the sun had gained the upper hand and it looked like what remained of the afternoon would be settled. Being close to Valley Forge, the area was fairly open with long stretches of greenery and trees, and, due to the unusually lazy slide into the fall season this year, the breathtaking colours of the local flora were still very much in evidence. Bronze, gold, flaming reds and scorched earth – the changing leaves provided a visual feast hard to match anywhere.

Sad, I'd always thought, that nature's reward for putting on such a spectacular annual show was an agonisingly slow death . . . Whoa! Time out! I pulled myself up short. All this grade-A philosophical musing was beginning to drag me inexorably towards a large black pool of moroseness. I was depressed enough by the gruesome stream of images from this morning's horror constantly whistling back and forth through my beleaguered brain. Adding the plight of dying foliage to the pot was definitely asking for trouble . . .

We reached the intersection with Route 422. To the left, Evansburg National Park was only a few miles away, but our destination lay dead ahead, to the north of Fairview Village.

Since the roads had been quieter than expected we arrived with about ten minutes to spare. The Institute itself looked like a premier Dr Frankenstein ex-rental. A classic piece of early twentieth-century insane asylum design – if you weren't mad when you arrived, you certainly would be after a couple of weeks in the place. I think to compare it to the fabled *House of Horrors* would be doing that particular residence a serious injustice – dark, pseudo-Gothic architecture, barred windows and conicalled roofs. All that was needed were a few bats flying around and the scene was set for the next Dracula remake.

'*Gott in Himmel*,' Sondra exclaimed, already infected by the Transylvanian genre, 'I hope you've packed the garlic and wooden stakes. The Hotel California's got nothing on this monstrosity.'

'What?' I queried, totally lost.

My companion shook her head. 'Why is it, Clock, you're never with the programme? You've heard of the Eagles – famous Seventies US rock band? Well-known song called?'

Ball in my court, I sifted through my patchy rock and roll music archives and yes, there it was, right next to ELO and

Elvis. Not the best filing system in the world, I'd freely admit, but at least it worked – occasionally.

'Got it!' I exclaimed triumphantly. "Hotel California", the relevant phrase being, "you can check out any time you like, but you can never leave" – right?'

'Sort of,' came the less than impressed reply. 'Come on then, let's hope we can find out something useful here. Keep your fingers crossed the interior decorator wasn't Boris Karloff.'

Thankfully, Mr Karloff's services had not been employed. In stark contrast to the gloomy and threatening exterior, the layout inside was both pleasant and modern. The entrance and reception areas were bright and airy. High-quality carpet, recently laid unless I was very much mistaken, covered the floor as far as I could see. A mixture of reproduction impressionist and contemporary paintings adorned the walls, and the staff, wearing pale blue uniforms, were friendly and eminently approachable.

After registering at reception we were escorted to a first floor office by a jovial lady of Japanese extraction. There, we met the Institute Director's secretary, Carol Ann. This most attractive and efficient lady greeted us like long-lost family, insisted we try a cup of her freshly brewed coffee then unloaded the bad news. Due to circumstances beyond their control, there had to be an unavoidable delay of about half an hour to our scheduled appointment. Consolation cups of coffee in hand, we were summarily shown into a small waiting room and assured that we'd be seen as soon as humanly possible. I could tell Sondra knew what I was thinking the moment Carol Ann closed the door behind us as she left. This was as far as Natalie had got on her quest. The question now was, would we suffer the same fate and be plunged into a Dalian world of alternate memories and rotating identities? Thirty minutes in any waiting room, or even the prospect of it, filled me with dread. You just know that after twenty-five minutes of torture with your hopes of a reprieve gradually sprouting roots, some sadistic bastard will come along and announce another delay. Today, however, my dark theory was to be exploded. After only fifteen minutes exchanging fanciful theories with Sandy about the morning's blood-curdling events, Carol Ann returned with good news. The director was ready to see us.

Once inside the remarkably unpretentious office, I was up for my first surprise. Dr Lesley T. Stravinsky turned out to be a homely looking middle-aged lady instead of the thirty-something male lawyer-type I'd imagined. We did the usual three or four minutes small-talk thing then got down to business. There was no doubt that without the influence of Sandy's powerful contacts we wouldn't have made it past the front gate. It was also obvious that the previous operators were not among Dr Stravinsky's list of favourite people. Several quite senior staff members, we were told, had recently been indicted on charges of negligence and malpractice. A number of other cases were currently under investigation, and further charges were likely to be brought. In fact the only reason we'd been granted an audience at all was that one of the Institute's new doctors heard our story and specifically asked to see us. Lines of engagement clearly marked out, the director made her apologies and left to attend another meeting.

No sooner had the door closed than a young man in a white coat, claiming to be Dr John Arquette, breezed into the office unannounced.

'Thank you for making contact with the Institute,' he began in a cultured English accent. 'I'm very much hoping that your visit will turn out to be mutually beneficial.' Dr Arquette leant against the windowsill and came straight to the point. 'I'm not supposed to talk about issues related to the former administration of this Institute,' he said in a deliberately low voice. 'Since the authorities found out what was going on here about a month ago, the FBI were brought in and immediately imposed a media blackout.'

Sondra frowned. 'But I thought it was just a case of new owners taking over.'

'That's the cover story,' he confirmed. 'Until the investigations are complete, the Institute's being run by Washington. The staff you've seen have all been drafted in from various government agencies and the military.'

'If so,' I interjected, suddenly feeling less than comfortable, 'then presumably you're part of the team. I don't understand why you're talking to us.'

Arquette nodded. 'Fair comment. I'm actually on secondment from the British army. I was assigned to the US military last year to help out with Gulf War casualties. My specialist area's psychological trauma. To be honest, I'm not really into all this *X-Files* caper. I'm only interested in helping as many of the poor blighters who've suffered in this hell-hole as I can.'

Sondra was looking distinctly perturbed and, I suspected, was not at all encouraged by the implications for our quest. 'You know why we're here?' she asked.

'You're looking for a young woman who disappeared some three years ago,' the amiable doctor recounted. 'For reasons as yet undisclosed, you believe she might have been admitted here. That's all I've been told.'

Sandy glanced at me as if seeking support for her next question. 'That's right,' she acknowledged. 'But before we go any further, are you willing to explain what happened here? Why all this secrecy?'

'As I said,' Dr Arquette began cautiously, 'strictly speaking, I shouldn't even have told you about the FBI presence. If Dr S or any of her lads and lasses finds out, I'll certainly be for the high jump. Anyway, since I'm hoping you can help me . . .' He relinquished his position by the window in favour of reclining on the desktop. For whatever reason, he clearly had no desire to assume the seat previously occupied by Dr Stravinsky. 'As far as we can ascertain, part of this Institute operated as a *bona fide* psychiatric clinic. The other half, however, seems to have been set up for the sole purpose of making people disappear. For example, if you needed to have your old aunt committed so you could claim her fortune – mad or not – everything could be taken care of here: naturally for a price. Of course there was never any risk. People who weren't insane when they arrived certainly were by the time any legal assessments became necessary.'

I winced, reminded of my thoughts on the very same subject less than an hour before.

'In addition,' the doctor went on, 'there were definitely a number of suspicious deaths. Needless to say, records are incomplete, have been altered or simply don't exist.'

'So given the FBI's involvement, it's thought organised crime was running the show?' I postulated.

Arquette scoffed. 'That's the tourist version. If you ask me, looking at the names of some of the residents here – well, as I said before, I'm not an *X-Files* fan.'

In return for the good doctor's candour, Sondra and I explained in some detail what we knew about Elena Pascal. We'd agreed on the plane coming over that a certain degree of artistic licence would be essential in order to create a convincing story that masked the truth. Basically, this was a straightforward missing persons case. The British police had tried and failed to trace the girl, the last of her family had recently passed away, therefore we, as her only remaining friends, had decided to mount our own private enquiries. All issues related to Kathy Murkett's disappearance, Gogmagog and Natalie McCarthy were definitely not part of the package. The most challenging point was the issue of photographic identification. Natalie had never referred to her partner's appearance, and a missing persons investigation without a photograph or even a verbal description was just a tad unbelievable. In desperation we'd simply made everything up, picked out an old poor-quality shot of one of Sondra's nieces, and 'Bob's your uncle'. Most people spend their lives bluffing their way into or out of all sorts of situations, so what was so different about this?

By the time the Q and A session that followed our account was over I couldn't decide whether Arquette had bought it or not. We were now well and truly in the middle of a FBI hornets' nest. For all I knew, pleasant, caring Dr Arquette could be a skilled secret agent, the room bugged and banks of computers checking our records as we spoke. On balance

181

though, I preferred to believe his story. Either way, we'd doubtless find out pretty soon.

Whatever the situation, the doctor seemed prepared to move on to the next stage. He revealed that despite a series of intense investigations, even the names of some of the patients remained a mystery. Although many of the former workforce had been detained and questioned, a handful – mostly senior medical staff – had managed to evade arrest. Their whereabouts unknown, and with no other means of verifying the authenticity of the limited records unearthed, identification efforts had been seriously hampered. The patients themselves were, without exception, seriously disturbed. Most lived in their own isolated worlds, lost and terrified, while others simply couldn't or wouldn't speak. It transpired that a young woman belonging to the latter group had sprung to the doctor's mind when he heard of our enquiry. This patient, when she did speak, had an English accent, and a set of basic records believed to be hers dated back three years. We were warned that communication was invariably difficult and frequently impossible. I took a chance and asked if the girl looked anything like our photo. The answer was both distressing and intriguing – her face had been deliberately disfigured by plastic surgery. Given the circumstances, I wondered why Arquette considered a meeting to be of any value. According to our story, we were only friends not family. Chances were, therefore, that we'd have a hard time recognising her, and in turn she'd harbour no recollection of us. Nevertheless, he preferred to try. A word, a phrase, perhaps the tone of voice or something in the eyes might trigger a response – such was his slender hope.

We were shown into a bright, colourful room furnished with a bed, TV and chest of drawers. The floral-patterned curtains fluttered gently in a slight breeze sneaking its way beneath an old paint-encrusted sash window. Dr Arquette arranged for two chairs to be brought in and, as we seated ourselves, the patient arrived. Her escort, a well-built black female nurse with a smile broad enough to heal the world, ushered the ghostly figure into the room. She positioned her charge beside the bed then, as if testing out the results of a prolonged training programme, caringly but with a firm voice encouraged the girl to sit. There was a brief hesitation and a marked degree of trepidation about complying with the request, but after a few more words of reassurance, the patient crawled onto the bed. Sitting more or less in the centre of the mattress, the girl clasped her knees close to her chest then began to nervously inspect her new surroundings. The nurse took the only other chair in the room and placed it by the window. Before sitting, however, she went outside, returning moments later with a large drawing book which she laid on the bed.

When settled, she addressed us in the same soft manner employed to manage her patient. 'Now, you folks don't pay any attention to me,' she began. 'My name's Abi, and I'm just gonna sit here quiet in case Rosie there – that's what we're callin' her till we find out who she really is – gets herself into a state.'

'Is there anything we need to know?' Sondra asked. 'Dos and don'ts?'

Impossibly, Abi's smile became larger. 'No honey, yuz be yerselves,' she recommended. 'Only thing to watch for is if Rosie asks ya for a mirror. Best to pretend ya have one and act like ya handin' it to her.'

The girl had, by now, retrieved the drawing book and, with it carefully positioned at her side, was slowly turning the pages. She was indeed a sorrowful sight. In many respects she resembled an old woman – thin, listless and with a slight tremor constantly torturing her limbs. Her long auburn hair was recently washed and had been painstakingly combed through. With her head bent, sections of it fell forwards, concealing much of her face and the scars that ravaged it. In reality, her disfigurement wasn't as severe as I'd imagined. There was no mistaking the extensive scar tissue evident on her forehead and cheeks, but as far as I could tell the area around her sad, deep-blue eyes had not been tampered with.

'Hello,' I began. 'I'm Jerry Clock, and my friend here's Sandy Warwick. We've come all the way from England to see you.'

Without moving her head, Rosie glared at me through her fine strands of hair. 'C-l-o-c-k,' she repeated slowly, as if the word were difficult to pronounce. 'Hickory dickory dock, the mouse ran up the c-l-o-c-k.'

Shifting her seat closer to the bed, Sandy took up the thread. 'That's right,' she agreed. 'The mouse ran up the clock. Do you remember having a clock where you lived in Cambridge with Natalie? You remember your friend Natalie, don't you?'

There was no response, but I had the strangest feeling that somewhere locked behind those fathomless eyes, Sondra's words had rapped on a secret and long-forgotten door.

'Was Elena Natalie's best friend?' I ventured. 'Elena Pascal?'

The girl suddenly reacted with a start, slammed her book shut then stared at the window. 'Mirror, mirror on the wall. Who's the fairest of them all?' she recited. 'Rosie should have a mirror: a mirror for the fairest of them all. Do you have Rosie's mirror?' Caressing the uneven surface of her maltreated face, the girl slowly focused first on Sondra then on me.

In line with the nurse's advice, I pretended to withdraw something from my pocket and handed it to her.

'Thank you,' she said, receiving the invisible mirror then admiring herself in it.

For the next ten minutes we tried every approach we could think of which might elicit some form of positive response. There was still no evidence that Rosie was in fact Elena. Her accent sounded typically English, but it was hard to detect any trace of a dialect. In terms of age it was possible the girl was in Natalie's peer group, but the physical and mental damage she'd suffered made that equivocal.

184

It was becoming obvious that Rosie wouldn't be able to take much more questioning. The nurse indicated another five minutes then left, explaining that she wanted to ensure that her patient's room had been tidied up in preparation for her return. I looked at Sondra and shrugged. We were both out of questions.

As I watched, Rosie's gaze slowly shifted from her book to the window to us then at length focused on the chest of drawers. This performance repeated several times before the order in which the fixed locations were being viewed changed. She continued in this vein until her companion returned, then abruptly stopped.

'That's one of my little girl's special games,' Abi laughed, stroking Rosie's hair. 'Doctors think it could be important. Trouble is, none of 'em knows what she's doin', do they, hon?'

In that instant a bright shard of divine inspiration lodged in my brain. Rosie wasn't just looking from one object to another; she was following something that was travelling to and fro through the air.

'How many fairies can you see?' I asked, looking around the room as if I too was tracing the path of some airborne creatures.

The girl's expression softened. She pointed to the ceiling, looked at me and said, 'Two are squabbling up there. I think two more are hiding now, but a fifth, he's sitting on your shoulder. Can you hear what he's saying?'

'Not really,' I confessed. 'I often see the fairies, but sometimes I can't hear them.'

For the first time Rosie smiled. 'That's because you're too stuffy,' she scolded me. 'The one on your shoulder – he's called Cam – says you don't pay enough attention. If you try harder, then you'll be able to hear quite clearly.'

Mention of the name Cam set Sondra's eyes alight. 'Could you tell us the names of your other friends?' she requested.

'Will you be kind to them?' the girl asked, her tone noticeably protective.

Sandy nodded. 'I promise to be extremely kind.'

'There are many,' Rosie continued. 'Not all have names, but today we have Cam, Tilly, Scal, Lena and Thea.'

It was like being allowed into the presence of a deity or experiencing the moment when an ancient text is finally deciphered. All four names were the second half, or minor modifications, of the two girl's names, Elena Pascal and Natalie McCarthy.

Quickly hoping to capitalise on the breakthrough, I gestured towards the drawing book. 'Do you have any pictures of your friends?' I asked.

Rosie snatched up the pad, crushing it against her knees, and the less-troubled expression of a few moments ago transformed into mistrust. I did my best to be calming, but it was beginning to look as if I'd gone a step too far.

'Come on now, Rosie girl,' Abi suddenly piped up, at least as excited as if not more so than me by the preliminary breakthrough. 'Let that there nice gentleman have a peek at your drawin's. He's sure to like 'em as much as I do.'

The girl hesitated then slowly looked at her nurse like a small child seeking support. Abi nodded her head and waved an arm towards me. 'Go on girl, don't be a spoilsport.'

Reluctantly Rosie relaxed her grip, placed the book by her side then edged it inch by inch in my direction. I couldn't really tell at what point it was acceptable to reach out and take the prize, but after another two shoves I decided to take the risk.

With the book on my lap, I checked to see if there was any sign of panic or attempt at a retraction. The girl, however, was now staring at the ceiling, totally engrossed, I hoped, by the antics of her quarrelsome friends. Sondra quietly returned her seat to my side and together we turned the pages.

Not surprisingly, the drawings were stark and threatening. Most were of a hospital room – presumably Rosie's – or scenes depicting fairies. Occasionally there was an inset showing a river lined by old buildings, which at a stretch could have been the River Cam running along the Backs. After six or seven such drawings the theme changed. Gloomy pictures of dark beings often standing in torrential rain dominated page after page. Then the lighter subject of figures seated in a park, the sun shining and two girls playing emerged, but it didn't last. Towards the end of the pad were a series of macabre portraits. As far as I could tell, each was of a girl in different states of disfigurement. Again, perhaps due to my pressing desire to discover clues, aided and abetted by an overactive imagination, I was convinced that all were either self-portraits or of Natalie. Then came the final entry. Essentially a montage, its central theme was a stone building surrounded by grey streets and amber lighting. Strange-looking figures, seemingly young girls dancing, were set throughout the work. Sometimes in isolation, sometimes merged together, the overall impression created by the girls was, to my mind, that of a wild party. As I started to examine this most enigmatic of the sketches in more detail, Sondra pointed to some writing above the door of the building. 'The Way We Were' it read. I looked at her, puzzled.

'Apart from a romantic movie starring Ms Streisand,' she whispered in my ear, 'that's the name of the most celebrated transvestite club in downtown Philadelphia.' My guide then traced her finger across the picture to the left-hand side, where a confusion of scribble had been applied to hide something underneath. It was hard to make out, but I could just discern two images – one a large black mass, the other drawn in white crayon. Attached to the arm of the latter was a tiny detailed drawing just beyond the outer edge of the scribble. I glared at Sandy.

'The effigy,' I mouthed. 'The Gogmagog effigy.'

11

36D

We hadn't been arrested – that had to be a good sign, surely? Just the opposite, in fact. Our exit from the Institute had been remarkably smooth. No unscheduled interviews, no detentions, not even the odd suspicious glance. I didn't like it one bit. For the hundredth time I peered through the rear window of the car, certain that by now there had to be some kind of black sedan carrying a trio of suited dummies hard on our tail.

'Jerry, will you stop doing that?' Sandy demanded, on the verge of blowing one of Julian's famed gaskets. 'Look, for the last time, take it from someone brought up on *Dragnet*, *The Untouchables* and *77 Sunset Strip* reruns. If the FBI or any other of our wonderful law-enforcement agencies were after us, we'd be sitting handcuffed in the back of a beat-up Chevy by now with a couple of stiffs reeling off the Miranda.'

'Who's Miranda when she's at home?' I interjected, quite befuddled.

Sondra let out a feigned scream. 'Jerry, I don't know why I bother. Haven't you got any idea where the "on" switch is on that relic of a TV set of yours? Oh, just forget it. Look it up next time a New York cop breaks into your apartment and hits you on the head with a Big Mac.'

I was in trouble again. Ah well, I sighed to myself. At least Sandy being upset with me was proof that I still had a handle on reality. After today's experiences, *Lord of the Rings* seemed more like a soap opera based on a day in the life of Dr J than a fantasy for students.

Idle banter apart, I was deeply disturbed by our meeting

with poor, sweet Rosie. There was no doubt in my mind that the sad, frail and horribly abused figure steeped in her own private world of make-believe was in fact Elena Pascal. How she came to be in such a place, three thousand miles from home, I had no inkling. Equally unclear was how such appalling misfortune could have befallen an innocent woman who probably hadn't a single enemy in the world. Well, at least we'd found her. I only hoped the wonders of medical science would, one day soon, be able to restore not only her face but also her beleaguered mind. If there were a just God, then perhaps a time would come when Elena and Natalie, set free from their living hell, could once again resume their life together. Who knows? I could only hope . . .

All of which was fine. The problem was that one helluva lot of sorting out had yet to be done before people had the slightest chance of rebuilding their lives. As Dr Arquette had so succinctly put it, 'An apathetic society had allowed this malevolent tumour to flourish. If it now wanted rid of it, immediate surgery was the only solution.'

And what of the good-hearted doctor? Definitely more to that gentleman than met the eye. Nevertheless, at no time during our visit had he furnished grounds causing me to doubt his sincerity. After our meeting with Elena, he'd seemed genuinely delighted with the results. Unfortunately, there'd been little we could do to conceal our findings. Nurse Abi made sure of that. It was hard to blame her since it was patently obvious that she cared for her Rosie deeply. But when it came to keeping a lid on things – forget it. The good lady had turned out to be more efficient than the BBC in broadcasting what she described as a miracle. In less than five minutes I wouldn't have been surprised if the entire junior staff of the Kremlin hadn't been fully apprised. Left with no other option but to tell the truth, we'd promised Dr Arquette that upon our return to the UK we'd immediately inform the police and allow them to liaise with the Institute directly. As a scenario, that was great – one for the lecture room. In reality, it didn't bear thinking about.

But then Sandy was probably right when she'd said later, as we drove out onto the highway, 'Was it really likely that Arquette, Stravinsky or any of the other players involved were simply going to sit back and wait for the Old Bill to give them a bell? Hello-o!!'

Still, I wasn't sure. Was the doctor just a secondee from the British Services interested only in helping the sick? Was the FBI story kosher? And was it reasonable to believe that homely Dr Stravinsky was CIA, MI5, NSA, or any other of a thousand three-letter abbreviations?

Tired of my mounting paranoid questions and theories, Sandy eventually put a cap on the subject. 'Okay, Jerry, let's leave it like this,' she proposed. 'Since the FBI haven't picked us up, we'll assume we're under twenty-four-hour surveillance. This is good. We're getting close to the heart of this mystery, and sooner or later the shit will hit the fan by the shovel-load. When it does, what better than to have your own personal cavalry just waiting to come to the rescue?'

I was sorely tempted to pursue the matter by asking how long a jail sentence could we expect following the rescue, but I thought better of it.

Cavalry or no, I could gain no respite from the vivid pictures I'd recorded of four tragic lives, and all in less than twelve hours. Art and the religious madman – dead. Elena – physically and mentally ruined. And then there was the fourth. Quite unexpected, almost like a throwaway line concerning something vital delivered at the end of a long, exhausting speech. Rika.

Our wrap-up session with Dr Arquette at an end, we'd been on our way to pay the Director a courtesy farewell call. Arquette was leading the way when suddenly one of the blue-uniformed staff came rushing up to speak with him. The upshot? Could we briefly visit another lost soul before we left, hopefully to conjure up a second miracle? At first Arquette had dismissed the request, but the woman wasn't to be denied. It was further evidence that news of our works of wonder had spread far and wide. A deep sense of shame had descended on me like a dark cloud as I watched the nurse plead her case. With the strong religious theme percolating through my life at present, I couldn't help but be reminded of Jesus and the multitudes that clamoured to receive the touch of his divine healing hands. But I wasn't Jesus and I certainly had no desire to be seen as his disciple. Yet, despite my resolve to avoid being dragged any further along this treacherous road, I couldn't help but feel great admiration for the dedication and concern shown by the unyielding supplicant. To prevent further distress I'd therefore indicated to Arquette that if he had no objection other than that he believed the visit to be a waste of our time, Sandy and I could at least look in on the patient.

In the event, the victim turned out to be another young girl. Like Rosie, the poor creature had no past and had been subjected to a similar degree of facial surgery. Due to her stunningly classic-Indian appearance, the staff had decided to call her Rika – a name I thought to be well-chosen owing to its regal connotations. Her enormous dark eyes stared sightlessly past us as we entered the room. She was sitting in a chair, humming softly while cradling a small doll. In contrast to Rosie's case, we were told that Rika had never spoken, spending each day in exactly the same way. The nurse who'd begged our presence explained that the girl had at one time exhibited some signs of recognition while being shown an atlas containing photographs of famous cities. I hadn't been at all surprised to learn that Rika's reaction was observed when she'd come across a picture of Cambridge.

For about ten minutes Sondra and I had asked questions, surreptitiously dropping in the odd key word from our recent experiences. Rika hardly blinked. I asked if the girl had ever written or drawn anything, but the answer was no. As a last resort I'd called for some paper and a few coloured crayons to see if I could encourage her to draw. Again, not the slightest hint that anything outside her totally closed and isolated world was being registered. It was only after we'd decided to concede defeat that the tiniest of breakthroughs occurred. I'd handed the pad and pencils to Sondra while I held Rika's hand and talked. Without my realising, my companion began to sketch. As I was speaking I noticed that the young girl's gaze had, for the first time, shifted a fraction and seemed to be focusing on something – my partner's drawing. I'd cautiously attracted Sandy's attention, and slowly but surely she'd responded by leaning forward so that Rika could see more clearly what was being drawn. As quickly as possible, Sondra dashed off a series of simple outlines – Cambridge, Gogmagog – then, when nothing seemed to be working, a picture of a thin, white woman standing with a large, black man. No result, so the pad was handed back to the nurse, who placed it at Rika's side just within her reach. We made our apologies for our lack of success then said farewell. We'd literally just stepped out into the cool afternoon air when the door behind us had been flung open. There, pad in hand, still breathless from his exertion, stood Dr Arquette. He retrieved one of the pages from the book and showed it to Sondra. It was her drawing of Black and White. On careful examination, however, it was clear the picture had been added to. Above the black figure's head a crude image of a large book with a cross on the cover had been drawn. Next to it, scrawled in almost illegible capital letters, were three words, *JESUS LOVES ME.*

'So d'you think Rika was yet another victim in a long line of Elenas and Natalies?' I said out loud, prompted by my troubled mind to share the burden.

Sondra thought for a moment then nodded. 'No doubt of that,' she agreed. 'I don't know about you, but I've a nagging feeling that we've got ourselves sort of trapped into just a single segment of this whole affair.'

'Sorry, I'm not sure I catch your drift,' I admitted.

'Well, I'm pretty sure that we're looking at a fair-sized operation here,' she explained. 'Probably scores of girls are involved if our theory's right regarding the porno movies. Presumably things generally run smoothly. But when they don't . . .'

'That's when our friends Black and White get involved,' I interrupted, stealing other people's punchlines having recently become my new hobby for some reason.

'Exactly,' Sondra exclaimed. 'Natalie and the other two girls, Twister and Art – problems requiring a quick solution. So when the people at the top require such a service, then who're they gonna call . . . ?'

'If it's true that we've mostly been caught up in the problem end of the business – and I agree, it's looking like a dead cert – then it would significantly aid our chances of finding out what happened to Kathy and why, if we had a way into the mainstream works,' I remarked.

Sondra patted me on the leg. 'It would indeed, Dr Clock. And that's exactly what we're gonna do, starting tonight.'

I should have known that Sandy was up to her old planning tricks when she'd insisted on driving us back. From the first day we met, if the girl had a problem or needed a plan, then she'd drive. Didn't really matter what mode of conveyance – pedal bike, car, rowing boat. As long as she was at the wheel she'd have a direct line to the ruling deities of strategy and solution.

It took a few more minutes before the captain was ready to reveal her proposal or, to those who knew her, orders. To Sandy's way of thinking, the most auspicious means of finding out about the elusive business empire we'd been chasing and of accessing the mainstream was to somehow get involved at the grassroots level. From that vantage point, as she so graphically put it, we could look up in safety to see what was happening since those at the top never look down. I had to admit she had a point. All we needed now was access to some grassroots – and guess what? The Way We Were Club, centrepiece of Elena's crucial drawing, was to Sandy the key to a veritable half-dozen meadows-worth.

Suddenly there it was again, coming straight at me with

no chance of escape – another God-forsaken late night. After the day we'd just had any normal person would have been desperate simply to flake out for a week. But oh no, not Clock and Warwick – or Warwick and Clock – whatever. No, the Mulder and Scully of the amateur investigative world were on twenty-four-hour assignment. Who was it who said 'rest is for wimps'? No idea really, but it was probably me during one of the annual management meetings at Van der Heijden.

'You want us to do what?' I almost spat the words across the dashboard.

'Deaf as well as daft these days then, Jerry. We *are* tumbling head-first into senility, aren't we?' Sondra replied with just a hint of sarcasm. 'Look, it's simple enough,' she retorted, 'transvestites are, in one sense, not born, they're made. If you're a guy but prefer to be a gal, you need to give nature a helping hand.'

'Yes, I know all that,' I interrupted. 'And I'm in full agreement with your hypothesis that a doctor or one of the clinics that offers that type of service may have links with our case . . .'

'But despite that real possibility,' Sondra argued, 'you refuse to check out the 3Ws club?'

'Sandy,' I said softly, hoping to diffuse the mounting tension, 'think what we've been through in the last seven hours or so. We're tired, exhausted, not to mention mentally flattened.'

Sondra frowned. 'Well, you might be, but. . . Oh shit, Jerry. I'm sorry. You're right as usual. I'm getting all hyper. Not enough sleep and too many shocks and knocks.'

I touched her hand, hoping it would relax the vice-like grip she had on the steering wheel. 'I'm as angry as you are about the way whoever's behind all this seems to delight in using people like Play-Doh. I think after this afternoon I'm also more or less convinced that Kathy Murkett's trapped on the same conveyor belt as Elena and the others were. Even though it might already be too late, even though we've unexpectedly run into the path of the authorities, I still want to do everything I can to help.'

Sondra's repentant expression suddenly exploded in a brilliant smile. 'Excellent! Then we're on for tonight,' she proclaimed. 'Good on yer, Jerry. Still as reliable as Old Faithful.'

Bugger it, I'd been suckered again, I rebuked myself. I couldn't believe it – the oldest trick in Sondra's book, and I'd fallen for it hook, line and cannonball. There was no longer any doubt – I'd lost the finely honed edge that kept me one step ahead of the pack at VdH. I was past it.

'Okay,' I sighed. 'A bit below the belt, but you win. Here's the deal. You get us back to the hotel by seven. We set aside a couple of hours to freshen up, have a bite to eat and make a quick call to the home troops so we're ready to leave at nine. Traffic permitting; we should be ready to sample the mysteries of 'The Way We Were' from ten o'clock. Agreed?'

Sandy saluted, and the pact was sealed.

Despite the occasional snarl-up on the expressway near King of Prussia, we were able to maintain our schedule. There was little new information from Cambridge, which under the circumstances was just as well. I let Sondra provide an edited account of our traumatic day then did my best to assure Julian that we'd find Kathy soon safe and sound. Of course I failed, but at least he drew some consolation from the fact that Elena – lost for a full three years – had turned up alive.

With forty-five minutes to go before our ETD, the not insignificant question of what to wear raised a hand demanding to be addressed. Neither of us could claim expertise when it came to mixing with the transvestite community, especially in one of their hallowed shrines. Given our ages, general appearance, available clothing and time, options were severely limited. In the end it was decided that I was better off going in my full corporate finery. 'Blind them with style and quality' was my partner's primary tack. Sondra's case, however, presented more scope for adventure. She was tall, slim, wore close-fitting suits and had considerable experience with make-up. With a bit of effort and a pinch of imagination, Ms Warwick may well be able to pass herself off as a young gentleman albeit on the effeminate side.

At nine p.m. precisely I knocked on Sandy's door. When she opened it, I had to admit to being extremely impressed by the transformation. It was truly remarkable what a few stitches, an eye pencil and a tub of Brylcreem from the hotel shop could achieve.

'You look fantastic,' I crooned. 'If it wasn't for your obvious feminine charms, you'd be quite the dapper chap.'

Sondra's expression, slightly apprehensive I'd noticed when she first appeared, underwent a drastic collapse into a mixture of profound anguish and embarrassment. I was certainly taken aback. It was a side of her I'd never seen before. Surely my furtive remark couldn't be responsible for such a reaction?

'Oh Sandy, I'm really sorry. I apologise for whatever I've said that's upset you. God knows it wasn't intentional.'

'No cause for alarm, Jerry,' she replied, recovering by a degree or two. 'Nothing to do with your mediocre attempts at wit. Better come in. Time I told you what's been at back of my odd behaviour these past years.'

'Told me what?' I questioned, unable to comply with Sondra's 'no cause for alarm' assurances. I accepted the offer of a seat and waited with bated breath for whatever dark secret my troubled friend had decided to reveal.

'Three years after marrying Tim, I became pregnant,' she began with a sigh.

'I didn't know . . .' I started to say.

Sondra waved me into silence. 'Please, Jerry, just let me run through this in one shot,' she appealed to me. 'Like I said, I was pregnant. About a month later at a routine check-up a small lump was discovered in my right breast. To cut a long story short, seven months later I'd lost the baby and undergone a double mastectomy. Tim tried his best to support me, but the miscarriage and the sight of my newly rearranged chassis were too much for the poor schmuck. His divorced secretary was built like Dolly Parton and seemed able to have babies more easily than shelling peas, so off he went . . .'

At first I couldn't take it all in. It was as if someone had changed TV channels without warning and one drama had been replaced by another with a totally unrelated storyline.

'Anyway,' she continued in the absence of any verbal response from me, 'upgrading to male impersonation is no more difficult than replacing a light bulb. All that's required is a large dose of emotion suppression, i.e. shame, embarrassment, vanity . . .' As she spoke she slid out of her jacket, unbuttoned her shirt and unclasped a specially modified bra. 'Not quite as you remember, is it?' she quipped, her face ravaged by a deep-rooted sadness.

My heart sank, tears blurred my vision, and at that moment I realised I loved this woman more than anything else life could offer. Without thinking I took her in my arms, crushing her scarred body to mine as if intent on merging our two separate forms. To begin with, Sandy didn't respond. Perhaps she thought my action was born out of pity or sympathy; perhaps – well, whatever she was thinking, it was wide of the mark.

'Come on, girl,' I murmured. 'It's me: your one and only Jerry. You must know I never stopped loving you. And if you think the size of your bra's important, you're an even bigger dummy than I am.' At last I felt her body relax and for another few minutes we remained locked in each other's arms. When Sandy finally broke our embrace, it was obvious that she too had suffered a bout of the silent waterworks. I helped her back on with her clothes and let her correct the flood damage to her make-up.

'Thanks,' she said at length. 'That must have been a shock, and you handled it well.'

'Stuff the handled part,' I retorted. 'I meant what I said. So, as I've heard you say to some of your students when you're doing your tough US professor routine, just get used to it, it's part of your life.'

Sondra smiled, and the road to recovery looked well under construction. Later than we'd planned we prepared to set off on our journey into the unknown, but before we left my companion tried to give me a signal that she'd be okay.

'So then, Clock,' she called out, holding up her bra. 'Do you think 36D's a bit on the optimistic side? I must admit it's bordering on cheeky, but I've got a couple of other sizes. Comes in handy when shops don't have my size or the cut's too tight. Novel concept, eh, changing the shape of a person to fit the clothes?'

It was a fair point.

Although we didn't appear too far removed from our normal appearances, for one reason or another we found ourselves making a fairly hasty exit from the hotel then across the car park. My turn to drive, we beetled along the Schuylkill at a steady fifty-five mph, despite Sondra's assurances that the highway patrol wouldn't flinch unless we started stroking sixty-five. Inevitably, the conversation ping-ponged between the truth behind Art's murder and the ubiquitous Ms White and her mate. The fact that Elena had drawn their images and for some extraordinary reason picked up on the effigy was astounding. Add to that Rika's response, which we agreed had to be the influence of the Reverend, and everything became that much more bizarre. The involvement of the silent holy man was particularly perplexing. How he'd come to reconcile strongly held religious beliefs with his mobster sideline was a real brainteaser.

I successfully found a convenient parking lot only five minutes walk from our destination on South 13th Street. Even though it was nearing eleven o'clock, there was still quite a crowd out. Much to my relief, the appearance of these fellow humans was extremely varied, ranging from homeless down-and-outs rummaging through garbage stands to the wild-party brigade heading for clubland.

The Way We Were club turned out to have a distinctly Romanesque feel to it. Above the entrance the name, in gold cuneiform letters, had been carved into black and grey marble, which in turn formed the main feature of the premises. The revolving doors were constructed of tinted glass set in a gold framework and were flanked on either side by white stone Corinthian-style pillars. To greet and presumably vet arriving guests, we found a very large Hawaiian looking gentleman with a baby face and a twenty-five-inch neck. On this occasion I was more than happy for Sondra to do the talking. Once again, a certain amount of 'dropsy' was required to facilitate administration procedures, etc., but with considerable flair and *joie de vivre* a favourable result was soon forthcoming.

Inside, the theme drifted away from that of ancient Rome to New York and Chicago in the 1930s. Tables, bar and staff reflected the period with remarkable accuracy. Even the jazz band and lounge singer could have been transported in time to ensure authenticity. A very attractive young lady in a beautiful black silk evening gown showed us to a table and alerted one of the serving staff. So far, I wasn't as uncomfortable as I'd imagined. Perhaps seventy per cent of the clientele were females dressed in everything from leather hotpants to full petticoats and frocks *à la* Doris Day.

'Do you like the girls?' Sondra whispered in my ear.

'Certainly do,' I confessed. 'There are some real stunners.'

'Good,' came the satisfied reply. 'But don't forget, dear, they're all men.'

I'd forgotten. 'Bloody hell,' I breathed, 'you're having me on. I was just in half a mind to chat up those two hot-looking chicks sitting by the bar till you spoilt everything,' I joked. 'You wouldn't have minded, would you?'

'I don't mind now,' Sondra revealed, continuing the ruse, 'but be warned, the type of guy who uses expressions like "chat up" and "hot-looking chicks" doesn't stand a snowball in hell's chance of getting to first base with any girl in this town, male or female.'

Firmly put in my place, I continued to marvel at how naturally feminine most of the 'ladies' were. On prolonged inspection I saw one or two exceptions, but to my chagrin Sandy assured me that these rejects were in fact real women. When it came to women dressed as men I felt on much firmer ground. I scored a much higher hit rate and even won a few points back from Sondra.

Well, this was all very pleasant and entertaining, but what next? Most of my discussion with Ms Warwick had centred on how to gain entry to the club and various back-up plans if the task proved difficult. Ironically, we'd got in without a hitch, but were now short of a follow-through strategy. While I was trying to clip together several of my celebrated scenario plans, I noticed a Marilyn Monroe lookalike giving Sondra the eye. Before I could comment, the blonde bombshell wiggled up to our table and in a deep voice, which totally destroyed the illusion, asked my partner to dance.

Bloody cheek, I thought.

As far as I could tell, no one was paying the slightest attention to me. But then I had to face facts. I was an old guy in a smart suit who looked like an old guy in a smart suit.

Jealousy's a funny thing. There I was, watching a guy dressed up as Marilyn smoodge the dance floor with my girl, and I was seriously pissed off. Thankfully, when the number being played ended the two broke up and Sandy rejoined me. Unfortunately, my green pallor mustn't have faded sufficiently, as she smiled and gave me a peck on the forehead.

'Don't worry, hon,' she purred. 'Marilyn's looking for another Marilyn, if you catch my drift. But, and it's a big "but", if you pardon the expression, I picked up some potentially useful information.'

'And let's just hope that's all you've picked up,' I squeezed in sarcastically, completely unable to resist the temptation.

Sondra winced. 'Listen,' she instructed, 'in about half an hour there'll be a short cabaret show. While my friend and I were chatting, I took a risk and asked if she, or he, had any contacts in the cosmetic surgery line.'

'That was a bit previous, wasn't it?' I remarked. 'Not the sort of thing you usually ask someone two minutes after you've met.'

'True,' Sondra agreed hesitantly. 'But to be honest, I wasn't the one who brought the topic up.'

I sighed. 'Go on, let's have it.'

'Ms Monroe thought you were a new recruit. You know – just about to make a commitment to your true female self,' Sondra explained. 'Well, nothing personal, he wanted me to assure you, but he felt you'd need quite a lot of work to effect a worthwhile transformation.'

'Very delicately put,' I conceded. 'Most considerate, cheeky bugger!'

Fortunately, at that moment our drinks arrived. I hadn't tasted bourbon for a while, so the slug both pleased my senses and repressed my anger. While I waited for a refill, Sondra explained that one of the performers – a Cher impersonator – was apparently the best person to speak to about my 'problem'. Marilyn had promised to introduce us after the show and felt confident that, if we hit it off, Cher might, for a price, be prepared to drop a name or two.

My second and third bourbon safely tucked away, I sat back to resume my people-watching exploits. The time passed quickly, and before I'd even completed a forty per cent survey of the guests, a grotesquely fat lady bounced onto the stage. She wobbled and gyrated an enormous set of breasts at the audience then announced in probably the smuttiest voice I've ever heard that it was show time. As if the word 'grenade' had been yelled instead, dancers abandoned the floor in a flash in favour of their seats.

Sabrina, as the rolling lard-ball professed to be called, began slagging off a selection of well-known US Congressfolk and the odd TV celebrity. This annoyed me greatly, since I had to admit the vulgar rhetoric flowing from her slobbering mouth was clever and quite funny. Slowly but surely the subject matter of the jokes descended to unexplored depths of depravity, and at one point I found myself calling on Sondra for interpretations. Worryingly, these she seemed easily capable of providing without the slightest hesitation, which made me wonder about the company she'd been keeping since condemning me to a life of corporate misery all those years ago.

With the intro having successfully whipped up the audience's party spirit, it was time for the first act. Inevitably, I suppose, it had to be Madonna. The lights dimmed, the music exploded from a cartload of gigantic speakers, and a figure adorned in vintage Madonna costume launched into 'Material Girl'. I hadn't asked Sondra how much she'd had to bung the Hawaiian sumo at the door, but it probably wasn't enough. I was totally mesmerised by the quality of the imitation and overall presentation of the performance. On the odd occasion when I remembered the artiste was a man, it was a real battle between eye and brain as to which harboured the truth. Following an equally laudable rendition of 'Papa Don't Preach', Tina Turner took to the stage and blasted us with 'Simply the Best'. In many respects this particular gentleman could have made a strong case that he *was* the best. His legs alone got my vote; but in truth these still only came a poor second to his face, which could easily have been stolen from the original. It was then time for our act to perform. Like her two colleagues, Cher was a work of art, or perhaps considering the plastic surgery involved, a work of science. Of the three, this guy had set himself the most difficult challenge. Sporting a skimpy semi-see-through top, tights, G-string and suspenders, he wore the least clothes. And, as I remarked to Sondra, if that really was a man, I was Queen Elizabeth II.

The exhibition so far had convinced me unequivocally of one all-important point. We were scalding hot when it came to uncovering a lead that would eventually take us to the heart of Kathy Murkett's disappearance. There was no doubt in my mind that if we could only track down the doctor or doctors who were performing these masterful transformations, we'd be well on the way to solving the whole puzzle.

To a chorus of whistles, shouting and fevered applause, the show concluded. True to her word, Marilyn signalled that we should follow her through a narrow door off to one side of the stage. There, we found ourselves in a corridor lined on either side with dressing rooms – some fitted with the stars' names, others blank. Cher, hardly surprisingly, not only had a personalised door sign but also one of only two large shimmering gold stars as a backdrop to her name. Marilyn knocked and, when called, entered, leaving us outside. Some moments later the door reopened and confirmation was given that we'd been granted an audience.

Being afforded the opportunity to view my new idol at close-quarters might, I feared, prove a mixed blessing. On the one hand, I had high hopes that my rosy impressions would remain undiminished. On the other hand, logic insisted on preparing me for a fall. As it turned out, logic was the only thing taking a dive. If I died and went to heaven at that precise moment, I'd have no qualms in swearing to St Peter that I'd met Cher in person. Even in the less than salubrious environment, away from all the special lighting and fancy sound systems, the person I shook hands with would be the lady herself for the rest of my life.

Once Marilyn had been shooed away, we were invited to sit.

'You two cops?' Cher began unceremoniously. 'Look like Vice ta me. Well, yer out o' luck tonight, boys. I'm clean. So if that's all, why not do me a favour and go fuck yerselves. I've got another show in an hour.'

It took some very fast talking and a truckload of assurances to avoid being summarily ejected. A crash dive seemed inevitable when I suddenly remembered I still had my passport with me.

'Jeremiah Orville Clock,' Cher repeated, thumbing through the pages. 'Shit, that's one helluva name. But ya're a Brit, so I guess ya could be on the level. Sonny, God rest his soul, always liked the Brit rock scene, so for his sake I'll give ya five minutes. Talk ta me.'

Sondra took over the reins and very skilfully, I thought, outlined our needs. She explained that I was extremely sensitive and only wanted to commit to a regime of physical reconstruction if the doctors involved were the best. Money, of course, was no object.

While she listened, Cher set about revising her appearance for the next performance. A slight dab of make-up here and there, a change of wig, and the star of the Eighties became the superstar of the Nineties. Incredible!

'Sounds like a load of crap ta me,' she concluded. 'Jeremiah here doesn't look the type for hormones and titties. Besides, he's no spring chicken, is he? But you Brits are a pretty fucked-up bunch of jerk-offs. All that cocksucking and ass-fucking at public school, I guess. Okay, here's the deal. I ain't sayin' I'll do nothin', but you come back tomorrow about six before the place opens. I'll speak to some people and see if they're interested. It'll cost ya five hundred to get that far. So what d'ya say? Ya in or out?'

We were in, but only by the skin of our teeth. Trying to make it look as if doling out five hundred bucks was no more of an event than breaking wind took some doing. Not having anticipated this kind of outlay so early in the proceedings meant we only had five hundred and nine dollars thirteen cents between us. Nevertheless, some fancy sleight of hand and Sondra succeeded in slipping me her contribution while Cher was preoccupied changing her knickers. I didn't really know where to look for the best nor had I time to consider what to expect if I did decide where to look. In the end I bottled out, but then by chance looked up to find myself staring at her almost naked body reflected in a mirror. Our eyes met.

'So, this is what ya want, sugar?' Cher said, chewing gum. It was a disturbing sight. The face, breasts and body of a female marred – if that's the right word – by a set of male genitals. I was dumbstruck and only too grateful when Sondra responded.

'It's what we want,' she stated with creditable confidence.

'Well people, it's no picnic, I can tell ya,' Cher volunteered. 'All that dieting, liposuction, electrolysis, and that's before ya start the tablets and surgery. If ya ask me though, the biggest problem's the pecker. Ya keep it – it ruins the line of yer knickers. Ya lose it – ya can't change yer mind. A bitch if ya meet some foxy beach bunny ya just gotta fuck.'

I could appreciate the dilemma, but I wasn't really in the mood to debate the issue. My genitals were already aching just from the thought of being removed to improve a knicker line. It was definitely time to go. I handed over the monkey, confirmed we'd be back by six the next day and literally dragged Sandy out of the room.

'I'll be needing another drink before we go,' I said with theatrical emphasis. 'That's the last time I fall for one of your hare-brained schemes. After this lot I'll probably be mentally scarred for life.'

'Stop overacting,' came the unsympathetic reply. 'Like you said to me recently, you're lapping it up, you can't tell me otherwise.'

My secret laid bare, I kept silent and struck out for the drink. In our absence the club had filled to capacity and no empty tables remained. Fortunately – or unfortunately – Marilyn and a newfound friend spotted us emerging into the body of the club and insisted we join them. Ironically, after moaning that no one seemed interested in me, Marilyn's partner immediately started emitting affectionate vibes in my direction. A very girlish looking Afro-American lady/ gentleman – Virgin, as she introduced herself – was archetypal jailbait, whatever sex she was. This young lady, I soon found, possessed the unique talent of managing to find a reasonable excuse to maintain bodily contact with me at all times. For centuries women have accused men of having octopus arms. Well, it was payback time tonight. Hardly surprisingly, Marilyn reacted unfavourably to the switch in Virgin's attentions and was obviously beginning to regret her invitation when Ms Grotesque the comedienne flopped back on stage. She launched into another sequence of witty anecdotes and snide remarks, which I would have enjoyed more if I hadn't had to keep removing Virgin's hand from my crotch every thirty seconds or so.

Feeling distinctly uncomfortable in that particular region of my anatomy due to all the excessive attention it was receiving, I excused myself and headed for the rest room. Barely had I left the table when a kerfuffle suddenly erupted by the entrance. The house lights responded by flicking back to life just in time to pick up a gruff-looking gent in a powder-blue suit swaggering into the club. Apart from the two sultry blondes he was toting, one on each arm, a couple of very heavy-looking bodyguard types waded in and began to clear away some of the crowd that had already started to mob the entourage.

I moved back to Sandy's side and whispered in her ear. 'Any ideas?'

'Plenty,' she replied, taking my hand and standing. 'I think we can safely say we're definitely on the right track.' Then, in answer to my puzzled look. 'Take away the toupee and the make-up, and I think you'll find we're in the presence of the revered Mr Wayne Millard.'

12

AC/DC

Another trip back to base in good old West Conshohocken. I was beginning to feel like a commando holed up on the fringes of enemy territory. Despite the peril, my sister-in-arms and I attempt each day to penetrate deeper and deeper into the heart of the aggressor's lair. Time after time, with resistance mounting and the fighting evermore fierce, we nevertheless go in flags flying. In the end, casualties limited to our own battered minds, we so far always manage to sneak back across the border and on to the relative safety of the Marriott West.

Tonight's mission had perhaps yielded the greatest success of the campaign so far. I had to believe that fate was now gradually beginning to favour our cause. Certainly, for five hundred dollars I was expecting something more than just another dead end. Yet potentially of far greater significance was the startling appearance of the convicted murderer, Wayne Millard. Even my logic had no trouble accepting that if this bloke was banged up in San Quentin, he couldn't be swanning around in a transvestite joint in Philadelphia. This find had set the scenario-planning element of my brain whizzing around like a demented horse-fly. All the key words were up for grabs – crime, substitution, disguise. The result? A number of intriguing possibilities, but perhaps the most disturbing consequence of all my cogitating was the notion that all of these things when added together spelt mayhem and chaos: two frightening concepts, which just happened to fit in nicely with biblical associations of Gog and Magog.

Sondra uncharacteristically said very little as we drove through the largely deserted streets. The night was the coldest I'd experienced since we arrived and, apart from a couple of tramps fighting over who should sleep atop one of the city's many steam vents, most God-fearing folk were no doubt wisely tucked up in bed. After mentally bidding good night to the illuminated boathouses along the Schuylkill River, I couldn't maintain the silence any longer.

'Is there any way we can get a hundred per cent confirmation that Millard's still in the clink?' I began somewhat rhetorically. 'You don't think he was able to cut one of those deals you hear about? You know, witness-protection programmes.'

'Yes and no,' Sandy replied, clearly preoccupied.

I waited a few moments hoping for further elaboration, but none came. I tried answering my own questions, feeling confident that this was guaranteed to provoke a response. It usually did, and always in the form of a direct contradiction. 'Shouldn't be too difficult to double-check on Millard's prison status,' I speculated. 'Very unlikely that the authorities would have had any truck with a man like that anyway, whatever he might have to offer them. And as far as the witness-protection scheme . . .'

'Okay, Jerry, you can lose the psychological manipulation routine. I'll talk if you want.'

It wasn't a typical Sondra response. Something was troubling her. . . Of course, how bloody crass and insensitive could one human being be? We'd just spent the past few hours in the company of men who'd been able to transform themselves into some pretty fair examples of womankind. During the whole of this episode Tick-tock the Dick Doc had droned on about how great they all looked. Listening to this was my poor, sweet Sandy who had that very same evening just revealed one of the most tragic secrets a woman could harbour. Pillock, stupid pillock.

For once I was unsure what to do for the best: stay silent; change the subject; or try to apologise for my thoughtless behaviour. In the end I opted for the daftest course and turned the car radio on. I suppose on reflection, it could have turned out worse. The pre-selected station was at least one churning out golden oldies, not heavy rock 'n' roll or some irritating chat show. It didn't take long for me to realise that Sondra had already seen straight through my ploy. Sometimes I find female insight a real bugger. Inwardly I accepted defeat but, as my finger approached the on/off switch, Barbra Streisand of all people saved the day – 'The Way We Were'.

A smile brushed Sondra's lips as she tapped my hand away from the controls. 'I don't know how you managed to arrange this one,' she said wryly. 'But I guess I have to give you nine out of ten for being able to bribe coincidence.' So we sat, surrounded by darkness in the overheated atmosphere of the car, listening to Barbra wail her lungs out. And by the time she'd finished our world had been put to rights.

In the morning we decided it was time to move our centre of operations. We were through with trips to the mall and the Gellar Institute. Our focus now was the great city itself. More phone calls and faxes yielded good results. The Four Seasons Hotel on Logan Circle was able to accommodate us, and Sandy's contact confirmed that Mr Millard had never stepped foot outside the prison compound since entering it some five years ago. Conspiracy theories even more rife than before, my partner and I spent a good hour conjuring up endless fantastic tales to explain the facts we currently had to hand. Eventually, my head throbbing with a premier league headache, we decided to call home.

Today's news, while not particularly startling, at least continued to support the emerging picture. Norma's Internet activities had come to an abrupt end. Over the past day, links to GM-related websites had been disappearing faster than tickets to a new A. L. Webber musical. As of that morning, nothing at all remained. Julian had gone as far as he could in trying to find out more about people on the list who'd already been released from jail. And oh dear – shock, horror, probe – he could trace the whereabouts of not a single one. As a long shot I asked if he or Kathy had ever had dealings with the transvestite community or had ever heard mention of the 3Ws club. The young man responded in the negative to both questions, but eagerly undertook to approach members of his business circle who might know something or themselves have contacts.

We said goodbye to West Conshohocken after finally sampling one of Billy C's Philadelphia cheesesteak sandwiches. Half a portion was usually more than enough for me, but since I hadn't eaten much the previous day, the whole thing plus a large tub of curly spicy fries and a couple of beers disappeared before I knew it.

Like the Marriott, I was familiar with our new accommodation. Among the top few hotels in the downtown area, the Four Seasons wasn't cheap but if you could afford it, it was a great place to stay. Of particular note was the Fountain restaurant: without doubt one of the best hotel restaurants I've ever had the pleasure of sampling. Under the present circumstances though, I had little or no enthusiasm for leisurely dinners, however excellent.

Mid-afternoon arrived and all we had to do was prepare for our reunion with Cher at the 3Ws club. From earlier in the day I could tell that Sandy was brewing up another of her schemes and so, as we sat in her room half-watching the TV, I decided to pre-empt the issue.

'So, what's today's intrigue?' I asked casually.

My companion unconvincingly pretended not to understand the question.

'Come on,' I bludgeoned. 'You're always doing that sort of thing to me. Don't like it when the shoe's on the other foot, do you?'

Rather unseemly, I thought, Sondra put her tongue out then smirked. 'No one likes a smart-ass, Jerry. You, of all people, should know that. Anyway, I suppose I do want you to consider an idea I've been kicking around.'

'Which is?' I said, feeling that for once I had the upper hand.

Ms Warwick adopted one of her dreaded professorial postures.

Not good, not good at all, I decided, anxiety beginning to stir somewhere in the background.

'We managed reasonably well last night,' she began. 'The main problem though, I'm sorry to say, is your credibility.'

'Credibility as what?' I repeated like a dummy, knowing full well what she meant.

Sandy glared at me.

Rumbled again. 'Well, it's not my fault,' I complained. 'It could be worse. I could have a beard and a tub of a beer belly. Then what?'

'Then I'd have to shave off the beard and put you on a diet,' came the gleeful reply.

'Meaning?' I drawled.

My companion offered me a seat by the mirror. 'Meaning, Dr Clock, we've got a spare hour or two. More than enough time to effect a few improvements to your appearance.'

'Oh shit!' I exclaimed. 'I'm not having you make me up like a woman. Absolutely not, so you can just . . .'

A loud knock on the door sliced the 'forget it' off the end of my demand.

'Who the hell's that?' I grumbled, flinging open the door.

A middle-aged woman and an older man carrying sundry bags and cases stood on the threshold, beaming at me.

Sondra coughed. 'Yes, Jerry dear, I agree completely. I'm not going to make you up, they are!'

'Sod it!'

Like they always say, 'Time drags when you're not having fun.' For me, the time wasn't dragging; it had almost come to a complete stop. It was all so obvious now. Ready agreement to move to the city, stay at the Four Seasons; and then there'd been all those extra phone calls. All part of the grand design to set me up for a *fait accompli. . .* But, like most things these days, I'd have to overcome my natural resistance and adapt. In this case it was after all eminently reasonable to assume that if we did expect to progress beyond the first stage with Cher, I'd have to seriously sharpen up my act and become at least an order of magnitude more convincing.

The make-up artists turned out to be old friends of Sondra's from way back. Don and Silvi ran a successful beauty salon not far from the intersection of 8th Street and Pine and, like my scheming companion, did a spot of theatrical moonlighting on the side. I'd no idea what kind of cock and bull story Sandy had spun them, and I thought it best not to ask. Whatever it was though, they treated me with great understanding and, given their amiable manner, it didn't take long for the sharp edge of my anger to dull.

About halfway through the makeover proceedings, another delivery arrived: this time clothes. By now I'd abandoned all hope of renegotiating Sandy's plan, so I just uncrossed my legs, metaphorically speaking, and thought of England.

To my surprise, the facial treatment took less time than I'd feared. Don shaved me to within an inch of my life and took charge of the foundation work. Silvi was obviously the sadistic type, seeming to gain enormous job satisfaction from pulling, ripping and tweezing extraneous hair away from places I never knew had any in the first place. Particularly painful was the eyebrow-plucking ceremony, which if I ever had to torture someone for information, would definitely be my method of choice. After some disagreement, it was finally decided that I'd best suit dark make-up. A variety of coloured powders were applied to my cheeks in order to create a gaunter look. This, I was assured, formed an excellent match with my golden-brown eye shadow and deep-red lip gloss. Eyelashes, a little mascara plus a few more strokes with an eyeliner, and I was ready for the wig. Don had brought along several styles, but everyone including me settled on a jet-black, shoulder-length number – centre parting, fringe and curled in to hug the neck.

I wasn't too bad at all . . . On a dark night, with no moon, hiding in a doorway, down an unlit alley, I could be mistaken for a woman. A Venusian woman maybe, but who's to say a Venusian man mightn't be interested.

With less than thirty minutes to go before we needed to leave, it was time to experiment with the selection of clothes. Wisely, Sandy had drawn the line at any form of skirt or frock. Even with opaque tights, one look at my spindly pair of pins and I'd have my provisional transvestite licence permanently revoked. Size was, not unexpectedly, the deciding factor. Despite Silvi's enthusiasm for a dark-green trouser suit, my strangulated nether regions couldn't have survived intact. After a double recount, the final vote went to a pair of classic black trousers, silver crocheted top and a fitted black blazer with silver trim. A stylish black-and-tan chiffon scarf to hide my chest hairs, a set of Monet clip-on earrings and I was the finished article.

Sondra's plan also turned out to include her own meta-morphosis. She emerged from the bathroom as my make-up team was helping me on with an ankle-length overcoat, which if nothing else was a great piece of camouflage.

'Well, Jerry,' she grinned. 'Don and Silvi have done you proud. You're a tad heavy here and there, but I've seen much worse.'

To be honest, no one in the room was paying any attention. The reason? No one in the room had ever seen Sandy decked out in that way . . . There she stood, just like a model lifted from the pages of a magazine. She was wearing a black turtleneck minidress and a full-length per-fectly tailored camel-coloured coat. Her shoes, belt and earrings, made of high-quality simulated leopard skin, yielded an inspired combination.

'Thank God for that,' I said once I'd finally recovered my voice. 'At least everyone will be looking at you. It's amazing, you look like a dream.'

Sondra gave a nervous laugh. 'Kind of you to say so. Let's hope, as the odd couple, we're sufficiently absorbing to maintain Cher's interest.'

By now we were running late. Don, evidently aware of our deadline, quickly ushered his partner out of the room to give us a few moments alone before we embarked on our debut. I wanted to give Sandy a good-luck kiss, but under the circumstances decided against it. Too risky – the make-up would smudge, I told myself. The journey from room to lobby to taxi proved to be a big disappointment. No one paid any attention to us at all. Why? Well, it could have been that as we hit reception a scruffy group of yobbos – purportedly a well-known rock band – arrived and stole the limelight.

'Bastards!' I whispered to Sandy. 'I go to all this trouble and not one wolf whistle, wink or even a glance!'

Despite our delayed departure from the hotel, the taxi dropped us in front of the 3Ws club precisely at six o'clock. Unfortunately, the place seemed completely closed, with no sign of Cher or the Hawaiian wrestler. I tried knocking on the covered revolving door, but no reply. After about five minutes, we decided that standing in one place was a sure-fire way of being picked up by the police for soliciting, so we began to stroll in the general direction of the Liberty Bell exhibition. A few blocks on, we retraced our steps, but still no one. By now my feet were feeling as though they were about to drop off. My companion had been consider-ate enough not to subject me to the ignominy of having to walk in stilettos. Instead I'd been kitted-out with a pair of men's fashion platforms, which although marked with my size, appeared to have been constructed with a stick insect in mind. When another twenty minutes adopting a similar holding pattern proved fruitless, it was agreed that we'd probably been the victims of a neat hustle operated by Cher and her mate. Left with no other option, Sandy flagged down a cab and we headed back to the hotel.

As we drew onto the hotel's forecourt, a large white limo was blocking the way. The driver was leaning on the bonnet, and neither he nor the hotel staff seemed about to shift it. Cursing, I started to get out of the cab, only to find myself being pulled back inside.

'Look!' Sondra hissed, nodding towards the main entrance. 'See who's leaving the hotel? That's them, isn't it?'

I looked, I saw, and then I almost choked. Heading towards the limo was none other than Ms White with the Reverend Black bringing up the rear. The driver rapidly jumped to and opened the back door for the lady and her escort. I glanced at Sondra, but she was already uttering the three words I thought never to hear outside a movie theatre.

'Follow that car.'

Unlike in the movies, our driver failed to respond and could only be persuaded after a handful of bills bearing the portrait of President Jackson was thrust in his direction. Although we got off to a late start, the limo immediately got stuck at lights entering Logan Circle. After that, the chase was relatively straightforward since the target car was easy to identify and, sticking to the downtown area, it moved at a snail's pace. For some time we seemed to be travelling in a wide arc and I began to suspect we'd been spotted and were being led around in a circle. Fortunately the limo suddenly broke with its previous course and, after cruising a series of shady-looking back streets, emerged onto South Street. There, it immediately began to slow down and stopped in front of a large grey-stone building. Sondra signalled the driver to go past and pull in twenty or so yards ahead. Through the rear window we could clearly see the occupants alight and proceed up a flight of steps to a vaulted entranceway. Just when things seemed as if they couldn't get any better, our driver, in response to my partner's query, announced that the limo had parked outside the Andreas de Mello Tower, current home to the St Joan the Blessed Martyr Hospice and Clinic. For a few more deceased presidential portraits, our man also revealed that the clinic was well known for its charitable works treating drug addicts and AIDS victims. He also disclosed that to fund such philanthropic activities, the facility operated a number of private floors catering to rich clients and their special needs. Bingo!

Since we'd literally bought the cab, our driver now seemed quite content to spend the remainder of the night pandering to our every whim. We therefore decided to watch and wait. Knowledge about who went in and who came out could be of inestimable value if this was in fact some kind of covert operations centre.

For more than an hour we maintained our vigil, but during that time not another soul approached or left the clinic. Another hour passed with the same result, then another and another. At eleven the limo suddenly departed, and as far as I could tell without a passenger. Chances were, therefore, that the driver had been contacted by mobile phone and had received instructions to collect another party. The question now was what of Black and White? They'd been inside for over four hours. What on earth could possibly command their attention for such a prolonged period at this time of night?

As so often is the case, fate always seems to push you to the point of surrender before it sees fit to show its hand. Tonight was no exception. Eleven forty-five just turned; our driver, despite his hefty fee, was becoming fractious. Sondra and I looked at one another and knew it was time to pack it in, at least for that night. Only when this silent agreement had been made, did the unseen forces that rule our lives take up a prodding stick and begin to poke around . . .

'Look!' Sondra exclaimed halfway through giving our driver leave to return to the hotel. 'The limo's back.'

Sure enough, the vehicle returned to exactly the same spot, allowed three people to disembark then again drove away. The trio spent a few moments debating while standing beside the kerb. Despite the lateness, the street lighting was good and more than adequate for us to ascertain that all three were men dressed as women. Unlike the crowd at The Way We Were club, though, this group were far less impressive. Furthermore, it appeared from the way they behaved that one of them was trying to convince the other two to accompany him into the building. Finally, their dispute reached a climax. One individual, clearly unhappy with the situation, stormed off, leaving his companions calling after him. Left alone, the remaining couple pointed towards the building, exchanged some kind of packet then skipped up the steps to the entrance.

Since our cab driver had reached the point of no return, we had no choice but to let him go. Although it had been the most expensive taxi drive I for one could remember, the extra cost had not been entirely wasted. We'd spent nearly five hours in each other's company, during which time I'd noticed the man ogling Sondra frequently, but apart from an odd glance in my direction he'd displayed no sign of horror, amusement or revulsion at my appearance. It was true I'd only spoken to Sondra in whispers and never to him directly. Nevertheless, I felt it was a good test result and in a perverse way pleasing, since I was becoming quite comfortable with my custom-made female persona.

Standing on the pavement, I suddenly began to feel decidedly unsafe. It was cold, dark and menacing, to name but three adverse conditions. Besides that, a visit to a rest room wouldn't have gone amiss and, judging by Sandy's posture, I could tell the same was true for her. So it was make your mind up time. Continue our surveillance and freeze, hail another taxi and return to the hotel empty-handed, or go for it. I always find it incredible that apparently well-educated and sensible people, when placed in unusual situations, always manage to opt for the most irrational course of action. . . Not wishing to be the exception that proves the rule, Sandy agreed that we had no choice but to 'go for it'.

With absolutely no idea what we were getting ourselves into, and armed with not even the vestige of a plan, we trolled up the steps and into the hands of destiny. We got off to a less than laudable start. Try as I might, I couldn't open any of the doors. Beyond the glass barrier I could see what appeared to be a reception desk, and although the area was lit I could see no evidence of a nurse or guard. It was then I noticed a small button attached to a miniature

217

intercom box, which was mounted almost flush to one of the metal doorframes.

Believing that a local voice would engender a more favourable result, Sandy gave it a shot. Eventually, an elderly gentleman in a noticeably fancy guard's uniform sauntered into view, evidently in no particular hurry. He reached the desk, peered at us through half-inch-thick bottle-bottom glasses and then released the lock without a word spoken. In we went and on up to the desk, almost prepared to tackle our first serious obstacle.

'Hi, I'm Sondra,' my companion announced positively.

'Sixth floor,' came the disinterested reply.

'Well, that was easy enough,' I thought, grabbing Sandy's arm and propelling her towards the lifts. 'Never look a gift horse in the mouth,' I said quietly in response to her startled expression.

The elevator doors opened onto a fairly extensive hallway and yet another reception desk-cum-nurses' station, this time staffed by a formidable-looking spinster-type sister.

'Appointment or referral card?' the woman said with a disapproving air.

Deciding I was well overdue for a turn and particularly in view of my appearance, I did the honours. 'I'm afraid I don't have either on me,' I said in my best English accent.

'Stop right there,' I was instructed. 'No documents, no consultation. Why can't you people understand? I suppose that fool downstairs just waved you through without checking. The man's worse than useless.'

'I'm here on the recommendation of . . .' I had more or less decided to go with 'a contact from the 3Ws club'. Pretty lame I knew, but it was better than nothing. As I hesitated though, my eye caught sight of the nurse's computer screen. On the display was a main menu containing four names: three doctors and a Ms White. Of course! The voice of understanding cried out in my head – Twister surrounded by all that medical paraphernalia, my own drug-induced interrogation. Ms White was some form of qualified physician. I coughed to disguise the prolonged pause, and in that split second conjured up a totally new scenario.

'Sorry,' I apologised. 'Slight allergy, you know. Now where was I? Oh yes. Recommended by Dr Arquette.'

The Tartar squinted at me over a pair of half-spectacles and I could almost see the neon sign behind her eyes reading, 'So what?'

Not to be deterred, I switched to scenario B. 'Dr Arquette told me he'd contacted your Dr Setnika,' I brazened, noticing that of the four entries on the screen, three had engaged signs blinking next to their names while my choice warned, 'Do not disturb'. 'By the way, my name's Dr Stravinsky.' I took out my wallet and handed old dragon-face the name card Stravinsky had given me. She read the card and then for the first time exhibited signs of indecision. Progress! When in doubt, name-drop your way out!

The woman began to shake her head, apparently seized by a fit of pique. 'Most irregular,' she murmured, then staring straight at me. 'Dr Setnika's in a very important meeting and can't be disturbed. I could make a provisional appointment for you tomorrow to be confirmed after I've spoken to the doctor. However, if you say it's urgent, you can wait if you wish and I'll let him know you're here when the meeting breaks up. But it'll definitely not be before one, and I can't be held responsible if he won't see you.'

I nodded, smiled and graciously accepted the latter option. The waiting room was in the corner, some distance from the reception desk. Perhaps just as well given Sondra's obvious need to succumb to an acute attack of the screaming heebie-jeebies.

'Jesus Christ, Jerry. What the hell was all that crap about?' she exploded.

It took a few minutes to explain my discovery and strategy, and then eventually she began to calm down.

'Let's look at all the facts,' I continued. 'This isn't the secret headquarters of an international gang of super-

219

crooks that we expected. The guard, the nurse; even the people who came in the limo – I think this place is primarily what it seems: a regular hospital. And like the cab driver said, its charitable work's funded by rich embarrassment money.'

'You mean treatment on the quiet when Felicia comes home pregnant, on dope, with AIDS and demanding a sex change?' Sandy exaggerated.

'But I still believe it's a cover for part of what we've been looking for,' I insisted. 'I'll bet you anything this is where at least some of the mainstream work plus the odd special case is handled. And it's here we'll find Kathy Murkett, I can feel it in my water.'

Sandy shrugged. 'Great, so we've got a charitable institution, viable only by virtue of cover-up money from the rich and famous, operating side by side with an organised-crime porno racket,' she summarised. 'Very entrepreneurial.'

'Even more worrying than that,' I added. 'We seem to have Ms White and the Reverend doing a fair old Jekyll-and-Hyde routine. By day, one treats the sick while the other presumably ministers to the dying. By night, they both turn into psychotic killers with a flair for the theatrical.'

'Okay,' Sandy responded sharply. 'So you've figured everything out and successfully arranged for us to be sitting in this waiting room like a pair of prize turkeys. Now what?'

'As I've already explained,' I replied, checking the nurses' station for any untoward activity. 'We find Kathy. If we come across any secret records just lying about, that'd be a nice bonus, but I'm not planning on holding my breath.'

'Good,' Sandy remarked as if she were talking to an idiot. 'I see, we short-circuit the video surveillance, bash the old girl on the head then run through the building shouting ' "Kathy, it's Heathcliff!" Are you mad?'

I pretended to think for a moment then smiled. 'What me, mad? Dressed up like a tart, pursuing villains through the streets of Philadelphia at midnight. Of course not.'

Jocularity born of nerves and fear put to bed, I described

my plan such as it was. Basically, it started with the trip to the rest room we both craved. As we'd entered the waiting room I'd spotted a sign for the requisite facilities suspended from the ceiling. My proposal was that we make a point of letting the nurse know where we were going then, on the way back, slip away down the back stairs. In the elevator I'd noticed that all the floors were labelled: Administration, Obstetrics, Pathology, etc., except levels four and five, which were left blank. At least it was somewhere to start. With regard to security, nothing could be done. If for some strange reason Black and White decided to scan the monitors, what was there to see? A pathetic specimen of a man dressed up in woman's clothing with a flash-looking bird they'd never seen before . . .

Reluctantly, Sondra gave the idea a green light, so I launched into action. To avoid skidding off the track at the first bend, I followed my companion into the Ladies rather than possibly cause a commotion in the Gents. Since it was empty, I decided to repair the wear and tear to my appearance caused by six hours of valiant service. As I was finishing up, a young nurse wandered in to rearrange her hat. Spying the small maintenance kit Silvi had furnished me with, she asked if she could borrow my eye pencil. I could see Sandy stop breathing, but the encounter went off without a hitch. It was a proud moment for an apprentice transvestite. Accepted by a real female in the most sacred of houses: the ladies' washroom. What greater challenge could there be?

Stage one done and dusted, we crept along to the stairs and made our way to the fourth floor. In contrast to the sixth level, the reception area was a hive of activity. Medical staff, intermingling with the occasional well-wisher, buzzed around, paying little attention to our presence. Adjacent to the nurses' station was a set of double doors controlled by a keypad locking system. Fortunately, so many people were flying in and out that the door, never quite able to make it back to base, frequently remained open for a spell. Putting on our best 'concerned visitors' expressions, we marched up to the barrier just in time to prevent its closure and swept into the corridor beyond.

The new layout appeared just the same as any other hospital ward, with rooms occupied by patients lining the hall on both sides. Since many of the doors were propped open, it was easy to take a peek inside without arousing suspicion. First I thought it odd that there should be so much activity at that time of night, but it soon became clear we were in one of the charity wards. Quite a few down-and-outs were being examined and treated for minor conditions, leading me to conclude that this floor was used more as a triage operation set up to separate the wheat from the chaff. In a way this was a disappointing find. Only two floors out of twenty had been unlabelled on the elevator panel and, given the function of level four, chances were that level five would turn out to be the corresponding admissions ward.

After a quick check around just to make sure there were no hidden rooms or corridors, we made our getaway via the lift. Working on the principle that cream always floats to the top, this time I opted for the twentieth floor marked 'Ward M'. As in all the best films, the elevator car stopped on nineteen and refused to go any further. The design of this level turned out to be different yet again. To the right beyond the lift doors was a wide corridor bathed in soft lighting and lined on one side only with a number of utility rooms, or so their notices claimed. Eventually the walkway opened out into a circular expanse. Into this, several other corridors converged onto a multi-component nursing station manned by an equally ferocious and no doubt close relative of the sixth-floor dragon. This time there was little room for manoeuvre. The gatekeeper, highly suspicious of our presence, informed us that we were on a private maternity floor. Visitors other than immediate family were clearly not expected or welcome after nine p.m. without prior arrangement. Since we met neither of the two entry criteria,

I decided it best just to apologise for the mistake and retreat.

Still intrigued by what lay hidden on the twentieth floor, we tried the stairs. At the summit of the stairwell there just had to be another locked door and another keypad control. This example, however, gave some cause for optimism. Its outer casing was cracked; its buttons faded, and several wires were in evidence poking out of its side. Definitely an occasion when the content of a lady's handbag was worth its weight in platinum. For no charge other than a pleading smile and a veiled promise, Sandy allowed me free rein with her collection of tools. A nail file, some scissors and my particular favourite, a pair of tweezers, gave me all I needed to well and truly bugger up the electronic circuitry. . . We were through, but nowhere near home free. Adjacent to the bank of lifts was a guard office past which all visitors clearly had to travel to gain entry to the main body of the floor. By a stroke of good fortune, the area was empty and only one guard, seated with his back to us, was on duty.

'I'm beginning to suspect the gods aren't as with us as I thought,' I whispered.

Sandy paid me no attention, preoccupied instead in trying to get a closer look at the guard station. Eventually she turned towards me. 'My eyesight's not perfect these days, but if I'm not mistaken Sonny Boy over there's eye-balling a copy of *Playboy.*'

'Is that good?' I asked, lost as usual when my companion started her 'communication via riddles' routine.

'Very good,' she confirmed. 'Listen, you stay here but be ready to come if I signal. If my hunch's correct, we're as good as in.'

Before I could ask for more details, Sandy slipped out in front of the lift, adopted a posture as if she'd just arrived and was looking for something in her purse then coughed. As the guard responded by hastily closing his magazine and swivelling around, my partner walked confidently towards him. Following a noticeably over-friendly greeting, Sandy somehow managed to get herself invited into the guard-room. A minute or so later, she waved me over, parted from her new chum and, linking my arm, walked through the main entrance as the guard released the doors.

'Very impressive,' I murmured. 'How on earth did you manage that?'

'You're not the only one who can play the business card trick,' Sandy gloated. 'Easy as pie. I simply flashed a little leg then told the guy I'd been employed by his management to secretly check on security standards.'

'That would certainly grab his attention,' I agreed.

Sondra grinned. 'You could say that. Anyway, I explained that his station was the last to be tested. I was feeling tired and, since most of his colleagues had performed poorly, I felt like giving him a break. Nothing to do with the fact I thought he was cute, of course.'

'Sexual manipulation,' I sighed. 'How very feminist of you. So how did you get him to let us in if his job is actually to spot the ruse and kick us out?'

'Reveal the plot then explain the best way to handle it to gain maximum points,' came the nonchalant response. 'First: the plot. I'm a famous history professor and have a name card to prove it. I pretend I'm sneaking you in to see one of my students who's a patient here. The usual sort of reason – the two of you are involved but his parents have told the hospital to deny you access. In truth, we're reporters doing a touch of opportunistic scandal-hunting. Second: how to foil the plot. Being an "on the ball" kinda guy, the guard immediately suspects a scam but, instead of just turning us away, lets us in then stops us on the way out.'

I couldn't help but laugh. 'Pretty cunning stuff,' I drawled. 'That way his company not only finds out what we were up to, but also gets to take any action it likes since they have proof "we done it".'

'QED,' Sandy concluded. 'Give the folks enough rope and let them hang themselves – works every time. Needless to say, none of this will happen. When we're ready to leave, I'll flash a bit more leg and promise to write him up as security guard of the year.'

With me still marvelling how all this had been achieved in what seemed only minutes, we strolled along the corridor, occasionally taking a peek behind any unlocked doors we came across. Based on the type of patients we saw, this at last appeared to be a ward dedicated to reconstructive facial surgery. However, it wasn't a case of rooms full of young girls either disfigured or looking like film stars. People of all ages and conditions were being treated, the discovery of which had me questioning the validity of all my grand theories. I was about to consult Sondra as to her thoughts when I realised she wasn't with me but was staring through an observation window into one of the patient's rooms. I retraced my steps and, as I reached her, she clutched my arm.

'Jerry,' she breathed anxiously. 'What's big, black all over and has a religious bent?'

I followed the line of her gaze. 'Oh fuck!' I mouthed. As the vision of my dark nemesis branded itself onto my brain, a set of amber lights positioned all along the corridor sprang to life. There was no accompanying siren, no bells ringing, but I'd no doubt what it meant – intruder alert – and there were definitely no prizes for guessing the identities of the particular miscreants.

'Quick!' I exclaimed. 'Let's see if there's another way out.'

First we walked, then we marched, then finally, as people started to emerge from all manner of doors, half of which I hadn't even noticed, we ran. They were like grubs gnawing their way out of a rotten apple. They were everywhere. We raced from one corridor to another, one room to another, but could find no exit. The combination of Sandy's stilettos and my excruciating platforms ensured that our efforts at racing were severely limited, but by God we did our best. Startled patients were now outnumbered by medical staff and security personnel. It really was looking as if we were the ones suddenly holding all the rope and had more than enough for a double hanging.

After hitting two more dead ends and with our return

path blocked by the advancing posse, it was time to give up and face the consequences. I drew Sandy to a halt then turned, only to find myself confronted by a door marked, 'Director's Office and Emergency Exit'.

'Our last hope?' I questioned in the form of a prayer. Literally as we were about to be seized, I almost crashed through the door, catapulted Sandy inside and slammed it shut. For endless seconds my heart pounded, my muscles tensed waiting for the hordes outside to attempt a forced entry. Strangely, nothing happened. Instead, the clamour abruptly faded and, through the glass door panels, I saw the flashing amber light shut down. It was then that the room lights came on and I felt Sandy's hand on my shoulder.

'Dr Clock and Professor Warwick, welcome,' a deep, husky female voice called out. I swivelled around to find three women entering the room from the rear. 'A great pleasure to meet you both at last,' the voice continued. 'Allow me to introduce myself. I'm Greta Oakridge, and I believe you already know Ms White and Ms Murkett.'

13

Come into My Parlour

Greta Oakridge wasn't at all easy on the eye. A lady of perhaps sixty, she was a good five stone overweight for her five feet four inches. Her chubby face could have been a saving grace, but for some extraordinary reason she'd opted for the use, or more accurately overuse, of a chronically anaemic-looking foundation powder. In combination with dark purple eye shadow, pencilled in eyebrows and ruby-red lipstick, she reminded me of a recently touched-up corpse ready for display. If challenged to select Ms Oakridge's most attractive feature, I'd be hard pressed. To be fair though, her short curly blond hair, although totally out of step with the rest of her appearance, seemed natural enough and possessed an unusually soft, silken quality. The final calamity was her dress. An odd lime-green sequinned creation, it was too short, too tight and definitely too low-cut by any standards even I could imagine.

'Come on in, come on in,' she sang out, waving us towards her. 'Take a seat. Looks to me like you folks have been doin' some pretty serious runnin' about.'

I understood the words, I understood the meaning, but the response centres of my brain were completely fried to a crisp. My legs wouldn't or couldn't move. All I could do was stare at Kathy, with the occasional glance towards Oakridge and Ms White.

In the absence of any response, our hostess gestured towards her two companions, who in turn set up a couple of chairs in front of a large desk and physically guided us into them.

'I know all this is a bit of a shock for ya both,' Oakridge

continued, settling her considerable bulk into a huge leather chair behind the desk. 'And I do sympathise, believe me, I really do. But let's be fair. The sight of you, Dr Clock, dressed up like a ten-dollar hooker hasn't helped to calm me down none neither. And perhaps now would be as good a time as any to remove that ridiculous hairdo, don't y'all think?'

Still, I found it hard to concentrate on what was being said. Even the presence of Ms White, resplendent as usual in revealing white costume, had little impact on my perception. All I could focus on was Kathy standing silently at the back of the room, her eyes looking in my direction but not seeing. Finally, my delayed action reflexes kicked in and I dragged off the wig.

'Are you all right, Kathy?' I croaked, my tongue finally breaking free of the anaesthetic that had numbed it since I first caught sight of her.

There was no reply: in fact not the slightest evidence that my words had even reached her.

The older woman frowned. 'Nope, I don't think the good doctor's firin' on all cylinders yet,' she remarked glibly. 'Ms White, better escort Kathy next door for a while until our guest's operatin' system gets back on-line.'

I wanted to object, to call out that she mustn't leave in case she vanished again, this time perhaps forever, but the words crumpled together at the back of my throat.

It was only as the two women disappeared through the door that I realised how different Julian's lady looked. No longer was she the fragile hippie with a pasty face and Indian-style frock. She was a much more familiar sight to me – a businesswoman. Her long hair had been tied back and fashioned into a tight bun. She wore a deep brown two-piece fitted suit *à la* Versace or perhaps Lacroix, and circular-framed spectacles. Nowhere near as pale as I remembered, her new, much healthier colouring looked to be the result of a few days exposure to real tropical sunlight rather than anything conjured up out of a bottle. Perhaps it wasn't Kathy after all, I began to consider. I'd already seen one attempt at a duplicate, so why not another?

My chance of finding out the truth vanished through the door, leaving the convivial Greta as the only source of information. The sight of her made me wonder. Had we at last stumbled across one of the infamous group's core elite, the orchestrator of all the nightmares we'd experienced? Or was it so far beyond the realms of possibility to believe that Ms Greta Oakridge was in fact leader of the pack: number one, the boss, the Godfather even? A million and one questions were spinning around my sorely confused and punch-drunk head. I felt like a wonky washing machine stuck in a fast spin cycle, slowly but surely shaking itself apart. But I wasn't about to break down yet. Not after all we'd been through. Answers were at hand and, as God was my witness, I was going to extract them even if I had to wrap my hands around this awful woman's throat and choke them from her.

I noticed Sandy shifting in her seat and begin to speak, her voice filled with suppressed fear and anger, but a loud knocking on the door behind us drowned out her words.

'Come in, Reverend,' Oakridge called.

Slowly the door opened and, in his characteristically methodical and lethargic style, the colossus paced across the room to take up the seat vacated by his partner.

The old crone leaned back in her fancy swivel chair and regarded Sandy and I quizzically. 'Pretty much recovered now, are we?' she said softly. 'I sincerely hope so, as time's a luxury I haven't had for – oh, nigh on thirty years.'

With the arrival of the Reverend, the atmosphere in the room changed. Not only that, but Greta's tone suddenly lost a fair percentage of its original good old Southern hospitality. It immediately reminded me of how Ms White seemed to have two personas: one in the presence and one in the absence of the taciturn hulk. I looked at Sandy and, drawing upon the special unspoken language that had developed between us from our days in Cambridge, let her know I was okay and ready to enter the battle of wits I suspected was about to commence.

'I'm recovered sufficiently, thank you,' I replied, trying to strengthen my voice. 'Since you've been kind enough to inform us who you are, perhaps you'd also be willing to tell us something about your position?'

Oakridge erupted in laughter and turned towards the Reverend, who clearly wasn't as amused. 'Very English,' she coughed, moisture forming in her eyes. 'Ms White said y'all were good value for money, and it looks like the girl wasn't jivin' me. I'm sorry, Doc. Rude of me laughin' out loud like that, but you're funny. Anyone ever told ya that? No, come to think of it, guess not.' At this point she paused then weighed me up and down as if trying to decide whether I was worth wasting any more time on. Eventually she nodded as if she'd reached a decision. 'Listen, Doc,' she resumed. 'It's like I told ya before: my time's cruelly limited. Sure, I'd like nothin' better than to sit here for a couple of hours with you two fine people and tell y'all the story of my life over a nice cup of Earl Grey, but I can't. Ya see, I'm not sole arbiter of my diary now, am I, Reverend?'

The Reverend slowly shook his head in confirmation.

'I know ya have a wagonload of questions but, to be honest, my answerin' 'em won't help ya one little bit. Problem is, ya interfered. Not only that, but ya kept on interfering. If ya'd only just left well alone, but . . .' Here, she paused and again fell back in her seat.

Now it was my turn. 'Have you any idea how crazy all this sounds; how crazy you sound?' I stated calmly. 'Look at the people surrounding you. A deranged woman with a mono-tone dress sense and a similarly afflicted holy man who plays with a whip. Don't you think you'd be better off seeking professional help instead of killing people or ruining their lives?'

Greta didn't bat an eyelid. She just sat regarding me like a cockroach she'd decided to squash underfoot.

My first attack and not a single target damaged, never mind destroyed.

'Valid point,' she observed, pre-empting my second strike. 'Some people see me as brilliant, some, like you, think of me as insane; while others, well, they regard me as evil. Not a very flatterin' word that, evil, but an interestin' concept all the same. Men have never doubted that God was one of 'em. Okay, I'll go along with that. But if so, ya can be damn sure that the Devil's gonna be one bitch of a woman.'

'Oh, I see,' I interrupted. 'You're not mad, you're the Devil.'

My assertion clearly didn't sit well with the Reverend Joseph. With uncharacteristic speed and agility, the big man rolled off the edge of his seat and came at me like a bull.

'Reverend Black!' Madam Oakridge called in a voice that clearly revealed her role as Commander-in-Chief. 'Please be seated. I'm sure Dr Clock regrets his remarks, don't ya, sir?'

Under the circumstances I decided I did and clumsily retracted the inference. It took another step, however, before the raging beast could check his momentum, and by the time he did I was less than a breath away from extinction. His fury sucked back into the bottle, Black ambled back to his seat then glared at me, clearly intent on transmitting his unspoken thoughts – next time, I was a dead man.

'All right,' I breathed. 'It may be that even if the Angel of Death here doesn't tear me limb from limb first, my days are numbered. Not something to look forward to, but if that's the way the die's cast I don't expect there's much I can do about it. However, I drew Sondra into this and surely Kathy Murkett can't be that important to you. Please, if you have to make an example of someone, let it be me and allow them to go free.'

Oakridge's expression softened and a faint smile graced her lips. 'A mighty pretty plea, Dr Clock,' she acknowledged. 'And one I feel deserves some reward. In my experience, selfless acts are rare. Most of the scum I come across only have their own interests at heart – everyone else, well they can just go screw 'emselves. You know, I think I ought to thank ya. For a few seconds there ya almost restored my faith in that tired old concept of human kindness.' Again this strangest of creatures lapsed into thought. It seemed an age before she spoke, but when she did even Archangels would've been compelled to pay attention.

'Well, Dr Jeremiah Clock, as reward for your self-sacrifice, I've decided that before ya leave us, so to speak, I'll grant ya some peace of mind. To do so means delayin' my schedule, and no one's provided sufficient cause for me to do that in nearly twenty years. Ya might not appreciate it in this lifetime, my boy, but ya're uniquely honoured.'

My dealings with the mentally microwaved were extremely limited. Under sentence of death and consumed by anxiety for the eventual fate of Sondra and Kathy, I could hardly think straight. My expectations that the worst I could have faced was a verbal swashbuckling session followed by a sound pulverising at the hand of the good Reverend now seemed like a gross underestimation. The woman sitting before me had decreed I was to be eradicated and, short of divine intervention, I could envisage no other means by which this decision could be reversed. Perhaps if I behaved according to expectation, it may afford the ladies a glimmer of hope and grant me the satisfaction of understanding some of the circumstances that had led to the sealing of my fate.

'Thank you,' I said simply. 'Your concession's much appreciated and I'm genuinely grateful.'

Greta nodded majestically. 'Firstly, I'll confirm what I expect a clever man like you's already guessed. Secondly, ya can ask me three questions.' Without waiting for a response, the old woman stated her interests in such a matter-of-fact way that you'd have thought she manufactured knitwear or sold greetings cards. It was all so simple. She was in the business of producing people to order. If a pornographic filmmaker needed a famous figure to star in his epic – no problem. If a convicted criminal wanted someone to serve time on his or her behalf – no problem. If someone famous died at an inconvenient time and a substitute was needed to carry on until the spin doctors could put their propaganda in place – no problem. All that was needed was money to pay for the service and people willing to sell their souls for it. Supply and demand. Both were there in abundance. All Ms Oakridge did was oversee proceedings and make sure the two always walked hand in hand.

Astonishingly, the explanation was over in less than five minutes, and listening to her speech I began to sense that I was wrong about her. Greta Oakridge wasn't mad, unhinged or even evil. She was no more than an extraordinarily gifted businesswoman. In many ways she was no better or worse than the people I used to work with at VdH. Shit, she was no different than me. Originally, her territory had covered the darker side of human nature and, as a result, you would expect her to become involved with some unquestionably strange people. Unlike Ms White, I believed her when she claimed that in the majority of cases everyone was happy with the arrangements and no one got hurt. Even the people who went to prison on another's behalf were content. They were carefully selected. Men and women who'd been dealt a bum hand in life. The lonely, the desperate, sometimes even the ill or dying. For short-term assignments, the money they received together with a guaranteed new face and fresh identity offered them the chance to start over. Not only that. Second time round they could be 'reborn' with an advantage. Those accepting prolonged stretches or, due to illness those not expecting to survive the term, could provide anonymous life-long financial stability to family members or friends. As Oakridge herself put it, there were mainly winners in her line of work. How many others could boast a similar claim?

So far in accordance with our telepathic agreement, Sandy had held her peace. Given the circumstances and her character, it was no mean feat; I knew that all too well. Greta's last statement, however, finally shattered the limits of her endurance.

'Oh please!' she exclaimed. 'It's like listening to Adolf Hitler explaining how he helped the Jews to a better life. A week ago I'd no idea an organisation such as yours even existed. Since then at least three people have died and we've come across another three horribly abused. What riches have they reaped from your all-caring benevolent society?'

The old women listened patiently while Sondra unleashed her hostile attack. At its conclusion she looked at me like a judge who, having entertained one lawyer's comments, turns to the opposing counsel for their response. 'Would you like that to be question number one?' she said calmly.

In truth I hadn't even considered the issue of my three questions, but it was clearly time I did. The relationship to the old children's story in which a boy is granted three wishes as a reward for releasing a genie from a bottle immediately sprang to mind. As in this and many variations on the same theme, the tale always contained a warning or some painful lesson in morality: 'Beware of what you wish for, you just might get it' being among the favourites. A harrowing statement, and one Greta Oakridge no doubt had the copyright to. But who was I trying to fool? I'd as much chance of formulating the perfect set of questions under these conditions as I had of beating the Reverend in an arm-wrestling match. I could feel Sondra's eyes burning into the side of my face in anticipation. So, what the hell? It was as good a start as any.

'Yes,' I said at length. 'I would like that to be my first question.'

'It's your nickel,' Greta shrugged. 'But you already know the answer. However . . . Regrettable consequence of a large and complex illicit business,' she breathed. 'That's it, pure and simple. These days it's all about delegation and empowerment. You, Dr Clock, should know that more than most. Trouble is, it doesn't matter how good the people are in the middle ranks; instructions, orders, plans or objectives – everything's open to interpretation.'

Sondra scoffed. 'So you're saying the tragedies we've witnessed weren't a direct consequence of your orders?

They occurred due to the fault of poorly trained and under-supervised minions misunderstanding their instructions?'

'Professor, now really,' the old woman jeered. 'This isn't a faculty debate. I said nothin' about fault. The people I deal with are professionals. They've special, sometimes unique, talents. When there's a job to be done, they do it. How they do it? Well, deary, that's up to them. I might have thoughts on the methods used, and sure, every group would handle the same task differently, but the result's always the same. And to be honest, that's all that counts... Next question, Doc.'

Oakridge was right. Although the context was hugely different, I could understand her position. I'd been there, God help me. I'd even liked it. As to the next question, that was easy enough. If nothing else, I at least had to find out how Kathy was involved in all this and the reason for her elaborate disappearance. I asked.

'More interesting,' Greta responded. 'Kathy Murkett falls into a unique category when it comes to extraordinary talent. Back in 1979 I was visitin' Kresge College at the University of California, Santa Cruz. Let's just say I was there on a recruitment drive. Ms Murkett, at the time a young student on a UK Arts Council grant, was studyin' the history of American culture and its influence on modern art. In those days people used to study all kinds of crap. Anyway, she'd that special somethin' I was lookin' for, so I signed her up, trained her up and sent her back to the UK. Over a decade she undertook a series of assignments for me, all of 'em accomplished with remarkable efficiency. The girl was good, maybe even the best. As a result I set up a full UK franchise and put Kathy in the drivin' seat.'

Although I'd had no serious trouble accepting the answer to question one, this was beyond belief. Quiet, almost invisible little Kathy some kind of criminal mastermind heading up a UK syndicate – incredible! I was mystified. Of the hundred new questions that immediately sprang to mind, top of the list by a head and at least half a shoulder was how Julian fitted in. He couldn't possibly be involved, I was absolutely certain of that. If so, then what was going on? Suddenly my own words boomeranged back on me. 'Quiet and almost invisible'. If it were true, what better character to have in charge than one who could travel through life without anyone – not even the person they lived with – harbouring the slightest suspicion?

'All right then,' Sandy interjected, her expression betraying a greater degree of disbelief and bewilderment even than mine, I suspected. 'I like a good fairy tale as much as the next person, but I'm not sure about the ending here. What's the point?'

'Question three, Dr Clock?' Oakridge enquired.

I shook my head. 'No,' I said firmly. 'I'm prepared to make a stab at answering Sondra's question myself.' With our host's leave, I ventured forth. 'Everything that's been happening suggests the winds of change are being whipped up by one almighty storm. Something of monumental importance is in the offing around here, and it's time to recall all the key commanders back to base. Since they won't be returning, their previous lives have to be erased permanently. What better way than a series of unrelated natural deaths, fatal accidents or murders? Just everyday life, and of course there's always a body to bury.' As I was concluding my account, Greta unobtrusively left her seat and allowed Reverend Black to help her on with a heavy mink coat. She waited until I'd finished, whispered something to her companion then signalled him to leave.

'Time's up?' I enquired casually.

'Regrettably so,' came her distracted reply. 'The Reverend will just be a minute, so if ya wanna go for yer final question, now's yer chance.'

'Bit risky, isn't it?' I suggested. 'Allowing yourself to be alone with the two of us?'

Greta raised an eyebrow. 'Don't get too excited,' she warned. 'Either of ya moves and I'll shoot ya both dead: the professor first. Now, d'ya want to ask a question or not?'

'I'll ask the question,' I conceded. 'What's the connection with Gog and Magog?'

'Oh deary me, honey, what a dismal last question after you did so well speculatin',' Greta sighed. 'I felt sure you'd have come up with somethin' more probin' than that. Nothin' to it, you'll be disappointed to learn. Just a personal interest of mine. Like the professor here, history fascinates me. And, like the Reverend, certain parts of the Bible, particularly Revelations, make me wonder. Combine the two, and Gog and Magog for some reason popped up and caught my imagination. Perhaps you'd care to see some of my research? You'll forgive me if I don't give ya a guided tour. Oh, and you bein' intelligent folks and all, I expect I can trust ya not to damage anythin'?' With that, Oakridge, looking no more concerned than if she were on her way out to a night at the opera, swept past us to the door. 'A pleasure talkin' to ya both,' she commented. 'I hope I was able to at least clear up some of the mystery and maybe fill in a few blanks. *Adios, amigos.*' Then, with her mink coat swirling behind her, she was gone.

I immediately stood up, only to be confronted by the sight of the Reverend Joseph receiving whispered instructions from his mistress. Time stood still, and all I could think about was how odd that Greta should use one of Julian's favourite parting salutes. Had she learnt it from Kathy, from him or vice versa? My mind was obviously beginning to develop more hairline cracks than I thought.

Abruptly the momentary trance I'd slipped into was knocked for six as the Reverend re-entered the room then herded us through a door marked 'Emergency Exit'. Sondra and I found ourselves in a large study. Dark oak wood panelling covered all walls and, suspended from the white plaster ceiling, a huge crystal chandelier dominated the space. To our left stood rack after rack of books, manuscripts and ancient texts, guarded on either side by six-foot wooden statues of two strange giants. According to their nameplates, replicas of Gog and Magog on view in the Guildhall, London, they seemed to be watching our every move, ready to strike at the slightest provocation. Set some distance away from the opposite wall was a white alabaster desk in front of which, located almost at the centre of the room, were two extensive glass display cases. Each contained an abundance of artefacts ranging from stone carvings to faded parchments and etching plates. The walls to our right and behind us were covered with a wide variety of paintings, drawings and photographs, all depicting the same theme, many of which I judged to be of considerable value.

Having allowed us a few moments to become acclimatised to our new environment, the Reverend unexpectedly vacated the room, locking the door behind him. Given the sudden release of tension by being left alone, Sondra and I instinctively caught hold of each other. It wasn't a hug; it wasn't an embrace; it was something much more. My heart lifted . . .

'Well, despite the heavy hints to the contrary, I'm still in one piece,' I tried to joke. 'More importantly, Ms Oakridge didn't actually threaten you and she's still keeping us together.'

When our grips finally relaxed, I refused to part from my companion completely. Hand in hand like the lovers we'd been two decades before, we stood together, each supporting the other. Our curiosity aroused by the extraordinary collection around us, we spent a little time examining the content of the display cabinets and bookshelves. The whole room was indeed a source of great fascination, and under different circumstances it would have been a singular pleasure to become absorbed in this shrine to the tales and legends of Gog and Magog. However, we urgently needed a way out, so, repressing academic inclinations, we began to search for any kind of feasible exit – nothing. The room possessed no windows, maintenance closets or openings of any kind. As far as I could tell, the only way in or out was via the door – the locked door.

I beckoned Sondra to sit beside me, choosing a leather settee positioned against the picture wall adjacent to the entrance, evidently designed to allow its occupants a grandstand view of the cased exhibits.

'Looks like it's all down to the hand of fate,' I proclaimed, attempting to make a potentially negative statement seem positive. 'You know, the one thing I still can't come to terms with is the idea that Kathy Murkett's an underworld genius. It's just, well, unbelievable.'

Sandy's expression softened in a gesture of sympathy for my disappointment. 'Come on, Clock, don't be glum,' she encouraged. 'Look at it this way. You've succeeded in your quest and discovered the lost damsel alive and well.'

'True,' I smiled. 'But I'm buggered if I know how to explain it all to Julian, assuming we ever get out of here.'

'To be honest, Jerry,' my companion said, gripping my arm. 'It's only the last part that concerns me. I know it sounds selfish, but if you meant what you said back in the hotel room, I just want you with me. You've done all you can now. Let's focus on escape and leave the authorities to sort it out from there.'

It was all I needed to hear. Sandy wanted me. I drew her close; our lips touched then locked in the magical kiss I'd been dreaming of for years. My Sandy had returned to me, bugger the lip gloss.

After a prolonged breathless embrace, we spent the time it took to wipe my make-up from Sandy's face to speculate on what could be so great an event to precipitate the present upheaval in Greta Oakridge's empire. Was she expanding into fields anew or in some way consolidating the operation? We simply didn't have enough facts. One point on which we both had no trouble in agreeing, however, was that the Gellar Institute must still in some way be a key factor in the scheme of things. The whos, whats, wheres and whys were once again just more unfathomable conundrums.

Lulled into a false sense of security by the return of my lost love, the shock of seeing Ms White and the Reverend Black march through the door had double the impact I'd have expected.

'Well, look at the two lovebirds,' Ms White crowed. 'Having a cosy time, are we? What a shame we have to spoil everything by breaking you up.'

Caught off-guard, we both reacted slowly to the rude interruption, and before I knew what was happening, the Reverend yanked Sandy from my side and hauled her out of the room. For a moment I could hear her fighting against her enslavement. She called my name, another door closed, then nothing. Instinctively I stood up and moved towards my tormentor, who blocked the exit.

'That's far enough, lover,' she purred. 'Be a good boy and sit over there by the desk. That way the Reverend won't have to harm your special friend.'

Reluctantly, I complied.

'Excellent,' she continued, striding over to my side. 'Now, all that's required before we can have an intimate little chat is the application of some simple precautions. Better safe than sorry, as they say.' With that, she grasped both my hands, wrenched them behind the chair back and bound them together with handcuffs similar in feel to the ones I'd removed from Toby Farthing.

'What's all this in aid of?' I protested.

There was no answer. Instead the young woman retrieved a roll of wide packing tape from the desk drawer and proceeded to bind each of my ankles to a chair leg.

'So at last we're finally down to violence?' I persisted, desperate to say anything to abate my mounting fear.

'What a vivid imagination,' Ms White answered as she put the finishing touches to her handiwork.

'Where's Godzilla taken Sandy?' I yelled. 'If that bastard so much as . . .'

I was shushed into silence. 'Don't go on so,' she demanded. 'I've already told you, if you co-operate the professor will be fine, at least for the time being anyway.'

Again I exploded. 'What the hell's that supposed to mean?'

My plea once more fell on deaf ears. It had taken a few minutes, but I'd finally got the message. Ranting and raving wasn't going to work. From my last encounter with the lady in white, I'd come to understand something of her complex character, but nowhere near sufficient to manipulate the current situation. Perhaps, a calm questioning approach would yield better results, I reasoned.

'Okay, no more shouting,' I promised in a tempered tone. 'But one thing's really puzzling me.'

'Only one?' came the slightly amused reply.

I feigned a smile. 'Of the many things puzzling me,' I rephrased the comment. 'Something you said to me during our previous interview. You indicated that neither I nor anyone associated with me was any real threat to you. So why all this?'

Ms White nodded her head approvingly. 'Ever the scenario-planning specialist,' she said almost to herself. Then, focusing her full attention on me, 'Yes, to be fair, I did say that. In point of fact, I should confess that "all this" as you describe it is a direct result of your proving me wrong.' I was confused, and my companion could see it. 'Let me make it simple for you,' she continued. 'After I left you to recover from your psychedelic experience, I thought that was it; our paths had crossed for the one and only time. But, like I said, I was mistaken. Not only did you persist, but you progressed, advanced; even managed to gain the attention of and then actually meet Ms Oakridge.'

'So I've been promoted to "worthy opponent" status?' I ventured, hoping that my claim would in fact be refuted.

Ms White gave a wry smile. 'You have indeed,' she confirmed – strangely excited by the idea, I thought. 'And it's because of that I've asked for you to be my bonus this year. I'm sure you remember all about bonuses from your executive days. Lump sums, share options, long-term incentives. Well, before I do what I'm afraid has to be done, you're going to be my share option, and guess what? You've just become vested.'

I tried hard to convince myself that I'd no idea what she meant, but it wasn't going to work. It was an interesting dilemma. Which should I fear most – the threat of pleasure or the threat of pain? Like a slide changing in an automatic projector, the whole atmosphere seemed to switch from real to surreal. The young woman's eyes flared with wanton desire, her lips moist and alluring, glistened in the soft hue cast by the chandelier. The temptress had returned.

'Don't be frightened, lover,' she pouted. 'This isn't going to hurt too much. In fact I've just had a deliciously inspired thought, which I'm sure you'll simply adore. You like to play questions and answers, don't you, Jeremiah?'

'Depends who's asking the questions,' I replied, unable to stop my temperature from rising.

'Why both of us, of course,' she purred. 'It's no fun otherwise. And you do know I want you to enjoy being my bonus now, don't you?'

Before I could think how to reply, my self-appointed sexual fantasy began to gyrate – slowly, sensuously, irresistibly. 'Let's try an example,' she breathed. 'Do you like lap-dancing?'

'What's that got to do with anything?' I protested.

'Hmm, still very tense I see,' she remarked with exaggerated concern. 'Perhaps a short demonstration might help.'

Half of me wanted to scream and yell, to struggle against my bonds, but the other half craved the demonstration. As if listening to the intoxicating rhythms of some sexually charged music playing in her head, she began to rock and sway. Her body flowed like a field of corn teased by a summer breeze, her burning eyes mesmerising. She circled around me, touching, caressing my face, while all the time directing her heady perfume to invade and captivate my senses. With her back turned, she lowered herself into my lap, stroking, pressing, tantalising me with her soft but firm buttocks. I had no control, probably I never had. My hardness was straining to break free of its confinement. It was agony. It was divine. Then it ended. As I felt the point of no return bubbling through my loins, there was no release.

'Did you like that, lover?' she whispered in my ear. 'Think carefully now, but if you're not sure, there's a huge clue poking its head up just about here.' She grabbed my erection and squeezed. My heart racing, breathless and with perspiration dampening my brow, resistance was a long-forgotten whimsy.

'Yes.' The word whistled past my teeth as if it were my last.

'Very good answer, my handsome man. Now you can ask me a question. I knew you'd like this game.'

I was a physical and mental wreck. Excited beyond endurance, ashamed beyond measure – God above, I didn't know what I was feeling. Stripped of most of my finer mental functions, I managed to find a few shreds of logic still intact and with their aid somehow strung together a question.

'You and the Reverend,' I panted. 'How do you fit into the Oakridge Corporation?'

Ms White fluttered her eyelids. 'I see, straight into the personal arena. Well, that's easy enough to answer. The Reverend spent many years in Africa ministering to people dying of AIDS, leprosy, cancer and the like. He believed that the poor souls, physically weak at the moment of their passing, were easy prey for the Devil. His goal was to make them spiritually strong enough to fight their way free and ascend to the Holy Kingdom. That's why he always likes to leave our clients a few well-chosen words from the Scriptures. A last opportunity for them to seek salvation. He did, however, have another career before he "saw the light" so to speak. Let's just say he was a caretaker for a group of very unsavoury characters. When he met the boss, she harnessed both his skills and applied them to our present work.'

'And yourself?' I interjected, feeling that I'd got the general drift.

'Nothing special,' she replied coyly. 'I'm just a virologist with a flair for electronics. Together with the Reverend, I help Ms Oakridge maintain her hospital and charitable interests as well as provide certain specialist services when required.'

'Like damage limitation, clean-up operations and coercion in support of her primary business,' I proposed.

Ms White only smiled then wandered around behind me and began gently massaging my neck.

'I feel another question coming on,' she announced. 'Rape. Do you believe it's actually possible for a woman to force a man to have sex against his will?'

Another weird question, I thought. What in creation was she doing? Was this another mind-game: a prelude perhaps to a further drug-induced interview? Or was I in fact under the influence already? All I could do was play along, assuming of course that my body could hold up under such intense sexual bombardment.

'Without question,' I concluded. 'No healthy male could suppress certain physical reactions from occurring when faced with any half-decent-looking woman with sex on her mind. And if constrained it . . .' I didn't complete the sentence, suddenly realising what I was describing.

'Another good answer, lover,' my companion exclaimed. 'Your turn again. Still enjoying yourself, I hope.'

'Okay,' I began slowly. 'You told me that killing people wasn't part of your primary MO, yet since we met three people have died and you've had a fair shot at trying to snuff out at least three others. Am I missing something?'

'It would appear so,' Ms White replied in a considered tone. 'I think I know the incidents you refer to, and I have to say I'm very disappointed you deem me a liar. The mall – that was nothing to do with us. Another department altogether. Your boating accident was the result of a slight misunderstanding between the Reverend and myself rather than a serious attempt to kill anyone. As for the young boy and that fat queer. One was a pathetic would-be black-mailer: a blasphemer who foolishly interrupted our work. The other, simply ungrateful vermin. Needless to say, the Reverend had no tolerance for either. That answer your question? Yes, of course it does. My go again!' Finishing with the massage, my strange partner stood before me. Her breathing was gradually increasing, and I could almost feel a new wave of sexual fever invade her body. 'This time,

244

lover, I want you to pay close attention and give me your honest opinion,' she requested.

As I watched, she purposefully began to caress and feel her breasts then ran her hands slowly but deliberately down her sides, over her hips and on to the hem of that shortest of clinging skirts. By degrees, she teased the cloth toward the top of her stunning legs, leaving me totally aghast. It took only seconds before the tops of her stockings and suspenders were revealed and only a few more breaths before I realised she wore no vestige of underwear. Look away – I couldn't. Close my eyes – impossible. I was caught in the most powerful grip a man can experience – the sex of a woman.

'See how the light catches the soft delicate hairs on my cute little pussy. Don't you think it's attractive? You do,' she said without my saying a word. 'How kind. What would you like to ask me now?'

I was losing control and Ms White, the bitch, saw it. She knew what I wanted to ask, but I wasn't about to give her the satisfaction. 'What's the story behind your warped theatrics?' I croaked. 'Natalie soaked in blood even though you planned to incinerate her, Twister hooked up to that Dr Phibes' contraption, and Toby Farthing . . .?'

The fantasy shook her head, unzipped the side of her skirt and stepped out of it. 'Oh, that's far too many intimate questions in response to mine. I'll tell you what. I get another shot, and if you answer correctly, I'll tell you everything you want to know. . . Fair?' She paused, then delivered her devastating question. 'Would you like to fuck me, lover?' she almost growled. 'Do you want to fuck me here and now in Ms Greta, all high and mighty, Oakridge's office?'

I swallowed hard. The answer was obvious; we both knew that, yet I couldn't give in, not only for Sondra's sake but also for my own self-respect.

'No, thank you,' I stuttered.

'Really?' came the disbelieving reply. 'What a shame, and you were doing so well. How unfortunate to fall at the last hurdle with the wrong response when in fact you knew the right answer all along. Ah well, never mind. No more information for you. But since you've been such a good sport, I think you deserve a consolation prize.' Ignoring my protests, the young woman knelt in front of me, released the buttons on the side of my pants and pulled them to my knees. Carefully she licked the tip of my erection through my straining briefs. I moaned, pulled against my restraints, but the rout was already on.

'Stop it!' I cried. 'For God's sake, woman . . .' The remainder of my plea evaporated as she pulled away the flimsy cloth barrier she'd so painstakingly saturated. Her hands immediately began to caress and fondle my manhood, driving me crazy. For an agonising moment she ran her tongue languidly up and down the shaft of my raging erection. Then she paused. For one sadistic moment she moved away, fixing me with a smouldering glare. The thought of being left like that – driven to the verge of ecstasy then deserted – was too cruel. Rationally I wanted her to desist, practically I felt as if I'd die if she did. But it was all part of a calculated tease, a ploy to demonstrate in the clearest of terms who was in charge, who the more dominant. Rising gracefully to her feet, my seducer turned her back toward me and gradually lowered herself onto my throbbing member. Heaven and hell fought for the deeds to my soul as she moved backwards and forwards, riding me like a horse. For a man who hadn't been with a woman for five years this had to be the worst and best re-initiation ceremony imaginable. She began to moan then groan as I involuntarily responded to her attentions. I thought I would explode. She stopped again, but this time long enough only to exchange positions. Now straddling me face on, she tore away her jacket, hiked up her top and pushed her smooth, ample breasts into my face. Like a dog subjected to a Pavlovian experiment, I responded by licking, sucking and biting her nipples, returning some of the glorious torment she'd inflicted on me. Suddenly she began to increase the speed of her rhythm, the perspiration of our straining bodies freely mingling. It was too much. I had to let go, crashing into the welcome arms of release. Seconds later she too cried out, then again and finally a third time before her need was at last satisfied.

Breathing deeply she ran her hands through my hair then, with unexpected consideration for my exhausted condition, carefully dismounted. Without a word spoken between us, she dressed and tended to her appearance. Then, like a mother concerned for her child, she turned her attention to me. Considering it pointless to resist, I allowed her to replace my clothes and wipe away the smeared make-up from my face. Checking first that no evidence of our encounter remained, Ms White walked towards the door, pausing as she took hold of the handle.

'Pity there wasn't time for you to ask me about the coffin in your garden,' she remarked rhetorically. 'That's one question I'd have gladly answered. Anyway, doesn't matter now. Thanks, Dr Clock. It was a good performance, especially for a man of your age. Educational, too. Seems you were right about men and rape.'

14

Men Don't Mind, Boys Don't Matter

'My God, Jerry, what've the bastards done to you? Have they hurt you?' The sound of Sandy's sweet voice filled me with both joy and sadness. Joy that we were reunited and she was safe; sadness because, well, because I was no better than an animal. I didn't deserve sympathy; I deserved only scorn.

I gave her a hug, but I felt dirty. It was definitely one of those times when a natural disaster, especially a devastating earthquake with its epicentre preferably beneath my feet, would have come in really handy.

I'd no idea of the time when the Reverend finally came to release me from my prison. On several occasions, sleep had almost managed to creep up on me, but I was too frightened to succumb; scared out of my wits that if I slept I'd dream, and if I dreamt then what? Images of primitive, abandoned sex with Ms White? Or visions of cradling Sandy in my arms? I just didn't want to find out. The big man had, as usual, said nothing and betrayed no knowledge of what had taken place. Like a pre-programmed robot, he simply performed the task he'd been set – to transfer me from prison A to prison B.

So here I was, Sandy fussing over me, but hardly a word did I have for her. Somewhere in the recesses of my mind, I could hear her desperately trying to get through to me – repeatedly calling my name and asking if I was injured. But Jerry Clock or what was left of him was at the bottom of a deep, deep well, cowering from the light, afraid to be seen. Funny really. I used to think my voyeuristic leanings – way out there in risqué-land – were cause enough for shame, but now. . . I tried to speak, struggling to let the one person

248

who really cared for me know that although I might have wished to be dead, I wasn't. Finally, sleep mounted a surprise attack. I was unprepared, outflanked and, given no other option, surrendered.

When I awoke Sandy was sitting by my side, her hands touching mine. 'How're you feeling, sweetheart?' she said softly.

I felt like shit but I said, 'Okay'.

For the first time I paid attention to my new surroundings. Another room with no windows and only one exit – yes, another locked door. In many respects I couldn't really complain. The accommodation we were in was more like a five-star hotel suite than the rat-infested cell I'd prepared myself for. Two queen-size beds occupied the main section together with a wardrobe doubling as a TV cabinet and a chest of drawers. The design was pseudo-Regency: classic striped wallpaper, tasteful carpet, co-ordinated curtains covering a fake window, and plush bedding. Through a wide entrance to the left was a small sitting room containing a second TV plus VCR, a settee, two armchairs and an extensive Chinese-design coffee table. Opposite lay the ensuite bathroom – marble fittings, shower, bidet, even a whirlpool bath. What more could you ask for with an 'on spec' booking? Perhaps the most fascinating feature was a small dumbwaiter, which Sondra informed me delivered food and other supplies on a regular basis.

The same image I'd considered recently of a condemned man treated to princely service prior to his execution rumbled back into my thoughts but in truth I just didn't care anymore.

I shaved and showered, managed to eat a few mouthfuls of a brunch that turned up, then threw on a tracksuit, which had been considerately provided. Finally, I knew I couldn't put Sondra through my silent, moody routine any longer. She deserved better – much better. I glanced at the bedside clock. One o'clock on the same day. Was this my final day on earth? I wondered. Or would I have to wait one, two or more unseen sunrises before someone finally came to do the deed? Well, at least I'd meet my maker having confessed my sins to the one I loved, even if it did mean incurring her hate and loathing. I took several deep breaths, asked her to join me sitting on the couch and confessed my crimes.

When I'd finished Sandy stared at the ceiling as if seeking to locate the most appropriate point through which to summon a lightning bolt to blast me to ashes. But I was wrong. Eventually she looked at me and shook her head.

'Must've taken some guts to come clean with that lot,' she remarked. 'Can't say it fills me with joy to find out that ten minutes after I tell a guy I want him with me, he's bonking some cute piece of ass with legs up to the zoo. But I don't see what else you could've done. At least this way I get to find out before I'm too sucked in that your equipment hasn't rusted up over the years.' She smiled.

'Jesus, Sandy, how can you joke about it?'

'I should say, Jerry, that under the circumstances I can pretty much do what I like, wouldn't you? Better to deal with it through humour than screaming fits, deep depressions or silence.'

There was nothing I could say.

'Come on, Jerry, stop beating yourself up,' she commanded. 'The same thing could've happened to me. Have you thought of that? And if it did and I told you, what would you say? How would you react?'

I could sense that this was one of my companion's shock tactics, and I had to admit it was a good one. It hadn't even crossed my mind that anything like that could happen, but it was a valid point. How would I feel if it had? A classic case of easy to say when it's only hypothetical, but totally different when it's stark reality. I thought about it carefully. The answer? – I just didn't know exactly. What I did know was that after I'd cut the offending cretin's bollocks off and pushed him into the nearest snow-blowing machine, I'd never let Sandy out of my sight again. My whole being would then be dedicated to helping, comforting and supporting her. But most of all I'd want her to know I loved her. Anything else I might feel just wouldn't matter. I explained my thoughts, and by the end she'd taken my hand.

'I haven't forgotten that neither of us may have a great deal of time left,' she reminded me. 'If so, I don't want to be standing in front of St Peter wasting valuable cloud nine smooching time arguing the toss about this. On the other hand, if you stopped sulking into your beer and got us out of here that would be better. But then, I wouldn't want to start my new lease on life with you worrying about the slut from hell. Let's just agree to adopt one of those modern US smart-ass phrases, "Get over it". You try. I'll try. *Pax vobiscum.*'

'Hell has no greater fury than a woman scorned.' A popular misquotation that most people know well. But at that moment I wondered if there was an opposite phrase: something along the lines, 'Heaven hath no greater strength than a woman loved.' If not, there should be. I was looking at a living example. In that special indefatigable way by which one human being is able to let another know that permission to approach is granted, Sandy made her position quite clear. I took her in my arms and crushed her to me with such force I almost knocked the breath out of her.

'Careful, Jerry,' she coughed. 'I might be one tough cookie, but even those lousy ones you make'll break if you try hard enough.'

But I wasn't about to let go, and if we could have stayed locked together like that forever that still wouldn't have been long enough for me. Unfortunately, in the end the ethereal imaginings of the mind are always coerced to yield by the base demands of the body. Sandy needed to visit the toilet, I had a crick in my neck and, last but not least, there was the small matter of how to escape.

Funny how things so often repeat in twos and threes. Come across one problem and you can slap a fiver on it that another's bound to crop up before you know it. For us, this was the second time in less than half a day that we'd been obliged to search for a way to break free of a confined space. With irritating predictability, no road to freedom, obvious or obscure, presented itself. Apart from the door, the only other direct connection with anywhere outside our prison was the service shaft, and that was microscopic. Not even Harry Houdini would have been able to spirit himself out of this place with or without divine intervention. It was even worse than you see in films. At least in such contrived situations there's always some hapless idiot opening the door to deliver food or medical supplies. Not for us though, the chance of clobbering someone on the head and racing off into the distance. No, we just had to have a bloody dumbwaiter.

At the end of our exhaustive efforts all we'd managed to discover was that the phones didn't work but the TV did. Perhaps more into spy stories than me, Sandy decided there must be some form of surveillance system to monitor our activities. I didn't like to remind her that I was probably only checked in on a short-term basis and after I'd gone she'd be released, or so I wanted to believe. *Ergo* no need for the extra expense of secret cameras or a mike. Nevertheless, to keep my lady happy we foraged around for a while until at last by mutual consent we jacked in the search. Then, as if to taunt us by demonstrating that in fact we were being watched after all, tea and a plate of snacks materialised in the dumbwaiter.

'Ruddy marvellous!' I exclaimed. 'Well I'm pleased someone's having fun. I'm buggered if I know where they've got a camera stashed.'

'Never mind, Jerry,' Sondra insisted. 'Let's just be thankful for small mercies. The accommodation isn't half-bad, they keep feeding us and we're together. What more could you ask of a prison?'

I nodded. 'And I suppose it's free,' I joked. 'Although I'd be happy to pay twice the rack rate of the Four Seasons if I could only check out.'

'Speaking of checking out,' Sondra remarked, 'I still don't quite understand what you were getting at with all that talk of "winds of change" in the Oakridge empire. Care to elaborate for a simple country gal?'

Even though Sandy was from the rural suburbs of Philadelphia, the last thing she was was simple. Nevertheless, I suppose I had been a trifle over-poetic in my earlier commentary.

'Nothing too earth-shattering,' I announced. 'I've the strangest feeling that Greta and Co. are engineering some form of corporate restructuring in response to either a merger or take-over. It's as if they're shutting up the present shop in preparation for a grand reopening in a new location or under a new product banner. Shame really that I couldn't have got any more out of Ms. . . well, you know what I mean.'

Sondra became pensive. 'Makes you wonder what Kathy Murkett was up to as head of the UK branch office,' she mused. 'Does look like the list of names we found was her handiwork, though. Think of it. Forty-two people have served or are serving jail sentences, not one of them the actually convicted criminal. It just seems completely beyond belief.'

'A few weeks ago I'd have been the first to agree,' I replied. 'These days I simply don't know anymore. You hear about contract killings, government conspiracies and secret goings-on in the news all the time. Problem is it's so commonplace no one takes much notice. My concern now is that there actually could be all sorts of horrors going on beneath the daily exposés. It's a frightening thought.'

'Especially if what Oakridge is involved in is merely one example, and perhaps only a small one at that,' Sandy added.

For a while we fell silent. I launched another search for monitoring gadgets but without success, then, in the late afternoon with nothing else left to do, we watched TV news programmes. Nothing but war, disaster and mayhem were reported, leaving me even more depressed than before.

The experience did, however, yield one result: a renewed debate about the relevance or otherwise of our old friends, Gog and Magog. Sondra had already highlighted some of the legends surrounding these figures in my living room on the night of the explosion. Up until now I had a fair recollection about some of them but was a bit hazy on the biblical tales. Listening to Sandy again it was clear there were in fact more stories about the pair than soft mick. Still, it was the religious connotations that attracted my interest, in particular the difference in concepts to be found. In Revelations, Gog and Magog are described as two malevolent forces under the control of Satan released upon the earth prior to its destruction. On the other hand, in Ezekiel, Gog is a prince and Magog the land of his origins.

'Sounds to me like the usual hocus-pocus that surrounds legends,' I piped up as the discussion began to falter. 'A thousand versions and probably none of them based on fact. If you ask me, it's just a ploy by crafty historians to keep you all gainfully employed. Oh dear, getting short on government grants. Let's reinterpret the odd legend and convince everyone that a few more decades of research will reveal the lost secrets of medieval jockstraps.'

Sondra frowned. It was then I noticed the time. To my surprise our conclusion-less jawing session on G and M had taken us well into the evening. Dinner arrived, was consumed and returned. I felt so strange. Every few minutes I had to contend with a handful of vividly differing emotions all ducking and weaving, each determined to sneak by my defences and seize control. Hope, fear, optimism, pessimism, occasionally despair. Why couldn't they annoy each other or perhaps just talk amongst themselves quietly – anything, but leave me alone. Eventually we agreed to turn in, try to get some sleep and hope that a miracle or two would gestate overnight ready to burst forth in the morning and whisk us to safety.

With a certain degree of clumsiness, we each gravitated to our own oversized bed and lay down. I switched off the lights, said goodnight and began staring at the dark ceiling.

After five minutes, I'd had enough. I rolled to the edge of my bed, only to find that Sandy had beaten me to it.

'Your place or mine?' she whispered.

Her place sounded good, so I joined her under the sheets for some extensive cuddling. Probably because I'm a complete moron, it didn't occur to me that a time would come when I'd have to decide either to finish what I'd started or retreat. That time came earlier than either of us expected. Hugs soon gave way to kisses, and kisses seemed quite naturally to demand the presence of caresses. Suddenly I felt my love pause. She gently released herself from my embrace, sat up and switched the light back on.

'I'm sorry if I went too far,' I apologised. 'God knows what you must think of me after last night's performance.'

Sandy gave an embarrassed smile. 'Wrong end of the stick again, Jerry,' she tried to joke. 'Still not that good at understanding we complex females, are you? Let me give you a tip for the future. If a girl invites you into her bed for a cuddle, she probably wants you to go too far.'

I looked into Sondra's eyes and there, sitting towards the back pretending it didn't want to be noticed, was the answer. 'You're worried about your upper deck, aren't you?' I smiled. 'You think I'll start to make love to you, undo your top and then freeze.'

'Clock, what the hell's an upper deck?' she complained, still trying to disguise her discomfort.

'One of Julian's more imaginative expressions for that region of a woman's anatomy above her waist,' I replied softly. 'To me that means arms, chest and head, of which the latter's the most important. The others are just there to keep it in place and to do its bidding.'

Sandy gave me a playful shove. 'You've eaten too much. A piece of carrot must've got stuck in your brain. This isn't a joking matter. It's serious.'

'Half true,' I corrected. 'It's no joking matter, but it isn't serious. If you think I'm affected by the absence of a couple of mounds of flesh which, if I remember rightly, you couldn't see anyway when you were flat on your back, man, are you in for a shock.' As I spoke I began to tickle her sides, something she used to love in our long-distant past. She started giggling and squirming about like an eel out of water.

'Bugger off, Clock, you bastard. You know I can't stand that. What about . . .' Before she could finish, I pulled her down on the bed, pushed her flat and sat on top of her.

'You were saying?' I breathed in the corniest sinister manner I could manage. 'Oh yes! What about . . . these!' As the word 'these' took flight from my lips, I ripped open Sandy's pyjama top and started avidly kissing her all over her neck, chest and stomach. 'You should know by now, men don't mind, boys don't matter,' I concluded my performance. I covered the whole area with wet smooches then joined them all together with my tongue. My partner was still screaming when I broke off the assault and leaned forward to mount a similar offensive on her lips and cheeks. Barely had I begun when the shock of a cold hand grasping my manhood pulled me up short. We looked at each other, Sandy still panting from the exertion of her laughing fit.

'Not finished down there, have we, Jerry boy?' she growled softly and sexily. 'Get down there and don't come up until the job's properly done.'

Orders received and understood, I pecked my way like a starving sparrow from mouth to neck, neck to breast and finally on to the stomach. Then, having filled her belly button with saliva – always guaranteed to provoke enhanced writhing – I pulled off her pyjama bottoms and set to work on my given task. My attentions met with immediate response, and after only a few moments exploring that most feminine of charms with my tongue, I felt her erupt in a quaking orgasm. Further treatment yielded a similar result, but a third invasion was blocked. I felt Sandy's fingers tickling my ears: another sign from the past meaning time to return to the surface for ground manoeuvres. In accordance with tradition, I rolled over, lay flat and allowed my beautiful angel to peel away my clothes and caress me with her wings. Her tender ministerings complete, she positioned herself over the monument she'd created and completed our union. As we loved I held her hands, traced the scars on her body with my fingers, and, through our inseparable gaze, convinced her of my unending love – a love I'd thought lost, found anew; never to be lost again.

We slept in each other's arms, woken twice by our bodies' unquenchable desire to be reunited. For me it was like being granted a second chance. Sandy had been returned to me and, despite the destructive force wielded by Ms White, we were still together. It's one of the strangest differences in the world – the feeling of sex with love compared to that without. I would never forget my shame. Rightly that was my burden, my penance. As for the lady in white, I could only feel pity – pity that she seemed incapable of spiritual love and therefore would never experience the true ecstasy I knew she craved.

Two more days passed without any change to our routine. We arose, washed, ate and slept. The rest of the time we loved. It was almost as it had been in my Cambridge rooms, the only difference being the absence of sunshine filtering through threadbare curtains. Our needs continued to be met, with even a change of laundry appearing on the second morning. As the hours passed I couldn't help but hope that I'd been granted a reprieve: that the ordeal would soon be over. Sandy too, I could sense, was gradually becoming more optimistic.

Towards the end of the third day I idly switched on the TV, seeking to catch the news. During the course of my habitual channel-surfing the familiar sight of King's College blazoned across the screen caught my attention. I backtracked as quickly as possible and discovered that the picture was being broadcast by the BBC World channel.

'Sweetheart,' I called, 'there's something on about Cambridge.'

As Sandy joined me, I clicked off the mute setting and listened. To my horror, a vaguely familiar face and an all-too-familiar name popped onto the screen accompanied by the announcer's words, 'Found dead, possibly murdered'.

'Oh God, no!' I cried. 'They finally got to Natalie.'

Unfortunately I must have joined the report towards its conclusion, as almost immediately the topic changed. Frantically, I tried all other available stations but, in the end, had to wait half an hour before the BBC report was repeated. In fact the full piece contained precious little more than we'd already heard. In essence, the badly charred remains of a young woman believed to be one Natalie McCarthy had been recovered from a burnt-out second-floor flat not far from Robinson College. Police were treating the death as very suspicious. It was another terrible shock. Natalie had repeatedly stated that she didn't expect to survive, but I suppose I just chose to ignore her. Now she was dead. Perhaps only a week after Julian had saved her, she'd finally suffered the fate originally planned for her. Sandy did her best to console me, but I felt wretched. If only I'd gone after her when she ran away. If only I'd insisted on tracing her immediately instead of blithely deciding that if she needed help she knew where to find it. If only, if only . . .

Utilising our very handy hot-beverage making facility graciously provided by our attentive hosts, my concerned partner plied me with tea until I began to come round. For a while she let me ramble on about what I should and shouldn't have done, then asked if I'd mind entertaining a couple of points she'd picked up on about this most terrible of affairs.

'Sure,' I said. 'Sorry to go on, but I can't help feeling . . . well, you've already heard it ten times in the last five minutes. What's caught your attention?'

'Might not be much,' she began, 'but remember, we believed that Natalie had been hastily done up to look like Kathy Murkett. Our understanding was that the poor girl's body would be burned after death, thus obliterating any remaining telltale signs that she wasn't actually Kathy. Odd, therefore, that despite the body being badly burnt, the report named Natalie and showed a photo of how she must have looked before the plastic surgeons got to work.'

The lady had a point. Caught in the midst of an emotional torrent, my mind had simply focused on three words – Natalie, burned, dead. I realised that I'd still been thinking of Kathy and had dismissed the photograph since it was clearly out of date and of poor quality. The evidence, however, now suggested a drastic change of plan.

'You're right!' I exclaimed. 'What could've happened to force them to reverse everything?' I started to ruminate over this bizarre occurrence, but then remembered that Sandy had used the phrase 'a couple of points'. I asked her about number two.

'The second thing's pretty insignificant, but still it doesn't quite fit,' she replied. 'Basically, why let us see this? They've given us a TV so they know we'll come across the report sooner or later. What's the deal?'

This observation I found, in fact, to be more worrying than the first. It was relatively easy for me to dredge up a whole series of scenarios that were all equally plausible and equally unsavoury. Given that we'd had enough depressing talk for one day, though, I let it go with a noncommittal, 'Could be something or nothing, but I'll give it some thought anyway,' then changed the subject.

For the next few hours we kept the TV constantly on. Mostly we stuck with the BBC, but occasionally I checked to see if CNN or other major US broadcasters were running the story. It wasn't very likely, but the suspicious death of a girl in Cambridge might just have attracted the odd programmer's interest. No more details were released until the end of the midnight bulletin, when the announcer indicated that he'd just received some additional details on the McCarthy case. Two new photographs were displayed – a man and a woman. The newsreader's words echoed in my ears. 'Being sought by police for questioning.' The photographs? Dr Jeremiah Orville Clock and Professor Sondra Elise Warwick.

'Shit! It's a set-up,' I hissed. 'That's what all this's been about. The bastards stuck us on ice while they rearranged the plan, killed the girl, then fitted us up like premier chumps.'

Sondra grabbed my arm. 'Jerry, I know what it looks like, but I've a nagging feeling that there's something missed out: something we don't know yet.'

Even as a child I came to respect female intuition. I often cursed it; I always doubted it, but I also found it paid to heed it. Since Sandy was no ordinary woman, her premonitions and hunches usually turned out to be solid gold fact. In this case I genuinely hoped she was right, for the situation wasn't looking good at all. Surely it couldn't possibly get any worse . . .

That night neither of us slept a wink. Most of the time was spent slurping back gallons of disgusting hot chocolate made up from sachets. We went over and over a thousand scenarios, trying to work out what Greta Oakridge was planning. As the alarm started to cough out its irritating electronic pulse to announce seven-thirty, we were totally exhausted. No further news had been forthcoming, and our best idea? We'd both turn up dead somewhere in the desert with notes pinned to our chests citing Natalie's murder as the reason for our suicide pact.

At eight o'clock breakfast arrived, so at least they were still feeding us. Trouble was, what for? I was definitely beginning to feel like a turkey being fattened up for Christmas.

It wasn't until after lunch that the content of the news bulletin changed. I should have known it was bad news as soon as I realised the story had been moved from fifth to second place in the running order. As luck would have it, I was in the bathroom when it started. I rushed out in response to Sandy's call just in time to catch the intro and first story. Then it came – perhaps the most extraordinary experience of my life. First a picture of Natalie, then our photographs, and finally video footage of Professor Warwick and myself, hands cuffed together, being escorted into a police van.

'Jesus, Jerry!' Sandy exclaimed in astonishment. 'We've been arrested on suspicion of murder.'

It was a neat trick, perhaps the neatest yet. In all the hours we'd spent struggling to figure out what was going on, neither of us had come anywhere close to this baby. However, at least one thing was certain. My companion hadn't lost her touch when it came to premonitions. I couldn't decide what to feel for the best. Should we be honoured that so much trouble had been taken on our behalf, or should we prepare ourselves for imminent execution now that, to all intents and purposes, we no longer existed? Finally, I knew how the lead character must have felt in *Invasion of the Body Snatchers* – and I didn't like it one bit.

Caught unawares, neither of us had time to snatch a good view of the poor buggers who'd been suckered into acting as our doubles. Strangely, that particular topic afforded us the only light-hearted moment of the day. After fifteen minutes of intense discussion, I suddenly realised that over half the time had been spent worrying about how we looked being herded into the Black Maria.

It wasn't much after that I noticed Sandy was looking tired. However, as I tried to persuade her to lie down for a while I realised I didn't feel too clever myself . . .

I half-awoke in total darkness, a sledgehammer pounding out a catchy little number in the centre of my brain. It was stiflingly hot, and even though I felt I was lying on top of the bed, it was difficult to move. I raised my head, only to have it crash into something soft yet hard. Now I was fully awake.

'Christ above!' I called out. 'Where the hell am I?' The sound of my voice came back to me muffled. I tried to move, turn, bend my legs, but all actions were blocked by the same padded surface my head had met. I was in a coffin.

Jesus God, a coffin. I yelled, screamed, smashed against the sides and lid, all with the fury of ten men, but to no avail. My heart was beating out of control. Fear had wiped away all trace of rational thought. I was in free-fall and the ground was coming up at an incredible rate of knots. Suddenly hit by a momentary wave of claustrophobia, I started gulping for air. Involuntary reactions were sparking off throughout my body. Teeth clenched, eyes closed, fingernails biting into the palms of my hands, electric shocks zigzagged up and down my spine. The ground seemed almost upon me when, from somewhere in my soul, a message managed to break through the chaos and reach my brain. Sandy – was she okay, hurt, nearby, in another coffin? A mushroom cloud of questions and concerns about my precious lady shattered the glass on my fail-safe mechanism and a dozen parachutes released, unfurled and guided me gently to safety.

Gradually I collected my splintered wits together and damage control kicked in. Logic in part restored, I began to assess my situation item by item. A re-examination of my environment confirmed that I was in a box, and although inexperienced when it came to spending time in such containers, I was reasonably sure it was a coffin. I was alive. How was I sure? Well, as far as I knew or in fact hoped, dead people didn't have headaches, aching joints or have to keep breathing. This conclusion brought me to the issue of air. Although not in plentiful supply, I had the impression that it was percolating through the structure. I was able to breathe and, assuming I'd been incarcerated for a reasonable time, the conclusion must be that there were air holes somewhere. At least this observation gave some cause for optimism. I wasn't dead, I was uninjured, and I had air – for the moment that would have to do.

Next item on the agenda was to construct a catalogue of events. Things were still far from clear, but at a best guess the lunch must have been drugged. A little amateur detective work in the form of self-analysis revealed that I didn't feel hungry, so it was reasonable to assume that no more than four hours had elapsed. With regard to why circumstances had changed after so many days of inactivity? Odds-on favourite – confirmation of our, or at least our lookalikes', arrest. Now I could concentrate on my main concern – Sondra.

I tried calling out, but there was no reply. Knocking and kicking the top and sides of my sarcophagus similarly yielded no result. What else could I do to make myself heard in case my poor love was nearby and in similar circumstances? I couldn't think. But then what if . . . ? What if there was an air vent either in the lid or on the side of the coffin around about the region of my head? If I could rip away part of the lining, there may be a chance I could locate the spot by touch. There may even be a source of light.

The operation proved far more difficult than I'd imagined. Either my strength was giving out with old age, or – just my luck – I'd copped for a top-of-the-range last resting-place. As it happened, my luck had been boxed in with me. Once I'd managed to pull away a handful of material above my face, I could feel the wooden lid and, hey presto, a small hole covered by some sort of metal filter. A definite result, I thought, but only half my wish was granted. No light.

I'd literally just completed my first stab at interior decorating when in the distance I heard a faint moan. The sound faded then returned with greater clarity. Suddenly a stifled scream set my heart racing again.

'Sandy!' I yelled. 'Sandy, is that you? Don't be frightened, love. It's me, Jerry. I'm with you.'

The screaming continued: more frantic, more desperate by the second. Without doubt Sondra had been condemned to the same horrendous fate as I.

I called out again and again but couldn't make myself heard.

On and on: the hysterical cries seemed set to last forever. It tortured the very core of my soul to think of my sweet love terrified out of her wits. Another memory from the past jumped to the fore. Sandy had suffered from claustro-

263

phobia – not seriously, but confinement in a coffin would hardly prove therapeutic.

I doggedly persisted in my efforts to make her hear me, but still without success. As a last resort I attempted to time my calls to match the fleeting moments when she was forced to breathe. More agonising seconds of failure goose-stepped by, then finally there was a pause. I bellowed out her name repeatedly, almost like a football chant. At last I heard a reply. Weak, frightened, exhausted, but it was definitely a response. One word.

'Jerry?'

Endeavouring to be as clear and succinct as possible, I reassured her; tried to guide her to a calmer state. Step-by-step I made progress. At last she was ready to receive instructions on how to access her own air vent to improve the quality of our communication.

'What are they going to do, Jerry?' Sandy's trembling voice drove me wild, charging me with an overwhelming urge to smash the woodwork restraining me into a million splinters. Alas, the strength of Superman was not mine to command. All I had was the power of words.

'It's okay, sweetheart,' I called. 'Just think, if they wanted us dead or were still contemplating killing us, they wouldn't waste time sticking us in air-conditioned coffins. We've probably been packaged up so we can be transported elsewhere without being seen.'

There was no reply. Chances were that normal conversation wouldn't be enough to combat Sandy's fears and phobia. I urgently needed to devise a different strategy – very urgently. Sifting through my memories, one possibility courteously skipped into the spotlight. The Tarot. My interest in these ancient cards had fascinated Sondra. She'd enjoyed the fortune-telling sessions I occasionally laid on for her, but more importantly the use of the cards as an aid to meditation never failed to capture her imagination. It was worth a try . . .

To my relief I received a positive response to my proposal, so I gave it my best shot.

'First of all, focus on your breathing,' I instructed. 'Do what you can to relax. Breathe deeply, rhythmically, then close your eyes and think of your favourite card.'

'The magician,' came the slightly stronger reply.

'Okay, the first card of the Major Arcana.' It was a good choice. 'Now, with an image of the card fixed firmly in your mind, minimise your breathing rate and let the tension flow away through your extremities,' I encouraged. 'Concentrate on your feet first, then imagine all stress, all anxiety, draining away from each part of your body in turn. Legs, thighs, stomach, chest, arms, then finally the neck and head.' I waited two or three minutes, listening intently for any sounds that might indicate my directions were proving difficult to achieve, but all seemed well.

'If you're ready to begin,' I ventured. 'Let the scene depicted on the card fill your mind and tell me what you see. Just like we used to practise.'

Sandy confirmed she was ready. 'A young man,' she began. 'Strong, handsome: holding a flaming wand in his right hand. He's got long black hair. It looks like it's being tossed by the wind. Above his head there's an infinity symbol and on a table in front of him, four objects: a coin, sword, baton, and a cup. The four suits of the Minor Arcana. By his feet I can see flowers growing – lilies and roses, I think.'

'Anything else?' I asked as softly as I could, but still loud enough to be audible.

'Yes,' came the considered acknowledgement. 'The Magician's wearing a large red cloak fastened across his chest by two white cords. And he's pointing to the table, perhaps towards the coin symbol, but it's not clear.'

It was a very good description and, if I wasn't mistaken, accurately described the card from one of my early 1970s sets.

For those inclined to believe in the Tarot, the Magician was a positive card. It professed power through knowledge, marvels achieved through skill, and reflected a powerful male influence. All I could hope was that Sandy would

265

interpret the image in the same way, perhaps even associate it with me – if that wasn't being too arrogant. As long as she'd forgotten that, when inverted, the Magician becomes a trickster who wrongly applies his skills, we'd be fine.

Description complete, I moved on to the last and most important stage of the meditative process. 'Allow yourself to cautiously enter the scene before you, taking great care not to disturb the surroundings or attract attention. Then, once you're inside, find yourself a comfortable place to sit and watch what happens. Don't forget, if you tire or want to stop, follow the reverse process, stage by stage. I'll be here waiting for you when you get back.' It was a daft thing to say, but it was the only comforting words I could think of . . .

My promise, however, was ill chosen. No sooner had I decided to adopt my own advice and meditate using the Tarot than I heard a door open and footsteps. I experienced a slight rocking motion, sensed I was being lifted, then to my horror realised I was moving: being wheeled away. I called out, but the door slammed shut. Had Sandy heard me? Was it the tail end of her cry I could hear ringing in my ears or just wishful thinking? I couldn't be sure. God help me, I couldn't be sure.

15

Northern Lights

'Well, fuck me with a Portuguese banana. If it isn't Jeremiah Orville Clock in the flesh.' Despite the crude nature of the greeting, the voice was unmistakable – Cher. It was dark, but as I looked about me bewildered and confused, the lights came on. Incredible! The Way We Were Club. For some reason I'd been taken back there. But why? Seated alone at one of the tables not too far from the dance floor, I caught a glimpse of the lady in question approaching from the wings.

'Jerry boy,' she continued, 'where the fucky-ducky have ya been? Me and Marilyn have been wearin' our butts off waitin' for ya to turn up.'

Now I could see her clearly, dressed in the same get-up as when last we met, she looked less convincing than I remembered. It was as if the spirit of Cher she'd managed to coin from somewhere had completely drained away. Certainly she looked like my idol, but she was no longer 'her'.

Before I could respond, Marilyn appeared on the stage then sat on its edge, her legs dangling into the small defunct orchestra pit. 'Hi, poopsy,' she purred. 'Marilyn's missed ya too. Ya've not been holed up in some two-bit motel with my little Virgin, have ya now, fucking her brains out like a naughty boy? Cos if so, I'm sad to say the girl's probably given ya one mean mother dose of the clap – ouch!'

The whole scene was extraordinary, almost unreal. I felt reasonably okay. A tad woolly-headed maybe, but nothing too serious. At least I was out of the coffin and somehow back in my own suit. Question was, where was Sandy? I enquired of my two hosts, but they just looked at each other and exchanged knowing smiles.

Noticing that I was continuing to regard my surroundings, Cher sat beside me and held my arm. 'No need to worry, sweetness, we're all alone. No one's goin' to find out yer little secret. Now I've got good news for ya. I told my friends about what ya want and they've decided to help.'

I gave a strained smile. 'That's great. Thanks very much,' I said. 'When do I get to meet them and where?'

Cher stood up and slinked over to Marilyn.

'No problem, lover boy. For five hundred bucks we come to you.' Stumbling to my feet, I spun around to face the new speaker then almost fell to the floor. The one person I hadn't expected or wished to meet again – Ms White. She advanced a few steps and, as if following on a lead, the space she'd just occupied was immediately filled by the unmistakable Reverend Black. My heart was already in my throat and, try as I might, I couldn't speak. Apparently there was no escaping these two characters that, like malevolent shadows, seemed bound to dog my every move.

The shock of their dramatic appearance had momentarily caused me to shut down most of my sensory perceptions. As these returned, I realised that the pair no longer wore their familiar uniforms of black and white, but were dressed in deep red. It came as no surprise that the change in colour detracted nothing from Ms White's devastating appearance, but the Reverend – well, red just wasn't him. If anything he now looked more like a flamboyant Chicago boxing promoter, or even a clown, than a sombre man of the cloth. Either way, his new outfit had no impact on the way he looked at me. As in Greta Oakridge's office, I still had the strong impression that he was just waiting for an excuse to turn me into pâté.

'We just can't seem to avoid bumping into one another, can we, Dr Clock?' Ms White said, sitting herself at my table. 'I have to admit I was very surprised to learn you were in the market for a sex change. Why not sit down and tell me

268

all about it? I'm sure we'll be able to accommodate you in one way or another.'

'What're you talking about?' I snapped, maintaining my standing position. 'This your idea of a joke?'

Ms White looked genuinely shocked: a sight which derailed my line of attack. 'Oh, I'm sorry,' she exclaimed. 'But my associates told me they were quite convinced of your sincerity. So you didn't give Cher five hundred dollars to make preliminary enquiries on your behalf?'

'Yes,' I admitted stupidly. 'I gave her five hundred dollars, but it was only a ploy. At the time we were trying to trace doctors who might have been involved . . .' Here I hesitated, suddenly unsure of how to describe the situation.

'Involved?' Ms White begged the question. 'Involved in what? Helping people perhaps, giving them new lives, granting them a chance to start over? Any of those ring a bell? I think you've been standing on your brains too long. Sit down here and give them a well-deserved rest.'

I was about to refuse when I noticed that the Reverend had moved. A second later I found out where – behind me. Before I could react I felt a metal cable wrapping around my neck – the infamous steel whip. It snapped closed in an instant, choking the air from my windpipe. Suddenly the end was pulled even tighter but then yanked downwards, forcing me to drop to my knees. As I gagged, my face inches from Ms White's knees, the pressure released and the cord slid away from my neck like a snake slithering back to its lair.

'Much better,' Ms White decreed. 'Now then, down to business. Five hundred dollars isn't much, granted; but since it's you I think I'll be able to offer you a very reasonable deal.'

'Why are you still going on about this?' I coughed. 'Another one of your torture routines, is it?'

At that moment Cher interrupted. 'Hey, just a minute,' she cried, evidently not too pleased, 'it cost me over five thousand bucks to have my face done and another two thousand for my ass. Five hundred's not enough for a circumcision. I'm fucked if he's goin' to get the works for that.'

At that, the Reverend, whip in hand, sauntered over to the two ladies and entered into a war of whispers. Not surprisingly, the Reverend's contribution was minimal, but after several exchanges the matter was evidently resolved.

'Okay,' Marilyn concluded. 'We've got the picture, and it's cool. Just make sure he doesn't get any fancy stuff. I hate it when you smart-ass doctors go dealing out freebies.'

The former lady in white nodded her head. 'Thank you so much, girls, for your understanding,' she remarked sarcastically.

'Oh well, suck my cock with those red ruby lips,' Cher responded indignantly before flinching under the Reverend's glare.

'Look,' I said, scrambling onto a seat, 'you've had your fun. I'm confused, frightened, not to mention well and truly beaten. You win. Just take me back to Sondra and then, if you're going to do away with us, just do it.'

Ms White leaned closer to me and stroked my face. 'Don't worry, lover boy,' she said softly, as if not wishing her companions to hear. 'Take no notice of them. You'll get good value for money.'

'Oh shit!' I exclaimed. 'Give it a rest, for God's sake. You're not even a plastic surgeon.'

Ms White reacted as if gravely offended. 'Well that's as maybe, Dr Clock, but I've had lots of practice, and I'll prove it. Reverend!'

I looked around just in time to see the big man's huge hands descending on my shoulders. He hauled me to my feet, spun me around, then with a blow from his forehead knocked me senseless.

I came to lying face-up, strapped to a small square table. My head and legs dangled over the edges while my arms had somehow been tethered beneath its surface. The Reverend stood at my side, apparently cleaning his metal whip, occasionally pausing to make sure I wasn't trying to wriggle free. By the bar I could just make out the three ladies. Ms White had donned a surgeon's coat and mask while Cher and Marilyn, drafted in as assistants, were squabbling over who should wear the one nurse's hat they had between them. Their preparations complete, they joined the Reverend and all four began to eye me as if I was a frog about to be dissected. My analogy was aptly chosen.

'Ready, Dr Clock?' Ms White asked.

'Ready for what, you mad bitch?' I cried. 'Let me go. Stop all this play-acting. I'm not impressed.'

'Oh, I think you will be,' came the excited reply. 'After much debate I've agreed that the fee you've already paid, taking into account commission for Cher and Marilyn, comes to two hundred dollars. That being the case, we'll do the operation here. That way you'll save on hospital charges. The Reverend's kindly agreed to act as anaesthetist, and although these two ladies only have limited nursing experience they've agreed to assist me. So I think that's all. Oh silly me! I haven't discussed what we're going to do yet.'

I was now terrified. It seemed as though I was in the hands of a group of insane-asylum escapees. I'd no clue what their objective was, but if it was merely to have fun scaring me shitless, they were doing a great job. Unable to move let alone struggle, all I could do was yell. For what seemed like minutes my four spectators appeared mesmerised, listening to me squeal. Finally, the Reverend roughly stuffed a course woollen sock in my mouth. It tasted and smelt foul, causing me to gag and choke.

As if no time had elapsed since she last spoke, Ms White took up where she'd left off. 'Under the circumstances I think it's best if we focus on the essentials,' she explained clinically. 'To start with I'll make a few modifications around the eyes, move on to the neck, then I'll remove your penis and testicles. How's that sound?'

My head filled with shrieking, my eyes bulged. I shook my head frantically from side to side, trying to dislodge the revolting sock from my mouth, but it was hopeless; everything was hopeless. A wave of panic gripped my straining heart then squeezed it as I saw the Reverend step back. He raised his arm. The whip unfurled. I saw the lash, sensed the tip hurling towards me. Crack!

Something was pressing on my eyes. It felt like moistened lint, but it was difficult to say. My brain instructed my hand to check the situation out, but there was no response. In fact when I thought about it, I couldn't sense my hands, arms, or any other part of my body. Suddenly the grotesque image of Ms White and her three demonic accomplices unfolded before me. Oh my God, what had they done to me? The feeling was indescribable. Terrified by the thought of what horrific mutilation I'd suffered yet unable to confirm it by touch, was worse than being roasted alive. An involuntary moan left my larynx, but my mouth remained closed like a steel trap. So far the only consolation I had was that the filthy woollen sock was gone, as were its taste and smell. Not much under the circumstances, but for some inexplicable reason it stopped my mind from going belly-up. Time had lost all meaning. With what was left of my body unable to make its presence felt, I had the notion that my situation must be akin to being in a sensory-deprivation tank. All I needed now were a few healthy hallucinations and I'd have experienced the full treatment free of charge.

Gradually I became aware of feeling thirsty. The condition worsened until my mouth was bone dry and my throat was like the inside of a vacuum-cleaner hose. Without realising I called out, but this time I heard my voice. I could speak again. In a way, I didn't really expect anyone to come. Why should they? After my illegal operation, where would I have been taken? To a hospital, a clinic, a doctor? None seemed very likely or probable. Nevertheless, although I was still missing two of my five senses, I had the unaccountable impression that I was somewhere safe and being cared for. I called again.

'Well, well, well, you're finally back with us then, Dr Clock. That's good, very good.'

The joy of hearing another human voice – a friendly female voice and one definitely not belonging to Ms White – was beyond description.

'Who are you?' I croaked. 'Where am I? What happened?'

'Oh now, ya don't want to go askin' a whole lotta fool questions soon as ya wake up. Rest's what ya need most at present. Questions can wait till later. Expect y'all be needin' a drink. There ya go.'

To my relief I felt a straw poked between my lips. For a moment I hesitated, wondering whether or not it was safe to take anything on trust. It was another fool question. I wasn't exactly in a position to check or analyse anything. This was definitely a case of 'beggars can't be choosers', and I was without question the most desperate of beggars. Drawing the cool liquid into my mouth, I was relieved to discover it was a kind of mixed-fruit cordial. Only a few sips were granted me, but it was enough to keep me attached to my life's thread. I began to ask more questions but received no answer. Either the angel of mercy was ignoring me or had left. Hopefully, if the latter case then I had reason to hope that a doctor – a properly qualified physician – would be on his way to see me soon.

Yet it was not to be. I waited and waited but no doctor, nurse or other soul came to relieve my anguish or allay my fears. Time once again turned against me for reasons I couldn't imagine, determined to be my enemy. At length I drifted into a tormented doze, which in turn evolved into a restless sleep. Awakened by the vivid reality of a pitiless nightmare, I endeavoured to reassess the measure of my condition. Imperceptible changes there might have been, but to all intents and purposes I was still an anxious spirit trapped in a lifeless shell.

When even hope seemed on the verge of abandoning me, the angel returned to quench my burning thirst. I pleaded for information: news of Sandy, my condition and finally just to know the date. Again I was condemned to be left ignorant and alone. On the third visit the voice was different. Still female, still caring, but this time not American: more probably Central European. I spouted off my standard series of questions, already resigned to receive empty promises or evasion as my only reply. But not so.

'You must be patient, Dr Clock,' the voice insisted. 'You've been very ill. The fire nearly claimed your life, you know. It's a true miracle that the doctors were able to save you. However, it won't be long before you're physically well, then I'm sure your mind will heal just as quickly.'

Fire, injury, mental illness. What on God's earth was the woman talking about? If I'd any physical ailments they could only have been caused by Ms White. Surely there must be some mistake. Forced to dance with despair, I did my best not to stumble. I called out to Sandy again and again, but received only the echo of my own voice by way of reply. Purgatory, damnation, fire and brimstone – I began to regard these as mere trifles compared to what I was suffering. Inch by inch I was being manoeuvred into praying for death. Heaven, hell – it didn't matter. If only I knew that Sandy was free and well, my soul was available at a knockdown, rock-bottom price to the first bidder.

'Dr Clock, isn't it?' A young girl's voice nudged me from my dreamless sleep. 'What a surprise. I didn't expect to see you here.'

I opened my eyes to find myself sitting in a wheelchair in a darkened room. It took a handful of seconds more before I suddenly appreciated the change to my circumstances. Although unable to rise, I could see, feel, move. A wave of joy swelled through me like a spring tide. Then I remembered – Ms White, the operation. Perhaps as any man would, I checked my genitals first. Still there, thank heaven. Then my face. Much harder to tell if there was anything untoward. Maybe a dream, I speculated after my initial elation. Perhaps, but at least it was my first experience of anything other than horror, abandonment and fear that I could remember in recent times. Why not just take it for what it was? If, in a moment, it disappeared in a cloud of vapour, then so be it. I would have a memory to feed my starving hope and, if sufficient remained, a small present for my beleaguered heart.

I looked about me to locate the speaker but could detect no one.

'Over here by the window,' the voice rang out.

Given the poor light, the existence of a window seemed unlikely, but as I repeated my survey I caught sight of a shadowy figure seated with a faint light at their back. I wheeled myself closer until the face of the creature became visible. It was a girl: a youngish girl, sitting in a straight-backed wooden chair, holding a large drawing pad. From my new position I could see now that behind her there was a window, but external shutters had been closed to exclude most of the light. Despite the weakly lit conditions, the girl's face became quite clear as my eyes grew accustomed to the dark. A pretty lass, she had long auburn hair, full cheeks and a beautiful smile. Inhibited by my less-than-perfect colour sight under darkened conditions, I was unable to determine the colour of her eyes, but I had the impression they were blue. Given her general appearance and the presence of the pad, I took a chance.

'Elena?' I asked gently. 'Elena Pascal?'

'That's right, doctor,' came the enthusiastic reply. 'But I'm surprised you recognise me.'

'Yes, to be honest I wasn't sure,' I confessed. 'When I last saw you, you weren't . . .'

'Well,' Elena finished my sentence. 'I know, but I'm all right at the moment.'

'At the moment'. It was an odd turn of phrase, but then 'odd' was rapidly becoming the all-too-familiar norm for me. Best not to question, I decided.

'Do you know where we are?' I asked hopefully.

'Heaven, I think,' the girl replied. 'Well, that's as soon as they come to open the shutters.'

Goodbye reality, I mused. It seemed like another great opportunity to play 'guess the scenario'. Were we in heaven? Was I insane? Was this a dream? A fascinating puzzle on any other occasion, but I was weary of living in a surreal universe. This particular environment was comfortable enough, and perhaps if the shutters were removed it could become positively pleasant. Since there seemed to be no other sparkling alternatives on offer, might as well bide my time here, I concluded.

Elena put her hand out towards me then pulled my chair closer. 'Would you like to see some more of my drawings?' she offered.

'That's very kind,' I replied. 'I'd be honoured.'

Just to add an extra quirk to the situation, the pictures were exactly the same. The fascinating thing on this viewing, however, was that the girl began to describe their meaning.

'This is me when I worked at the Gogmagog Video shop in Cambridge,' she explained to my very great interest. 'Standing next to me is Ms Murkett. She was the manager. I liked working at the shop, but I did something very bad and had to be punished.'

'Can you tell me what?' I asked, unable to guess the deed from the pictures.

Elena looked embarrassed and seemed reluctant to go on, but unexpectedly decided to do so. 'I found out information about Ms Murkett's other work, helping people to change places,' she confessed. 'When I asked for money not to tell, she was sad and said I'd have to leave.'

'And did you?' I enquired.

'Greedy people like me eventually reap their own reward. That's what Ms Murkett warned me when I wouldn't listen to her,' she explained. 'She was very patient and understanding. It was all my fault. I just wouldn't let it drop. Then one day . . .'

'One day you met Ms White and Reverend Black,' I

interrupted as she turned to the next drawing, featuring their crude images.

'Yes,' came her forlorn reply. 'After that many things happened to me. I visited strange places, met unusual people, behaved improperly. In the end I became sick and had to spend a long time in hospital.'

I took her hand and held it as she closed the drawing book. Much of her story came as no surprise. Based on what I'd gleaned from Natalie and a variety of other sources, the pieces of this pitiful tale easily slotted into place. The only aspect of my encounter with Ms Pascal so far that troubled me was her manner of speech. She spoke like a naïve teenager rather than the young woman she was. Whether this was a manifestation of her mental condition, my imagination or the fact that none of this was real, didn't warrant closer scrutiny.

After a short rest, I enquired about Natalie. This part of our conversation was perhaps the happiest for both of us. Elena obviously had a deep love and affection for her partner. They'd been well matched, and during the all-too-few years fate had allowed them to be together there had been much joy. As far as I could tell Elena knew nothing of what had become of her companion. She clearly remembered sneaking out a letter to her, and I had a sense she knew Natalie had travelled to the US to find her, but no more than that. Unfortunately, the mystery of why Natalie had fallen prey to the invisible dark forces that had stalked the Gellar Institute remained unsolved. My only thought was that the girl's arrival might have been taken as evidence of potential danger, another blackmail attempt or just a loose end that had to be tied up. Even Greta Oakridge and Ms White had admitted to misunderstandings within their ranks and, as I knew only too well from my own management experiences, that inevitably led to mistakes. With Natalie gone and the likely perpetrators of the crime doubtless scattered to the four winds, it now seemed as if the truth would remain skulking in the world's great library of the unknown forever.

'I'm afraid it's time for me to go,' Elena announced quietly. 'Thank you for coming. I've enjoyed talking to you. I hope you're soon well again.'

Unable to persuade my companion to stay longer, I watched silently as she gingerly rose from her seat and shambled across the room into the parading shadows. Once her form had disappeared, I heard her voice like a distant echo calling to me.

'Don't worry. You won't be lonely. My friend will come shortly. She'll keep you company till it's time to go.'

Time for her to go, time for me to go, or yet another riddle? I debated.

Left to my own devices, I decided to explore my shaded surroundings. Presumably there had to be a door through which Elena and I had arrived, and perhaps a second through which she'd just left. I wheeled myself away from the window to embark upon my quest. Strangely, the intensity of the darkness dramatically increased with every yard I travelled. Ahead, total blackness awaited me, beckoning yet intimidating. It was a direct enough message and one I didn't feel confident enough to ignore – go back. Thwarted before I'd even got started, I swivelled around and, using the faint light framing the window as a beacon, rolled back to my original spot. As I approached, the sound of a small bell tinkling distracted my attention. I affected a three-hundred-and-sixty-degree turn in my chair, but could see nothing.

'You seem lost, Dr Clock,' the voice of an Asian-sounding girl came from behind me.

Again I launched into a circular sweep of the room, but before I'd reached mid-turn I felt someone grasp the back of my chair and begin wheeling me away from the window.

'Who are you?' I exclaimed, alarmed and feeling acutely vulnerable.

'Indira,' the voice replied. 'But you only know me as Rika.'

Restricted by the chair and hampered by the growing darkness, I was unable to confirm the speaker's claim. We seemed to travel for an inordinate amount of time: far longer even than if we'd circumnavigated the Albert Hall. Suddenly a swathe of bright sunlight caused me to shield my eyes. The feel and smell of fresh air filled my nostrils and, as I grew accustomed to the brilliance, I realised we were in a small garden.

I was parked near an oval cedarwood table and two chairs then, at last, my unsolicited helper walked into view. For a moment she stood before me, resplendent in a breathtaking green and blue sari patterned with gold and silver. Her face, all trace of blemish vanquished, was perfect, and as her surrogate name had suggested to me she did indeed look every bit an Indian princess. She smiled, bowed in traditional Indian style, then took up one of the seats.

'Where is this place?' I asked, looking about.

'It's my secret garden,' Indira revealed. 'I spend much of my time here. Quite beautiful, isn't it? Perhaps you'd care for tea while we chat.'

I nodded in the affirmative, still struggling to come to terms with my new change of scene.

From a pocket concealed within her dress, my refined hostess produced a finger bell and gently rang it. The sound was the same as I'd heard announcing her arrival. It possessed a sweet, peaceful quality: highly musical, like the refrain you'd expect bluebells to make if they had the ability to ring. Presently an old gentleman materialised, carefully supporting a long silver tea tray. A Sikh military officer, I surmised; the man acquitted his duty then retired without speaking a word.

'Please accept my apologies,' Indira began while arranging the cups and saucers. 'When you came to see me, I wasn't able to speak. My rudeness was inexcusable, but I found myself in a difficult situation.'

With the arrival of the tea I'd taken advantage of the interruption to complete my cursory examination of the garden and the young lady entertaining me. In a peculiar way I felt they were one and the same. The garden was walled with bricks of considerable age. Rare and more traditional flowers, shrubs and plants lined the perimeter in a glorious celebration of colour and delicate fragrances. A handful of young oak and yew trees had been planted at strategic points along the edge of an immaculately kept lawn which sparkled in the sunlight. A mood of serenity – majesty even – drifted through the air, filling me with the strangest conviction. It was as if this idyllic sanctuary itself had created Indira from its essence to reside within its protective walls so it could tend to her every need. In return, the garden thrived and flourished, nurtured by the presence of her boundless grace and beauty.

'No need to apologise,' I finally replied. 'Your difficulty was obvious to me. I only wish I'd been able to help you in some way.'

'Ah, but you did,' the girl insisted. 'Sharni – that's the little doll you saw me holding – and I are most grateful. After you left we suddenly found ourselves transported away from the horrible grey and shadowy world that had enslaved us, to this forgotten corner of Utopia.'

We paused to sip the tea: a delicious milky concoction highly flavoured with just a hint of sweetness, quite unlike anything I'd previously experienced. When I'd finished, Indira refilled my cup then regarded me as if trying to decide something about my purpose.

'I fear you must leave soon,' she said finally. 'And you have yet to hear my story.' Without waiting for my response, she recounted her sad tale. 'I'm afraid I was a most unruly youth,' she confessed. 'I rebelled against my family, my traditions and my religion. Eventually my father became so angry I ran away from home, soon to be absorbed into the hopeless life many runaways succumb to. Drugs ravaged my body. I fell pregnant, but the chemicals killed my baby. Life became a curse from which I could think of only one escape. It was a cold winter's day when I sought the comfort of a supermarket toilet to end my misery.' Indira paused as if caught up in the terrifying memory of that fateful day.

'You met someone?' I prompted.

The girl nodded. 'A woman found me, snatched away my

needles and took me to see a man: perhaps her husband. He was very kind – a funny, charming character. He took me to hospital, gave me money and his phone number. When I was well, he said, if I wished he could find me work.'

'In erotic videos?' I ventured.

'Not exactly,' came the slightly surprised reply. 'My job was helping the girls in the films. General duties, wardrobe, sometimes even advice on eastern make-up styles.'

'This man,' I interjected. 'His name was Julian?'

'Yes,' Indira replied, 'that's it. I'd almost forgotten – Julian.'

'What went wrong?' I asked, acutely fascinated by this strangest of odysseys.

'My own foolishness,' she replied. 'I decided I wanted to be in the films, but Julian said it wasn't the right way for me to go. Once again I ran away, returned to my old ways. Crime became my friend: a lucrative source of income to buy drink and drugs. One day I was caught breaking into a newspaper shop. I had a knife, and someone died.' Choked by the painful vision, Indira was forced to break off her story for a second time. When she'd recovered sufficiently, she asked if I would forgive her, for she felt unable to continue.

It was a difficult situation. On the one hand I desperately wanted her to finish, but on the other I didn't want her to relive what must have been a hellish recollection. As an alternative I gained permission to ask questions and, based on the answers, pieced together my own version of events.

There was no doubt that Indira had turned to her former saviours for help. Purely by coincidence, she had traced her way back to Cambridge at a time when Julian was away on business, and therefore encountered only Kathy. Given the damning facts, there was only one suitable recourse. A deal was struck and the fugitive was spirited away to the US. There, by the cruellest twist of fate, complications had developed during the preparative surgery for her first assignment. The result – brain damage. A tragedy or, as some might choose to regard it, the rightful handing-down of justice.

By now the light was fading. It was an eerie scene, and as the shadows lengthened I felt a tingling in my spine. Although no words were spoken, it was time for us to part. Indira left her seat and wheeled me back inside.

As we re-entered the darkness, I asked, 'Can you tell me where we are now? Is it the Gellar Institute?'

'You are close to home,' my guide replied enigmatically. 'I am exactly where you saw me.'

'Are there others like you?' I persisted.

At first she made no response. Instead I was gently drawn to a halt and the wheelchair brakes applied. Then I received my answer.

'Not so many. All are gone now. Only Rosie and I remain. Goodbye, Dr Clock, I must go now. Sharni will be lonely without me.'

There was a moment when fear breathed deeply at my side, but then it vanished. I wondered what would happen next. Would there be others to meet? Was I about to wake up, or would I be left sitting in a wheelchair surrounded by darkness for all eternity? I tried to rationalise the meaning of my two interviews, to make sense of what was happening, but my mind was too tired, too fatigued. Sleep was perhaps best. When I awoke – if I awoke – there'd be time enough for further pondering.

Dream or reality I couldn't say. All I knew was that my brain was active again, and on this occasion had chosen to lead me to believe I was back in hospital. Still unable to move a muscle, eye pads firmly in place, I couldn't decide whether time had jumped backwards, forwards, or come to a dead stop.

'Good day to ya, Dr Clock, and how are we doin' this mornin'?'

Now I had an Irish voice to add to my collection. If nothing else, my dreams were imaginative and varied, I told myself. So far I hadn't a single recurring vision to complain about. At present, however, I wasn't in the mood for pandering to any more amorphous, invisible or shaded figures. I wasn't going to play along.

'Quiet as a dormouse,' the voice observed. 'Ah well, it's to be expected, so it is. Anyway, let's be havin' these pads away and see what we shall see.'

Novel, I thought cynically. Haven't come across this ruse before. Can't have old Tick-tock getting better – spoil all the fun. Trouble was, I couldn't ignore the fact that it did feel as if someone was touching my face and bandages were being removed from around my eyes.

By degrees I became aware of light: faint at first but unquestionably growing more intense. Glasses – dark glasses – were placed on my face, and gradually I could make out figures moving to and fro before me. Despite my resistance to accept that I was experiencing reality, optimism insisted on pulling the sheet from over its head. A series of bright flashes caused me to screw up my eyes, then one almighty flare sent me reeling. When I finally summoned the courage to look again, I was in for another jolt. I was standing outside, holding onto a barrier rail that skirted the edge of some kind of large balcony or platform. It was evening, very cold, and the sky was a vivid mixture of red and purple. It took me a few moments to gather my thoughts, but there could be no doubt. I was standing on the observation deck of a small airport. There was little sound: only the wind whistling across the rooftop of the terminal building behind me registered in my ears. Everything appeared to be real enough. I could see lights, the occasional stationary plane dotted about but, most encouraging of all, people. Interestingly, I was wearing the same tracksuit I'd been issued with in my hotel prison. My watch was still in the pocket where I'd left it, and a handkerchief I'd had occasion to use was stuffed inside the jacket. Could it be that I'd somehow survived a mental ordeal? Perhaps I'd blacked out in the coffin due to lack of air and everything I'd suffered since then was all part of some warped CO_2-mediated psychological aberration. The proof I needed lay in the hands of my fellow humans. Communication. If I could only talk to someone about food, football or the price of beer and receive the usual litany of moans and complaints, there'd be no doubt I'd finally resurfaced in normality.

I abandoned my plane-spotting position and headed for the terminal doors. As I approached I caught a fleeting glimpse of a woman: a woman dressed in a tracksuit identical to mine. My step quickened, Sandy's name forming on my lips. Then, horror of horrors, two figures clothed in red appeared from nowhere, set on a direct-intercept course with my lady. I hesitated then, in a knee-jerk reaction, ducked as the sky above me exploded in a shower of flickering lights. Red pulses merged with greens and yellows, erupting like a thousand tiny volcanoes. Puddles of colour rippled across the heavens as if a small child were dripping paint into a basin of water. Although I'd never seen it before, all I could imagine was that this spectacular display of nature was the Aurora Borealis – the Northern Lights. Why it should appear now, of all times – at this most crucial of moments – was beyond my imaginings. Was it a sign, a portent or just coincidence?

I recovered my concentration and rushed towards the entrance, but it was too late. The tracksuited woman, her two pursuers, vanished into wisps of vapour. I threw my head back to scream at the dancing lights, only to find that the performance had ended. There was only blackness – the blackness of the sky and the blackness in my mind as I slid into oblivion.

16

Of Gog and Magog

'D-Doc, can you hear me? Come on, Doc. You're frightening BJ,' Julian's voice echoed somewhere in the distance.

Oh shit! More hallucinations, I decided. How much more of this do I have to take? Where am I supposed to be now, for God's sake – a frozen Alaskan riverbed with my neighbour trying to wake me from another trance? Bugger off and let me die in peace.

'He ain't dead, is he?' the illusion persisted.

'Of course not, dummy,' Norma's voice joined in the fun and games. 'You can see his breath when he exhales. Doc, please, it's me. You've got to come round.'

'Go away, me,' I murmured in the vain hope of banishing whatever nuisance wanted to have a go at tormenting the remains of my mind.

'Try the whisky,' the girl's voice recommended.

An acute burning sensation took away my breath. I retched, coughed, then opened my eyes, only to be blinded by intensely bright light. 'What's happening?' I cried. 'Get away, leave me. . . Julian, Norma? It can't be. You're not real.'

'Was this mornin',' Julian replied. 'Jeez, am I glad you're okay. Gave me one helluva fright there for a spell.'

For the nth time I wrestled with the information being transmitted by my senses, trying to separate fantasy from whatever remained of actuality. Hands were helping me up and guiding me into a sitting position. My eyes flickered, endeavouring to retreat from the unrelenting lights, then they adjusted, clicked into focus, and there I was. Good point. Where was I? First impressions – I was resting on ice-

285

cold ground with my legs dangling over the edge of a large hole taken up mostly by an open coffin. Standing over me were Julian and Norma, looking like a couple of amateur grave robbers. It was a bright, chilly day: the air was crisp, the sky blue, and all around was good old English countryside. I looked at the two concerned figures before me then took a deep breath. This was real, without a shred of doubt. By some miracle I was alive, I was home.

My journey to Julian's VW was hazy, to say the least. No one knew what to say for the best. In fact no one knew where to begin let alone who should start. In the end, all I remember was being forced to consume several more swigs of whisky, which in this one rare case probably did me more harm than good. After that, I'd been propped up against a tree and buried, this time fortunately only in blankets. Harried by Norma's constant badgering, Julian had hastily filled in the hole from which I'd apparently emerged. By then I was feeling very sleepy and decidedly light-headed. A wave of fear did a fly-past as my eyelids suddenly closed. Where would I be when I opened them? Another dream, another mind-bending experience? With a determined effort I forced one eye half-open. It was all still there, praise be to God. In the background I could hear my companions talking, but their words made no sense. Something about my appearance, something about how they'd found me – but I couldn't be bothered to ask. In fact I hadn't the energy even if I'd wanted to. Come to think of it though, I did catch BJ asking Julian what I was doing feeling my crotch. Luckily they didn't ask – and I wasn't telling. It was all there and that's all that mattered. After what seemed like a couple of days with my backside becoming progressively more frozen to the ground, the pair had hauled me to my feet, then in a gut-wrenching, brain-sloshing manoeuvre I'd found myself slung over Julian's shoulder.

The next thing I knew, a stream of hot air from the VW's heater was blowing in my face. I felt disgusting to start with, but as I began to warm up. . . At that moment the expression 'death warmed up' took on a whole new personal meaning for me.

As we negotiated the large M11 roundabout, the change in vehicle momentum gave me sufficient of a jolt to prompt speech. 'Is Sondra okay?' I asked, temporarily forgetting much of what had happened since our detention in the hotel prison.

There was a long pause before anyone spoke, giving me ample warning of the likely reply.

'Sorry, Dr J,' Norma said slowly. 'We don't have any news.'

My heart sank, but in my confused state I convinced myself that since I'd somehow made it, she surely would too. It was only a matter of time – it had to be. I toyed with the idea of asking after Kathy, but before I could make my mind up one way or the other, Julian jumped in.

'Best not talk till we get you home, Doc, and check you're okay,' he insisted. 'There's a heap-load of stuff we all need to say. Scrub up, chow down first; powwow later.'

I couldn't argue with that, so I sat back, prayed for Sandy's safe deliverance and let the remainder of the whisky in my system dissolve a few more thousand grey cells.

Before I knew it we were home. I'd no idea how I managed to skip across the Atlantic or to what degree the distorted memories of my encounters with Ms White, Cher, Elena and the others were fact or fiction. In the half-hour or so it had taken to complete the journey, my body, limb by limb, had acclimatised to the warmth of its surroundings and was now aching with a vengeance. Still unable to support myself, my friends marshalled me out of the van and into Julian's living room. I was given hot coffee, force-fed half a dozen slices of jam-laden raisin toast then carted off to the bathroom. With Mr Stammers putting in a valiant performance as orderly-cum-nurse, I took a bath. I felt in desperate need of a shave, but the young man advised against it for the moment until I was stronger and less likely to have an accident. We then worked our way through a medical checklist to determine my condition, mentally ticking off the boxes as we went. To our relief I seemed to be in fair fettle – a selection of stiff joints, one or two alarming bruises, but otherwise not bad for someone who'd just been dug up out of the ground. By the time my ablutions were concluded, most of the alcohol I'd swallowed had worked its way through and I could think more clearly. A fistful of painkillers swilled down with a gallon of orange juice, and I was ready and eager for our mutual debriefing session.

Julian's living room was selected as the venue for the meeting. I was fixed up with a heavy dressing gown and plonked down so close to the roaring fire I was almost part of the fuel. Once again we were back to the weighty problem of who should go first and where to begin. For me the choice was easy. I needed to hear all that had happened during my absence, including anything that might help us to recover Sondra. At the moment my main concern was that she might still be in the States. If so, I had to get back there, whatever the personal risk. Somehow, for some reason, the fate promised me by Greta Oakridge and later referred to by Ms White had not come to pass. Whether there'd been a change of mind, heart or plan wasn't important. All I had to cling to was my earlier thought – if I'd been freed, however bizarre the circumstances, Sandy must also have been granted a similar reprieve. So it was decided – a home team kick-off with Ms Bates as spokesperson.

'I've been keeping a diary since we first met, so I've got a full written record to refer to,' she explained. She turned to Julian for some ethereal moral support then kicked off with a blockbuster question.

'What d'you think the date is?'

Interesting question, I mused. One I'd asked myself a number of times during my hair-raising journey through the deep and misty caverns of an addled mind. 'Well, let's see,' I replied. 'It was mid-October when we left for the US.

If I say a week before things got nasty, and a week's worth of swimming around in LSD – early November.'

The look in BJ's eyes was enough to confirm that I was well shy of the mark.

'Go on then,' I encouraged. 'Let's have the worst.'

'Eleventh of December, Doc,' Julian stepped in, handing me a copy of the morning paper.

There was no denying I was surprised, but if challenged to set a score between zero and ten where zero represented 'expected' and ten the opposite, I couldn't have gone higher than four. After what I'd endured, or believed I'd endured, it was unlikely that in future the concept of surprise would ever be particularly 'surprising' again.

I handed the paper back. 'Same year,' I announced. 'Could have been worse. At least I've still got fourteen shopping days left till Christmas.' It was a puerile remark, but I sought only to ease the pressure on Norma. I could tell, as soon as I got the date wrong, she'd instantly grown uncomfortable with her role as chief storyteller. 'Don't worry,' I reassured her, 'you just reel off what you've got to say, then later we can do the "Never! Surely not? Can't be!" routine. How's that?'

'Thanks,' she replied then, flicking through the pages of her diary, she began the saga.

The first chapter afforded me some degree of confidence since it was just as I'd have expected. When our friends stopped receiving daily calls, they became gravely concerned. A couple of days phoning all the places in the US they could imagine we'd be proved expensive but fruitless. Then the news of Natalie's murder was released. Before they knew what to think, our pictures were in the papers and the police arrived to crawl all over my house. The next day, when we were arrested, Julian had rushed off to Cambridge police station, hoping to see us. He was turned away. I apparently had made it clear that I wished to see only my lawyer: a position echoed by my female partner-in-crime.

Chapter two, which Julian related, was more intriguing.

289

Being unable to convince themselves that we'd simply popped back over from the US then hung around the police station until someone decided to arrest us had prompted drastic action. Julian dug up the coffin in my back garden.

'Jeez, Doc. That there gravediggin's some mighty tough work,' he volunteered as I pressed him for details.

'But what about the electronic device I told you about? Did you find it?'

Norma smiled. 'Yes, we found it. Turned out to be a tamper-indicator device. You know, touch it or what it's linked up to and it records the time, etc.'

'Is that all?' I exclaimed, not at all convinced.

'I thought so at the time,' she conceded. 'But it turned out I was wrong.'

My 'In what way?' was rolled over by Julian reclaiming his right to his part of the testament.

'Before we get into that,' he insisted, 'you have to know what we found inside the box.'

More insensitivity on my part. In focusing on the device outside the coffin, I'd momentarily forgotten that whatever else might have turned up it was more than likely that Twister was the one guarding it. But wrong again.

'Wasn't the young fella after all,' Julian announced. 'Just a pile of steel boxes.'

'Forty-two to be precise,' Norma chipped in. 'All wrapped in plastic bags and all locked up tight with some fancy electronic gizmo. Couldn't open a single one.'

Definitely not what I'd expected to hear at all, I mused. Instead of confirming my previously held suspicion, two new conundrums had sprung up. Where was Twister? And what did the boxes contain? Yes, as BJ was hinting, there were forty-two names on the list we'd found in GM Video. However, was it really plausible that these were in some way connected? Personal belongings or case histories for each individual? Well, I supposed the answer had to be yes. I'd already learnt of the Oakridge consolidation or merger programme and of the Gogmagog identity-eradication campaign.

290

Under the circumstances, it wasn't that difficult to accept that the forty-odd ongoing or recently completed projects under Kathy's control would also have to be reclassified as loose ends. Then there was the 'two birds with one stone' crack made by Ms White. 'Hide the evidence and frighten me' was just as believable as 'Hide Twister's body and frighten me'.

'So can I see the boxes?' I asked excitedly, confident that my as-yet-untested skills as a safecracker would be up to the challenge.

'Sorry Doc,' Julian apologised. 'Things ain't that simple. You're way ahead of yerself. Best let BJ finish.'

Irritated beyond endurance, I sat back and held my peace.

'We placed all the boxes in your garage for safekeeping,' Norma explained. 'Trouble was, the next day they'd gone. Bastards left the place in a right mess. Had the nerve to leave us forty-two empty plastic bags to clear up, and well, this . . .' Norma produced a blue metal box with an opened envelope stuck on one side. 'Oh, by the way,' she added, 'the others were all silver, so this one's extra. Also, as I was trying to explain earlier, I'm pretty sure the tamper device contained a transmitter. That's how they knew to come.'

I took the container and examined it. Custom-made for sure, I decided. And, as far as the locking mechanism was concerned, it had to be extra-terrestrial, or at least Japanese. Resisting the temptation to shake, invert or tap the object, I set it on my lap and focused on the envelope. On the outside the words 'To the friends of Dr Clock' had been written with a thick, black felt-tip pen. Inside, there was a note that read:

Loyal friends,
All is not as it seems. Dr Clock will be returned to you soon. When December comes visit Wandlebury daily. Mr Stammers will know where to look. When found, the doctor will seem different to you, but there is no need for alarm. Until he reads this note, however, do not allow him to see his reflection. Dr

Clock may open the box by means of the one he held most precious.
Yours in absentia,
Of Gog and Magog.

'Very Edgar Allan Poe,' I murmured to myself, looking at my two companions. 'What's all this about reflections?' I demanded, anxiety swiftly seating itself at my table. 'I thought it a bit strange when Julian didn't want me to shave and I wasn't allowed in the bathroom until the mirrors had steamed up.'

'Like the note says, Dr J,' Norma hastily replied, 'there's no need for alarm. It's just you look a little different. Nothing much, really.'

Memories of Ms White and her promise of cut-price treatment, the lint eye-pads and the tingling sensation I'd felt around my face since I was rescued bobbed to the surface.

Before I could say another word Norma unzipped her bag and held out a hand mirror. Taking a deep breath, I accepted the glass and stared into it . . .

Unnerving, unsettling, unbelievable – the first three of at least a dozen 'un' adjectives that flooded my thoughts as I squinted at my reflection. It was me, but then again it wasn't. There was little doubt that my face had undergone a number of changes, but all were subtle, barely perceptible. Only when the whole was taken as a package did it become obvious that I wasn't quite the same Jeremiah Clock I had been a few weeks, or more correctly, a month or so ago. Words failed me. As if suddenly charged with energy, I stood up and marched to the door. All I could manage as I went was a backward wave to my concerned friends, indicating that they should stay put.

In the bathroom I undertook a millimetre-by-millimetre examination before flopping down on the side of the bath to reflect. All in all, I had no choice but to admit that I didn't look too bad. In fact, if anything I seemed a tad younger. The bags under my eyes had been reduced, and I generally appeared more taut around the jowls. My nose was straighter than I remembered, and my hair had become an order of magnitude whiter. Finally – although I'd missed it at first – two of my less than sturdy teeth had been replaced and a third given a rather smart gold crown.

Once again it was back to the 'question and no answer' game. I'm captured, imprisoned, given an *ex gratia* makeover – which would no doubt have infuriated Cher – then dumped back in the UK. Why?

By now Julian had come to collect me. 'There ya go, Doc.' He gave a wry smile. 'Like the little lady said, nothing to go frettin' about. As they say, ya look a new man.'

I couldn't help but laugh. A new man, that was good. I liked that.

BJ rustled up some more coffee while back in the living room I fiddled with my other present – the blue box. Julian left me in peace, clearly aware that I needed time to consider not only the reasoning behind my new face but also the nature of the grander plan surrounding it.

Although it was very hard to accept, I was rapidly being forced to conclude that I was being helped. The advent of my new face clearly put me in the same category as all the other substitutes created by Oakridge Associates Inc. A duplicate of the original JOC was in jail pending a murder trial while a modified version – me – was at liberty to move freely about in society. All I needed now was a new identity, which brought me back to the containers. Perhaps they didn't house case histories or personal belongings as I'd originally surmised. More likely that each contained IDs, new and/or old. If so, then the answer to the questions 'Who was impersonating me?' and 'Who was I now supposed to be?' probably lay in my hands. Time to forget the money and open the box.

Normally, I'm all for crossword puzzles and cryptic clues, but for one only just returned from the dead it was less of a challenge and more of an insoluble problem. According to the note, I was supposed to be able to open the box by means of 'the one I held most precious'. Well it had to be Sandy: that seemed plain enough. The one part of the clue I found especially disturbing, though, was the word 'held'. Why not 'hold'? That would sound much more positive for the future. Not at all comforted by such thoughts, I punched S-o-n-d-r-a into the lock's combination keypad, then S-a-n-d-y. Nothing: not even the odd encouraging click or whirr. Then it occurred to me, cruel but obvious. I'd always loved Sandy and always would. There were no past tenses in our relationship. Yet, in the distant past, there had been a moment – an all-too-fleeting moment – when I had held one most precious to me in my arms. Jasmine, the daughter Trish and I had made, survived in this world for less than an hour. Another heartless trick of fate, which from that day saw the beginning of a rift between us that could never be healed. Self-recrimination, blame, guilt – all combined, driving us into our separate careers, separate worlds. How could anyone know of this tragedy or wish me to be reminded of it in this way? A perverted mind or a clever mind? Perhaps both.

There was only one way to test my hypothesis. . . I typed in the letters, the mechanism released and the box opened. My God, who were these people walking among us? It was frightening, truly frightening . . .

The container's content, neatly packaged in individual plastic bags, was no less than a life. Passport, driving licence, birth certificate: every conceivable document that proved an individual actually existed on this overcrowded planet. Dr Clock was dead, long live Dr Clock: a newly manufactured character by the name of Matthew Woodrow Clock. I was now a Doctor of Anthropology, brother to the dastardly Jeremiah, who now awaited judgement by his peers in the cells of Highpoint Prison. Fortunately, I was a younger sibling by a grand total of two years and a long-term resident of Australia, where I had apparently spent most of my adult life. Conveniently unmarried and with no special attachments, I had recently returned to England to continue my work and visit family. And what an obliging family the

Clocks were. Apart from a few distant cousins, the only remaining relative was good old Jerry. Packet after packet contained details of my life: photographs as a child, at school, graduation, even some with Jerry and our deceased parents . . .

Like most people, I'd heard of the US witness-protection programme. I'd even considered it as an explanation for Wayne Millard's reappearance, but this? This went far beyond anything I'd imagined possible. Piece by piece, block by block, I was finally beginning to appreciate the scale of Greta Oakridge's business. To be able to effect these miraculous substitutions and replacements must involve countless experts, specialists and government officers. But how could such an incredibly complex and illegal process be kept secret? How could it possibly operate in a society where the slightest whiff of strange goings-on was guaranteed to be plastered across the front page of at least half-a-dozen newspapers before you could blink? I hadn't the slightest idea, and probably never would have.

When Norma returned with the drinks – plus more food just in case I wasn't still bursting at the seams – I handed round my new identity. Julian and BJ sat silently glancing through the paperwork and photos, occasionally expressing incredulity at the scope and quality of the work. For me the *coup de grâce* was a clipful of documents relating to the house. The bottom line? Jeremiah had recently made Matthew joint owner in order to raise capital. In essence, I was now an equal stakeholder in my own house. At least, as Julian observed, I still had somewhere to live, thus freeing him from the possibility of having to put up more than one guest!

Once we'd finished ogling my new holiday snaps, my companions reciprocated by showing me the set of newspaper cuttings they'd kept of Natalie McCarthy's case, and my and Sandy's subsequent arrest. As I followed the story I began to see how contrived it all was. Evidence conveniently found: not so obvious as to make it suspicious, but not too obscure so that the local constabulary would have been in danger of overlooking it.

By the time we'd each had our fill of the 'all-singing, all-dancing' Dr Matthew, mid-afternoon was upon us. Before dusk descended I made my excuses and meandered up to my garden. It was peaceful, quiet. There was no trace of a breeze, and with its absence I could sense Jack Frost chuckling at the prospect of a mischievous night's work. The sky was remarkably clear. I could see countless stars twinkling in heaven's boundless eye – forever watching patiently as humans hurried on to who knew where or why. I wondered, somewhere on another continent was there another soul gazing up into the vastness of space? Was my Sandy free, well, able to think of us? I hoped so; God, I hoped so.

It was freezing, and I was still a long way from being healed mentally or physically. Today had seen my deliverance from the jaws of death, my rebirth as a brother I'd never had. But, perhaps more importantly, I'd been reunited with Julian and Norma. How strange that the three of us – so different, so unrelated – should find solace in each other's company. For twenty years I'd worked alongside so-called clever people, smart, sophisticated men and women, some of whom professed to be my friends. In truth, one by one they'd all let me down, deserted or even betrayed me. Now at fifty-one, or forty-nine if I opted for my Matthew persona, my best friends – in fact my only friends – were a young man living in his own world and an even younger girl trying to find hers.

That was enough philosophising for one evening, so I wished Jack good hunting and returned to the warmth of Julian's fire . . .

'Well then, my saviours,' I proclaimed heartily, 'before we go any further, there are three things you haven't explained yet. How in the name of Hades did you find where I was buried? How did you manage to dig me up? And why am I still alive and not dead through cold, suffocation or dehydration?'

BJ shrank back in her chair and gestured towards Julian. 'All down to the amazing Tex Tucker, Dr J. I'm just the sidekick.'

'Thank ya much, thank ya much,' Julian crooned, exaggerating his Western accent even more than usual in what I took to be a friendly attempt at sarcasm. He paused, obviously pondering how best to proceed then, satisfied with his decision, began. 'Now, I don't rightly remember that TV programme – where that clever fella used to ask smart folk real difficult questions – but I seem to recall you could answer multiple questions in reverse order. If it's okay with you, Doc, I'd like to do the same.'

To be honest, I didn't really know what he was talking about since I rarely watched television, and in any case loathed quiz shows. However, any form of reply was fine with me as long as it was in English, so I agreed.

Julian began. 'You didn't die because ya couldn't have been buried for more than a few hours. Like it said in the instructions, we visited Wandlebury every morning and, as it turned out, at about the same time. Wandered around for a couple of hours then high-tailed it outa there. If ya ask me, people who put ya down there were keepin' an eye out so they'd know the best time. But that's not all. I reckon yer coffin was specially lined. Ya know – some sort of thermal stuff. On top of that, they'd fitted ya up with a couple of air pipes to the surface, and even had a bottle of juice fixed up with a straw taped to the side of yer mouth. Darnedest set-up I've ever seen.'

'Incredible,' I murmured as my memory came up trumps. When I first discovered my morbid encasement, I'd thought the padding was pretty heavy-duty. Then there was the air hole I'd discovered and, bugger me, the angel of mercy – a sip of fruit juice through a straw pushed between my lips. Could it have all been part of another Pavlovian training session?

Julian stroked his chin as if, having successfully managed the first question, the second was likely to prove more taxing. 'Okay,' he abruptly stated, 'number two. Of course we dug ya out with shovels. Why we had 'em? Well, we'd used 'em to dig up the box in yer garden. After we finished, I dumped everythin' in back of the VW to take home, but then forgot all about it.'

'Until this morning,' I interrupted, acutely aware of my neighbour's growing discomfort. 'They caught your eye, and something told you that a couple of spades might just come in mighty handy.'

Julian beamed at me. 'Now Doc, you're doing that imitation thing again. But yep, that's about the size of it.'

That was all I needed to know. My first question was now redundant. Much to BJ's annoyance, I winked at my anxious neighbour to indicate he was off the hook. I think he partly understood, but it was of no matter. I'd explain it to him later when we were alone. It was patently obvious that Julian had been unaccountably drawn to the correct location and had spotted the air pipes. How? Exactly the same way he'd known where to find the Gogmagog effigy. There was definitely a strange link between my trusting friend and the mysterious Iron Age fortress on top of Wandlebury Hill. What it was or why he should have it, I didn't care a jot. I was only too glad it existed, and by heaven did that work for me!

The next day I felt much better. It was like being set free from an immense burden: released from prison, miraculously cured after a long illness – hell, I didn't know, but at least one or more of the above. Despite my initial elation, the thought of Sandy still lost to me and the story I had yet to tell Julian about Kathy slapped me back down hard. With regard to Ms Murkett's situation, I'd been lucky so far. I could see Julian was bursting to ask me for news, but had apparently made a pact with himself to wait until I broached the subject.

After breakfast I persuaded my comrades to take me back to the Wandlebury gravesite. Not for further examination, I explained; only with the thought that lightning may deign to strike twice in the same place. There could be no greater calamity than to find Sondra returned under similar circumstances but to be too late to revive her. Hardly to anyone's surprise, we found nothing. I kept an eye on Julian at all times but, apart from detecting the embarrassment I was causing him, I perceived his radar screen to be blank. After a couple of hours, I agreed to abandon the search but only when given a solemn promise that we could try again the following day.

On the way back home I heard that Toby Farthing continued to make good progress. He'd been out of hospital for a few weeks and, according to Julian, had undergone a sort of mini-religious experience. Deeply affected by his narrow escape, the old boy had decided to mend his ways and hang up his whip and thong, so to speak. He could now be seen at raves and similar venues, talking youngsters out of appearing in porno films and expounding the virtues of sobriety, or at least cutting down a little. As for my icing business, the gods had indeed chosen to smile favourably upon it. The day after Sandy and I had failed to check in, Norma found out that the armoury wedding had been postponed until February due to some technical hitch. Not only that, but the industrious young lady, hopeful of our return, had arranged for my competitor to undertake additional contract work. As a result, all the cakes Sandy had remade had been taken to a fairly advanced stage of completion and now only awaited final decoration *à la* Clock. However, before proceeding, I suppose I'd have to decide one extremely important thing – was Matthew Clock ready, willing and able to move into the cake-icing business?

In the afternoon I decided it was high time I provided an account of all the extraordinary events surrounding my US adventure with Sandy. Before beginning, I took Julian aside and broke the news about Kathy's apparent double life. Judging by the expression on his face, I doubted he believed a word I said. There was no question that his only interest, quite naturally, was learning that his partner was safe and well.

'That's really great news, Doc,' he exclaimed, on the verge of bursting. 'I always knew my little lady'd be okay. Just like I always knew, you'd be the one to find her for me. Thanks Doc. I'm mighty, mighty obliged.'

The hardest part of the interview came when he finally asked the question I'd been dreading. When did I think his darling Kathy would be coming home? It was so patently obvious that he really had blocked out most of what I'd told him. I had no idea what fairytale rationale his mind had wrapped around my explanation, but a happy ending was obviously a major component. Partly to appease his tortured mind and partly to bolster my own fading hopes for Sandy, I told him both women would be back soon. I then felt compelled to go further and, although I knew it would make matters worse, speculated that the ladies were probably together, doubtless devising the most expedient way to exit Greta Oakridge's domain, and planning new ways to make our lives that irresistible blend of heaven and hell for which we loved them dearly.

Our spirits lifted on a gloriously bright cloud of make-believe, we rejoined BJ, and I unfurled my story as best I could. At Julian's insistence I left out nothing, and as I described my reunion with Ms Murkett I could tell Norma thought her lost to us forever.

The following day brought with it a light dusting of snow. Undeterred by the worsening weather conditions, we mounted our daily vigil around the Wandlebury and Gog-magog Hills, but again to no avail. Another day, another empty search, and then, during the fourth expedition I had an overwhelming desire to know more of Gog and Magog. To my friends' surprise and no small degree of concern, I pleaded with them to drop me at Cambridge railway station before they returned home. From there I took one of the faster trains to Liverpool Street and then on to the Guildhall Library by taxi. I'd no idea what I thought I'd discover – assuming there was anything to discover in the first place. All I knew was that I had to see the original statues of the two legendary giants for myself. Perhaps in some strange way I believed that if I faced them – maybe touched them – I'd be granted magical powers. Nothing too outlandish – just sufficient for me to cast a spell that would seek out my beloved and, in a shower of petals, materialise her at my side. Not too much to ask, surely?

In the event I found no trace of magic, but in a way something more useful and infinitely more practical. I found understanding. Furnished with a stack of photocopied articles and pamphlets provided by the helpful library staff, I made my way next door to the Guildhall. There, in the presence of the two imposing creatures, I read about their supposed origins and of their cruel fate. As Sandy had indicated, there were many stories and legends about Gog and Magog. What I didn't know was that the story surrounding the two chaps glaring down at me was even more complicated than I'd imagined.

Centuries before Christ walked the earth, ancient Britons fought against the might of the formidable Trojan army. Each side had its own great champion: Gogmagog of the Britons and Corineus representing the Trojans. The two opponents met in one last test of strength high upon the cliffs that trace the Plymouth coastline. There, Gogmagog was defeated and cast from the rocks to his destruction. So the tale was told of how New Troy was founded, a city which was destined to become good old London town. Strangely, as the centuries passed, the name of Corineus was forgotten and the populace decreed that the name of the other giant be divided between the two. Hence, Gog and Magog came into being. Many images of the two warriors had appeared throughout the ages. The charm ripped from Ms White's bracelet by the ill-fated Natalie must have been one of the earlier examples. Certainly, as far as I could recall, it bore no resemblance to any depicted in my reference texts. For me, however, that was unimportant. The significance lay in

301

the fact that Corineus had become Magog. That which had been one became two. That which possessed one name became another. It was exactly what Greta Oakridge and Kathy were all about. Taking two lives, mixing them up then reintroducing them to the world in different guises and with assumed names. No wonder Greta latched onto the legends, especially when you took into account the connections with biblical prophecy. What could be better? The perfect corporate vision . . .

It took about five more seconds for me to realise that my line of thought was nothing short of monumental crap. Nonetheless, I'd gained a modicum of understanding. By its very nature, the fact of a legend can never be proven. If it were, then the story would immediately transcend the realms of fantasy and enter the learned estate of history. The message was clear enough. I had to blast the Oakridge GM legends out of the shadows and into the light, where they'd instantly crystallise to fact. Once they were destroyed, Sandy would be released and at last we'd be free of the torment.

It was definitely time for me to be on my way. The hour was late and I still had a train journey back to Cambridge to contend with, not to mention a bank-breaking taxi ride home. At the station I picked up a paper and settled down to read it. In accordance with my quirky behaviour patterns, I began at the back, dismissed the sport and TV pages and scanned the business news. Not surprisingly, the hubbub of the city left me cold.

After a few moments I found myself thinking about my substitute: a man who, for some reason, saw a lengthy prison sentence as a more attractive option than a life of freedom. He doubtless had good reasons prompting his decision, but I still found it hard to imagine. As my thoughts continued to drift, I wondered what kind of man he was. I remembered what Greta had said about how she believed her services actually helped people. Perhaps, after all, she was right. It was quite possible that my lookalike was alone, ill, or in some other desperate state. Even so, I still had a major decision to make. Did I allow this travesty of justice to continue, or go to the authorities and explain everything? Ever since I'd thawed out from my ordeal in the coffin, the matter had weighed heavily on my mind. I'd managed to push it aside to some extent by convincing myself that any precipitous action before I found Sandy would be unwise. So far, the legal process was only at the remand stage. No urgent need, therefore, to go in with guns blazing. Yet what if?

But I wasn't predisposed to 'what ifs?' so I forced my attention back to the newspaper and on to a selection of general articles about lady vicars, new cars and holiday scandals. The train was not far from Cambridge when I finally made it to page two. Nothing unusual – just war, murder, football hooliganism and fire.

At first the report about a blaze in a downtown Philadelphia medical facility didn't register. All that changed, however, when I read the name of the clinic and its address – St Joan the Blessed Martyr Hospice and Clinic, Andreas de Mello Tower, South Street.

A bunch of blasphemous expletives formed on my tongue but had to be chewed off to avoid offending the genteel-looking old lady sitting nearby. The entry was short and contained little detail. What it did report, however, made my heart grow cold. Greta Oakridge, director; found dead at the scene. In addition, several other badly burnt corpses recovered by the fire services had yet to be identified. I couldn't believe it.

17

Revelations

And so the eradication of Gogmagog was complete. No visible trace remained of the clandestine operation Greta Oakridge had created, and now she herself had vanished. Of course I knew full well it was all just another illusion, another sleight of hand to lead the outside world down one more blind alley, but what could be done? My resolve, born of the understanding I'd acquired in the Guildhall, was looking a trifle lost at sea. I could hardly mount a major exposé when to all intents and purposes nothing remained to be exposed. Sure enough, Ms Oakridge would resurface in the not-too-distant future. The problem was, where and in what guise? For the length of the taxi ride home from Cambridge I pondered the imponderable. Mainly I was frustrated. Once again the goalposts had been shifted, and this time before I'd even kicked off. And what of my Sandy now? Was she one of the charred unidentified bodies, or had she been carted along for the ride? Had she been given a new ID in preparation for her return, or was she already part of the new Oakridge megaplan? Thoughts such as these were having a great time proliferating in my head. If I closed my eyes and visualised each one in turn, reproduction slowed. On the other hand, if I tried to ignore them, their numbers swelled beyond belief. Despite my morose condition, I was constantly reminded by some part of my psyche that hope sprang eternal. While I wanted desperately for Sandy to be alive, she would be; and since I'd always want the same thing, however unrealistic, the saying held its meaning.

Fortunately there was no need for me to break the hospital fire story to my friends. When I reached home I headed straight for Julian's place only to find him, newspaper in hand, literally waiting for me on the doorstep.

It had been two days since I'd reinstalled myself in my own castle, but the ghosts were too many and too loud. Much to my relief and eternal gratitude, Julian, quickly realising all was not well, had extended his invitation for me to stay with him. It was an offer I was only too willing to accept. I did occasionally spend time pottering about the old homestead, but only during the day and never unaccompanied. Like a novice vampire hunter, as soon as the light began to fade, I was out of there. If the spectres were comfortable, that was fine with me. They were welcome just as long as they didn't roam beyond the confines of the rickety walls.

Despite the late hour of my return, Norma conjured up something for me to eat. Since I'd been a guest in the Stammers' Hotel I'd become pampered. As soon as I appeared anywhere near a mealtime, food was instantly ready for me to consume. My hand never seemed to be without a cup of something, and the general level of attention and concern I received could easily have filled an over-sized Olympic swimming pool. Tonight, however, was special. My supporters were clearly on full red alert, looking for any telltale signs of a sudden deterioration in my condition.

Ironic, I thought, that Julian should so wholly give himself over to shoring up my weakened defences. He might be many things, but definitely not stupid. I could tell he harboured the same fears for Kathy's fate as I did for Sandy's. Yet here he was doing his damnedest to take my mind off the subject.

After I'd avidly consumed my repast, we all sat in front of the fire like three lost souls at a ten-thousand-year reunion party. If you took us as a group, there would have been more life in a glass of liver salts.

For some reason I began to focus on BJ. Having scanned

everything I knew and had experience of with her, two issues appeared on the 'items for further review' tray. The first was merely an observation. Apart from our initial meeting, I could recall no further manifestations of her behavioural problem. We'd been through some tricky situations, but the phenomenon hadn't recurred. Was that still the case? Secondly, she seemed to be a permanent fixture in Julian's abode. What about Mr Knott? Surely he was less than excited to find out that one of his foster children had been consorting with a potential killer. Unable to fathom an answer to either point, I asked.

Norma smiled. 'So after staring into the fire for half an hour, looking like you're about to solve the mysteries of life, that's all you've been thinking about?' It was a smart response and one that broke the tension which had surreptitiously crept up on us. 'Okay,' she continued, 'if you must know, I can confirm no more outbursts. Probably it's because my brain's too occupied making sure Tex here stays on the straight and narrow. As for Dad, I just told him it was all a big misunderstanding, and as soon as the police completed their investigations they'd realise that. In the meantime, I was keeping your business ticking over and staying with one of my new friends.'

'And that's been accepted all this time?' I remarked, somewhat amazed.

BJ shook her head. 'No, Julian said it wouldn't do and you'd be unhappy with him if he didn't come up with something more. . . seemly's the word he used. God knows where he got that from – probably watching some fancy drama on the telly, eh, Jules?'

Another clever crack from the lady. Well, it was good to see she was comfortable around us. As for 'Jules', he was loving every minute.

'Anyway,' she continued, after playfully throwing a cushion at her wannabe but never-be strict guardian. 'We agreed on a plan where I'd stay at home for a couple of days each week. Julian's been really great about ferrying me to and fro, and guess what? Mum loves him. Thinks he's John Travolta.'

At least that was a couple of things less to worry about . . .

Soon after that the lost souls group broke up and we all sidled off to bed. I'd stopped praying the day after I was told Father Christmas didn't exist. After that first major disappointment I had, on one or two subsequent occasions, considered trying to reconnect my severed line to the Almighty. Needless to say, something awful always cropped up just at the critical moment and the project was never completed. Since I'd lost Sandy, though, I did what most Christians of convenience would have done – stuffed the telephone lead into the socket and told myself God would understand. So I was all hooked up and just left hoping that the guys operating the exchange were prepared to patch the calls through. Julian and Kathy; Norma and Twister; Sandy and me – three relationships all knocked off the tracks in one way or the other. A fair package of misfortune and human suffering for me to bring to the table after a forty-year absence!

Several more days passed with no change to our routine and no new information. The bad weather made the Wandlebury expeditions increasingly taxing, not to mention distinctly more depressing. News of the clinic fire was nonexistent after the second day, obviously not interesting enough to compete with 'Confessions of a Lottery Winner' and a further cut in interest rates. By 19 December we were struggling badly, to say the least. The previous night I'd declared that unless something positive came to light within the next day or so, I was returning to the US. From my point of view the only remaining leads left open to us were in the Keystone State of Pennsylvania: the Gellar Institute and The Way We Were club. Somewhere in one or both of these establishments there had to be a source of useful information I could use to track Sandy and maybe even Kathy. I knew the risks. No one would think twice about making me disappear permanently if I started treading on people's toes, especially if those toes happened to belong to the people who'd arranged my 'second coming'. Be that as it may, I wasn't to be deterred. And, FBI or no FBI, I was ready to go down fighting. Also, rather selfishly, I didn't care too much about others who might be affected if my endeavours proved successful. I did, however, feel I had an obligation to ensure the safety of Elena and Rika. All I could hope was that if the house of cards did come tumbling down around me, one or two genuine souls would still be left to help pick up the pieces. If I were a betting man, I certainly wouldn't be inclined to waste any of my hard-earned money on Lesley Stravinsky. John Arquette, on the other hand, could still prove to be the individual with the potential to restore my faith in a just God. Since my return I'd been seized by the desire to phone him, but I'd decided against it. If he was one of the good guys and knew of my arrest, trying to explain everything away over the telephone would be a non-starter. I had to see him in person and somehow make him believe my story. So my mind was made up. As Matthew Clock, I should have no trouble entering the US, and with a new set of credit cards and matching bank accounts I was hardly financially challenged.

Halfway down my drive on the way to collect Julian and Norma for our morning constitutional up and around the Gogmagog Hills, I met the postman. A convivial chap, who always had a friendly word for Jerry, he was acutely embarrassed at having to face Matthew. Interestingly, though, he showed no sign of suspicion and said nothing about how similar in appearance my brother and I were.

I received the mail, fully intending to stuff it in my pocket for review later, when the letter being squashed under my thumb metaphorically jumped out at me. It was addressed to Dr Matthew W. Clock – the first correspondence of my new life. Postmarked in Scotland, the writing looked familiar, but for a moment I couldn't quite place it. Inside I found a heavily embossed card – an invitation – requesting my company for tea the following afternoon. And the kind person making the offer? None other than Dr John Arquette. There was no attached note, but on the reverse side of the card I found a scribbled message,

Very important we meet. I have valuable information you will want to hear. Come alone.

The added encouragement provided by these words was of course totally superfluous. Any chance, however slight, of a few minutes chat with Arquette would have had me climbing Mont Blanc to meet him, never mind accepting a formal invitation to tea. And it couldn't have been easier. The venue was a small café just off the market square in Cambridge. Not the most private of locations, but who was complaining? It was like a dream come true. The break I'd been hoping and praying for. If this led to Sandy's return, I swore by all that was dear to me I'd be the first to sign up for a lifetime of standing charges for my newly reconnected celestial telephone service.

Filled with optimism, I rushed along to Julian's to break the news. Of course we were all delighted and full of speculation about what I'd find out. Unfortunately, we all hit on the snag more or less at the same time. The meeting was nearly thirty hours away. How could we survive until then? 'A horse, a horse, my kingdom for a horse.' Well, you could forget that, but give me a time machine and I'd trade in my precious TR6 on the spot.

Eventually, when our initial jubilation had subsided, we agreed that we'd just have to carry on as normal. Since we'd no way of knowing what Dr Arquette had to impart, it would be foolish to abandon our ongoing activities before the meeting. So we sat down, made a plan and subsequently followed it to the letter. Wandlebury first, followed by a trip to Cambridge to check out the teashop. Not that there was a lot of point to the latter endeavour, but Julian insisted it was worth the effort just to see if any suspicious characters were casing the joint. As it turned out, the only suspicious characters were the three of us. Having attracted the attention of numerous passers-by, the owners of shops on either side of the target café and a couple of bobbies, we decided to quit while the going was good . . .

In the afternoon Julian had arranged a meeting in Cambridge with yet another of his chums. Coincidentally, this also promised to be of more value than of late, as the contact had a wealth of US experience and had actually been to The Way We Were club in Philadelphia within the last month or so. The meet was scheduled to take place in one of the pubs down by the river. Norma and I, excluded from the proceedings, skulked around the shops, making return trips to the pub every half-hour to see if our partner had finished. In the end we waited nearly two hours, and by the time Julian emerged – flushed in the face, having consumed too many bevvies – we were climbing the walls. For once, however, the cost of drinks and a little sweetener were not the usual waste of time and money. The contact had confirmed that rumours of FBI investigations into the 3Ws club's extra-curricular activities were rife. Stories of more than one well-known criminal, who should by rights be banged up in a state pen, making guest appearances at the club had even percolated across the Atlantic. In a sense it wasn't much at all, but at least it suggested that the authorities were close on Greta's heels. If Sandy was still being held by the GM conspiracy, then there must be the possibility that one or more US law enforcement agencies could reach her at any time. Encouraging news to fuel my optimism.

After another night pacing the floor of my temporary accommodation, it was up with the dawn and chomping at the bit, waiting for my friends to rise. Overnight more snow had fallen, and with the sun radiant in a bright blue sky Wandlebury was a picture postcard. We conducted our now

310

well-established search pattern, which this time yielded a few moments of excitement. As we skirted the perimeter of the ancient fortress, Julian started behaving oddly. He shot off at a tangent, finally coming to a dead stop in a small clearing surrounded by conifers and hawthorn. Norma and I hovered nearby, waiting to pounce if he displayed the slightest sign of special interest in his surroundings. After a few minutes of anxiously biding our time, a small hare bounced out from the undergrowth, prompting Julian to bend down and retrieve something from the ground. Like the released firing arm of a cocked pistol, we shot over to his side. Alas, a false alarm. The recovered object was nothing more than an old piece of lead piping. An odd place for it to have wound up, but of no value to us. At this rate it was beginning to look as if Julian could have an excellent future as a walking metal detector. Further research into the scope and reproducibility of his unusual gift would, however, have to be postponed to another occasion . . .

At last the most severe of patience trials was at an end. It was time for my rendezvous at the teashop. My companions agreed that after seeing me safely into the establishment they'd cruise the market place, and if the cold became unbearable move on to Lion Yard. I don't think I've ever been as nervous as I was approaching that tiny building with its narrow glass door and leaded windows.

Inside, about thirty per cent of tables were occupied, but none by Dr Arquette. Given a choice by the pleasant lady that greeted me, I opted for a corner booth capable of seating four and made a point of explaining that I was expecting at least one more companion. Out of courtesy, I placed an order for tea and a selection of cakes then glared at the entrance, willing my host to appear.

The tea was delivered by a rather large lady dressed in a traditional black dress and white cotton apron. She laid out my order, set the tray to one side then, to my astonishment, sat down opposite me.

'Hi there, Dr Clock, fancy meetin' you again,' she said

311

softly. 'Bet y'all didn't think to see me again. Well, I can tell ya, I certainly hadn't planned on seein' you either.'

'Greta Oakridge!' I exclaimed, the words almost too shocked to leave my lips.

'Not anymore, sir,' she smiled. 'And perhaps ya'd be good enough not to call me that. Just in case. Ya know, like they say, walls have ears.'

All I could do was stare. The personification of my worst nightmare had just sat down before me, having served tea. Could this really be happening? If it wasn't, it was definitely another five-star hallucination, that was for sure. This over-friendly waitress certainly looked like the Greta Oakridge I'd met in Philadelphia. In fact, apart from the change in wardrobe, toned down make-up and a different hairdo, she appeared just the same. I opened and closed my mouth, but no words emerged. Scores of questions all reached the same point in my brain at the same instant and totally clogged the exchange.

'Now there's no need to be alarmed,' she continued, having observed my oral gymnastics. 'A little'll do just fine. As usual, I'm on a tight schedule, and by rights I shouldn't even be here.'

The mention of schedules immediately brought to mind Ms White and the Reverend. Instinctively I must have begun to scan the room, as my companion was quick to respond.

'No one else but me here today, deary,' she assured me. 'But that reminds me, everybody sends their regards, and of course Dr Arquette apologises for not bein' able to join us.'

'Where's Sandy?' I blurted out, the crush of questions having at last jostled into some sort of priority order.

Greta waved a finger at me. 'Wrong first question, young man,' she chided. 'But I can see ya're still a mite off-balance, so I'll overlook it.'

Since it didn't look as if a clue to the right question would be forthcoming, I gave number two in my queue a try. 'Why did you change your mind and let me live?' I asked, gradually becoming more composed.

312

'Better,' came the considered reply. 'Actually, I should be honest, Doc. Wasn't anythin' to do with me. If it had been, I'm sorry to say ya'd be one stiff limey by now. What happened? I hear ya say. Simple enough. "You've got a friend", as Mr James Taylor would say. When yer case reached me, I just passed it on to our strategy boys and gals. And guess what? They decided ya had to be eliminated ASAP. Would've been fine by me, but Kathy stuck her neck out for ya. Asked to be assigned the case and accepted full responsibility – whole kit and caboodle. A high price to pay, my friend, make no mistake.'

I found it hard to respond. 'Thank you' seemed a bit lame. 'What for?' was probably nearer the mark. 'Why?' – even though it meant the same – sounded more concise. I tried it.

Oakridge shrugged. 'Don't know, didn't ask,' she admitted. 'I know this'll sound real mean and insensitive, but on a scale of one to a hundred, worryin' about *you* comes in at about minus fifty; and just so there's no misunderstandin', that, sir, is low.'

'If so,' I replied, acutely aware of my position in the scheme of things, 'why are you talking to me now?'

'Another good'un that, Doc,' the old woman breathed. 'Let's just say that now I've spent so much time and money on y'all, I kinda think of ya as an investment. I know Kathy does. She's the one who asked me to come.'

Well, at least that implied a degree of permanence, stability and hopefully a future. The only worry was what would I be expected to do when the time came for my investment to be cashed in? Perhaps if I asked the $64,000 question there might be a clue in the answer, assuming of course I actually received one.

'If, as you say, I'm now a company asset,' I ventured, 'how about filling me in on the purpose of all this restructuring that's been going on.'

'Fair enough request,' Oakridge replied. 'But don't go elevatin' yer status none, Doc. I said ya're an investment. That's office-junior status. An asset, well, that's a totally different matter. Ya'd be talking as high as vice president, and that ain't you, sir, not by a long stretch. Anyways, all ya need to know is that after years of independent operation, let's just say I attracted a fair bit of government attention both at home and abroad. What with the new millennium, changes in style of international politics, a united Europe, etc. etc. my services are becomin' much sought after. Time to face facts. The world's tired of petty dictators sparkin' off wars all over the place. Ya can't leave'em be, and ya can't knock'em off without a whole lotta trouble.'

'So enter the Oakridge solution,' I interrupted.

'Precisely,' Greta replied. 'Not only that, but there's those who already know or at least think they know about folks who'll be visitin' from, shall we say, further afield. And if they're right, it won't be too far distant neither.'

I listened spellbound while the old woman continued to deliver her explanation as if it were of no more moment then discussing the reorganisation of a sweet shop. In a way I still had my doubts regarding the reality of the situation. There I was in a teashop, surrounded by a handful of locals and tourists, being treated to information others would have willingly risked their lives for. Was Greta really alone? Were the clientele who they appeared to be? Or was it all just another elaborate stage production? I began to consider it a distinct possibility until one of the patrons seated by the window, unable to attract her server's attention, started calling to Ms Oakridge.

'Excuse me, we've been waiting more than ten minutes for a new pot of tea.'

Greta shot the unfortunate soul a look quite capable of turning flesh to rubble. After that there were no further comments about the service from anyone, so it all seemed natural enough. Chances were, therefore, that my companion was applying one of her novel psychological theories, i.e. if you want to keep secrets and don't want to be overheard, the best approach – talk freely in a public place. Nobody gives a damn, nobody pays attention, and if they do listen they won't believe or remember what you said anyway.

314

In many ways I got the impression that she was one of those people you sometimes read about in spy novels: no name, no background, no evidence the individual even exists. Given these circumstances, there was never any need for semi-permanent disguises or plastic surgery. When you needed to be someone else, you just created another non-existent character.

As usual, Greta only spoke for a few minutes. Her answer to my question had in fact been more of a warning than anything else, and I felt certain it was because she and Kathy wanted to impress this upon me that the boss herself had deigned to descend from Mount Olympus to deliver the goods. The message was clear. I'd been more fortunate than I could ever imagine. Not only had Kathy saved me from the recommendations of the Oakridge strategy group, but, more importantly, from their new associates, at further personal cost. Whatever the deal was, it came with an ultimatum to unload the past completely. All the original underworld projects, both large and small – minor sidelines, charitable cover-work, the lot – had to go. Under the new arrangement Greta's organisation was to become completely invisible not only to the criminal community, which had been its lifeblood, but also to any law-enforcement offices that had been involved. It was clear that Oakridge and her associates were the best at what they did, particularly when it came to pioneering as yet unheard-of plastic surgery techniques. Therefore, rather than allow her to continue selling her services to the highest bidder on either side of the law or political fence, a secret group with immense power had decided to sign her up to a single contract. A classic case of 'better the devil you know'... Reading between the lines, Kathy must have paid an enormous price to have my sentence commuted to rebirth. Exactly how high, I shuddered to think.

'So ya see, Dr Clock,' Greta said after a brief pause to sip her tea, 'ya've a simple choice to make. Leave well alone now, or try to stir up a hornets' nest. Be very clear though. My new associates are still mighty edgy about yer special situation. Ya give 'em the tiniest of reasons, and ya're a goner. Nothin' I nor Kathy can do ta save ya. Not only that, but there's the two folks taking yer place in the glasshouse. Like I said to y'all before, what I arrange makes most people happy. Yer man, well, poor guy's only got a few weeks at best. Details aren't important, but his family's in dire trouble because of him. It's a difficult situation, but we'll take care of it and then set 'em up with a new life elsewhere. The woman? She won't cop hardly any time at all. In exchange she'll be escapin' a brutal husband and gettin' a brand new start with the baby she's carryin'.'

I barely had time to assimilate this information when I noticed the café owner give Greta the eye. The old woman glanced at her watch and frowned.

'Sorry, Doc, but time for me to leave ya again,' she remarked. 'But before I go, Kathy asked me to apologise for the business with that coffin and boxes in ya back garden. I've heard the story. Shame about the youngster ya probably thought was down there, but at least in death he became a hero. Saved a score o' lives.'

In common with our previous encounter, Greta left her seat preparing to depart before I'd had the chance to ask the multitude of questions I feverishly sought answers to.

'What about Sondra?' I snapped. 'And Kathy? I have to tell her partner something.'

'Hard questions, those,' she exhaled. 'Just have ta tell her fella she can't be reached. As for the professor, she's not around anymore. But here, I have something of hers for ya.'

As her words entered my head I felt sure I'd taken my last breath. I vaguely saw a carrier bag being placed at my feet, but it held no immediate interest for me. All I could think of was that my only link with Sandy and the truth about her fate was about to leave.

'Greta!' I croaked. It was probably the last time I'd address her, and the name stung as if my mouth were filled with broken glass.

'She's gone too, Doc, remember?' Oakridge said softly,

on the point of departing. 'And who I am now don't concern ya. We won't be meetin' again for a long while. When we do, whether it's upstairs or downstairs, I'll buy ya another tea and there'll be all eternity for us to discuss whatever ya like. Take care now, Dr Clock. Nice renewin' yer acquaintance. *Adios, amigo.*'

I watched in abject despair as the bulky figure discarded her apron and walked towards the door. As she reached it, someone on the other side ushered her through and allowed another person to enter. At first I was so numb I could register nothing, but then something about the way the new arrival walked took my eye. The scene abruptly collapsed into slow-motion as I regarded first the legs, then the body, and finally the face of the woman approaching me.

'Sandy!' I cried. 'Oh my God, Sandy.' I leapt to my feet, clasped her to me and hugged her with every ounce of my being. Tears streamed down my face, blurring my vision. I was literally quaking. She stroked my hair then, with both hands, gently manoeuvred my head so that we faced each other.

'It's okay,' she said quietly. 'The ordeal's over. I'm home.'

I've no detailed recollection of what happened after that moment of unimaginable joy when Sandy flew back into my arms. Somehow the bill was paid and we were spirited away through the back of the shop by the owner. Heaven knows what it must have looked like to the other patrons, but frankly that was their problem. We found Julian and Norma – I remember that. I also recall my neighbour looking back anxiously towards the teahouse, no doubt hoping for his own miracle to occur. But it didn't and I, God help me, now knew why it never would.

The trip home was a complete blank, and it was only when Sandy and I were finally left alone that my memory started recording again.

'Where's Julian and Norma?' I asked vacantly.

Sandy smiled. 'They're being discreet,' she explained.

317

'Said they'd wait for us over at Julian's. If we're not "out" as Norma said, in about two hours, she'll give us a call.'

'Out of . . . oh, I get it,' I confirmed, still a little slow. Well, before you could be 'out', you had to be 'in', so despite my concerns about Sondra's condition we somehow found our way into the bedroom.

Initially we sat on the bed, unable to take our eyes off one other. Then I remembered my altered appearance.

'It's okay, Jerry,' Sandy assured me, 'I know quite a bit about what happened to you, and I've already seen the photos. Kathy said you'd look better in the flesh though, and she was right.'

'You spoke to Kathy Murkett?' I exclaimed, totally amazed.

'Sure did,' came the casual reply. 'Very clever woman; strange, but nonetheless quite brilliant.'

I shook my head in disbelief. 'So you know about the fire at the clinic, the background regarding our jailed lookalikes – all that?'

Sandy nodded. 'Kathy took a major gamble to save us. She had to make it look as if we'd been taken care of to please her new bosses, hence the episode in the coffins. After that we were smuggled out and sent to the Gellar Institute. As it happened, you were the one they most wanted rid of, so Kathy used you as the test case. Capitalising on the cover operation already in place here to mask our actual demise, she transformed you into your brother. Finally she got us out from right under their noses and essentially put you back in circulation – the whole thing carried out under a veil of total secrecy. It was some feat.'

'That's all very well,' I observed, 'but why wasn't I simply blown away as soon as these faceless boss characters found out what happened?'

Sandy shrugged. 'No need. Kathy'd demonstrated once again how a situation that would have traditionally been solved by violence could be dealt with more effectively.'

Back to my newfound role in life as an investment or, if I was a good boy, an apprentice asset, I thought. I explored the issue further but there seemed little more to be revealed. My partner had also been given hints about our being investments, but beyond that knew no more than I. In summary I'd survived because I hadn't caused a fuss after my release. The forces of malevolence had decided it was an interesting demonstration and, since their requirement for me to be dealt with had in a way been achieved, they'd lost interest. Again the message was hammered home. 'Sit still and be left in peace; rock the boat and . . .' It didn't need to be spelt out any further.

I learnt that it had been a direct consequence of the urgent need to reinstall me in the UK with a new ID that I'd apparently suffered my period of psychic distress. It was essential that neither I nor anyone else – other than the trusted few assisting Kathy – knew what was happening. All part of the demonstration to please and appease the brass. Of most interest to me was the revelation that Sandy had been close by for much of the time, albeit kept well out of sight for obvious reasons. Fortunately, her ordeal in the coffin had been only transient. Once safely delivered to the Gellar Institute, she was released into Kathy's charge. So, despite the cocktail of drugs used in conjunction with the surgery and to keep me deliberately disoriented, some of my dreams had a basis in fact. The eye-pads, doctor, nurses, even the business with the fruit juice and straw, were mostly real events. Perhaps the most extraordinary occurrence, however, related to our journey from the US. A private plane had been used to fly us from Philadelphia to a small aerodrome in the Scottish Highlands. There, before I was transported down south by road, I'd apparently gone walk-about and, of all nights, on one of those rare occasions when the Northern Lights adorned the heavens. As for my interviews with Ms Red, Elena and Rika, they would remain one of life's unsolved mysteries . . .

'Fascinating,' I murmured half to myself. 'But why plant me in a coffin and then make me suffer for over a week fretting about you?' I enquired.

'The coffin story, I'm not too sure about,' Sandy confessed. 'As far as I know, that piece of theatre was mainly for Julian's and Norma's benefit. I was told Julian had gone to the police station then subsequently dug up the coffin out back. I guess Kathy and her team thought it best to keep everything sinister, not only to encourage you to steer clear of the authorities but also to promote your friends' silence. My return was delayed until you'd convinced your would-be executioners that you were going to be a good boy and deserved a present. Not to mention Kathy was just a little tied up handling Greta's exit from Philadelphia.'

Suddenly the most obvious of thoughts butted its way into my mind – my partner's identity. With all the shock and excitement of her return, I'd failed to register that her appearance seemed fundamentally unchanged. Now I came to think of it, her make-up was noticeably heavier, more adventurous, and her hair was several shades lighter. When I commented, Sandy smiled and handed me the carrier bag Greta had left me.

'Kathy did offer me the option of a few nips and tucks, but it wasn't compulsory so I declined,' she explained. 'One advantage of being a woman – a touch of make-up and a bottle of hair dye and you can be someone different every day. The main issue was I had to have a new identity which would avoid suspicion. Given my past, Sondra Warwick had to be totally eliminated. Essential for you, me, and the girl impersonating me in prison, who'll hopefully have a happier life after all this is over. Better check out the contents of the box and let me know what you think.'

It took only a few seconds for me to flip through some of the documents and read who my love had become, and to decide I approved. Professor Samantha Germaine Clock, anthropologist, lifelong colleague, friend and recent wife of Matthew.

That was enough talk for the first session of our reunion, and besides there was only half an hour left before Norma would be on the telephone to see if we were 'out'. No more time to waste. Too much had been lost already . . .

Over the next few days we talked of all our experiences, occasionally with our two friends but usually when alone. What would become of the Gellar Institute? Was the FBI ever involved, or were they in fact primary stakeholders in the new Oakridge Corporation? Doctors Arquette and Stravinsky – agents, investigators? Or merely what they claimed to be? There were still so many unanswered questions, but that was the way it had to be. Everyone agreed to let sleeping dogs lie. At least Sandy was able to confirm that whatever happened, Kathy had promised Elena and Rika would always be cared for. That was all that mattered.

When by ourselves, Sandy passed along more information from Kathy about how to behave with regard to my imprisoned brother. We'd already read in the newspaper that the man had fallen seriously ill and wasn't expected to survive to stand trial. Nevertheless there were things I had to do and, since he knew of my existence, I'd been given leave by my benefactor to visit him if I so chose. It was the least I could do. With regard to Sandy's situation, once we'd taken the decision to accept our new lease on life there was little for her to do. On that first evening when we were together, however, I did find out one other revelation. Although no changes had been made to her face, the surgeons under Kathy's command had offered one additional option – reconstruction work on her breasts. Of course miracles weren't possible, but the result was quite remarkable. As I told her, it wasn't important to me, but I knew it was for her, and I was glad.

And so Christmas Day arrived. Christmas dinner was laid on at the Clocks', with Mr Stammers and Ms Bates as honoured guests. In keeping with the normal flow of family life, we had happiness, reflection and pain seated around the festive table. Happiness for Sandy and me, reflection for Norma as she wondered what heroic feat Twister had been involved in, and finally Julian, the bearer of pain. Everyone tried to make the occasion as joyful as possible and, after dinner, presents were handed out. Of particular note was a set of temporary tattoos my new wife had persuaded one of Kathy's make-up people to manufacture. For BJ, of course, they were all different styles and designs of a Blue Jay in flight. The most extraordinary present, however, Norma gave to me. It was a poem: a poem she'd composed especially for Sandy and I, entitled 'The Icing Man and the Historian'.

The Icing Man and the Historian

The icing man's a man I like
He's kind of fun and rarely glum.
When trouble comes he'll stand and fight
He doesn't care by day or night.
And if implored by ladies fair
He'll battle demons in their lair.

There have been times I've heard it said
When icing man was head of heads
That happiness blew faraway
And skulking in its hide each day
Refused to listen to his pain
But when he changed flew back again.

He has few friends but since I'm one
I doubt he'll mind if I go on
To tell you of his special love
The graceful don, historian.
She too is bright and mighty fair,
And fearsome are they as a pair.

The icing man oft speaks of care
Yet sometimes growls at those who dare
Approach him with a hostile air.
A secret, if you find him pleading,
Historian and I are teasing
But only since we know he finds it rather pleasing.

My eyes filled with tears, I made my excuses and headed for the bathroom. It took more than a few minutes to regain my composure, but my achievement was to be short-lived. As I retraced my steps back across the hall I caught a glimpse of a large black limousine drawing to a halt outside the front door. Fear instantly seized me as I saw the huge form of the Reverend Black emerging from the driver's side. He walked to the back of the car and opened the door. Two females alighted: one, dressed in red and looking like a million-and-a-half dollars, was Ms White; the other, dressed in a 1960s hippie-style frock, was none other than Kathy Murkett. I didn't know what to think. Should I alert the others, panic, run? No, none of those seemed necessary somehow. I couldn't say why, but for the first time since meeting Black and White they seemed wholly benign.

As if driven by a telepathic command, I opened the front door. By now Ms White was about to re-board, but paused when she spotted me. She blew me a kiss and, as Kathy reached the porch, shot me a smile sufficient to send ten men into a sexual frenzy. Ms Murkett looked me in the eye, then nodded. And in that moment I recalled Greta's words that Kathy had to pay a terrible price for her interference. What that could be I still had no notion, but here she was. Whether for an hour, a day, a week or forever – who could say? The only thing I could be sure of was that she was here because of Julian. Despite their worlds being so far apart, she obviously loved him, and perhaps that was part of the sacrifice: her career in exchange for her partner and his friends. If so, I just hoped and prayed it would be nothing more sinister.

The limousine with its two occupants was already reversing down the drive as I stood aside to allow Kathy to pass. Before she entered the living room I caught her arm and said the only word I could think of.

'Thanks.'

Again she nodded and stepped into the room. A shocked silence descended like a hammer. Our late guest looked at Julian, and then it happened – a sight I'd thought never to see in this lifetime – Kathy smiled.